THE
OTHER VIKI

BOB BENNETT

authorHOUSE®

AuthorHouse™
1663 Liberty Drive
Bloomington, IN 47403
www.authorhouse.com
Phone: 1 (800) 839-8640

Published by AuthorHouse 03/23/2017

ISBN: 978-1-5246-7021-4 (sc)
ISBN: 978-1-5246-7022-1 (hc)
ISBN: 978-1-5246-7020-7 (e)

Library of Congress Control Number: 2017902191

Print information available on the last page.

CONTENTS

PART 1

Leave or Die

CHAPTER 1

Harald Antonescu stood at the head of the table in the cramped common room of his parents' farmhouse in the small village of Niculesca, Romania. Three of his younger sisters and a younger brother sat on either side of the scarred tabletop, and his parents, Georghi and Olga Antonescu, stood at the head of the table with Mama holding the heavily bundled baby boy Viorel in her loving arms.

Through a tiny four-paned window, Harald could see it was still dark outside. A haloed moon illuminated the glistening white trimmed pasture and fence posts. The stove's fire had long since died down, so the room was freezing cold. In the weak lantern light, the family's mingled breath gusted clouds of vapor that floated up and disappeared into the low ceiling's exposed rafters.

It had been a long and difficult night—for his parents; for the youngest children, who didn't fully understand what was about to happen; and for the older ones, who did understand. Harald had spent much of his childhood as caretaker to his siblings while his parents toiled in fields owned by Mr. Lupescu. Now that he was twenty-one, that responsibility had once again fallen into his lap. Muscular, with a dark complexion, a thick mustache, and slicked-down black hair, he was much sought after by the young women in the village. His dream of finding a wife and of furthering his four years of formal education had been derailed—perhaps forever—by the economic disaster that had gripped the world. Harald disliked farming, but he had learned early on that he had no choice but to do what his parents said. "If you want to eat," they told him, "you must work."

Their small home had been built in 1890 by Harald's paternal grandfather, Ilie Antonescu, with the help of his friends and neighbors, as a wedding gift to Georgi and Olga. Constructed with adobe bricks and stucco, the house and its slate-capped roof had withstood forty-five years of perilous storms and ugly winters.

Harald's papa took out a handkerchief and mopped his eyes which were brimming with tears. "Your mama and I have been dreading this day for months," he said, "but now that it's here, we must all be brave and try to make the best of a terrible situation. Mr. Lupescu has laid off his farmworkers, so we have no income to buy what we need. Most of the food we get from our own crops is taken to pay the taxes the government demands. We must live on what we are able to preserve, and that isn't enough to feed the whole family until next year's harvests. All Romanians are suffering. We are no different. Your mama and I wish it wasn't so, but we can't control the Great Depression any more than we can make it rain and put an end to this brutal drought. You are old enough now to make your own way in the world."

He paused to take a deep breath. When he spoke again, his voice cracked with emotion. "Children, it's time for you to leave. So, hitch up the wagon and be on your way."

Eleven-year-old Ana jumped up from the table and threw her arms around her mother's waist. "Why do I have to go, Mama?" she cried. "I don't want to leave you."

"Young lady, you have known this day was coming for weeks," Harald reminded her. "You should be ready to leave as we had planned."

Ana buried her face in her mother's apron, shook her head, and sobbed.

Pretending to be a helpless baby was a game Ana played to get her way, and it often worked. Harald was fuming inside, but he softened his tone. "Of course you don't want to go," he said. "None of us do, but we have no choice. The five of us must leave, or we will all surely starve. Mama and Papa have the younger ones to care for, plus the new baby is expected later in the year. As I am the oldest son, Papa put me in charge of this move. And I agree we must leave—and leave now!"

Ana sat down on the floor, beat the raw planks with her heels, and bawled, "I don't want to go. Please don't make me go!"

"Well, you are going, whether you want to or not," Harald told her. "It's time you grew up and stopped thinking only of you. Do you think Elica, Dominik, Simone, or I want to leave the family? Papa and Mama chose you to go with us, so get busy. Collect your things and store them in the wagon. We must go now while the roads and fields are still frozen. We have to get as far as we can before the sun comes up. When the road begins to thaw out, it will turn to mud, and with our horse pulling the loaded cart and the cow tied to the back, our progress will slow to a crawl."

Ana wasn't listening. "Mama, I promise I will eat less," she begged from her seat on the floor. "I promise. Please just let me stay."

"I have heard enough from you, little sister," Harald said. He turned for the corner of the room and picked up the well-worn sliver of a tree branch Mama and Papa used to punish their disobedient children—Harald, too, when he was younger. A man on a mission, he twisted his sister by an arm and forced the slender girl to lean over the edge of the table. Raising the back of Ana's dress above her knees and pinning her chest to the tabletop with the flat of his hand, Harald savagely thrashed her bare legs with the switch. She writhed and kicked and screamed. Red welts appeared on her flesh. Harald was so furious with her that he couldn't seem to stop.

Mama quickly passed baby Viorel to Papa. She rounded the table and grabbed the upraised hand that wielded the branch. "No more!" she said. Her words snapped Harald back to reality. Shamed by his loss of control in front of the others, he threw the switch to the floor.

Mama bent down and took the weeping, trembling girl by the shoulders. Looking straight into her eyes, she said, "Ana is no longer a child. She will do as she is told. She now realizes she has no choice but to accept what is offered her—and she will go with you."

Her face red and tear streaked, Ana bolted away. She stomped into the cramped sleeping room, where the younger children were still tucked in their beds. Not caring whether she would wake them, Ana rummaged noisily, throwing things about. She reappeared moments later clutching an old gunnysack that held her few belongings. She shot Harald a look of hatred and defiance, as if all this were his doing.

The good-byes to Mama and Papa were mercifully brief, consisting of quick hugs and kisses on the cheeks. No one wanted to prolong the agony. Harald pulled on his heavy wool coat and opened the house's only door. Cold air blasted in. When he inhaled, it burned the inside of his nose.

"Girls, put on all your warmest clothes," he said from the threshold. "While you're doing that, Dominik and I will hitch up Mihai and tether Florin. Then we'll be on our way."

The ground crunched under the soles of his rubber boots as he and his sixteen-year-old brother stepped out into the farmyard. Dominik was an experienced farmhand. While not a big man, he was strong. Fair skinned with light brown hair, he favored his mother more than his father. He had already served a four-year apprenticeship constructing and restoring buildings for the landowner, skills that both Harald and his father thought vital to their survival at the new location.

The water-resistant canvas they had stretched over wooden hoops and fastened to the sides of the cart was coated in crystals of white frost. The fabric would offer protection from the sun and stormy weather while the family was traveling during the day and also as they slept at night. The bed of the cart was packed with expendable farm and carpentry tools, rope, wire, cooking gear, grain for the horse and the cow, and the vegetable seeds their parents could spare. Under Mama's watchful eye, Elica and Simona had gathered several containers of food, enough to last them until they reached their destination if they took only meager portions.

Elica, Harald's oldest sister, was nineteen and yet unmarried. Five feet four inches tall and with a dark complexion, black hair, and black eyes, she was an attractive, loving person well experienced in raising a family. From the time she was five, she had been expected to look after the siblings who followed. She had little formal education, just enough to read and write.

Simona, the family's second daughter, was thirteen, was two inches shorter than Elica, and had long brown hair, hazel eyes, and skin as smooth and soft as lamb's wool. She had only four years of education. As was the case for her other family members, her farmwork came first regardless of her age. And she didn't seem to resent the menial tasks she was given.

Harald and Dominik helped the bundled girls climb over the rear gate and get into the cart's dark and frigid bed. Ana, still sulking, hid her bag of possessions behind a bin of potatoes and then got under a tarp between Elica and Simona to stay warm.

Harald pulled himself onto the front bench seat. Dominik jumped up beside him. As the cold of the frozen wood plank seeped through Harald's coat and pants, numbing his backside, an unwanted and unhelpful thought resurfaced. Their parents were sending them away, casting them out without giving them a chance to live, a chance to create their own future, but agreeing to let them die out of sight and out of mind. He pushed the thought angrily from his mind. No, his mama and papa weren't like that. They would never be like that. And Elica, Dominik, Simona, and Ana would not die. No matter what, he would not let that happen.

Harald snapped the reins against Mihai's broad buttocks with a loud crack. Once the cart lurched into motion, he did not look back.

CHAPTER 2

Had it not been for the bright moon, the Antonescu siblings couldn't have left before dawn. The short narrow track that led from their farmhouse to the main road didn't get much traffic, so the cart wheels could easily follow the path of two pairs of deep ruts even in the pitch-dark. Once they reached the main road, the going became more difficult. The frozen ruts that had been cut by countless wagons and horses were a jumble of sharp ridges and potholes. The benefit of traveling before the road thawed was that there was no mud. The downside was a very bumpy ride.

"Damn, it's cold," Dominik said, pulling a tattered and filthy old quilt out from under the seat. He spread it across their laps and their legs.

As he held the reins, Harald alternated hands, hiding one of them under the coverlet to warm up his fingers and then the other. He and his brother were used to long hours of hard physical labor in bad weather, but this labor largely consisted of sitting still on an icy, bouncing board. The cart was noisy, too. Though tied, its contents still rattled, and the leaf springs creaked at every bump. The ride for the girls in the bed could not have been comfortable. There was no way, given the erratic motion and the racket, that they could have fallen back to sleep. His sisters were not used to this level of discomfort. The Antonescus were poor farmworkers, not gypsies. They slept in their own beds in rooms with four walls, not in a pile like cats to keep from freezing.

Though their journey had just started, Harald found it difficult to maintain mental focus. This was because they were traveling very slowly, not more than two miles an hour, and he hadn't slept well the night before.

"We have to be very watchful of Ana," he said to his brother in a low tone. He was confident they could not be overheard over the noise of the cart, the sound of hooves striking ice, and the animals' heavy breathing.

"Because she might get hurt?"

"No," Harald said, "because she might decide to run away, to take off for the farm while we're still close in the hopes that we won't go back for her and that Mama and Papa won't abandon the farm to return her to us."

"She thinks she's still a baby," Dominik said. "But she isn't."

"She's frightened of the change, that's all. It will pass. And after a couple of days, she'll be afraid to try to go back. We've got to distract her if we can, make it seem like she's an important part of the plan."

"You're not thinking about letting her drive the cart, are you?"

"No," Harald said. "We can't trust her with that. Half the time she's off in a daydream. And she doesn't have the strength to handle Mihai when he's pulling this kind of load. After the sun comes up, the traffic in both directions could spook him. When the road turns to muck, Mihai will have to be steered around the soft spots, sometimes taking routes he doesn't want to go. I don't honestly think Elica and Simona will have the strength for that either. In places, it will take both of us to manage it, one holding the reins, the other holding the bridle. The girls can spell us if we find a stretch of road that has good drainage, but otherwise it's too risky. If something happens and we break an axle, we're done for."

The cart started to crawl up a gradual upgrade. Mihai strained, his breath puffing clouds of white while steam rose from his broad backside.

The bits of sausage and cheese, and the cup of warm milk, Harald had had for breakfast didn't hold him much past dawn. His stomach was rumbling mightily as the sun began to peek over the treetops. They lumbered on steadily through shallow winding valleys and between the rolling hills. The slopes were a patchwork of stands of silver fir interspersed with cleared meadows. On either side of the road, hoarfrost began melting from the fields, the vapor rising like a wispy fog. In the shade at the edges of the tree line, clumps of winter snow lay mounded. He could see scattered small hillside villages in the distance—clumps of clustered houses surrounded by grazing land and forest. Points of golden light still shined through some of the tiny windows.

There were no road signs, and Harald had no map. If they got lost, he would count on asking for directions at a farmhouse or from a fellow traveler.

As the day gradually heated up, the traffic on the road increased—other carts, horseback riders, flocks of sheep—and the hard surface got softer and softer until it was a squishy mush. In places, the mud puddles spanned the entire roadway. On a long uphill grade, Elica and Simona hopped down from the cart, peeled off layers of hand-me-down and homemade clothing, and walked behind to lighten the burden on Mihai. However, Ana refused to budge from the bed which was just as well, because that way Harald didn't have to worry about her running for home when he wasn't looking.

As the cart crested the rise, the two girls climbed back into the cart. Harald turned to Dominik and said, "You've been keeping your thoughts to yourself about this whole venture. Maybe you didn't feel you could speak freely about it in front of Mama and

Papa? We're well on our way now, and our parents are miles away. Brother, please tell me what you're thinking."

"I'm like Ana," he said. "I don't like being forced to leave home. But I understand the consequences to the entire family if we'd stayed. I'm worried about what we will find at journey's end. Do you honestly believe we can clear and prepare the new land for planting by spring? Will it produce enough to feed us and pay all our expenses?"

"I haven't seen the land, Dom," Harald admitted, "so I don't know what it will produce or how difficult it will be to prepare. But I think the five of us can succeed at whatever we try if we are smart and determined, and keep our eyes on our goals."

Dominik nodded in agreement. Then he said, "Hari, I have one more important question: can you find me a lovely girl I can marry, like the one I'm leaving back in Niculesca?"

Harald laughed. "I believe we can make a new life for ourselves, but finding a lovely girl to marry is entirely up to you. May the good Lord be kind to you, Brother."

When the sun was directly overhead, Harald figured that eight hours had passed. And he guessed that with the ups and downs, they had traveled about fifteen miles. Before the sun began to set and they had to find a place to camp for the night, he thought they could do another eight miles. Over the sounds of the cart and Mihai's hooves, he could hear Dom's stomach growling, the rumbling nonstop. He steered the horse, the cart, and their tethered cow onto a broad grassy spot on the sunny side of the road. It was past time for them all, including the animals, to eat something.

As the girls began pulling lunch out of the cart, Harald and Dominik fed and watered the horse and cow. They sat on the ratty quilt that was spread out on the grass while Elica sliced mamaliga, the coarse cornmeal mush that is the Moldovan substitute for bread, and a little sheep cheese. Harald didn't want to waste the time building a fire to fry up the mamaliga, so they ate it and the feta cold. Ana complained, but still she gobbled it down in a blink. Although Harald's portion was about a tenth of what he would have normally have eaten, it stopped the complaints from his stomach.

After they had all finished eating, Harald said, "The journey ahead will be much like this morning: long, slow, and tedious. Papa and I believe it will take us five days and four nights to reach our destination; traveling that distance will be demanding of our stamina and mental awareness. If we make good use of our time and don't have any big obstacles to overcome, maybe it won't seem so far.

"Dom and I will do most of the driving," Harald continued. "As you have seen, the road conditions are challenging. We don't want to risk you girls getting hurt or the cart breaking a wheel on the way to our new home."

"But what if we want to drive?" Simona said.

"Then I suppose either Dom or I will sit with you and help you if you need it. For the rest of the day, and after the ice melts tomorrow, I think we should take turns walking behind the cart."

"I don't want to walk," Ana protested. "It hurts my feet to walk in these boots."

"Everyone's feet hurt," Harald assured her. "Taking turns walking will make the journey easier on Mihai. We need him strong and fit to help clear and plow the fields once we arrive. If he can't work, we will starve."

"We're going to starve, anyway," Ana muttered, loud enough for all to hear, and then she disappeared back into the rear of the cart.

"I guess Sister isn't going walk unless we tie her to the gate beside Florin," Simona said.

"Mihai won't notice if she rides," Dom said. "She doesn't weigh all that much."

"And what there is of her is mostly hot air," Elica said.

"Let Ana be," Harald said. "She'll come around when she realizes how boring it is being alone in back of the cart with nothing to look at but a cow's head."

After they packed up from their meager lunch, Harald told Dom to get into the driver's seat. As Dom gathered the reins, Harald helped Simona up into the seat beside him. "My turn to walk for a while," Harald told them. As the cart lurched forward, he fell into step behind it with Elica.

By midafternoon they were twenty miles from home and in territory unfamiliar to Harald.

Elica and Simona changed places, but Harald continued to walk. The steady, repetitive movement helped him focus on what he and his siblings were going to have to do to make a life for themselves, the tasks involved in preparing the land. He also considered the structures that had to be built to shelter them and the animals and to serve as a space to store food, tools, and supplies. They had never worked from scratch, starting with raw unimproved land, and had never designed and built their own house. It was the difference between being a farm laborer and a homesteader.

Mama and Papa have had to do, what they had to put up with to earn a living, and I don't want that. I want to work for myself and take advantage of that to move on and make a different kind of life. When the opportunity presents itself, the first thing I'll do is get out of farming and find another line of work, one that will please me better and be helpful and beneficial. I've known nothing but farming since I was old enough to walk. I want a job that will pay well and let me work indoors and among people. In the meantime, the responsibility for keeping everything and everyone together is mine. I have to keep thinking about what lies ahead of us, the next steps.

We are facing a huge challenge, but I know we can succeed.

CHAPTER 3

As soon as the sun dipped down behind the distant hilltops, the air temperature began to fall. All the clothes the Antonescus had taken off, they began to put back on. Harald could feel his legs starting to stiffen up and the tips of his toes going numb inside his rubber boots. He changed places with Dom and took the reins. There were still two good hours of light until dark. Although they hadn't traveled as far as he would have liked, it was time to call it a day. They needed a spot to camp.

Up ahead, Harald could see an unfenced open area close to the road that offered what appeared to be a convenient site for an overnight stop. It was bordered on one side by what looked like a small creek. Beyond the field, a faint dirt track led to a small farmhouse on a low rise. Hoping to get permission from the owner to camp on the land, he drove the cart onto the field. He told Dom and Simona to wait for him there, as there was no sense in their climbing another hill, and then he urged Mihai up the track. As he neared the house, he could see no animals or any sign that the property was occupied. The windows were tightly shuttered, and the yard was overgrown with dead weeds. Because the place seemed deserted, he thought it was safe to go ahead and use the field for the night.

Harald parked the cart on what looked like the flattest spot, and then he climbed down from the seat. Banging on the rear gate, he said, "Ana, we've stopped for the night. Time to get out."

After she jumped down, he said, "Ana, please lead Mihai and Florin to the creek and let them drink. Then pick out a nice grassy spot and hobble them there. After you peg the security ropes to the ground, feed them. Make certain the hobbles are tightly fastened and that their ropes are properly fastened to the pegs."

Ana didn't make eye contact, but she didn't object to the assigned task. She immediately set to work. *Perhaps the long ride alone has made her reconsider her stubbornness,* Harald thought.

"Dominik," Harald said, "your task is to make the fire and gather the foodstuffs for supper. And Elica, it is up to you to get supper ready. Simona, you and I will prepare the cart for sleeping, moving boxes and barrels out of the way so we'll be as comfortable as possible. These will be our tasks every evening until we arrive in Vioresca."

Elica once again sliced mamaliga and fried it in a little grease with tiny bits of spicy homemade sausage. There wasn't much of it to go around, but they washed it down with enough of Florin's milk to be satiated. After the meal was finished and all utensils were cleaned and put away, Harald gathered the family around the blazing fire to keep warm.

"Today was a good day of travel," he said. "Perhaps a little slower than I'd hoped, but uneventful. And uneventful is the best we can hope for. With any luck, the rest of our journey will be the same and we will make steady progress."

His sisters and brother were sitting on a crate, pressed hip to hip and bundled against the cold. Harald wanted to ease their doubts and anxieties about the family splitting up. Most of all, he wanted Ana to understand why she had been chosen to come with them, and to realize that they needed her as much as she needed them.

"I want to explain the reason why we're sitting around a fire in an open field instead of being home doing our night chores," Harald said. "You know the harsh conditions our family has had to live with. And you know how others are suffering under these same horrible conditions. You've heard and seen what it has done to our village. Families are desperate to find enough food to keep from starving to death. Many are begging from their neighbors, or walking the city streets pleading for whatever few coins they can get. There is food available, but no one has the money to buy it.

"Do you understand the torture Mama and Papa have been going through? When the Depression hit bottom, they began thinking about separating the family. They could see they were going to run short of the food needed to feed all of us. It was time for of us older ones to marry and move out to be on our own, but where could we go to find work enough to start a household and raise a family? None of the landowners were hiring farmhands, and the factories near the cities were letting go their employees. Our own landlord had to let his older workers go, including Mama and Papa.

"Mama and Papa decided the only answer was to find a piece of vacant land their older children could get and cultivate themselves. But where? There was nothing available in Niculesca. All its lands had been bought up years ago. So Papa thought perhaps he should visit Mr. Lucescu and see if he could come up with a solution to get us through this dilemma. The landowner had offered help before, if we children were ever in need.

"'I want you to meet Mr. Lucescu,' Papa said to me, 'not only to get to know him but also to learn how to negotiate with owners. You may have to do it yourself sometime.'

"Mama agreed with him and said Papa should take me with him.

"The next morning, I hitched up the cart and we made the trip to Lucescu's house in Suceava. It was a pleasant day, but a little chilly. The sky was a bright blue, with big clouds passing over. Lucescu's home was large and impressive, with iron gates and a gravel drive and tile-roofed outbuildings. After Papa knocked on the front door, we stood with our caps in our hands until it opened. Then we were admitted by a servant. When we were ushered into Lucescu's study, the landowner rose from behind his big desk. I knew he was a portly man, but this was the first time I had seen him without his straw fedora. He had very little hair.

"After introductions were made, Papa and Lucescu had a distressing discussion about the family's poverty and the difficulty of eking out a living under the present circumstances. Papa pleaded for aid to help us survive the Depression. Surprisingly, Lucescu seemed in a receptive mood. We couldn't believe our ears when he immediately said he had about fifteen acres of vacant land we could have in Vioresca, a small village near Saveni. I asked him, 'Did I hear you right, sir? You have vacant land you are willing to give us?'

"'Yes,' he said, 'it's yours so long as you live on it, cultivate it, and keep it producing. And when you die, you can pass it on to your heirs. But after you've seen it, you may realize that I didn't do you a favor. It's been more than a decade since it has been cultivated, and undoubtedly it is wild and badly in need of attention. Over the years, I have made it available to several families, but after inspecting it, none of them accepted my offer. It's yours if you want it.'

"'We want it!' Papa said. 'My children know what hard work is, and they will make the land prosper. We thank you very much for your generosity.'"

By the time Harald finished the story, the eyelids of his audience were drooping, their heads nodding. Harald couldn't be certain he had made his point or that they hadn't slept through some of it. For all of them it had been a long day. He followed his sisters and brother into the cart, and they covered themselves with worn woolen blankets and quilts. It took only a minute or two before he dozed off.

They arose long before the sun spread its warmth across the frost-covered pasture.

Dominik built a small fire. They breakfasted on warm milk and a bit of feta. As dawn began to break, they packed up and got ready to be on their way.

During their quick meal, Simona had insisted that she wanted to drive this day. Harald had relented, reasoning that if she could in fact handle the horse and heavy cart, it would be good to have a third set of hands for the driving. He sat beside her on the front seat as she coaxed Mihai onto the road. Ana and Elica were under the tarp in the bed, while Dominik walked. The two-cart-wide dirt and rock track was still frozen beneath a surface already softening to muck, but it remained frozen hard enough to keep the cart wheels from getting mired in ruts and puddles. It was the best time of day for Simona to test her driving.

"Simona," Harald said, "you've never driven on an icy unfamiliar road like this. You must keep your eyes open and look far enough ahead of Mihai for likely deep ruts and mire that could grip a wheel. If you see something that looks suspicious, you must steer around it as far as possible. If you get us stuck in a deep pothole, we've got problems that will take perhaps hours to fix."

Simona was so intent on what Harald was saying, and Harald so intent on getting through to her, that neither of them noticed a broad sheet of mud-covered ice dead ahead.

"Look out!" Harald cried, but it was too late.

Though Simona tried to change course at the last second, the right rear wheel broke through the film of ice with a crunch and sank into the hub with a jarring thud. Ana let out a yelp from inside the cart.

"See what happens when you're not paying attention," Harald snapped at her. "I told you, you have to stay alert while driving. Now do you understand what I'm talking about?"

"If you hadn't distracted my attention by talking so much, we wouldn't be in this mess," Simona replied with equal fire. "You didn't see it coming, either, big brother. Now what do you want me to do about it?"

"What I want you to do is stay alert and keep your eyes on the road. Don't let your mind wander or be distracted by anything, especially conversations. I know concentrating on the road is difficult and boring, but that's the job of the driver." He glanced down at the half-buried wheel and shook his head. "We may have to lighten the load to help Mihai pull the cart out of that hole. So you sit here and guide him while the rest of us push the cart until the wheel is back on solid ground. Hopefully, we can get it done without having to empty the contents."

Dominik knelt down and peered at the cart's undercarriage. "Axle doesn't look broken," he said.

"Then let's get to work," Harald told the others. "First, untie Florin. She'll only make it more difficult to clear the wheel." It took several tries, but after Harald had everyone simultaneously pushing from behind, Mihai was able to finally pull the cart out of the hole.

Once they were free, Simona climbed down from the seat and handed the reins back to Harald. "This job's no fun. I don't want it," she said. "I'd rather walk than listen to you berate me."

Day three began smoothly. The family made good progress until the terrain got hillier. The frequent upgrades meant that Mihai required more time to rest on the crests. On one occasion they had to make two trips to get all the contents to the top of the hill. Day four was more of the same.

When Harald woke up on the morning of the fifth day and looked at the back of the cart, he discovered that Mihai was nowhere in sight. Heart pounding, he looked all around and could see no signs of where the horse might have wandered. He shouted to the others, "Everyone, wake up! Mihai is missing!"

They all quickly jumped out of the cart. At the spot where Ana was supposed to have secured Mihai lay the hobbles and the ground peg. Apparently, she had not used them or else had forgotten to fasten them securely to his legs. That she was still fretting about having to leave home was no excuse for endangering them all with her carelessness.

"Ana, why didn't you hobble Mihai?" Harald shouted at her. "Why didn't you tie him down like you were supposed to?"

"I don't know," she said with tears running down her blushing cheeks. "I didn't do it deliberately! I was sure I'd done the job right, the way I always do. Now I can't remember. Where did he go?" She moaned, "Dear God, what are we going to do without him?"

No one spoke.

"There is no sign of which way he went," Harald said finally. "No hoofprints because the ground is frozen. Split up and search in different directions. I'll stay here and protect the cart, hoping one of you is successful in finding him."

Dominik, Elica, Simona, and Ana hurried away. After about an hour, they returned to camp, one by one. None of them had found any trace of Mihai.

"See what your negligence has done, Ana?!" Harald said. He knew his outburst wasn't helping, but he couldn't stop himself. "Until we find Mihai, we are stranded. We can only hope that he finds his way back here. We all know you don't want to be with us, but you are, and you must take responsibility for your actions, your poor attitude, and the poor quality of your work. Do you understand me?"

"Yes," Ana said, sobbing. "I'm sorry I failed to do what I was supposed to do. I promise I won't fail like this again. I don't belong here. It isn't fair that I am. No one asked me if I wanted to come, and I won't be content until I can return home. I'll try to do better the best way I know how, but I want to go home."

"While we wait, we might as well eat breakfast," Harald said. "It's been a long morning already."

As they started to eat, Ana pointed up the road and shouted, "Here comes a man leading our Mihai!"

"You don't know how pleased we are to see you!" Harald said as the man stepped up to them with their horse. He was dressed in worn peasant clothing, woolen pants, a tattered sweater, and rubber boots. "We are on our way to Vioresca. We have some land there that we plan to farm and make our home. This is our fifth day on the road. One of us forgot to hobble our horse. We cannot thank you enough for returning him to us. Is there anything we can do for you?"

"Maybe a cup of coffee and some of that sausage would be good."

"We don't have any coffee, only warm milk," Harald said.

"Milk will do fine. My name is Nichifor Niculescu. I own a small farm on the other side of that hill. I know how horses can get away and how appreciative I am when they are brought back to me. That is all the thanks I want."

"Then you know how we feel. Please, sit." Harald directed him to one of the crates near the fire, but away from the smoke.

"Well, consider yourself very fortunate for having some land you can go to," Niculescu said, chewing a bite of sausage. "At least you can scratch out a living, which is something that many thousands of others can't do. They are dying of hunger. Still others are leaving their villages trying to find anything that can feed them. Even bedraggled children are begging in the cities trying to keep their families from starving."

Harald nodded. "Because of this terrible Depression, our parents had to split our family. They didn't have food enough for us all. They told us, 'Either you go or we all starve to death.'"

"And we can't forget how many of our sons and daughters have moved into the cities to work in the factories and are now going hungry because the factories have no work for them," Niculescu said. "Yes, people are starving, and still the government continues building new plants. It's build, build, build! But no one is buying. And more are being laid off without income to buy what they need."

"Maybe Romania plans to ship the goods overseas to bring some income into the country," Harald said. "If that is the case, it isn't working, because the rest of the world is in a depression too and nobody is buying. Still, Romania raises our taxes and takes bigger and bigger bites out of what little we can produce. It doesn't make sense."

"Maybe it's their plan to equip the country in case there is war," Niculescu said. "Germany is building up its military like never before. A war in Europe could swallow up our country. Let us pray to God that doesn't happen. We haven't recovered from the First World War yet." Niculescu rose to his feet and wiped his callused hands on his pants. "Well, we can't solve the world's problems by sitting here. I must get to my work and let you get on with your journey."

"Again, I thank you, Niculescu, for being so neighborly and for returning Mihai," Harald said, shaking his hand. "Maybe someday I can help you. Who knows? May the good Lord look favorably upon you and bring you nothing but good luck."

"And to you, Antonescu, the same. And I pray the good Lord will guide you and your siblings safely to your new home, and be kind and generous through this terrible depression and drought." With that, he turned back for the road and was soon out of sight.

Quickly Dominik hitched Mihai to the cart, packed their scant belongings, and got under way.

CHAPTER 4

Harald stopped the cart on a rise for a moment so they could all take in the view. Their destination, the tiny village of Vioresca, lay at the head of a wide valley bordered on the east and west by two lines of hills. The surrounding land was level and ideally situated for farming.

"It's even smaller than Niculesca," Elica said.

From their vantage point, Harald could see four rocky lanes leading through the village. He counted fewer than a hundred dwellings and a multiplicity of dilapidated outbuildings at various stages of disrepair. Little attention had been given to the care and appearance of the properties. Harald guessed the peasants spent their days working to make the landowners' farms productive. What little time they had left was spent toiling their own garden plots for subsistence.

Many birds were flying around the village, including a flock of pigeons. High in the sky, a black hawk was slowly circling as it searched for its next meal.

Harald gave Mihai a light slap of the reins. The cart began to descend into the village.

Most houses were built of adobe and painted with a coating of whitewash, a mixture of lime and water. They were topped with rusting metal roofs or wood shingles. A few of the older buildings were roofed with thatch. Many of the outbuildings leaned precariously on weak foundations, and most needed new roofs. A larger structure in the center of the village appeared to be the community building. It too was adobe with a sheet metal roof.

The cart bumped and shuddered on the potholed, rock-cobbled street. It was worse than the road they had come in on.

The people who live here should be proud of their village and give it more attention than it appears it's now getting, Harald thought. I wonder who the leaders are here. I guess we'll soon find out.

It was early afternoon when Harald steered Mihai onto the nearest corner of their property. Climbing down from the wagon, he and Elica joined the others on a patch of green grass where they could take in a full view of the land stretching out before them.

With a big grin across his face, Harald extended his arms and said, "Look at that! Fifteen acres of farmable land and it's all ours!"

Elica dropped to her knees, threw her hands toward heaven, and shouted, "Hallelujah! Thank you, Lord." Making the sign of the cross, she closed her eyes and uttered a few words of prayer.

Dominik was somewhat less excited. "All I see is overgrown trees, rocks, and boulders everywhere, and people must have been dumping trash here for decades. It isn't that big of a farm, but there's too much work for us to get it done by ourselves."

"I agree," Harald said. "Getting our land ready for spring planting will not be an easy chore. Even with the five of us working hard, we are going to need help, but we will get it done."

"How much help will we need?" asked Elica.

"I'm certain our neighbors will help us when they see we need extra hands and tools," Harald said. "Our family never experienced that kind of thing because we've never been landowners before. It's customary for Romanian landowners to help each other out."

He shielded his eyes from the sun's glare with the heel of his hand. "I can see something that could be a problem for us, and it might be what Mr. Lucescu was referring to when he said he wasn't doing us a favor by giving us the land."

"What is that?" Dominik asked. "What did he mean?"

"I'm not absolutely certain, but my guess is he might have been talking about the small stream of water flowing along that edge of our property." He raised his other hand and pointed.

"What stream?" Dominik said. Then he said, "Oh yes, I can see it now. It's so hidden by overgrowth, I couldn't make it out. But what's the problem with having a water supply that close?"

"It looks to me like that stream at high water could block entry of horses or tractors onto the fields. We may have to build a sturdy bridge across it. But we'll worry about that when it comes time to plant."

"You mean this land is all ours?" asked Simona, apparently just beginning to awaken to the size of the gift that had been given to them.

"Yes," Harald said, "all of it."

"And we don't have to share our harvest with anyone?"

"Not a single person. It's ours to keep and use as long as we live. And after we die, we can pass it on to our heirs."

Harald squatted, took a handful of dirt, smelled it, and then crumbled it in his fingers. "I like the looks of this soil. It's black and will be easy to till." Brushing off his hands, he said, "Let's set up camp, empty the cart, and have some supper. In the morning, I'll tell you what your responsibilities will be."

After the family had eaten, the girls prepared the cart for sleeping while Harald and Dominik readied a temporary toilet. They dug a four-foot-long trench in the ground and spread two wood planks across it to stand on. A large piece of canvas strung to poles ensured the user's privacy. Satisfied by the day's work, Harald crawled into the cart with the others and fell into a deep sleep.

They were all up before the sun rose and eager to begin the first day of work on their land. Even Ana showed some enthusiasm. As they sat around the fire drinking warm milk and eating fried mamaliga, Harald explained his plans for the morning.

"Today we're going to start clearing the fields," he said, "but while we're doing that, there are some other tasks that need attention. Dominik, I would like for you to make a list of the tools and supplies we will need to build a shelter for ourselves, a well, and a more permanent toilet. Let me know as soon as you can, and I will do my best to get them.

"Elica and Simona, I would like you to be in charge of the food and the food preservative equipment and supplies. Make me a list of everything you need, and try to estimate the amount of storage space you will need to hold our meat and canned goods.

"Ana, you are responsible for maintaining the living quarters, and for furniture, eating utensils, and cooking and sleeping arrangements. Make a list of items you will need.

"I will work with you all in the field and keep track of what we can't do ourselves. Right now, I can see we will need a plowman and other workmen to help us prepare the soil for planting. Later today, I'll take Mihai and the cart, as I plan to go to Saveni to buy necessities. After that I will go to the record office and register our lands."

When there were no questions, Harald said, "Get the shovels and rakes. Let's go to work."

Harald's siblings followed him to a field and began the arduous task of clearing it by hand. From just looking around, it was obvious to Harald that only small sections of Mr. Lucescu's land had ever been farmed. Those sections were relatively flat and free of large exposed rocks, but they were dotted with scrub trees and patches of brambles. That was where the plowman and extra workers would come in handy.

At Harald's direction, his siblings started prying rocks out of the soil. The girls moved the smaller ones, and he and Dominik worked together to shift the big ones. They set the rocks in three piles based on relative size. Later these would be used to build rock walls around the field. The trash and deadwood that could be burned was separated from what couldn't, making two more piles.

As Harald threw a large rock on the pile, he saw three people—a man and two women—walking across the field toward them. They were carrying hand tools. The man was stout with a ruddy complexion, and he had a grizzled beard that covered his cheeks, chin, and neck. "I'm Stanislav Stanasila, your nearest neighbor," he said, extending a hand of greeting. "This is my wife, Stetiana, and my daughter Sophia. We heard in the village that you are taking over Mr. Lucescu's parcel, which has been fallow for so many years. We welcome you to Vioresca. And we would like to help you, if you will allow us."

The daughter, Sophia, was smiling at Harald. She was about the same height as Elica, and wore her long black hair tied in a bun at the back of her head. Her body was slim and her complexion fair. She had deep brown eyes that appeared to be compassionate.

"Good morning, neighbors," Harald said. He introduced his sisters and brother. "We are pleased to meet you. And we appreciate your willingness to help us get started."

Soon all were busily removing rocks, deadwood, and trash.

Unable to contain herself, Ana began complaining in front of the new neighbors—a fresh audience—about the hard work and the fact that she didn't want to be there. It was embarrassing to Harald and, judging from their expressions, to the other siblings. It made them seem ungrateful for the aid they were receiving. Harald pulled Ana out of earshot and told her to be quiet or she could work by herself in another field. The threat made her stop whining. She rubbed away her tears.

After they removed the visible debris from the field, saplings and limbs of dead trees were cut, trimmed, and piled to dry. The few surviving fruit and nut trees bordering the growing fields were pruned. Once Harald was satisfied that everything was under control, he prepared a lengthy list of the items his brother and sisters said they needed. When that was done, he made some estimates of what he thought it would cost them in units of grain and other farm products to pay his debts. Then he hitched up Mihai to the cart. On his way off the property, he drove over to where his neighbors were working. Sophia looked up at him and smiled. Her cheeks were rosy from her efforts.

"Stan," Harald said, "I want to tell you again how much we appreciate the help you and your family are giving us."

"Well, it's the only neighborly thing we could do for you. And I'm certain there will be times when you will be returning the favor. To survive this depression and drought, we must help each other. And from what I'm hearing, we will be fighting these things for a least two more years. I don't envy you having to start out anew like you're doing. You've got a big challenge ahead.

And, by the way, look up Bela Ionker in Saveni. He owns Ionker's General Mercantile Store and can be a big help to you."

"I'll do that. Thanks."

Sophia waved at him shyly as he started to drive away.

The village lane leading to the Saveni road was narrow and potholed, making for a bumpy ride, especially with an empty cart. Although the distance was only about four miles, Mihai could only go two miles an hour with the cart behind him. The slow trip gave Harald time to think about his new property and the mound of debt he was about to ring up. *We'll be poor like all the farmers,* he thought, *but at least we'll be alive.*

Saveni was much larger than a village. It had a population of about sixty-five hundred, and there were schools, government buildings, a library, and many business outlets. As Harald approached the center of the city, he passed by a clean, inviting park. There were several benches scattered around the neat gravel pathways, but only two of them were occupied. A few older residents were enjoying the clash between squirrels and pigeons over scattered bits of stale bread. Farther along, a small canopied carousel rotated and played music. Laughing children rode the colorful and artistically carved horses.

Harald had no time to visit the park today. His first stop was Ionker's General Mercantile Store, which was just off the main square, in a two-story building. A back door led to an alley where trucks and carts could pick up their purchases. As he entered the front door, he was met by a clerk who offered his help. Looking around, Harald could see the store was well stocked with furniture, and tools of all sorts. Wooden barrels of seeds were stationed around the store. There were two more clerks handling other customers. The store showed few signs that it was suffering from the depression, except for the mere handful of customers on a weekday afternoon. After Harald described his needs and mentioned how he wanted to pay for his purchases the clerk referred him to a back office, where he encountered Bela Ionker, the owner.

"I'm pleased to meet you, Mr. Antonescu," Ionker said. "Welcome to Saveni. How can I help you?"

He was short, about five foot three, and wore a double-breasted pinstripe business suit protected by a white linen apron. He had a deep red complexion and sported a drooping mustache that hid most of his mouth.

"I've just moved into Vioresca, along with my sisters and brother," Harald said. "I need food, tools, and seeds to start my farm in Vioresca on some land given to me by the owner. There are five of us. I was referred to you by my neighbor, Stan Stanasila. He recommended I see you about helping me get started."

"Yes, I know Stan very well. He's a good customer. If he recommends you, then I'm willing to work out an arrangement that will satisfy both our needs."

"I'm pleased to hear that."

"Well, my arrangements are based on what crops you'll have available to trade me for my merchandise."

"What are your payment terms?" Harald asked.

"I prefer to be paid with grains," Ionker said, "mostly corn and wheat, at the going market rate per basket at the time of the transaction. I expect payment in full within thirty days after your harvest."

"If I paid before that, could I get a discount?"

"Yes. If you pay before the thirty days, I'll give you 3 percent discount."

"I would rather get 5 percent," Harald said.

"No," Ionker said, "my going rate is 3 percent. But since you are moving into Vioresca and planting new grounds, I'll give you 4 percent. Take it or leave it."

"I'll take it," Harald said, shaking Ionker's hand on the deal.

With the help of two clerks, Harald was able to acquire everything he sought, from cooking oil and staples to tools and table utensils. Filling the list was costly, but he was pleased he could accomplish so much in such a short visit.

On his way home, he couldn't help but think about the distance to the city and the time it took to travel back and forth by horse and cart. *It would make more sense,* he thought, *if there was a retail*

*outlet in the village that could satisfy most people's needs. Hmm,
maybe I'll look into that when I have some free time.*

That evening, Harald took Ana aside and said, "You shouldn't
have expressed yourself so loudly this morning in the front of our
neighbors. You upset me so much at the time that I wanted to use
the stick on you. Your sisters and brother would have taken turns
after I was finished."

"I'm sorry, Harald," she said, her eyes brimming with tears. "I
realize now what a shameful thing it was to do. Please, Brother,
don't hit me."

"Since you apologized for what you said, I'm not going to
punish you. But I do want you to understand something once
and for all: you are not going home. You might just as well get it
through that head of yours: you are staying here with us!"

"But I was only trying to …"

"Enough! Now let's eat our supper and get some needed rest."

The mood around the campfire seemed to lighten as the
siblings got food in their bellies.

"I bought something today that I hope you all will appreciate,"
Harald told them. "A section in Ionker's store sells military surplus.
I picked up a World War I German tent. The canvas is in very
good condition. The tent is three times the size of the cart and
should be more comfortable to sleep in. We'll put it up after we
eat and have it ready to use tonight."

Dominik, Elica, Simona, and Ana looked at him in amazement
and then let out a big cheer. It was the first time since they had left
home that Harald had seen them all smiling and happy.

CHAPTER 5

After a month, when the weather began to warm up, Harald and Dominik laid out the plot for their first solid shelter. Digging the perimeter ditch was much easier when the ground wasn't frozen. In the ditch they layered a foundation of tightly stacked rocks, on which the shelter would be erected.

"We'll start putting up the house on Monday," Harald said. "Is everything ready?"

"Yes" Dominik replied. "We've got all the bricks we need and some lumber we can use. I had to buy more materials and supplies, but I feel we are ready to go. I'll be so happy to get it done; I'm tired of living in that old tent."

Early the next morning, a group of villagers arrived on the site. They included carpenters, bricklayers, inside finishers, glaziers, and several laborers. Dominik immediately set them to work. Progress was swift. By the end of the week, the shelter was completed, including a steep roof made of sheets of corrugated metal.

"How do you like it?" Stan asked Harald.

"It isn't intended to be our permanent home," he replied, "but it's certainly a lot better than living out of that cart and sleeping in that mildewed army tent. The shelter can be used for other purposes after we build our real home."

"That makes perfect sense to me," Stan said. "When my family first moved onto our land, that's what we did."

Behind them, Dominik let out a scream. "Ow! I've been cut. Someone help me!"

Everyone dropped what they were doing and ran to help. Harald got there first. A bloody ax lay on the ground where Dominik had dropped it.

"My God!" Harald said, pulling his brother's hands away from his thigh so he could see the wound. "That's a nasty-looking gash. You need attention, and quick. That wound will have to be stitched. Can anyone help?"

"I can help," Stan said. "Let's put pressure on the cut and get him to my house. I can stitch him up and, if necessary, place a poultice on it."

Harald and Stan picked up Dominik and placed him in a wheelbarrow, his legs hanging over the edge.

"I'll push this thing, Stan," Harald said. "You run ahead and get everything ready. I'll hurry as fast I can to get there."

"Ouch!" Dominik screamed as the old barrow bounced over the rocky surface of the roadway.

"Just grit your teeth and hold tight," Harald urged. "We'll soon be there. Keep pressure on the cut."

"It seems like you're taking forever," Dominik moaned.

Stan met them at the front door. "Everything's ready," he said. "Let's get him out of that wheelbarrow and sit him in the house, where I can get a look at what I need to do."

Lifting Dominik from the wheelbarrow was a struggle. They carried him into the house and stood him in front one of the threadbare easy chairs. He groaned when Stan asked him to drop his pants so they could better see the wound.

"Hmm, that's not as bad as I thought when I first looked at it," Stan said. "No major blood vessels are cut. I'll just clean it up, put in some sutures, and bandage it. You can sit down now."

After the treatment, Harald and Stan put their hands under Dom's armpits and raised him to his feet. "Just stand still until you can steady yourself," Stan said. "How do you feel?"

"My leg hurts like hell."

"Do you think you can walk?"

"I'll try."

On the first step, his injured leg almost crumpled under him.

"Whoa!" Stan said, holding him steady. "Rest a minute and try it again, but don't put your full weight on it just yet."

After a couple of minutes, Dominik found he could stand on the injured leg. After a few steps, he was able to tolerate the pain and walk, albeit with a pronounced limp.

"You're all right now," Stan said. "But give yourself time to recuperate before going back to work, and when you do, be extremely careful not to pull out the stitches and reinjure yourself."

"How can we thank you?" Harald said.

"Don't even think about it. Let's just consider it something that goes along with being a good neighbor. Now we must get you home. I'll hitch my cart and drive you there. You certainly don't want to be jolted back in the wheelbarrow."

When the rig was readied, Harald, with Stan's help, placed Dominik and the wheelbarrow into the cart and soon had them home to Dominik's berth in the tent. The wheelbarrow was returned to the toolshed.

The villagers, interrupting their house-raising celebration, rushed to the tent to see how Dominik was doing. "I'm fine, I'm fine!" he shouted. "It looks a lot worse than it is. Just go ahead and have a good time. Don't let me stop you. If I find that I can maneuver on this agonizing leg, I'll join you."

The yard soon filled with the workers' families, who brought what little food they could spare from their meager larders. A few brought musical instruments. Soon the classic music of Romania filled the air, inducing all to dance to the festive rhythms and familiar sounds. Harald opened his supply of *tuica*, the national plum brandy. Holding his cup up high, he shouted, "Drink up, everyone. For all your help. My siblings and I thank you very much for coming to our aid. I am proud of what we've accomplished and am very thankful for having your friendship."

And celebrate they did.

Before the Antonescus planted their first seed, Harald set up financial and production records for their property. He had learned how to do this from his father and neighbors in Niculesca. When he needed help with his mathematics and spelling, they had come to his aid. He spent many evenings working on the details of these records.

By the first of June, the fields were plowed, harrowed, and almost completely seeded.

Finding himself short of seed to complete the planned work, Harald went to the local seed exchange to get what he needed. The exchange had been established many years before when one of the more successful farmers in the village saw the need. He had partitioned off a corner on the ground floor of his barn and covered the space with small barrels of various seeds to be swapped for extra seeds the farmer had to offer.

"Hello. I'm Alexandru Constantin," the farmer said, extending a gnarly hand as Harald stepped into his barn. The older man wore a floppy cloth cap, a plaid sports coat that had seen better days, baggy corduroy pants, and rubber boots.

"I'm glad to meet you. I'm Harald Antonescu. I need seeds to finish our planting."

"I figured you would be showing up," Constantin said. "I heard you and your family had moved in and were going to farm that open land near the Saveni road. I'm here to help."

"I need mostly corn and wheat, and possibly some clover and flaxseeds. I don't have anything I can give you in exchange for what you give me, but I promise I will repay you the original amount, plus whatever extras I find I can't use."

"That's all I can ask for," said Constantin. "I'll fill some bags for and wish you well with your crops this year."

"What are your thoughts about this growing season? I'm hearing various guesses about how good this season will be. And some of what I hear bothers me. I keep hoping that we are seeing the end of the Depression and the drought. What do you think?"

"Well," Constantin said, "you probably know as much or more than I do, but it's my opinion that we won't see the end this year. But I do see an easing up of both."

"I feel sorry for those who have died in these terrible times," Harald said, "especially those who left the farms to work in the plants. Many were laid off. With no income to feed themselves, they starved to death."

"That's why I'm thankful I'm a farmer," Constantin countered. "Farmers are better off because they usually have something to eat. Meager though it may be, it is sufficient to keep us alive. As far as what the future holds for us, it is hard to say. But with the prospects of war materializing and the demand for our products increasing, I believe we'll soon be coming out of it. I just don't know when. All I can say now is good luck, and may your harvests be more than what you are hoping."

"Thank you, Mr. Constantin."

"Incidentally, if you're interested, a few of us get together here in the seed exchange on Friday afternoons to discuss the events of the week and maybe have a little tuica to ease our pains. I'd like to have you join us if you are interested."

"Yes, I'm interested. I'll try to be here this Friday. I don't know if I can add much to your discussions, but I'd like hear what all you have to say."

CHAPTER 6

When it came time for Harald and Dominik to erect a barn and build a durable chicken coop and a tall pigeon cote, their good neighbors once again assembled and helped them get the projects finished. The barn was built the way Harald wanted: an open-air structure with a steep and sturdy metal roof that would let the snows slide off before they got too heavy. He also wanted some open space under the building enclosed by lattices of tightly woven saplings and tree branches that would keep animals out and give him extra room to store preserved food.

As soon as the building was completed, Harald hitched up Mihai and paid a visit to the man half a mile away who owned a farm and bred animals to sell. When Harald told Andrei Dalca that he wanted chickens, ducks, geese, a female pig, and pigeons, Dalca asked him how he was going to pay for them. Harald told him he was willing to put liens on the property if that was acceptable. And it was.

On the way home, Harald felt a cold rush of air. When he looked over his shoulder, he saw that dark storm clouds rolling over the hills and rushing toward him. His first thought was, *Thank the Lord, at last we'll get some rain.*

But the initial drops quickly turned a heavy shower, and then to a torrential downpour. He stopped the cart long enough to pull a tarp over the cages of animals he had bought. The pig was securely tied to the side of the bed. By the time he climbed back up to the seat, pea-sized hailstones began raining down, driven by hard gusts of wind. The noise was incredible as the ice pellets bounced off the roadway a couple of feet in the air. Harald would have hidden under the cart to get out of the hail, but he knew he had to get back to the farm as quickly as possible. In a span of minutes, the ground around him was white and the hail inches thick. He urged Mihai onward.

As he turned down the dirt track to the farm, the hailstorm began to fade. He could see Dominik, Elica, Simona, and Ana bent over in their garden, still trying to cover the budding crop of vegetables with pieces of cardboard, feed bags, horse blankets, and any other material they could find to protect the plants.

Harald jumped out of the cart and ran toward them. What he saw in their garden made his heart sink. The hail had destroyed a lot of the plants. It lay heaped in the furrows like snow.

"We saved what we could," Dominik told him. "Some of the plants that look dead will recover."

Harald had hoped to use some of the garden produce to help pay down their debt with Ionker. Now they would have barely enough to feed themselves. And what they could not pay this year would be added to next year's debts, plus interest on the unpaid amounts. There would be no discounts, obviously. It would take a lot of bickering and promises to get Ionker to agree to the new deal.

"We'll replant what we can," Harald said, "and hope to have a late summer harvest. We've got to make it last through the winter and into the start of the growing season."

"God finally answered our prayers for rain," Elica said, her face and hands smeared with mud. "But it's our fault for not telling him how much we would need."

The work was unending and the days long. The Antonescu siblings cut hay from red clover, cured it, and pole-stacked it in the field until it was needed in the barn to feed the animals. Animals had to be kept watered and fed, and sheltered from rain and snow.

Through the summer growing months, vegetables and fruits were either eaten fresh, dried, or canned in jars and stored until the new harvest began in late spring or early summer. A variety of fruit trees, nut trees, and vines surrounded the property: apples, plums, walnuts, cherries, pears, and grapes. Grapes were used mostly to make wine, the popular drink with meals and for special occasions. Harald had a portable still hidden beneath the barn that he used to distill his favorite plum brandy.

Wintertime was the preparation period for the upcoming growing season, a good time to make or repair tools and equipment, furniture, clothing, and leather goods. Reeds from the water's edge were used for thatching, flax for weaving into linen cloth, old clothing for weaving rugs for floor coverings, wool for weaving the cloth to make clothing, and blankets for the beds and to cover the animals. On special occasions like weddings, clothing was designed and sewn by the local seamstress or tailor in exchange for agreed amounts of fruit, vegetables, grains, and/or animals.

It was all an excellent learning experience, especially for Ana— although she continually let it be known she was homesick, did not belong there, and was leaving as soon as she could get Harald to agree.

The shelter, the well, the outdoor oven, and other outbuildings were completed, and the corn and wheat harvest was much better than Harald had estimated, enabling him to pay off his debts except those related to the shelter and barn, which were extended up to ten years.

The shelves in their shelter were filled with canned vegetables, fruits, and some meats. A large ceramic crock contained sauerkraut made from fermented cabbage cured in salt water. The barn was packed with hay and seed enough to last to the next harvest.

Their cow had given birth to her calf, and both had wintered the ice and snow quite well. The hog had given birth to eight piglets. Two were kept for food; the others were sold for cash money.

After butchering, every part of the animal was either eaten, cured for winter servings, or cooked and canned. Some meats were either placed in small metal smokers or hung in wooden sheds and smoked over wood fires. Neighbors helped with the butchering and shared some of the meats as payment for their services.

Harald even made some money taking excess products to the city and selling them at the farmers market. He made it his objective to always have cash readily available. And he knew how to barter.

The Antonescu brothers' and sisters' first year on their farm had come to an end. The main topic of discussion now was the start of the next growing season. Establishing their claim to the land had been difficult, but their achievements were many, and living was actually easier than they had imagined, a result of their unrelenting labors and the much appreciated help from their neighbors.

Over the slow winter season, their social life had been active and they had attended and participated in the village events and festivals. Elica had met all of the eligible men, but she hadn't found anyone who truly interested her, and certainly no one she wanted to marry. At age twenty, she decided she would return to Suceava and try to make a life with the boyfriend she had left behind.

"I know this is going to be a shock," she told the others over breakfast, "but I've decided to return home and find some kind of work. My boyfriend has written repeatedly, saying that he still loves me and wants to get married. And since I've not been successful finding a husband here, I'm going to return to him. I want a happy marriage and a family of my own. I don't like leaving you, but you've got things organized now and I know you can manage fine without me."

Harald had felt her distancing herself for many weeks. Despite his disappointment, he understood that she needed to move on and start her own life. "We will miss you, Sister," he said, "but we understand and wish you well. When do you plan to leave?"

"Just as soon as I can gather my things. Then, if you'll hitch up Mihai and get me to Saveni, I'll take the bus to Suceava."

"Will we have time to invite the neighbors over to say good-bye?" Simona asked.

"Of course," Elica replied. "I could not leave without thanking them again for all their kindness."

The party on the eve of her departure was happy and well attended. Everyone seemed glad for Elica. People's laughter and smiles mixed with their tears. Harald and Stan toasted her success with Harald's homemade brandy while Stan's daughter Sophia looked on adoringly.

Harald had been dating her regularly over the last five months, but nothing seemed to be developing as far as marriage was concerned. They acted more like close friends than lovers. He knew that many in the village believed a wedding would be the eventual outcome.

CHAPTER 7

The second full year in Vioresca went by in a blur for Harald. Most of the planned building projects were completed, but there was still work for everyone from sunrise to sunset. The resulting harvest was better than the previous season's. With it, Harald was able to pay down their debt to Ionker considerably. He had every reason to think their third year would be even better. Perhaps they could start work on a permanent, "real" house.

But after the fields had been replanted in the early spring of 1936, Dominik dropped a bombshell on Harald as the two walked back to the shelter from the barn.

"I'm sorry, but I'm leaving you, Brother," he said, his eyes downcast.

"Why? To do what? Aren't you happy here?"

"Happy to be with family, of course, but I am not using the skills I apprenticed for. There isn't any real construction work here in the village because everyone helps to put up the buildings, so I'm going back to Suceava to find employment with the contractors there. Now that the country is starting to come out from under the Depression, I've heard there is a big demand for people like me who have building experience and training. Who knows, maybe I can even form my own company or become a manager of a government-owned company."

"But what will your sisters and I do without you?" Harald said. "How can we run the farm, just the three of us?"

"We already hire some peasant labor for part of the field work," Dominik said. "And the plowing and harvesting are done by contract. The farm is a success. You can afford to pay more peasant workers now. You will do fine. Of that I am certain, or else I wouldn't be leaving."

Everything Dominik said was true, and there was no believable counterargument Harald could make. He knew begging his brother to stay wouldn't work. The farm would go on after he left. But it gave Harald a sour feeling in his stomach. While Dom and Elica moved on to pursue their own dreams and goals, Harald was left to deal with the management of the family land, something he had never aspired to.

Ilie Antonescu was born on December 15, 1934, the twelfth and last child of Georgi and Olga Antonescu. The baby was named after an uncle of Olga's who had recently passed away.

Nadia Codreanu, the midwife, and her reliable assistant, Roxie Milea, assisted in the delivery. Codreanu had assisted Olga in all twelve of her births since 1913, when she'd had her first child, Harald.

Ilie entered the world flaming red and small enough to fit in a shoe box, certainly not the robust kind of children Olga had previously birthed. He was the family runt, weighing less than five pounds. A healthy infant with a powerful voice, Ilie demanded—and got—immediate attention.

"That's it!" Olga said after the first week. "No more children. I don't care what the good Lord says. I can't take it anymore. I love my children, and I love the Lord, but enough is enough!"

"I agree," Georgi said. "Now is the time to stop. You have done more than your share, I believe—more than the good Lord could expect from anyone."

Ilie never matured like his siblings. Even though he remained tiny and thin, he was frisky and enjoyed a strong appetite. He learned to walk earlier than those before him, and was constantly banging on pots and pans with wooden spoons, first with one hand and then with the other, making as much noise as he could without dropping the spoons, which he was prone to doing. He seemed particularly clumsy and uncoordinated when switching hands, not knowing which one to favor.

On the boy's third birthday, his parents decided to put him in kindergarten to see if changing the environment would settle him and possibly teach him something, even though he was younger than the others. Surprisingly, he progressed well in school and was quick to learn reading, writing, and other subjects.

When he was five years old, they placed him in first grade. He did well there also. But around the house and farm, he was good for very little. He never took to farming. He was small in stature and showed no signs of maturing enough physically to take on strenuous farm chores. In the tasks he could manage, he was meticulous, but generally it took him twice as long to complete them as it had any of his siblings.

"Ilie, I don't know what to do with you," his father admitted. "I've tried and tried to make something of you, but nothing has come of it. You can't handle the horses, you can't plow the fields, you don't know how to milk the cows and sheep, you can't paint the buildings, and you can't even do work in the house. I don't know what you are good for."

After Dominik left the farm, the Depression began to weaken and the economy gradually regained some of its lost strength. For the family, farm production was better than expected and financial security was being achieved, enough so that Harald, at age twenty-five, was beginning to dream about the soft peal of wedding bells.

He had always considered Sophia more of a friend and a companion than a woman he wanted for his wife, that is until the day she was injured while trying to harness one of the horses to the cart. The animal lashed out with a rear leg and caught her with a glancing blow to the shoulder that spun her around and dropped her into the dirt. She was lucky the kick missed her head, but it hurt badly and brought tears to her dark brown eyes.

When Harald rushed to her aid and put his arms around her, he felt a closeness he had never experienced with her before. She was warm, tender, and helpless, and she needed him. It gave him such a warm feeling that he wanted more of it, which fact convinced him she was the person with whom he wanted to spend the rest of his life.

Sophia was a loving, hardworking woman who, he knew, would make an excellent mother to their children. Being a female, and the seventh child of twelve, she'd had very little education. Like holy water, Sophia always remained calm, cool, and quiet, letting Harald do the talking and generally keeping her thoughts to herself.

One evening during the 1937 harvest festival when he and Sophia were walking their favorite path, he stopped, gathered her in his arms, and blurted out the question. "Would you marry me?"

Almost before he finished getting the words out, Sophia cried, "Yes! Oh yes! I don't know why you waited so long to ask me. I would have said yes after that first day we worked together clearing your fields."

The next day, Harald approached her parents and received their blessings. The happy couple was married on June 18, 1938.

CHAPTER 8

The weather was freezing cold, the temperature hovering around fifteen degrees Fahrenheit. Flakes of soft snow floated in twirling circles as the wind gusts snatched them up and lay them gently atop the crusts of frost spread across the barren fields. Spring and summer were just a hurry-up winter's dream.

From the outside, not a sound could be heard. The animals remained calm in their shelters, awaiting better weather. Inside the house, Ana was having difficulties with her morning chores. Nothing seemed to be going right. In her haste to finish washing the dishes, she dropped a cup and saucer and watched the broken pieces scatter across the floor.

"Damn it," she said.

As she was gathering the broken pieces of cup and bowl, she began to cry.

"What's going on in here?" Harald demanded as he barged into the kitchen. "You've broken more dishes? Dishes are costly and money is hard to come by. Don't you realize that?"

"I'm going home," she shouted. "I can't take this place anymore. I've been here more than five years, and that's long enough. I'm going home." She wiped away her tears with the back of her hand. "I've had enough of this damn farm and this damn village. I'm going to leave for home just as soon as I can get my things together. And you're not going stop me."

"What are you going to do when you get home?" Harald asked. "You have to work. And Mama and Papa can't help you. They still have the younger ones to care for. You will not be able to move in with them. So where will you live?"

"I don't know, and right now I don't give a damn. I'll take care of those things after I get there."

"Are you sure this is what you want? Are you sure Mama and Papa will take you?"

"I'm hoping they can take me in for a short while until I can get work and find my own place to live."

"Who will I replace you with?" Harald said.

"You don't need to replace me with anyone. Now that you're married, Sophia is working with you. And you can hire others to do the work when the times come. You can easily do without me."

Harald made a doubtful face. "Well, let me think about it."

"There is nothing to think about," Sophia said as she entered the kitchen. "I overheard the discussion you were having with Ana—it was so loud that I couldn't help but hear—and I agree with her. She is almost sixteen years old and she needs to be out on her own now. She needs to marry, settle down, and raise her own family. You know how few good marriage prospects there are here. Would you have her take old Lungu the widower as her husband? And now that I am here, I can take her place and do the work she has been doing. As Ana said, you can hire additional people when you need them. You can afford it."

"I disagree," Harald said. "I believe Ana would be better off staying here. She has property here that she can have when she marries. And we can help her get settled."

"As I told you before," Ana said, "I don't want any of this property. I just want to go home. And I won't be satisfied until I leave here."

Harald looked pleadingly to Sophia for support, but she just shook her head.

"Well," he said with a sigh of resignation, "I guess if that is what you really want, then you are of course free to go. I've been hardheaded about not wanting to lose you because you are my little sister and I love you and want to protect you. You can leave as soon as you get ready."

CHAPTER 9

Harald was beginning to believe the soothsayers. It had been predicted that after a short respite, they would be back in the drought. It looked like this was going to be a poor year. And they said the next year would be just as bad, if not worse.

How was he going to pay off the debts incurred in getting the land to produce this season? He hoped that production would be sufficient to at least cover the bills. But the situation was looking bleaker and bleaker. The ground had dried up, and many of the plants now sprouted in the fields were dying. To keep their garden plot alive and growing, they would have to carry water from the creek. There was no practical way to water the wheat fields and the cornfields. Harald didn't know how he was going to handle the shortfall with their creditors, but he knew he couldn't delay. He had to go into the city to see what could be worked out. Perhaps they would extend more credit and rely on next year's production to take up the slack. As terrible as things looked, he knew the landowners were not as bad off as others in the village. The peasant families who labored for the landowners suffered the most because they had no other food sources.

The cycle of drought had wrought disaster in 1934 and 1935, but between then and 1938, farm production for the Antonescu family steadily increased, providing them with enough of a harvest to pay off all debts, except the house, for which the debt had been spread over ten years.

There were many times when Harald thought they wouldn't make it, but they had.

One week of unseasonal freezing temperatures or a sudden terrible rainstorm was all it would take to wipe out the sum of their labor. And with the way the world was going, he knew that even if they managed a good crop, they could lose it with increased taxes if Romania got drawn into the conflict between Germany and Russia.

Harald continued to have fantasies about what he would like to do to make a more dependable living and to leave farmwork—and risk—to others. The more he thought about it, the more he was determined to open a store in the village and become an owner in the merchandising business. *Maybe now is the time to do it,* he thought. When he discussed this with the other members of his family, all agreed he should pursue his dream.

In July of 1939, after completing his sixth four-hour round-trip to Saveni within a two-week period, Harald decided it was time to carry out his dream of bringing needed merchandise to Vioresca. On his seventh trip, he had a conversation with Bela Ionker to gauge the store owner's thoughts about opening a retail outlet in Vioresca.

"What would I have to do to sell merchandise in Vioresca?"

"So you want to sell merchandise in Vioresca? How interesting. You want to compete with me?" said Ionker with a smile.

"No, no! I want to work with you. Driving all the way into the city whenever I have to buy something is too much trouble and takes too long. And everyone in the village feels the same way. We all want a store that is closer and more convenient that fulfills our needs. I'm sure you can understand that. I don't want to compete with you; I want to work with or around you, but in a store in our village. What do you think?"

"You would first need a strong, spacious building to store and display the merchandise."

"Must I buy the merchandise from you and you take profits off the top, or should we work as partners and share all the profits?"

"Why don't you come to work for me and get some experience with buying and selling? Then I will let you take my merchandise and sell it, and we can share the profit."

"That is something I would have to think about," Harald said. "If I am going to sell merchandise, I would want to do it on my terms so I can keep the profit. Could I buy the merchandise from you at a discount, stock it at my own pace, and keep the profit for myself?"

"Yes, you could do that, but it would be to your advantage to buy your own merchandise from the suppliers and not have to deal with me as a middleman taking some of your profits. Or we can do it both ways: some merchandise I will supply, and some you will buy from the suppliers, like gas and oil for cooking, and lighting and machinery and tools, if you want to do that."

"I don't know," Harald said, "let me think about it. After all, the people of Vioresca are mostly poor farmers with little or no money to buy what they need. I would have to take their produce as compensation for their purchases."

"That is all right. You can sell the produce in the marketplace whenever you come to Saveni and still make money. I have operated that way for many years, and it works out well. It just means you have to come to town more often. Plus you have to stay and sell your products. There are many different ways the two of us can work this out. It is something we both need to think about, and then we'll decide which way is the best for each."

"Very well. The next time I come in, I will have decided what I can do, and we will come to some kind of a decision and go that way. In the meantime, I'll take what I came for and you can put it on my account."

Harald spent a day walking around the village looking for a property he could use as his store, but there wasn't a secure building large enough to hold all the merchandise he planned to stock. In the end, he narrowed his search down to two small buildings sitting side by side that, combined, could serve his needs and be readily accessible to customers.

Now, he thought, I just need to resolve the matter with Ionker.

The next time he was in the city, Harald met Ionker and found him in favor of proceeding with the plan.

"Go ahead and get the buildings," Ionker said, "and then we will work out an arrangement for how to supply them with the merchandise you want to offer. In the meantime, I can supply some of the merchandise to you. I'll also check with the other merchants in town and see if they would let you handle their merchandise too."

"I like that arrangement," Harald said. "Let's proceed with it until something better comes along. I'll go ahead and get the buildings ready."

Harald returned home, talked to the separate owners of the buildings, and worked out arrangements satisfactory to both. Harald agreed he would buy the buildings and renovate them. In return, he would give the sellers discounts on the merchandise they bought from him.

Within three months, Harald's twin stores were making a profit. The village people were glad to see them develop and enlarge. He had to construct extra rooms to store the grain and produce he received in exchange for the farm products he sold. He also set aside space enough to accommodate the group of men who generally assembled each Friday afternoon to discuss current events affecting the nation and the farmers in general—and to enjoy a little tuica.

At one of these Friday gatherings, as the participants sat around the woodstove sipping brandy, Aurel Radulescu seemed unusually upset. One of the village elders, his great-grandfather, had obtained about three hundred acres almost a hundred years before. He was considered one of the local leaders because of his excellent farm production and his active participation in village matters.

"Here we are still struggling to recover from the end of the Depression, and the government continues to raise taxes on us farmers," Aurel said, his weather-seamed face flushed with fury. He had an unruly shock of wire-stiff salt-and-pepper hair and a matching mustache. "And they continue to borrow money from foreigners to finance this so-called industrial development program. They keep saying it is time for Romania to catch up with the rest of the world. All I can say is … ah … what the hell for?"

"They say a lot of development is needed," Harald said. "And I agree. This country needs new and modern industries and the service facilities that accompany such growth, like more electric power plants and new mine openings, more oil wells, better roads, and rail lines built throughout the country."

"But is it prudent to get it all done now, at the expense of starving peasants?" Aurel said with venom.

"I would like to have electricity and better roads, but the rest of it doesn't affect me," Pulu Wadim said. "What I need is more products to sell so I can pay my bills. I can hardly keep up my payments for the land I bought in the 1921 land reform. I'm still no better off than I was then, and I certainly can't afford to pay more taxes." Pulu was another of the village's leaders and a staunch member of the school board.

"I'm up to my ass in debt," Zamfir Baboescu admitted. "And there's no relief in sight. But it's the growth of these industrial plants that really bothers me. My sons want to move to the city to work in those damned plants. I need them here on the farm. This national industrial buildup is placing too many burdens on the families and causing all of us to pay more money for hired help."

"Yes," Wadim said, "it's forced landowners to cut back on planting because of the shortage of the workers needed to cultivate the lands. And don't forget what it's done to the schools. Our teachers are leaving to work in the plants too, and fewer students are going into teaching as a career. All we have are losses."

"What about this talk of a second world war?" Harald said. "Now our government has broken its agreement with Russia and joined with Germany to declare war on the former. Anyone in his right mind knows that Russia can't be beaten in a war. It was tried in the last big war, with the Allies failing. Even Napoleon tried it and was beaten. It just can't be done. Russia is just too formidable to be overcome in battle. The weather, for one thing, is Russia's biggest defense."

"I read in the newspaper," Aurel said, "the allied forces of Romania and Germany are taking back the territory that Romania had been forced to turn over to Russia earlier—Bessarabia, Odessa, and Sevastopol. Then the combined armies will march across the Great Russian Steppe toward Stalingrad."

"That's only part of the story," Baboescu said. "Now Germany doesn't want to pay for the oil, grain, and industrial products we have supplied them as their part of the war effort and that is having a negative effect on our economy. Inflation is getting out of control."

Harald raised his glass and said, "Hail to the motherland! May she overcome her problems, celebrate her victories, and last forever!"

With that, they all finished their tuica and said their good-byes. As his guests were leaving, Harald added, "I'll see you all again next week. Good farming! Or whatever it is you'll be doing."

CHAPTER 10

Harald returned from the draft board in Botosani late in the afternoon of January 6, 1941. "I just received my final notice," he told Sophia. "I'm to report to the recruiting office next Monday to be sworn into the army and transported to a training base up north."

"Couldn't you get another extension?" Sophia asked, her face pale and suddenly showing shock.

"No. I already told you, the last time I was able to get one, the recruiting officer said it would be my last one, unless, eh, ah …"

"Unless what?"

"Unless I came up with a lot more bribe money."

"And?"

"I couldn't manage it. He was asking too much and I could not get him to come down, not even one leu. There was nothing more I could do."

"Oh dear God," Sophia said as she broke into tears.

He put an arm around his wife's trembling shoulders. "Bela Ionker will help us with the stores, and our neighbors will help with the crops. Don't be afraid. Everything will be fine." For her sake, he said this with much more conviction than he felt.

Harald arrived at the recruiting office in January 1941. Along with about fifty other farmers and laborers, he was sworn into the Romanian army, placed on a train, and shipped to the training base.

After withstanding ten weeks of basic training, Harald was pronounced a soldier of the Romanian army and was then sent home for a weeklong furlough to get his affairs in order. As he had hoped, Ionker agreed to manage the stores and his neighbors agreed to help Sophia keep their farm going. Upon his return to the company, Harald and the rest of the men were assigned to an infantry division and transported to an area east of the Dniester River past the border with the Ukraine. There they joined with other Romanian and German forces and began a huge operation against Russian forces. Battle after battle ensued. By the middle of July 1941, the lost territories were recovered and returned to Romania. The six months of fighting were brutal, as the rations were short and the Germans treated the Romanians like barbarians. Many lives were lost, and many more men were wounded, including Harald.

He had been scouting ahead of the company's advance when he took a sniper's bullet, which entered his left shoulder, ricocheted off the bone, and exited his back near the shoulder blade. The wound took him out of action and placed him in the nearest military hospital. After he underwent three surgeries and antibiotic treatments to kill a life-threatening infection, the medical staff was able to save his arm. Six months later, he returned to Vioresca, Sophia, and his stores. Harald's war was over, but the scars of the experience would last forever.

Three months after the German surrender, Harald, at age thirty-two, decided he needed more than four years of education. Realizing he had a long way to go, he enrolled in night classes for a course that offered an elementary certificate and guidance into a commercial and marketing curriculum. After a few years of study, he was awarded his certificate. It was a good excuse to celebrate.

Several men from the village met in the backroom of his store. They passed bottles of tuica around and lit the extra-firm and aromatic Cuban cigars Harald had bartered with an underground vendor for, costing him many bushels of quality wheat grain, but the expense was worth it. Everyone wished him well and congratulated his achievement, at the same time wishing they had done the same thing themselves.

CHAPTER 11

At first, Ana was happy leaving Vioresca and returning to her parents and the younger children, but she quickly realized home wasn't the same as when she had left it. In five years, the young ones had grown and seemed to have forgotten her. When she tried to tell them what to do, they ignored her. Mama and Papa had aged a lot and didn't seem too enthusiastic about her return. At times they acted as if she was just another mouth to feed. Their reaction made her wonder if she'd done the right thing leaving Vioresca.

After Ana had been back a couple of weeks, her mother said what all the others were probably thinking. "Why did you come back? You and the others were making a good living for yourselves on your own land. Why did you want to come back here, where we have so little to go around?"

"Because I was so terribly homesick and missed you so much. I hated Harald's domineering ways and the isolation of the farm, and felt I had to return to be with you here in Niculesca. But now I'm beginning to realize that perhaps I may have made a big mistake. I can see now that my presence is adding another burden to you and Papa."

Mama did not dispute the assertion.

"But I'm not going back," Ana protested. "Not ever! If I can't stay here with you and Papa, then I'm going to move into the city and get a job there."

"Papa and I think that would be a good idea. As much as we love you and were happy to see you, you are now a young lady and capable of earning for yourself. We believe you need to leave and find paying work for yourself."

Now what do I do? Ana thought. I wasn't expecting this kind of treatment. I was so wrapped up in my desire to return home to Mama and Papa that I failed to realize that the conditions have changed very much among the family. I guess I refused to grow up and accept the changes of life that come with growing up. I suppose I did make life unbearable for the family. I'm beginning to realize that I was not a happy child and that I made life more difficult for the rest of the family. Now what do I do? I've got to leave Mama and Papa and get a job and a place to live. Now I realize I am on my own and have to make my own decisions. And I don't know who to lean on. Now I really need Harald to help me make a decision. But I don't have Harald to go to. I must do it myself. Before anyone hires me, they'll want to know what skills I have to offer that they can use. And all I know is the household chores I learned when taking care of the younger kids. I'm not fully educated. I understand there are a lot of jobs working for the rich people who live in those big houses. Those people even provide living facilities for their help. I guess I'm pretty good at doing what Harald expected of me, like keeping records, ordering the food and supplies—enough to keep a good kitchen—how to get furniture for the house, and how to keep everything organized and clean. I guess I was doing much better than what I was given credit for. Yes, I made a lot of mistakes and could be very nasty at times. I kept the others upset having to live with me. But I believe I'm a lot stronger now that that experience is behind me. I understand now that I was a nasty, unhappy person in Vioresca.

As it turned out, the time Ana had spent in Vioresca was the best thing that ever happened to her. Because of her experience being in charge of the household duties and having to endure an endless number of hours listening to and taking orders from her brother, she quickly found employment as a live-in kitchen maid in the rich Rafael Bratianu family's mansion in Suceava. Fully accepting her responsibility as keeper of the pantry, she worked hard ensuring there was always plenty of stock and enough of a food supply to complete the menus for at least a month at a time.

She did so well on that assignment that she was soon recognized as being one of the more efficient and dependable employees on the staff. Within a year, she was selected to manage the household staff. Along with that came the authority to hire and fire people as the need arose.

Ana was a quiet person and never raised her voice when addressing people, yet she maintained a firm grip on her staff and treated them fairly. Being a determined person, she did a quality job handling even the tiniest of problems, solving them all to the satisfaction of everyone involved.

But her insistence on perfection eventually caused her to quit the job. She had fired a kitchen cleanup girl for failing to wash the dinner glassware after being warned about it twice. Her employer asked Ana to bring back the girl, but Ana refused to relent. When he demanded that the girl be rehired, Ana left her job and went to work in one of the new industrial factories near Suceava. She moved into a modern apartment building near the factory.

Ana met Ion Pavenic at a girlfriend's wedding and was immediately attracted to him. He looked tall and handsome in his bright, shiny state police uniform.

The son of Estra and Damian Pavenic, Ion had two brothers and two sisters. His father worked for the county government in the office of the police department, and his mother was a housewife with a high school education.

Ion had attended and graduated from the elementary and high schools, an average student who enjoyed sports and music—and girls. Powerfully built with a dark complexion, black hair, black mustache, and black eyes, he stood out among his peers.

After dating for about a year, Ion and Ana were married on June 16, 1945, in a blissful sacred ceremony attended by immediate family, other relatives, and friends.

Following the ceremony, the wedding party and guests flowed into a nearby fellowship hall where the banquet was set up and enjoyed by all those present. Ion took advantage of the music, the dancing, and most of all, the free-flowing drinks. The amount of liquor he consumed affected his poise and speech. Ana was both embarrassed and disappointed by the spectacle he made of himself.

As she would soon realize, it would not be the last time she felt this way.

CHAPTER 12

In the late 1940s, a devastating famine ravaged many areas of Romania, particularly where the front line of the war against Russia had brought about much destruction and havoc. While many blamed the terrible droughts of 1946 and 1947 as the principal cause of the suffering, Harald knew firsthand that there were other devastating circumstances that siphoned food from the villages.

In 1944, Soviet troops had entered the country, immediately requisitioned food from the peasants' barns, and savagely implemented those orders. This action added to the local and state government agencies' already demanded shares of food, which left farmers with very little to serve their basic needs. Starvation ran rampant through the villages. People died, particularly children.

Many were driven from their homes in search of food, defying police orders to remain in their villages. Some who did leave and who had sold their belongings to buy food for their families were prevented from going back home. Many were shot, or hanged and left swinging in the wind as a warning to others to remain in their homes.

The impact of the famine was not limited to the rural areas. The towns suffered too. Goods sold by the stores were heavily rationed, and what little was available had to be sold only at fixed prices.

"Have you heard the news?" Harald asked Stan Stanasila as they surveyed a field scorched by drought. "Last night three young children died in the village. Two were only four years old, and one just three. Their parents had nothing to feed them. This famine is so bad there isn't enough food in this entire village to have saved them."

"Nobody has food," Stan said, "and nobody can leave the village to find it. There are guards at each road and each path leading from the village. Now they put up a little store where you can buy food, but who has the money? No matter how low the prices are, if you do not have the money, you can't buy. They even keep the young ones from going into the cities to beg for money. So they just die from starvation."

"Yesterday, five families knocked on my gate begging for food. I felt so sorry for them, but what could I do? We don't have enough to feed our own." Harald did not elaborate, but he knew that if the Germans had not overlooked the trapdoor in the barn floor and the supply of extra potatoes and apples he and Sophia had hidden, he and his family might have starved to death long ago.

A shout came from the gate behind them. Harald recognized the voice. It was Sandu, who had once worked for him before the war. He had been coming around at least once a month begging for food to feed his family.

Harald left Stan and walked slowly to the gate.

"I will pay you back next year," Sandu promised as he stepped up. He looked terrible—dirty and gaunt, and his clothes were nothing more than rags. "You know I wouldn't ask to borrow from you under normal conditions, but I don't have food to keep my family alive. I have several children. I offer them to you. They can work for you to help pay you for the food you have given me. There will be no additional charge for their labor. They are good children and good workers. They can be a big help to you."

"I thank you sincerely for the offer," Harald said, "but I have all the help I need. And I don't want to let my current laborers go, because they only have a small plot for their livelihood. Like me, they are being ordered to give up what little food they have to supply the Russians."

The man clasped his hands together and started to plead.

"I wish I could help you and your children, but I can't. It's simply impossible." Harald turned away from the gate and left Sandu standing there, his face in his hands, softly weeping.

CHAPTER 13

Georgi Antonescu threw up his hands in disgust at his fourteen-yearold son. "Ilie, you are good for nothing," he proclaimed so loudly that even the neighbors could hear. "I have tried and tried to make a man out of you, but nothing I have done or said has helped. When are you going to grow up enough to take on a man's work?"

"I don't know!" Ilie shouted back. "Believe me, I don't like being this way. I want to be big and strong like my brothers, but I'm not. I can't do what you call 'a man's work.' I don't like it and it doesn't suit me. I'd rather be doing something I'm good at."

"You like to eat, don't you?" his father demanded. "If you want to continue eating with the rest of us, you've got to do your share of the work. As it is, you aren't. And I don't know what else I can do to get you to do it. I'm thinking about sending you to your brother Harald in Vioresca to see what he can do with you. What do you think about that?"

"I don't care. I honestly want to do my share, but I can't. All I seem to be good at is my schoolwork, but that doesn't help get the farmwork done. You can send me to Harald's if you think I will be able to do any better there, but I have my doubts."

With no further thought or hesitation, Georgi put Ilie on the bus to Vioresca.

It was already June when Ilie arrived. All the planting had been completed. Now the clover had to be cut, dried, and baled.

Harald showed Ilie around the farm and arranged for him to talk on the phone to his brother and sisters, hoping someone could get inside his head and make him understand his responsibilities and earn a livelihood with the work he could do. After their tour of the farm, Harald sat Ilie down and had a lengthy talk with him, emphasizing his responsibility to the family and to himself to provide the food they needed. Then he told the boy he was going to have a three-month trial, after which he would either stay on or go back to Mama and Papa.

Harald quickly realized that the runt of the family, the "good-for-nothing," wasn't sufficiently physically fit to work in the fields or in any of the outbuildings, particularly mucking out the barn, loading the cart with dung, and spreading the manure over the fields.

He watched in dismay as Ilie tried to hoist the hay bales from the cart into the barn. They were too heavy for him to lift and carry more than a few feet. Harald then thought he would give his little brother a less strenuous job—driving the mechanical equipment they used to cut and bale the hay. He rented the equipment and spent several hours showing Ilie how to drive the tractor through the fields, cutting, raking, and baling the hay. But when Harald turned the equipment over to Ilie to hook up and drive himself, he found that the boy didn't have the strength or any understanding of how to do it. He couldn't shift the gears, release the brake, or attach the cutter and baler to the tractor.

At the end of the three months, Harald told his brother, "I agree with Papa: you are good for nothing. I'm sending you back home."

After years of shuttling Ilie back and forth from Vioresca to Niculesca and trying to make a farmer out of him, Georgi,

Olga, and Harald all agreed to let the boy complete his education. Perhaps he could be more dependable and useful doing something less physically demanding, like accounting, managing, sales, or perhaps merchandising. He definitely was not meant to be a farmer.

CHAPTER 14

In 1948, the country's land-ownership laws were declared obsolete. Landowners were directed toward a new system that other communist countries had been implementing, a system whereby the farmers in a particular area were divested of their individual properties and the parcels were unified to form collectives that specialized in particular farm products. In Vioresca, half of the farms were selected to raise cattle and the other half to cultivate and grow grain to feed the animals.

Much to the fury of Harald's customers, they were presented with the new system. Not only was their land being confiscated, but also their other assets, including buildings, horses, carts, working tools, and applicable supplies. The owners were permitted to keep their homes, a small section of land they could cultivate for themselves, and their few animals, except working horses. While a few immediately accepted the offer, the rest had to be convinced that it was the only option available to them.

Martin Maniu, engineer, and Dan Dita, business manager, were moved into the village to establish the collective farms that would supply the state with a variety of beef products and the food necessary to feed the animals. Their initial task was to convince the landowners to willingly relinquish their properties. They called for a meeting of the villagers to explain the program and to urge the landowners to give up their properties to the government. Harald listened as his neighbors and friends were told they could keep their homes and the small plot of land they used for their personal use, and that they could continue to work the farm as they always had, except not as owners. They would be employees of the state.

A few of the peasants who were not making it as farmers believed they could live better by giving up their properties and settling for that steady compensation the government was offering. They had had enough of suffering through each year, not knowing whether they were going to produce enough food to keep the family alive. But the rest of the villagers were not convinced that this was the right thing to do. Their life as landowners was satisfactory. They had no desire to give up their property.

"I don't know what the world is coming to," Alin Ianculescu said as he and Harald left the meeting. "Now the government wants to take our villages and turn them into cooperatives. How can they do that to us?" Ianculescu was one of the larger landowners in the village. His family had owned farmlands in Vioresca since they were given to his grandfather in 1911.

"I only own five strips of land," Ianculescu continued. "That's more than three hundred acres of good fertile soil. Now the government wants to take them all and turn them into a huge cereal farm to grow grains and hay. Harald, did the government men talk to you?"

"No, they haven't said anything to me about taking my lands. I only have about five acres, and my brother and sisters have only the same amount. Perhaps the government is not interested in what little we have to offer. Were you visited?"

"Yes," Ianculescu said. "Dita came to my place and told me to get ready to sign the documents, because no matter what I do, my land will become the state's property this time next month. I can continue to live in my house, become a worker for the state, and be paid a monthly wage. Also, I can keep a small plot of ground for my own use. But I can't sell any of my produce or try to make a profit. He said that doing so is illegal and that could go to prison if I broke the law. This land has been good to me. I don't want to give it up."

"When do you have to give it up?"

"This afternoon, Dita is coming back with the papers to sign. I don't want to sign. What can I do?"

"I don't know, Alin," Harald said. "Have you explained how poor the land is and how difficult it is to farm because of spots of inferior soil, and how you've only been able to eke a living from the farm? Have you offered him a gift to maybe just look away and go look at another area for more promising properties?"

"No, I haven't. I'm not good at that sort of thing. Maybe you can help me? Maybe you can get him to look at other areas and leave us alone. After all, this is just a very small village with little to offer from our lands."

"What do you have to give him?"

"Not much. I have mostly my lands and farming equipment and my house. That's all."

"Do you have any money? You must have some hidden away with all the prizes you have gotten from the shows and exhibits. You must have some tucked away in your mattresses or buried in the backyard. And how about the money you got from selling your products?"

"Well, yes, I do have some money put aside. But I might need that if I have to give up my lands."

"Well, you'll have to decide what you want most: your farm or your money."

"I'd much rather keep my farm. I have maybe three thousand leu I could give up if I can keep my farm."

"Very well, go get it and bring it to me. I will take it and approach Dita this afternoon when he arrives in the village."

Harald spent the late morning and early afternoon watching for Dita to make his arrival. Finally, in the afternoon, he recognized the man driving through the village in that old black prewar government vehicle he had been seen driving. Stepping onto the street, Harald waved him down. He introduced himself and then said, "I understand you are representing the state and have made an offer to take Ionculescu's property to convert into a large grain-raising project. I'm curious to know if that project will also include my and my siblings' lands and property."

"No, it doesn't," Dita said impatiently. "Your properties are too small and are not in the plan. We are concentrating our efforts on building a huge grain operation here. We want only the property on the eastern side of the road. And we must have Ionculescu's property to give us the necessary land to accomplish our objectives."

"Yes, that's what I understand. I've been talking to Ionculescu. He tells me he doesn't want to give up his property, so he asked me to intercede for him. I suppose you know what you are doing," Harald said, "but have you looked at the sections of land in the next village? It seems to me that it would be better if you took those lands instead of these. Ionculescu's lands are good, but they are chopped up a lot for raising grain, what with the big pond and the big tree-covered hill. It seems to me that it would be very costly to convert his property into a productive grain farm."

"But I have already cleared it with my boss, and he says to go ahead with it. So I'm here to get Ionculescu to sign the papers and let me have his lands."

"Well, since he hasn't signed the papers yet, would it be possible to convince your boss to let this property go and accept another arrangement in its place?"

"Yes, it is possible, but he has already sent his plan up to his boss. It would be costly to make changes to it."

"Well, I would be glad to help pay for making the changes. How much do you think it would take?"

"I don't really know, but I would guess about three thousand leu."

"Well, I'll give you fifteen hundred, and you can settle that with your boss."

"No. That will help, but it wouldn't be enough to cover all the costs of making the changes we would have to make. I believe I could get it done if you gave me two thousand leu. What do you think?"

"I'll tell you what I can do," Harald said. "I'll give you one thousand and I'll help explain it to your boss. That is the best I can do."

"I'll accept that amount. And I'll do my own explaining, thank you."

"Very well," Harald said. "If you'll come back later today or in the morning, I'll have the money for you."

"I'll see you in the morning."

Upon returning to the office, Dita approached Martin Maniu, his manager. "I got an offer of eight hundred leu to change the plans and let Ianculescu keep his property. I agreed to accept it, because I too believe it will not be a good investment to develop that land for growing grain. I believe the lands in the next village are less costly and more promising. I think it would be better if we followed that route. I've got four hundred as your share."

"Well, thank you," Maniu said, "but I think five hundred for me would be better. After all, I'll have to take these changes to my boss. He will expect something in return."

"Yes," Dita said. "You are correct. Five hundred it shall be."

"Well, well," Maniu said with a big smile on his face. "Isn't this a fine coincidence at just this time? I was getting ready to tell you that we now plan to cancel collectivization of this village in this county in favor of forming one in the next county."

The collectivization program in Vioresca was put on hold, awaiting a more favorable time. Maniu and Dita were moved into the neighboring county to oversee the organization of a much larger collective specializing in beef and pork production.

Harald took the last empty chair at the weekly meeting. "Everyone in the country is under totalitarian controls," he said in disgust. "The newspapers and radio report that no one is allowed to change his or her dwelling without permission from the government."

"And not only that," Aurel Radulescu said, "but also it is reported that all movement between towns will be controlled by the militia. What kind of horse crap is this? What's this country coming to?"

"Yes," Ianculescu said, "and hundreds of thousands of people have been thrown into labor camps or sent to prison. And that's not all. Just yesterday I heard that thousands of men and women are being killed working on that damned canal connecting the Danube to the Black Sea. That's what happens to the prisoners and other criminals when they are sentenced to work there. At least that is what I heard people say when I went to the city."

"I heard that, too," Wadim said. "I also hear that the communists are killing the rich politicians and elite businesspeople and ridding the bourgeoisie of their wealth and castles."

"They also say," added Baboescu, "that it is getting difficult to persuade the peasant proprietors to give their land to the state to become a collective."

"Yes, it will take a long while for collectivization to be accomplished, but it will be done, just like it has been done in other communist countries," Harald said. "I look for the state to come after our lands again … and soon, my friends. Heaven forbid."

As Harald had predicted, the threat of collectivization arose again in Vioresca, but this time by the newly appointed village manager. His job was to convince the disgruntled landowners that the government knew what it was doing, and that it would be done the government's way or else.

Naturally, the landowners were still perfectly content to keep the free enterprise system and reap the benefits that came with it. But accomplishing that meant employing peasant workers to cultivate their fields and providing them with housing and small plots of land on which they could cultivate and raise their families. But under the collective system, with the government owning all the assets, the owners became employees of the state and were paid on a wage basis, just like the peasant workers.

Harald was shocked by what was going on in his village: the beatings, the intimidation, and the extra taxes—and bribes— the landowners were forced to pay to retain possession of their property.

Harald finally concluded that fighting collectivization was a no-win proposition and quickly ceded his properties to the government. He did not want to get involved in a forced buyout. Since he was just a store owner now, he knew he didn't have that much property to lose, only a few acres of land, a small barn, and a couple of horses he used only for transportation. He decided to take his chances with retaining possession of the store properties and their inventories.

"What are you thinking so hard about?" Sophia asked, pouring them some tea at their kitchen table.

"It's the way the government is taking over the villages," Harald said. "I don't understand their thinking and what they hope to accomplish with the properties they are confiscating. It's not right! It's not fair! I suppose they will take my stores too, and just pay me a salary to manage for them. Well, if they do, I hope the amount of pay will be comparable to what I'm earning now. If not, then I will have to consider doing something else to make a living."

CHAPTER 15

Aurel and Marianela Radulescu had been peasant farmers for more than thirty years. Their farm had been in the Radulescu family for almost a century, obtained from a rich boyar in the 1864 land reform.

Radulescu was a proud man, an excellent farmer who was considered rich and successful by his peers. Aware of what was going on with the new collectivization program, he wanted no part in it. The mere thought of being forced to give up his properties and working the lands as an employee of the state was nauseating to him. He was determined not to participate.

"The bastard Petru is coming tomorrow," Aurel told Marianela as they stood by their barn. His voice was full of anger. "I don't want to give up our land. They have no right to take it. It's been in the family for generations."

With tears in her eyes, his wife said, "It's the system we live under now, and it's what we must do. Everyone else in the village is faced with the same threat. I believe we must go along with it and take whatever we can get."

"I'm going to refuse to sign," he said. "I'm not going to sell this farm!"

"You must, Aurel! If you don't let go, they will beat you and take your property by force. Look at what happened to Negrescu. They almost beat him to death for refusing. They ruined his face and broke his left arm and right leg. They crippled him for life. Because he was no longer able to work the land, he had to move his family to the city and take a menial cleaning job with a machinery company. Now his wife is working as a dishwasher in one of the restaurants. They live in a run-down rental apartment in the middle of empty lots and stinking rubble. They have little furniture and no appliances. The children run around in rags. The only new clothing they get is the required uniforms students must wear. What is this country doing to its people?"

"It's doing to us what the other communist countries have done," Aurel said. "It's making lazy drunken bums out of most of us."

As had been promised, the next day the county's communist leader, Petru, appeared at their front door. Dressed in a baggy suit, with his thinning black hair plastered to his skull, he repeated the message he had been giving to everyone regarding the new policies passed down by the state government.

"The state must have your property, Radulescu," Petru said, "to add to a section specializing in the production of grains to feed the animals being raised in other sections of the collective. We already have four farms, and we want five more, including yours. We plan to use them to raise a variety of grains, all to make feed for the animals being raised in other collectives."

The smugness on the man's pudgy face made Aurel want to take a shovel to it.

"I'm here today to get you to sign over your farm for the amount I mentioned yesterday," Petru said. "The collective must have your property to complete its formation."

"I refuse to give it up," Aurel told him. There were tears brimming in his eyes, and his scarred hands were clenched into fists. "This land has been in my family for almost a hundred years. You can't have it."

"You don't understand what I'm saying," Petru said, a smile spreading across his face. "I'm here today to take possession of your farm, not to discuss or argue with you, or to try again to explain the government's program to you. As of this moment, this farm belongs to the government, and you have no more say in the matter. You must sign the papers."

"Where will we go?" Marianela said. "We have no other place to live."

"As I have explained many times, you do not have to move. You can continue living in your house and keep your garden plot and a few animals. We want only your lands, your working animals, and your equipment."

"But how can I make a living and clothe and educate my children without an income?" Aurel protested.

"You will have income, as I have explained to you many times before. The government will pay you wages, and you will continue to work the lands as you have, but all your production will belong to the government."

"No, no," Aurel cried. "I cannot do it. I will not give up these lands."

"Is that your final answer?"

"Yes, yes, damn you. That is my final answer."

"You will regret it, I promise." With that, Petru angrily turned and walked away, leaving Radulescu shaken and beginning to think that perhaps he should have taken the offer.

Aurel was sitting in on a bench behind the house with his head in his hands and tears in his eyes when Petru arrived in a black sedan the next day. Petru and two burly assistants walked through the kitchen to where Aurel was sitting.

"I'm here to take possession of your land," Petru said, thrusting an official-looking paper in Aurel's face. "Sign this where it's marked."

Marianela rushed from the kitchen and stood beside her husband.

"No, I cannot sign it," Aurel said.

Petru turned, nodded to the two burly men, and with a twist of his head signaled them to do their duty. They roughly grabbed Aurel by the arms and forcefully dragged him from the sleeping room, through the kitchen door, and onto the rough ground. As he tried to rise, the thugs attacked him with short lengths of iron pipe while Marianela screamed for them to stop. But they refused, continually beating him on the arms, thighs, and hands, sparing his face. Aurel had no chance to defend himself. He could only curl into a ball and cover his head with his arms. Marianela jumped in and tried to beat them off with a broom, but she only succeeded in getting punched in the stomach and kicked until she too fell to the ground.

"Leave us alone!" she screamed at her attackers. "We will sign! Give me the paper. I will make him sign. Just leave us alone."

Petru called off the two thugs. He leaned down and, in a calm voice, asked Radulescu if indeed he would sign the papers. Aurel nodded and soundlessly mouthed, "Yes, yes, yes." He had no other choice: it was either sign or he and his wife would be killed. He now realized he couldn't leave his children orphans, not in this cruel world.

The moment he signed the document, he lost his farm and all the assets that went with it. All he had left was his house, his outbuildings, a few animals, and the small plot of land he relied on to keep his family well and alive.

The three communists left the back of the house, got into their black sedan, and drove away in a huge swirling cloud of dust.

Radulescu limped to the gate to watch them speed away. "It'll be a great day for all," he said to his bleeding wife, "when those three die and go to Hades and are forced to jump into the blazing fires of hell."

Harald had never liked farming. Over the years, he and his siblings had let more and more of their lands go fallow, but not, of course, the small plots they retained and cultivated for personal use.

In 1955, Harald and his siblings agreed to sign their claim to the property and assets over to the government. When the village manager Petru came around to put a claim on their lands, it was an easy matter just to sign the contracts and give up the property. None were happy about the outcome, but they realized they had no other choice after seeing what the other owners in the village had had to endure.

The one thing Harald hated having to give up was his horses. That was like losing family members. And it left him without transportation. Fortunately, local buses were now available to get to and from the city.

At age twenty-one, Ilie was small of body but large in intellect. Physically he had changed little as he matured, eventually standing at five foot four and weighing around 135 pounds. Ilie's future lay in the academic world, not in agriculture, but he had to admit he had given the latter a good try. After completing his degree in psychology, he joined the state's education system and begun teaching high school biology.

He had married Adelina Amanar, a university graduate and a teacher of English in the local high school, on June 16, 1956. With the help of his neighbors, they built a nice two-story house on the edge of the city, where he and Adelina started a family. In 1958 their daughter, Doina, was born, followed by a son, Radu, in 1960.

In 1958, as Harald had sadly predicted, his two bodegas were acquired by the government. They were renovated and converted into convenience stores, and he was placed on the state payroll as store manager. He worked long hours at a meager salary. To supplement his income, he continued to sell his premixed feeds and other supplies to farmers in the more mountainous areas, where it was not economically feasible for the state to collectivize their scattered small farms. He always did his best to please his customers, and he could haggle with the best of them over price and gratuity. As a result, his service fees were always good.

PART 2

The Other Viki

CHAPTER 16

Ana Pavenic did not feel well. With a high temperature, achy muscles, and a nasty cough, she suspected it was something more than just her fifth pregnancy, which was already at full term. In their six years of marriage Ana and Ion had already been blessed with four sons.

Praying the illness would soon go away, Ana looked forward to the new birth, asking God to let her deliver a bright and cheerful girl to round out the family, because this was it as far as she was concerned. There would be no more children, no more pregnancies. She loved her rowdy quartet of boys, but enough was enough. Her thoughts returned to Ion. She knew he loved her and the children, but he was not a reliable father. His job with the state police consisted mostly of office work. He was good at it and was paid well, but it meant that he had to work long hours. By the time he was thirty-five years old, he was a habitual heavy drinker. When inebriated, he became loud, obnoxious, and incapable of doing anything. Ana was left to maintain the household and raise the children by herself.

He never has helped with the boys, Ana thought, so why would he help me with another child? What makes me believe he will be staying at home more? What makes me believe he will sober up? If anything, he will continue to get worse, staying out most of the night and coming home even more inebriated than the last time.

Two nights later, Ana awoke with her first delivery pains. Her water broke. After much shouting and shaking, she was able to rouse Ion from his stupor and let him know it was time to go to the hospital.

As he eased his wife into their secondhand car, he tried to comfort her and take her mind off how badly she felt. "I hope it's a girl," he said. "That will round out our family. And then we can stop having children."

"Get me to the hospital, damn it!" Ana cried.

Still a little tipsy, Ion drove at reckless speed, but he arrived safely and got her checked in. He nervously paced the waiting room floor as the staff prepared her for the delivery. He was surprised when after a few minutes the doctor came out to speak to him, a grave expression on his face.

"Is something wrong?" Ion asked with concern. "What's wrong?"

"Your wife has double pneumonia," the doctor said. "She's a very sick woman."

"Is she strong enough to deliver the child?" Ion asked. "Will the baby be all right?"

The doctor looked him in the eye. "Yes, she can safely deliver the baby, but the pneumonia is serious. After the baby is born, we will go from there. As it looks now, however, we will keep your wife in the hospital until she has made a full recovery, and that will likely be a long stay."

Ion was alarmed, but he realized there was nothing he could do but await the birth and pray that Ana and the baby came through it. Any other outcome was too terrible to consider. *I wish I had brought some brandy to settle my nerves,* he thought.

Ion had noticed something was wrong with Ana from the way she struggled to look after the boys and maintain the household. She had let some things slide. He knew he wasn't much help around the house, but he didn't feel guilty about it. That was women's work. Because he was a policeman, he had to spend a lot of time away from home. And he enjoyed drinking with his fellow policemen when he wasn't working.

After what seemed to him a long time, Ana gave birth. Not to one, but two healthy, squirming, squalling babies—both girls.

Ion blinked in shock when he got the news. "You said twins, Doctor?" he asked. "I don't believe it. We were praying for one, but two?"

"Yes, two tiny girls," the doctor replied, "but Ana is terribly weak. She doesn't have enough energy to nurse the babies. Until we can clear her lungs and she can regain her strength, she won't be able to feed them. That could take several weeks, if we are lucky. The babies are so small that they will have to stay here until they gain the weight and strength to be taken home."

Ion could see that the twins were identical in many respects. They both had the same dark brown hair and similar facial features, and they were the same size. The births of Viorica and Maria had been easy, but Ana looked bewildered and showed little emotion. She only wanted to sleep.

Ion immediately sent a brief message to his in-laws, Georgi and Olga. The next afternoon, they appeared in the ward.

"Ana's very sick," Ion told them in the hall outside her room. "She won't be able to go home. The doctors can't tell me how long she will have to stay."

"What's the matter with her?" Georgi asked. "Your message didn't say."

"She has double pneumonia, and because of her weakened state it is serious."

"I want to see her and I want to talk to the doctors," Olga insisted, her eyes spilling tears. "We've got to think about the babies and how they will be cared for. I want to understand what the hospital is doing and how long the girls will have to stay here."

After entering the room with Ion, Olga and Georgi seemed shocked at their daughter's condition. She could barely open her eyes to greet them, she was on oxygen, and her breathing seemed labored. Finally, she managed a weak smile and enough of a soft whisper to say hello. Then, seemingly drained by the effort, she slipped back into a deep sleep.

Quietly sobbing, the new grandparents left her bedside and Ion, and walked into the baby section to view their grandbabies sleeping in their cribs. As they marveled at the beautiful sleeping twins, the doctor arrived and introduced himself.

"As you no doubt know," he said, "your daughter is very ill. At the moment, I have to tell you there is some question whether or not we can save her. If we can cure her, it will take many weeks of medicine and complete rest. She is unable to care for her babies now, and they were born so small—about four pounds—that we can't let them go home yet. We should keep the girls here at the hospital until they weigh at least five pounds. That shouldn't take long as they are close to that weight now, and they show every sign of having healthy appetites."

"How long do you think you'll have to keep Ana?" Georgi asked.

"That's difficult for me to say at this time, but we know that we will have to clear her lungs of the disease and, at the same time, strengthen her enough to be released from the hospital as quickly as possible. I can't give you a firm answer, but you can rest assured we will take good care of her for however long it takes.

"What are we going to do?" Olga asked Georgi, a desperate edge creeping into her voice. "We can't care for them. They're just tiny babies, and we haven't had tiny ones for almost twenty years. We are in our sixties and too old to be starting over again, never mind changing diapers and fixing food for two babies who will keep us up all hours of the night with their squalling."

"Why do you think I should know what should be done with them?" Georgi asked her. "I realize that someone has to take charge. At some point in time, the babies must leave the hospital. You and I both know that Ion should be making these arrangements, but he can't be depended on to do anything. He can't even care for the boys he has at home now. If they get any attention, it's from the neighbors."

"What about our children?" Olga asked. "Do you think any of them could offer to help?"

"We can ask them, but I think they would all turn us down," Georgi said. "They are too busy caring for their own to take on this added burden—except for Harald and Sophia. They have no children, and both are healthy and strong enough to handle it. We both know that Sophia has been trying to get pregnant for many years without success."

"That's a good thought, Georgi. I'll write a letter to Harald and ask him and Sophia to give us some help until Ana is well enough to take care of the babies herself. What do you think?"

"I think that's a good idea. But what do we do in the meantime? We may have to take the girls home with us and care for them until Harald and Sophia make up their minds to help us. Are we able to do that?"

"We are, but not for long," Olga said. "It won't be easy, but that is the only solution available to us right now. We are too old to be caring for young ones."

Harald rolled over, yawned, and stared up at the ceiling. He had spent a long night tossing and turning. His thoughts had been disturbing and circular: memories of what he had seen in the war and the pain he had suffered, coupled with his disappointment at the way his plans for a good life in Vioresca had gone sour due to circumstances beyond his control. *It was just one of those bad nights,* he thought. *I'm not going to let it ruin a perfectly good day.*

When he looked out the bedroom window, he was greeted by the bright sun filtering through the surrounding treetops. It was growing warmer day by day, and the time was nearing for sowing seeds and planting the tender seedlings that had sprouted in the kitchen. The new season's garden was something to look forward to.

Harald's mind turned to Ana and how much she had needed his attention as a child. He had to put up with her surly, stubborn attitude and felt he had to reprimand her for her homesickness because it poisoned the mood of the others. *She is a special person. Of that there is no doubt,* he told himself. *But she is also hardheaded and determined to do things in her own way.* And now with Ana having four young boys barely a year apart and another child about to be born, he worried that she was going to have more problems than she could handle. Plus, up to now, Ion hadn't been any help to her.

Mama has always been good about keeping us informed about the family, Harald thought, but we haven't received any letters recently. Ana must be doing well with her pregnancy. Otherwise, we would've heard something. We should keep in closer contact with Ana and Ion. But we live so far apart.

Harald remembered the years of being responsible for the care of his siblings while Mama and Papa worked in the fields. Sure, there were some anxious moments and it was not always easy, but there were many more happy and amusing times.

Harald thought again how nice it would have been to have had a family of his own to raise. Sophia had known for years that she could never have the children she so deeply desired. It worried him knowing how much she wanted children. It left him feeling helpless and sad for her.

Sophia was already dressed for the day and was busy preparing their breakfast when Harald entered the kitchen. "You know," she said, looking up from the eggs frying in the skillet, "I've been thinking about Ana a lot and wondering how she's doing."

"I've been thinking about her too."

"This child will give her five to love and tend to," Sophia said. "I hope Ion will do his duty and help her."

"Well, he could," Harald said, "if he made up his mind to stop drinking and stay at home for a change. But I don't think that will ever happen. He is who he is, and nothing is going to change him. I'm afraid Ana is on her own until she can get some help from her sons—and because they are still so young, that won't happen for years."

Twice a week, on Tuesdays and Fridays, the postman from the city delivered the village mail to Harald's stores, where his customers would pick it up. As he sorted the mail, Harald saw a letter from his mother. Suspecting that it might be news about Ana, he opened the letter and slowly read it.

His mama's handwriting was not the best—she had little formal education—but he could make it out. As expected, the letter pertained to Ana and the childbirth.

Dear Harald and Sophia,

The news here is both good and bad. First the good: Ana and Ion had been praying for a beautiful little girl. Instead, the good Lord gave them two.

Now the bad news: Papa and I need you. Ana has double pneumonia and must stay in the hospital until the doctors can clear her lungs of the disease. This may take weeks or months … the doctors make no promises. But it does mean that Papa and I will have to take the babies home when they are discharged and care for them until Ana is strong enough to do it. Ion is certainly not reliable, and he has the boys to care for. The doctor said the girls might be released from the hospital within the next week.

This is where you can make our life a lot easier. I'm not strong enough to care for two babies, and Papa is not well. You are the only ones we can turn to. Will you and Sophia come as soon as you can and relieve us? We know the journey is long, but we really need you.

Mama

At lunchtime, Harald took the letter home. After Sophia read it, he asked, "Can we help them?"

"I have mixed feelings," Sophia said. "I'm happy that she got the girls she was so eager to have. On the other hand, I'm sorry she must stay in the hospital for such a long time. But what really bothers me is that your mother and father are the only ones who've agreed to take the babies. You have other siblings who are closer—and younger than we are. Why did they ask us and not them?"

"I can only assume they asked and were turned down," Harald said. "I suppose they turned to us because we have no children of our own. What should we do?"

"If your parents have to give up the girls because they can't take care of them, I think we should take them and care for them until Ana is able to do it herself."

"You are probably right," Harald said. "But first we must get to Niculesca before we make a decision. I don't want to make any commitments until I have considered the responsibilities that come with caring for tiny babies. Actually, if I had my way, I wouldn't take either one or the both of them for that length of time."

"Why not?" Sophia demanded. "Don't you want to relieve your parents of that burden? We must do something to help them."

"Yes, we've got to do something. But if we took either one or both of the babies, I know that we would not want to give them up when it came time to do so. We would love them so much that it would hurt us terribly to have to give them back to Ana. But we have to go and see what we can do to help Mama and Papa. So, let's get ready."

CHAPTER 17

It took Harald and Sophia a week to make all the arrangements for the trip to Olga and Georgi's home. The two-hour bus ride—with three bus changes—gave them an opportunity to discuss the situation. On the day of their departure, strong rays of sun gleamed through a scattering of clouds that floated across the valley. While the world on the other side of the window seemed very bright and cheerful, Harald and his wife were very apprehensive about the journey and the end result.

"I am deeply concerned about this situation." Sophia spoke up. "While we've grown up looking after our brothers and sisters while our parents labored in the field for the owners, we've never had our own to raise and love. I do believe, however, that we could at least care for one of the girls until Ana leaves the hospital. What do you think?" she asked, looking Harald in the eyes.

"My answer is still the same," Harald said with a rising voice that displayed his frustration with the decisions he knew he was going to have to make when face-to-face with his fragile mother and ailing father. "I know that I will learn to love her so much that I wouldn't want to give her up. When is Ion going to act like a man?" Harald said in his loud voice. "He should shoulder the responsibility, not your parents. They've raised their family; they shouldn't have to bear that burden again.

"He has proven he is incapable of being a proper father to his children," Harald said, raising his voice louder in anger. "All he cares about is drinking and staying out all night with his policeman friends."

Harald saw other bus riders turning their heads toward him, but he continued talking loudly. "He's not around the house enough to discipline his boys. From what Mama has said, the neighbors are looking after them. Sophia, I don't want to have to deal with the man. I don't even want him to come around my house. He is always drunk and obnoxious. I don't like him, never have. I don't know why Ana married him. The only thing they seem to do together is make babies. Now she has six to bring up by herself."

Sophia put a calming hand on his arm, warning him that other passengers were listening in on their conversation. They both lowered their voices and only whispered to each other for the remainder of the trip.

Twenty-one years had passed since Harald and his siblings were forced to leave home. In that time, the country had survived the world's most devastating depression, a terrible world war, a horrendous drought killing hundreds of thousands from hunger and related diseases, changes of government from monarchy to communism, and collectivization of the area's rural farms.

This last change was the biggest to the economy of Niculesca. The government had combined it and surrounding villages into a collective specializing in dairy products. Unlike what happened in Vioresca, the people in the collective had elected a governing body to establish and enforce the rules and regulations to steer the village leaders.

The tiny village square and the layout of the roads was the same. Harald and Sophia got off the bus and began walking hand in hand toward the little two-room farmhouse where he and all his brothers and sisters had been born. As they passed through the rusting front gate, he was struck by how small the house looked—much smaller than he remembered. It made him sad to see that patches of the adobe exterior had fallen away. It made him think his father was too old to keep up the place.

They were greeted at the door by Mama and Papa with hugs and kisses on the cheeks.

Everyone immediately moved to the crib in the main room, where Viorica and Maria lay swaddled.

"They are so beautiful!" Sophia said. "They are perfect!"

Harald was immediately taken by their dark hair and eyes, their fat little rosy cheeks, and their smiles as they looked up at him.

"Your papa and I are so glad you've come," Olga said with tears in her eyes. "We love Ana's babies as much as we loved our own, but I know I can't care for them both, and Papa is not in any condition to help. He didn't want me to mention it, but his heart has gotten bad and he can barely get around by himself."

Harald could see that his father was embarrassed by this revelation of weakness. He had always been a proud, strong man.

"Sophia and I agree that you and Papa should not be left to bear this burden," Harald said. "If Sophia had her way, she would take both girls and give them good and loving care. The issue we have with doing that is the long time it might take for Ana to be released from the hospital. In that period of time, we both would learn to love the girls so much that we would want to keep them forever as our own. It would break our hearts to have to give them up. And we realize that keeping them both wouldn't be fair to either Ana or Ion. Viorica and Maria are their children, and we know they love them and would want to raise and cherish them as their family."

"Would you then consider taking one?" Olga asked.

"Before we left home, we discussed and considered that as a choice, but we turned it down for the same reasons we just talked about, namely that our love for the one we chose would just be too much for us to have to let her go."

As he spoke, he couldn't help but glance down at the two babies squirming in their bed, kicking their little legs, and waving their tiny arms. It urged him to pick up one and kiss and cuddle her. The more he looked, the more his hard-line stance softened. He knew how happy it would make Sophia if they took one of the babies, as she had always wanted a girl to raise and pamper. Plus, when the child was older, she could help around the house and be someone whom Sophia could depend on as needed. It would be the answer to Sophia's prayers.

"Mama, I have changed my mind," Harald said. "We will take one of the babies, but only with the understanding and acceptance that she will become our child to love and educate with no interference from any of the family."

Then, to emphasize his position, he repeated: "We will take her, raise her, educate her, and treat her as if she were our own birth child. I want to be certain Ion and Ana fully understand our wishes and will accept our decision before we move forward."

"Papa and I accept your proposal," Mama said, "but you're going to have a hard time getting Ana and Ion to agree to it. We'll go to the hospital this afternoon and discuss it with them should Ion be present."

Sophia, who had been quietly listening to the conversation between Harald and his mother, threw her arms around him and cried, "Thank you, thank you! You've just made me the happiest woman in the world. Thank you."

"Which of the girls will you take?" Georgi asked.

"Yes, Harald," Sophia said. "How will we ever choose?"

Harald realized that there was no emotional way to make the decision, so he fell back on his mercantile experience. "We will take whichever one weights the most," he said.

They weighed the babies with the old spring-loaded scale that hung from the ceiling in a corner of the room. Firstborn Viorica was the heavier by two ounces.

"The decision is made," Harald said. "Viorica will be our daughter."

Olga agreed to keep Maria and care for her until Ana was released from the hospital, however long that would be.

"Now we just have to get Ana and Ion's approval of the plan," Harald said.

"How dare you even think of such a thing?" Despite her weakened state, Ana found the strength to shout at them. "You call yourselves my parents? You call yourself my brother? You are stealing my child when I am too ill to fight you!"

"If we take Viorica," Harald said, "we will love her as if she were our own and without any interference from you or Ion. We will care for her and see that she gets a good education. Those are our terms."

"I will raise my own daughter," Ana cried. "I'm not twelve years old. You can't bully me anymore, Brother. My husband is a policeman!"

"It is no secret to any of us," Harald said calmly, "that you are in over your head with four boys and that you get no help from your policeman husband. How are you going to manage with two more children, all of them less than six years of age? We promise Viorica a good life in our home, and for that we ask for your acceptance and blessing."

Ana understood what Harald was saying and the conditions under which he and Sophia would agree to take Viorica. She remembered how determined Harald could be and the firm positions he always took in his dealings with her. She remembered

how he used to beat her with the switch—his last-ditch method—
to make her obey.

The more Ana thought about the four of them ganging up on
her, the angrier she became. But the resulting flood of emotion
so drained her reserves of strength that after a few minutes she
could barely keep her eyes open. Tears began to stream down her
cheeks. She knew in her heart that once again Harald was right.
She wasn't going to be able to take care of her daughters now, and
she couldn't depend on Ion to do anything. *I should have divorced
him years ago,* Ana thought. *I realize my family can't survive without
him. We are too dependent on his financial support.*

I realize Mama and Papa can't care for both my babies the
length of time I'm going to have to remain here in the hospital,
Ana continued to think. I'm thankful they, at least, can care for
Maria. And I know Harald and Sophia will care for and love
Viorica, but I can't tolerate them keeping her as their own child. I
don't want to let Viorica go, yet I know that Harald and Sophia,
being childless, can give her a better life than what Ion and I can
offer. At least she'll be loved and still remain within the family.

"Ana, what do you say?" Harald pressed her.

Her eyelids closed. She weakly nodded her head.

On the bus trip back home, there was silence between Harald
and Sophia. He knew they were both thinking about the situation
they had created for themselves. Questions ran through his mind:
how to feed the baby, how to clothe her, and how raise her to be
a responsible adult.

"What about the neighbors?" Sophia said, breaking his
concentration. "What will we tell them and the other villagers?
Word gets around so quickly. They will know she is not our child.
We will need to explain the circumstances, and you are the one

who will have to do most of the talking. People will come in the store and ask you about it. Don't forget, it was your idea that she become our daughter."

"I know I said that," Harald told her, "and that is just what I meant. We will care for her as if she is our own daughter and see that she gets a good high school education without any interference from anyone, especially Ion. I don't want him coming around to see her. That's the way it will be, or else I will return her to Mama and Papa."

As they were discussing this new and exciting change in their life, the baby lay asleep in Sophia's arms, contently sucking on a new pacifier. Harald looked at the peaceful child and smiled. "Viorica is the name Ana and Ion gave her, but now that she's our baby, I'm going to call her Viki."

As soon as they arrived home with Viki, Sophia went to her parents' home and borrowed the cradle, diapers, powders, and bottles her mother no longer had use for. She had explained to her parents why she needed these things, knowing that soon the entire village would spread the news that they had brought home one of Ana's twin babies.

Three months after being admitted to the hospital, Ana was released to go home. She took a few days to readjust to being back with her family, and then she traveled to her parents' house to get Maria.

Georgi and Olga were overjoyed to see her up and about after the long bout with pneumonia.

"Papa and I are so grateful to the good Lord for the miracle of your recovery," Olga said. "We had almost given up hope of ever seeing you out of that hospital bed."

"I too am relieved and happy to be feeling better and in my own home again," Ana said. "Now I'm ready to take Maria off your hands. I'm so grateful you and Papa were able to help me. Next I must get Viorica back from Harald and Sophia. I know it won't be easy, but I must have my own blood back. Is there any way you can help me?"

"That is something you will have to work out with Harald and Sophia," Olga said. "We don't know what we would have done without them. Caring for the one baby almost killed us both. We believe, as I know you do, that they will care for her and see that she does not want for anything. I would like to see Viki get a good education and a good job afterward, and then get married so we can have lots of great-grandchildren."

"Certainly I'm thankful that Viorica is being given good care, but she is my child and I want her at home with her twin sister. They should not be raised apart. I'll take the burden of Maria off your hands now. I can't thank you enough for caring for her."

With that said, Ana wrapped her baby in a warm, soft blanket and walked to the bus stop to take her daughter home.

CHAPTER 18

Viki was a feisty baby, quick to let everyone know when she wanted to be changed and fed. And she had the lung power to express herself. But once satisfied, she would lay back and sleep the night away. She was a curious, active baby. Once she could walk, she'd search in cupboards and drawers looking for objects to make noise.

Harald hovered over her and took every opportunity to teach her the difference between right and wrong. He also taught her that a farmer's life was an all-day endurance: working in the daylight hours on growing and preserving the ingredients of life, and in the dark hours making and maintaining clothing, using the tools for making looms, using the pressing iron, and cleaning and using the gas lanterns—not forgetting showing her how to use the outdoor equipment like the cart, the harnesses, and the tools for planting, harvesting and utilizing the value of the produce.

As Viki aged and grew, she was given light chores to do inside and outside the house. She learned how to clean and store dishes and sweep the floor. Outside she was taught how to feed, water, and clean up after the animals, and in the garden she learned to pull weeds and pick the produce. In the evenings after eating, Sophia showed Viki how to sew, and do embroidery patterns. Viki learned easily but could be stubborn if she disagreed with what she was told to do. And she was quick to defend herself.

When Viki turned five years of age, Harald sat her down one morning and said, "Viki, the time has come to get you started in kindergarten."

"Do I have to go to school?" she asked him.

"Yes. Not only is it compulsory, but also you have to get your education so you can succeed and have the life you want. You'll have to know how to read and write and do arithmetic, and you'll have to learn a lot of things about Romania and the rest of the world."

"Can't you teach me these things?"

"You need to go to school because the teachers there know these things better than me. They have been educated to teach what you need to know. And like I just said, the government says all children must go to school and get educated. So tomorrow I'll take you to the teacher and get you enrolled."

"If you say so, Papa."

The next morning, bright and early, Sophia dressed Viki in one of her pretty dresses and Harald walked her to school. The kindergarten teacher had a long, pale face and nose, and her black hair was tied up in a bun.

"Miss Arcos, this is my daughter, Viorica, but most everyone calls her Viki. She is ready to come to your school when you start in September."

"Yes, I know who Viki is. I was wondering if you were going to enroll her, as many of the local parents do not enroll their children in kindergarten. And it's a shame, because they do not get the start in education that benefits them most when they enter the primary grades."

"Yes, I have noticed that," Harald said, "but most of the parents are poor and can't afford to enroll their children, even though the government pays most of the costs. They can't afford the clothes and the meals. Plus, the children are needed to work on the farm, even though they are not capable of doing much. But what little work they can do is helpful to the family, particularly if the parents are not capable of working. Will Viki have to wear a uniform dress?"

"No, uniforms are not necessary at the kindergarten level," Miss Arcos said. "They may be at the secondary levels, but only where the schools require it."

"Thank you very much, Miss Arcos. You will have the pleasure of working with Viki starting in September."

"I look forward to it, Mr. Antonescu."

A week before the start of kindergarten, before Harald set off from home to work in his stores, Ana and Ion appeared at their front door. Apparently Ion had forgotten Harald's warning never to show up at his place seeking to take Viki home with them. But he was there. And because of Ana, Harald couldn't turn him away. Ion looked clean and sober, as if perhaps Ana had finally been able to straighten him out.

Harald was disturbed to see them, but still he welcomed them into his house. Sophia seemed equally surprised when they walked into the kitchen. To keep Viki from hearing the discussion, Harald sent her outside to tend to the ducks.

Ana pleaded her case about Viorica being returned to them. Harald kept repeating, "She is ours."

Ana kept repeating, "She is not."

The standoff continued. Ion remained silent during this exchange, apparently satisfied that Ana knew what she was doing.

"Yes," Ana said, "I can see that Viorica is happy here and seems contented and well cared for, but she belongs to us and I want her back. Her sister Maria also wants her back so they can grow up together. They are sisters. Maria needs her."

"Do your kids know about Viki being Maria's twin sister?" Harald asked.

"Yes, they do, and they don't understand why she lives here and not with them. We try to convince them that this is only temporary and someday she will return. In fact, when we told them we were coming to get Viorica, they were very happy and excited about her coming home. We don't want to disappoint them."

Ion finally spoke up, but about a different subject. "Do you have any tuica?" he asked Harald. "I'd like to have a drink with you."

"Yes I do, but we shouldn't drink now." Ana nodded her head in agreement.

But Ion wouldn't back off. "It is good to see you again, Harald, and I'd like to have a drink with you. After all, it has been a long time since we last saw you and Sophia."

Thinking one drink would be all right, Harald brought out the tuica bottle and poured them each a shot. The women declined. Harald sipped his. Ion, after gulping his straight down, offered his glass for a refill. Harald was hesitant, especially when he saw the dark look Ana was giving him, but he went ahead and poured another, which Ion again swallowed in one gulp. Harald pushed the bottle toward him in disgust and said, "Help yourself."

As the conversation continued, Ion did indeed help himself, and as a result he began to get louder and louder and kept repeating himself as if he couldn't think of anything else to say or as if he had forgotten that he'd just said it. "Yes, Ana and I came here to take Viorica back with us. We don't want to disappoint our children."

Harald held strongly to his original position. "When we took Viki from Mama, we promised you and Mama we were going to raise her as our own and give her the best we can. I don't see any reason why we should back down now. We will not give her up.

You might as well leave, because she is ours and we plan to adopt her as soon as we can."

While he had considered adoption before, he had not set a timetable to get it done until now.

Sophia spoke up and said, "We have grown to love Viki as if she is our own. We've made plans to place her in kindergarten Monday, and we intend to go ahead with it. We also have future plans to see that she gets educated through high school even if we have to move to do it. She will get the best education we can get find."

"Apparently then," Ana said, grimfaced, "you are not willing to let us take her back with us this trip?"

"That is correct," Harald said. "Not now. Not ever."

"Viorica is our child. We are going to take her back with us today," Ion said, slurring his words.

Harald noted there was very little brandy left in the bottle.

"No, you're not!" Sophia shouted back. "We will keep Viki until the time comes when she needs to know that she is your daughter. Until then, we don't want to confuse her by telling her that we are not her parents. I'm sorry you made this trip for nothing, but that is the way it will be, whether you like it or not."

Ion got even more upset at this and began to shout and call Harald and Sophia names unfit for a child's ears, like the thoughtless monster and complete ass he was. Ana turned her anger on her husband. She took him by the hand, looked him straight in the eyes, and yelled in his face, "Shut your dirty mouth! Viki is in good hands. I'm beginning to agree that Harald and Sophia can do more for her than what we can. We will go home without her."

With that, Ana dragged Ion out of the house.

CHAPTER 19

The kindergarten was only six houses down the street. Students arrived at 8:00 a.m. and stayed until 4:00 p.m. They learned to sing patriotic songs in Russian and how to write their names and the alphabet. After lunch they took a nap. Each student had his or her own plate, bowl, and utensils, and a designated space on the floor to sleep. Food was prepared and served on the premises each day.

Behind the school was a small lake surrounded by willow trees and reeds. The adjoining open field was a good place to play games. One day when she was not able to nap, Viki slipped away when the teacher's back was turned and played around the pond. The teacher noticed her missing and found her skipping flat stones across the water to see how many skips each made before sinking.

"You know you should not sneak out of the building like you just did," Miss Arcos said angrily. "It is my job to protect you while you are in school. I can't do that if you are sneaking away and putting yourself in danger. Suppose you fell into the pond. Who would be there to pull you out? You could drown. If you do that again, I am going to tell your parents. Then if you keep it up, I will arrange to expel you from the school. Do I have your promise you will not do it again?"

"Yes," Viki said contritely, "I promise I won't do it again if you promise not to tell my father. I don't want him to know. He will get angry and talk to me, and when he talks, he doesn't know when to stop. Will you promise?"

"Yes, I won't say anything if you keep your word. You're a bright student and will do well in school, but you must follow the rules."

Several weeks later, little Eugen Korzha couldn't sleep during nap time because he felt the immediate need to relieve himself. When Miss Arcos left the room, Eugen sneaked out the back door to the field near the pond. He went to where the outdoor toilet was located. But realizing he couldn't hold out long enough to reach the toilet, he dropped his pants, did his business, and then returned to the classroom and his sleeping pad unnoticed. When the teacher came back, she roused the students and resumed her lessons until recess time.

As the students were playing around the pond during their fifteen-minute recess time, Ioni Novescu stepped in what Eugen had left behind and was walking around with it stuck to his shoe, much to the amusement of his classmates. When the teacher saw that, she demanded the students tell her who the culprit was. No one spoke, so Miss Arcos turned on Viki and said, "You did it! I'm going to tell your parents as I promised I would if you ever slipped out of the classroom again!"

"No, I didn't!" Viki said, tears welling up in her eyes.

"Yes, you did. You must have slipped out again during quiet time."

"No, I didn't!" Viki spun on her heels and ran out the door and to her home, crying all the way. As she entered the house, Harald wanted to know what had happened. He asked her if she had been injured in some way.

She told her father what had happened and said that she was not going back to school anymore. "I didn't do it," she cried, "but

I know who did. Everyone knows who did it, but no one wants to tell the teacher. I'm not going back."

"Yes, you are," Harald said. "We are going back right now to assure the teacher that you are not the one who is at fault. You don't have to tell her who it was unless you know for certain who did it. If you don't know, don't say anything. But if you are absolutely certain who it was, you must tell her."

By the time they arrived at the school, the students were back in the classroom and teaching had resumed. When Harald confronted the teacher, she brought the class to attention and asked Viki if she knew who did it. At first Viki hesitated, but then, remembering what her father had told her to do, she pointed her finger at the culprit and said, "He did it! Eugen Korzha did it."

Eugen began to cry at once. "Yes, I did it," he wailed. "I promise I won't do it again. Please, oh please, don't tell my father. He will punish me with his belt."

Viki was exonerated and the matter was closed, except that Harald had to take five minutes and censure the teacher for making accusations and chastising someone without actually knowing who the culprit might be.

Viki felt better and was glad she had followed her father's sage advice. It gave her the knowledge that she could handle situations like this without creating a lot of trouble, especially if it absolved her of frightful events that could be held against her.

In first grade, Viki accidently bumped third grader Roxie Nicule while chasing a slow-rolling soccer ball, knocking her to the ground. Furious, Roxie jumped to her feet, confronted Viki, and shouted for all to hear: "Why don't you watch where you're going, you, ah, you ugly gypsy! You knocked me down!"

"I didn't see you," Viki responded. "I was watching the ball and I didn't see you." Then, with fists clinched and teeth tightly shut, she looked her adversary straight in the eyes and shouted, "And I am not an ugly gypsy!"

"Yes you are, and you should have been watching where you were going!"

"If I was watching you, I wouldn't have seen the ball that was kicked to me. And besides, if you hadn't been primping around trying to act smart and like a know-it-all, you would have seen me coming and would have better protected yourself."

"Well, you had better start watching, you, you, ah, ah, gypsy." Roxie stuttered, trying to find a mean word to describe Viki, while looking around to make sure others were watching. Satisfied they were, she shouted, "Yes, you are. You're a gypsy! The Antonescus are not your parents."

"I am not a gypsy, and what you say is not true! They are my mother and father."

"They are not, and you know it."

"I do not!" Viki screamed.

But this was not the first time this accusation came from the village kids. She had ignored it, believing they were just making it up to tease her. Now the time had come to ask her father.

She knew she would get a truthful answer.

"Papa, today a student in school said you and Mama are not my real parents. Is that true?"

"Why do you listen to what others say?" her father said. "How many times have I told you not to pay them any attention? Yes, you are our child. We raised you from a baby. You are mine, and Mama is your mother."

"But you always said you got me from the gypsies."

"Many people say that babies come from storks, but I prefer to say babies come from gypsies, who are always coming around trying to sell us something. In spite of what the other student said, you are a beautiful girl and very intelligent. Always remember, we love you. You are our daughter, and we will do everything we can to get you a good education and a good husband and children of your own. Tell the other children they don't know what they're talking about. You're our child and you always will be. We love you."

"And I love you too, Papa. When I get older, I want to marry you."

"We'll think about that when the time comes," Harald replied as he put his arm around her and kissed her on the forehead.

Viki accepted his answer and let the matter drop. As time went on and she continued to get the same taunts from her peers, she defended herself proudly and let it be known that Mama and Papa were indeed her parents. They loved her and she loved them, and that was all that mattered.

CHAPTER 20

The next morning Sophie and Harald were sitting at the kitchen table finishing their second cup of coffee and thinking about the goods in his bodegas he had to inventory, label, and shelve.

Sophia rose from her chair and moved to the small window facing the east. She watched the morning sun slowly come up over the eastern hills, throwing its vibrant colors through the fleecy white clouds scattered across the blue sky, bouncing a mixture of vibrant colors off the tall grasses of the meadows.

"We've got a beautiful sunrise this morning," Sophia said as she adjusted the window curtain. She hesitated a moment and then said, "After what happened again yesterday in the school yard, wouldn't today be a good day to tell Viki about her real family and how she came here to live with us?"

"It is going to be a beautiful day," Harold offered curtly.

It was obvious he had heard her, but still he was reluctant to broach the subject with Viki.

Sophia realized that once again he was doing his best to evade the question. She turned from the window. This time with more emphasis on each word, she said, "Don't you think this would be a good time to tell Viki she is not our child?"

"I heard what you said before, but I'm not ready to talk to her about it."

"Harald, she is six years old and is already in school. She's old enough to understand the situation and accept it."

"Yes, you are probably right," Harald replied, "but I'm still not ready to tell her about us not being her blood parents. I'm afraid we might lose her. Is that too much to ask?"

"She's got to know sometime," Sophia responded.

Harald was apprehensive about obtaining the adoption certificate because of the circumstances under which Viki had been taken from Ana and Ion. Before approaching the government clerk, Harald looked into the envelope he had brought with him to make certain he had enough cash to encourage the woman to prepare the document.

"What can I do for you?" the clerk said.

Noting her name on her identification tag, Harald said, "Adriana, I want an adoption certificate for my daughter."

"What's her name?"

"Viki Pavenic."

"Is she an orphan?"

"No."

"Who are her parents?"

"Ion and Ana Pavenic," he replied.

"What are the circumstances that enable you to legally adopt her?"

The reason Harald was apprehensive about obtaining the adoption certificate was that he would have to answer these kinds of questions. Taking a deep breath, he proceeded to tell the clerk all the details of how he and Sophia had found it necessary to take in and raise Viki.

"That was good of you and your wife to do this for your sister," Adriana said, "but I have to have their permission to let you adopt the child and remove Viki's name from your sister's family records and place her name on your records. I need a written statement from her and her husband that gives permission for me to make the changes and give you a certificate."

"It will take me a while to arrange that," Harald said. "They don't live near us. Is there any other way I can do it, Adriana?" he said, slipping the fat envelope under a book on her desk and pushing it toward her.

She removed the envelope from under the book, hid it in her hand under the desk, and counted the contents.

"That's generous of you, Harald, but, ahem, ah, my boss will need to sign the certificate and he would like to personally hand it to you. Perhaps you can help him with that?" She slid the envelope and the book back to him.

Harald reached into his pocket, removed several bills, slipped them into the book, and returned the book to her.

"Excuse me," Adriana said, "I'll take the certificate to him. He'll sign it and present it to you. It will not take long."

Within five minutes, the manager came into the room and gave the signed certificate to Harald. Shaking his hand with enthusiasm, he said, "Congratulations, Father, Viki now is legally your daughter."

Harald smiled and happily left the building.

"Well, it's done," Harald said as he showed the certificate to Sophia. Our daughter is now Viki Antonescu. It cost me a lot of money to get it signed, but it was worth it."

"I'm glad," Sophia said. "Now you'll have to tell her of her name change and advise the school."

"I'll tell her this evening, and the school in the morning.

That afternoon after school Viki came rushing in with exciting news. "I've been selected by the teacher to be a singer in our school chorus. I'm so happy I don't know what to do," she excitedly spoke out. "My good friend Krissy and I were the only ones picked from first grade."

"Well, I'm certain the teacher will show and teach you how to sing with the group. Now, I've got some more good news to share with you. Your mama and I have legally adopted you to be our loving daughter ... we've changed your last name from Pavenic to Antonescu. What do you think of that?"

"I like that, but I like my good news better than your good news. I wonder what songs the teacher will give us to sing." With that Viki turned and ran into the next room humming one of her favorite English songs she had learned from the radio.

"What do you think Sophia? Do you think she understood what I just explained to her?"

"It appears to me that she'll soon forget," Sophia smilingly responded. "It's obvious she is more excited about singing than having her name changed."

"I think you're right." Harald sadly responded.

CHAPTER 21

It was a nice late spring morning. Bright green foliage filled the trees and shrubs, hinting that perhaps, just perhaps, a bountiful harvest would be delivered when the warm season changed into the cool and frosty fall. Lush green clover fields were covered with white and pink blooms with almost enough growth to mow, bale, and store in the barn to await the need in the feeding stalls. This was the view Harald had out his window while he considered Viki and her upbringing. In fourth grade most children her age were already working in the fields and helping maintain the household duties. She was already fetching water from the well, feeding the chickens, ducks, and geese, and tossing handfuls of hay to the animals, but was time for her to take on more challenging responsibilities.

As he peered through the window, a fat goose waddled into view. It gave him an idea.

Summoned from a game of hide and seek by her father, Viki stood in the doorway ruddy cheeked and a little out of breath.

"Today," he said, "I want you to take the geese to the pond so they can swim and feed on the new grasses growing there. It will be good for geese, and your mama won't have to do it. She can use the extra time concentrate on her other chores. It will help you learn to assume more responsibility around the house."

"Do I have to?" she asked. Viki understood what Papa wanted her to do with the geese and how he expected her to do it because she had followed Mama many times. But she didn't want to herd geese. She wanted to resume the hide-and-seek game with Elena, her neighborhood friend. At the same time, she knew it would do no good to argue against her father's wishes. He always got what he wanted.

"No, you don't have to do it," he said, "but I want you to. You must learn how to get things done and be depended on to do them. All I'm asking you to do is lead the geese across the road and down the path to the Ionescus' pond. It has been over a week since they've been there to eat the grasses growing around the pond and the on the pond's bottom.

"They will follow you. But you must keep your eyes on them. Don't let them out of your sight for even one second, for they will scatter away and you will lose control, and only God knows where they will end up and whose property they will damage. Especially be alert when you pass near Ionescu's land. His garden is nice and green and especially inviting to the geese. They can ruin it in just a few minutes. Do you understand what I'm telling you?"

"Yes, Papa, I understand. I will do what you ask of me, and I'll do a good job of it."

She knew she had no other choice. She had learned early to do what she was told or suffer the consequences, which meant having to listen to one of her father's boring speeches. She preferred the switch over his long lectures.

That's the way he was with everyone. She had heard her father give orders and instructions to the people he hired to work the farm. He was strict and expected his workers to carry out his orders exactly as he gave them. If they didn't, he was quick to reprimand them, inflicting harsh language and lots of finger-pointing until he was assured they exactly understood what he wanted them to do and how he wanted them to do it.

In a few minutes, Viki had rounded up the geese and, with a long switch in her hand, started guiding them across the road and down the path to the pond.

As she passed the Ionescu property, the geese veered off and headed straight to the green garden her father had warned her about. Realizing the consequences of what they would do to the green plants, Viki swiftly headed them off with her switch. It was not easy. She came close to losing them, but she succeeded in getting them back on the path and headed toward the pond. Soon they were at the pond. The bordering grass was even greener and longer than her father had described. The geese quickly devoured it.

As Viki watched the geese filling themselves, she grew drowsy, but she remained alert enough to lead them into the pond, where they swam, flapped their wings, and stretched their long necks beneath the surface of the water, where more vegetation awaited their beaks. As she watched the geese swimming, she laid her head back onto the grass. Watching white clouds slowly drift toward the eastern hills, she soon fell asleep.

When the geese were full and ready to return, they assembled near where Viki was sleeping and, under the guidance of the leading goose, began their journey home. But before they arrived home, they decided to feed on Mr. Ionescu's garden plot, even though their gizzards were already full. They waddled quickly into the heart of the garden and began biting the new growth until all that was left were green stubs.

Stuffed, the geese waddled off toward home, leaving Viki alone in deep slumber until she was rudely awakened.

"Why are you sleeping and leaving your geese to roam freely in the meadow?" Mr. Ionescu demanded. "Do you know they ruined the entire garden my wife and I had spent so much time growing? Now we have nothing. We will have to start all over again. Come, I'll show you. Then I'm going to talk to your father and get this settled."

She could see that Mr. Ionescu was angry, but where were the geese?

"By the time I saw the geese in my garden," Mr. Ionescu said, "there was nothing left but stubble. I knew they were yours so I guided them to your home and saw that they got behind the gate. Then I came looking for you. Now I want you to see what you caused."

As they passed Ionescu's garden patch, Viki cringed at the damage that had been done and at what her father was going to say. When Ionescu marched her back to their home, Viki saw the surprise and concern on her mama and papa's faces. After he explained what had happened to his garden, he and Harald agreed on a settlement to compensate him for the damage caused by the geese. No one was happy at the turn of events.

Viki was deeply embarrassed and accepted the fact that she had failed. She had made a miserable effort to do as she had been told. Her negligence ruined another person's property. She vowed not to let that happen again. There was nothing she could do about it now except suffer the consequences.

"I was counting on you to manage the geese," her father said, "and I explicitly explained how it was to be done, but you didn't do what you were told. You shirked your responsibility. I'm wondering if I can depend on you to do it right the next time. And believe me, there will be lots of next times to do tasks as important as watching the geese. How can I trust you if you don't do the tasks you are asked to do? From now on whenever I tell you to do something, I expect you to do it and do it right. Otherwise, I will disown you."

"Papa, I know I did wrong, but I promise I will do it right the next time. I'm sorry it happened. I will try to do my best on any other task I am given to do."

Viki appreciated her father. He was her best friend whom she loved very much, so much that oftentimes she thought that when it came time for her to marry, she would marry her father. She always knew she could approach him for advice and assistance and come away feeling he had done the best he could for her.

CHAPTER 22

It was early Tuesday morning, April 16, 1963. Harald was shelving his last delivery of merchandise. The shop door opened and in walked the messenger from the telegraph office in Saveni. "What brings you here today?" Harald asked.

"I've got a telegram for you. It looks like it's from your mother."

Harald tore open the envelope dated the fifteenth and read the brief message: "This morning your father had a heart attack and died while working in his garden. He just fell and was gone. I need you to come help me with the arrangements. —Mama"

It had happened the day before. Georgi was seventy-one years old. He left behind Olga, his beautiful and caring wife of fifty-one years, twelve children, and thirty-one grandchildren. Georgi was proud of his achievements, particularly the successes of the five children he and Mama had sent to Vioresca to develop their own homestead. He and Olga had lived a hard life, suffering through depressions, wars, and agonizing economic turns as governments came and went. They had to learn the hard way to grit their teeth and do the best with what was handed them, or else suffer the consequences.

Following the memorial service, for which family and guests had gathered, Georgi's body was moved outside and laid to rest in the family's burial site. The graveside service was brief but poignant.

Harald held Viki's hand. He and Sophia stood way back in the cemetery to keep Viki away from the other children. Even though she was now their legally adopted daughter, they still hadn't told her that Ana and Ion were her real parents. Even in conversations with his mother, Harald stood his ground, but he knew someday he would be forced to tell Viki who her biological parents were.

The services didn't last long. Soon the families were back at the family homestead enjoying the delicious foods and drinks the neighbors had so kindly made for them. Harald continued to hold Viki's hand. Maria stared at her curiously, but she didn't approach the small family. The two sisters were twins, but they were not identical. There was a strong enough family resemblance that, at a distance, one girl could have been mistaken for the other—same height, build, hair color, posture. They could have merely been cousins. Throughout the funeral lunch, Harald kept Viki clear of Ion and Ana and their children. As soon as the grieving relatives and friends began to say their good-byes, Harald and his family moved quietly out of the house and walked to the bus stop.

CHAPTER 23

When Viki was in the fourth grade, she wanted to sing in the school's chorus. She had a strong voice for shouting, but at the time of the audition, as far as carrying a tune went, all she could manage was a gravelly monotone. The music professor suggested she might be more suited to playing one of the girls' sports.

Reluctantly taking her teacher's advice, she decided to play on the school's soccer team. She practiced dutifully and was chosen to play in every game. It was a good team, losing only one game that season. She was proud of her participation on the team and her part in its achievement, as were her mother and father.

At the end of that school year, with everyone in the class expected to participate in the annual stage production, Viki decided to audition for a part. Since she wasn't good at singing and had never tried to dance, she was given an acting role. She studied very hard to learn her lines. Having done well in rehearsals, she was confident and ready to perform on opening day.

Everything went smoothly until the last scene in the second act, when Christina Ivanescu, a close friend playing opposite Viki suffered a bad case of stage fright and had forgotten two of her lines. Viki didn't know what to do. She waited impatiently for Christina to speak up, but all the girl could do was look around for help. By this time, the noise of the audience was so loud that Christina couldn't hear the cues given from the wings. With hands on her hips and not knowing what else to do, Viki shoulder-bumped Christina and shouted, "You missed two lines. How come you missed two lines?"

Christina started weeping. No help was forthcoming. The curtain quickly closed. The set was replaced and made ready for the last act. The drama teacher was embarrassed, as was the audience, particularly both sets of parents sitting in the center of the front row. Again, Viki learned more lessons, this time in patience and understanding.

"It's too bad you had to experience that on stage," her father said after they returned home, "but failures like that will happen. Certainly it wasn't your fault, but you should have had the patience to wait until she could remember her lines. Or at least you should have had the understanding that these things always happen and that, in time, help would have arrived."

"But I don't understand how she could have missed those two lines when we had done so well in rehearsals," Viki said. "I was embarrassed and upset, and couldn't think of any way to help her. I could see that the audience was shocked, especially you, Mama, and Christina's parents. I suppose I should apologize to her parents, but I don't want to. I guess that makes me the bad culprit. But I still like to believe I did the best I could with my part."

Viki loved attending school. She had gained more friendships with her peers and enjoyed her position as being one of the smartest and friendliest students in the fourth grade. When she was promoted to the fifth grade, she and her peers were faced with a three-mile walk to the nearest upper-grade elementary school in Saveni. There was no local transportation. At least in the wintertime, the city school provided room and board.

"Viki," her papa smilingly said, "you're ten years old and it's time you learned to ride Mihai, our gentle and congenial horse. You never know when you will have to use him, so it's best you learn how to do it."

It was a nice cool October day with a light early frost glistening off the surrounding foliage and a bright sun casting its warmth upon Mihai. The anxious father prepared his terrified daughter for her first riding lesson.

"Do I have to, Papa? I'm not sure I want to. I'm afraid of Mihai, afraid I'll fall off."

"There is nothing for you to fear, Viki. Mihai is gentle; he'll give you a nice ride. Just learn how to harness and mount him, and then sit back and enjoy it."

Still apprehensive, Viki said, "Whatever you say, Papa. I'll try it if you are certain he won't throw me."

"I can't guarantee you anything, but if you just do as I say, you'll have no problems."

Harald gently seated Viki on Mihai and instructed her to pat the horse gently over the stomach behind the saddle to make him move. Viki did as directed, but Mihai didn't cooperate. He just stood still.

"He won't go, Papa. What do I do now?"

"Gently nudge his sides with your heels and he will move."

It was a good lesson, but still the stubborn Mihai refused to move. "Kick him a little harder," Harald said. As Viki did as instructed, Mihai reared, dropping the girl to the ground. Thankfully, she kept her balance.

"Damn you, Mihai," Viki yelled as she swiftly kicked each of the horse's back legs. Then, looking sharply at her father, she yelled, "See what I told you? I don't want to learn how to ride that damn Mihai. If ever I have need for a Mihai, I'll depend on my two legs to get me where I'm going. I certainly won't be up on Mihai!"

Viki continued to be more responsible when doing her assigned chores. When she made up her mind to do something, she proceeded to perform and act accordingly. Her motto was to do it now and get it over with; however, her headstrong nature kept her in trouble with her father. Even when she knew the action she was about to take would not be in keeping with his principles, she did it anyway. She wasn't always right, but she was satisfied to do it her own way and suffer the consequences of having to listen to her father rant and rave and threaten to disown her.

Eleven-year-old Viki and Krissy Popovici, her neighbor friend and fifth grade classmate, were dressed up on a Sunday morning and ready to walk to church together. With only a few wisps of clouds floating lazily beneath one of the brightest blue skies of early spring, it was a beautiful day—certainly better than the last five days of steady rain that had made a soggy mess of the grounds around the barn. The road was sloppy and the potholes were overflowing with sticky brown mud. Ionescu's creek had overflowed its banks and swamped the newly plowed fields.

Before Viki and Krissy could leave for church, however, they had to put the cow in the barn and feed her. It was the nine o'clock biweekly service. They didn't want to be late for Father Lucescu's second Mass of the month.

Krissy, a tiny slender girl with flowing dark brown hair, sparkling blue eyes and a curving smile, was not doing her part. Instead, she was dancing and frolicking back and forth, vying for

Viki's attention and admiration of the violet velvet dress she was wearing for the first time.

What Krissy didn't realize was that Viki had noticed her new dress, but, being jealous and annoyed by it, she was refusing to let herself be drawn into a big discussion of how pretty it and Krissy were. Instead, other less hospitable thoughts filled her mind.

Viki's own Sunday dress was plainly not as nice. It had been handmade by her mother from the colorful feed sacks her father had brought home from the feed store. While it was pretty and fit well, it didn't in any way compare with the store-purchased dress Krissy wore.

"Why don't you stop primping around and help me get this cow in the barn?" Viki shouted over the mooing of the cow. "If you don't help me, we will be late. And I'll tell Father Lucescu it was you who made us late."

"I am helping the best I can," Krissy responded, "but I want to show off my pretty new dress. Don't you think it's pretty?" Fluttering her eyelids and flashing a big smile, she spread the hem of the dress and made a little curtsy.

Krissy was always a nuisance, blustering about how smart she was, how she made better grades, and how much people commended her for her achievements, enough so that it made Viki want, in some way, to do something that would shut her up and bring her down a notch or two.

"You don't have to show me your dress," Viki said. "I have pretty dresses too, but I don't like to wear them when I have to put the cow in the barn. So when you stop prancing and showing off, we'll get this chore done and be on our way."

"I'm not showing off. It's just that I'm so pleased with my new dress that I want everyone to notice it and tell me how much they like it. That's all I want." Krissy resumed dancing with her head held high and her eyes sparkling. Krissy was elated; Viki was aggravated.

Suddenly Viki began to feel she had to do something to show Krissy that she too was important. It wasn't that Viki disliked Krissy, but at the same time Krissy wasn't really her favorite friend because of the showing off and boasting. Both were intelligent, and both did their best to outshine the other. Krissy was very good in mathematics and social science, but Viki was much better in reading, writing, and science.

Finally they got the cow settled, gave it some food, and started the walk to the church. All along the rough and wet roadway, Krissy continued talking of nothing other than how the people at church would swoon over her new dress and how good she looked in it. She was so happy singing the virtues of her father and praising the marvelous job he had done in selecting the dress.

This set Viki fuming. She started thinking about what she could do to Krissy to embarrass her and spoil that new dress, how to get it wet and dirty enough to embarrass Krissy before they arrived at the church.

Would I get in trouble with my father if I did something to soil the dress and embarrass Krissy? she wondered. Of course I would! And even if I did something and she told on me, would I feel better by getting even with her? I'd like a new dress too, but I don't think I can get Father to get one for me. But maybe, just maybe, by embarrassing Krissy I can make him understand my need for a new dress, and then he would get me one. Then I could flaunt it before Krissy and make her jealous.

But what can I do? She is always trying to impress me with her new clothes and playthings. Her father is always able to get things for her, and my father can't. I know we have to work hard for everything and there isn't enough left over to get us new things.

I don't know what to do, but I've got to stop Krissy from trying to impress me.

She thought if she could trip Krissy, she might fall and get dirt and grass stains on the dress, but that wasn't a certainty. Being near the creek, which the road followed, gave Viki the idea that she could push Krissy into the water and get her wet. But even that action was not enough to satisfy Viki's desire to really mess up the dress, as the stream wasn't deep enough to soak Krissy much higher than the ankles. Then she remembered the big mudhole up ahead on the road that had been there since the snows thawed. It was murky and slimy and deep. *That would be the perfect place,* she thought.

When they reached the mudhole, Krissy had no idea what Viki was planning. She seemed unaware that Viki was edging her closer and closer to the puddle. As she was about to step around it, Viki tripped her and nudged her hard enough to knock her off balance. Krissy, letting out a shriek, fell headfirst into the muddy pothole. The dress was ruined, and her hands, arms, and face were covered with mud. She looked terrible. Rising to her feet, she tried wiping the slime from her face and arms. As rivulets of grimy water dripped off the dress front, Krissy began to wail. But Viki was pleased, as Krissy's showing off had ended. Going to church, however, was out of the question.

Still in tears, Krissy jumped out of the puddle and ran for home. Viki watched with satisfaction until the girl suddenly changed course, heading for the Antonescus' front gate. Before Viki could catch up, the bedraggled Krissy was shrieking at Viki's parents, telling them what had happened and who was responsible.

Viki stopped in the road, her heart pounding.

"I'm so sorry Viki took her revenge out on you that way," Harald said. "I promise you, I will take care of it with Viki. And I will see your father and do whatever it takes to replace your dress."

Her mama had nothing to say—the look of pain on her face said it all.

Viki turned on her heel and went on to church as planned, not to hear Father Lucescu, but to delay the inevitable. She knew what Papa would say and do and she dreaded the thought of having to sit through his longwinded speech about what she did wrong and what she should have done instead.

He did not disappoint her.

"It would have gone much easier on you," Harald said, "if you had used your head before doing what you did to Krissy. If you'd wanted a new dress to show off, you should have let us know. Your mother would have bought one for you. Now the money it would have cost us to get you a new dress will instead go to Krissy to replace the dress you so foolishly ruined. That will be your punishment. And if you ever do anything like that again, I swear I will disown you. In that event, you will not call me Papa again."

CHAPTER 24

Viki seemed to have a dark cloud hanging over her head that spelled trouble just waiting to happen. She didn't go around looking for it. It seemed to come looking for her.

One evening when she was twelve, she got into a scuffle with a fourteen-year-old boy while watering Ioani, their cow. It was one of Viki's tasks after walking home from school to lead the cow to drink from Ionescu's pond. Oftentimes there would be several thirsty cows awaiting their turn to drink from the pond.

Ioani was almost always quiet and friendly, and always patient about waiting for an open pathway to the water. But patience was not one of the virtues of Nici Nicolai's cow. She did not like waiting to drink. With Nici's help, she usually pushed her way around those in front of her.

Viki's cow had had her horns shorn, whereas Nici's cow, being younger, still had long horns.

This particular day when Viki and Ioani arrived at the pond, they found the creek bank crowded with neighboring cows. So Viki, with a firm grip on the halter, settled down to wait for a chance to move forward. Soon Nici arrived with his cow and moved in beside her to await an opening to the water. His cow had other thoughts and began to paw the ground. Nici tried to calm her, but he was unsuccessful. Just then an opening appeared. Nici urged his cow to move into the spot ahead of Viki.

Viki didn't like Nici pushing ahead, so she tried to lead Ioani ahead of Nici's cow. Nici, however, not about to let Ioani get ahead of his cow, tried to push her out of the way. Standing her ground,

Viki pulled Ioani through the open gap and onto the bank. Before Ioani could lower her stubby-horned head to drink, Nici's cow gouged her with one of her sharp horns and made a deep gash in her right side, bringing blood.

Ioani was of a different temperament and did not try to defend herself, and Viki did not have the strength to get between the two animals to separate them. There was nothing she could do but look to Nici for help. Nici, however, just stood there laughing and urging his cow on as if as if he was enjoying the action. This compounded Viki's irritation. She began hitting him on the arms and neck. He retaliated, hitting back. Then they started wrestling, soon falling to the ground among the cows.

It was obvious that Viki was losing, what with Nici clutching her head in his hands and pounding it on the ground—that is, until the thumb of Nici's left hand accidently flopped into Viki's mouth. She promptly bit down hard on the second joint. He screamed. "Stop it. You're hurting me. Let loose."

Viki only bit harder.

"You're hurting my thumb, you dumb girl! If you'll turn it loose, I'll move my cow out of the way."

Again, Viki only bit harder and Nici shouted louder. Suddenly, Viki felt something separate under her bite. She could feel the first joint hanging loose. Her tongue could move it up and down. At that point she eased her bite enough for Nici to remove his flopping thumb. It was obvious she had severed something, because he had lost control of its use.

"You shouldn't have bitten so hard," Nici screamed. "Look at what you've done." And with that last retort, he hurriedly yanked the halter on his cow and speedily took off for home.

Viki, with a victorious gladiator's smile on her face, led her cow into the vacant spot on the bank of the pond and let her drink her fill.

"You should have let it loose," her papa said, trying to cajole her after she returned home. "If you had, he probably would have restrained his cow and let you have your turn at the pond."

"I agree, Papa, but at the time, after what his cow did to Ioani, I could think only to bite harder and harder. What else could I have done? I was trying to save Ioani."

"And I appreciate that, but cow wounds heal quickly. His thumb may never be right again. He needs strong hands to help his family make a living. You need to keep those thoughts in your mind. You need to protect yourself and your property, but the next time, just take it easy when you see you have the upper hand."

When Viki was in the seventh grade, she was walking down the road on her way home from school when she heard the footsteps of someone jogging up behind her. As she turned to see who it was, Nici Nicolai jumped into the big pothole she was standing next to and drenched her from head to foot with muddy water.

"That's for biting my thumb and making it useless," he yelled at her. "I'll never forgive you for that. I'll torment you as long as I live."

But Viki was not to be outdone. She was angry and knew she had to retaliate, but how? Having learned she could not beat him in a boxing or wrestling, she decided that she needed a weapon.

When she turned her head to look for something she could use, she saw some wood scraps by the side of the road. She picked up a short piece of lumber and began to beat Nici with it.

Viki was not just angry; she was livid. She was mad enough that the knowledge that what she was doing would not stand well with her father didn't stop her. She proceeded to whack Nici with the board until he threw up his hands and ran home with blood trickling from a nasty gash across his forehead. Also, he had a few splinters in his hands trying to ward off the blows.

Again Viki's father reprimanded her, talking and talking until she couldn't stand to hear it anymore. She had heard this message so many times that she did not want to have to sit through it again. She would rather he just take the trusty switch, whip her bare legs a few times, and turn her loose instead of forcing her to sit through his lecture.

As Viki grew older, she felt confident that she could care for herself. She knew that if she didn't, her father would preach to her to use her head in all matters and strive to do the best he knew she was capable of doing. Viki loved her father and was proud of him. The one thing that really hurt her was when he threatened to disown her and never again let her call him Papa.

Because of the love and support of her parents, Viki believed she could do anything she really wanted to do.

CHAPTER 25

It was a Sunday afternoon in late spring when a loud boom echoed across the valley, coming from the direction of Ionesco's pond. To Harald, it sounded as though someone had detonated a stick of dynamite in hopes of capturing some of the larger fish that inhabited the small body of water. As he stepped out of the house, in the distance he could hear crying and screaming. Something terrible had happened. A plume of dark, oily smoke spiraled up into the sky. Viki and Sophia came out to see what all the noise was about.

"Stay here!" Harald told them. Then he broke into a run.

Five boys were dashing down the road toward him, screaming for help. "What is it?!" he shouted at them. "What has happened?"

"We told Gregor not to touch it!" one of the boys cried. "But he did anyway, and it blew up!"

Harald followed them, full of dread, as they turned back for the pond. What he saw made him stop in his tracks. An area of the bank was blackened, making a ring twenty yards wide.

Victims' bodies and body parts were strewn all over the bank and floating in the water. A choking haze of burned explosive hung over the spot. It made him flash back to the things he'd seen in the war, things he wanted to forget. At the edge of the blast, the injured were trying to crawl to safety.

"We've got to help them," he told the boys who had led him there. He knelt down beside one of the injured, pulling off his shirt and tearing it into strips. "Press the cloth on the wound like this," he told one of the boys who'd escaped. "Hold it there firmly. It will stop the bleeding."

As he turned to apply a compress to another child's wound, he asked the boys what had happened.

"Gregor was throwing a rope into the water," the oldest one said. "It had a weight on the end with a hook. He said was trying to snag a fish. He hooked something heavy, and we all pulled on the rope to drag it out onto the bank. We could see it was a bomb. We told him to leave it alone, but he wouldn't listen. When Gregor tried to pry open the casing, it exploded."

A World War II bomb, Harald thought as he tended to the boy's jagged wound. Probably dropped by the Russians and intended for the village, it had missed its target and sunk, unexploded, to the bottom of the pond, a nightmare waiting decades to emerge.

When the village mothers and fathers arrived at the scene, they were stunned by the carnage. They searched among the dead and wounded bodies to find their own. When they did, they began screaming and wailing, losing control of their emotions. "Oh, my God, why have you done this to me?" Others bending over the bodies of their own, sobbed as they twisted their hands in agony, not knowing what to do or where to go for help. The scene was unbearably loud with cries and groans. The ground was literally covered with blood.

After what seemed like hours, the police and medical personnel arrived and took over.

The identified dead body parts were placed in boxes and transported to the morgue in Saveni. The wounded were bandaged and helped into ambulances for the journey to the hospital. Funeral services were conducted over the weekend and the bodies interred in the village cemetery.

"Viki will be entering high school in September," Harald said to Sophia one evening after supper, "and I've been thinking a lot about where she should go to get the best possible education. She has done well in her studies here, but I would like to see her do as well or even better in a high school where she can learn the accounting and economics curriculum her counselors recommend she follow.

"I know a little bit about accounting," Harald continued, "because of my stores, but I know absolutely nothing about economics. Her teachers say this is the way for her to go, and I agree. So, we'll move to Suceava as soon as I can quit my job here and am able to sell the house. There they offer more selections of schools that specialize in those fields. Plus, she won't have to walk as far as she does now."

"I think you're right," Sophia said, "but moving after all these years won't be easy. How about your work managing the stores? Do you think you can do as well in Suceava?"

"I don't know if I can do as well, but I believe I can get a decent job that will pay me well. There's a large need for good salespeople, especially in the feed business, and I think I'm a good salesman. Yes, I can handle that. If not, there will be something else I can do. After all, I'm fifty-three years old. If we are going to do it, now is the time. Viki is smart and needs the best education we can provide. This is how she will get a better job after school."

"What do you plan to do?"

"I plan to go to Suceava next week and buy a house that will satisfy our needs. Then, I'll get the two of you moved. After that, I'll try to get this house sold. Then I'll see what kind of work I can find that will satisfy me. I'll get my assistant to take over the stores while I take a few days to look over what is available and what it will take to rent, lease, or buy. Obviously, there is a lot that must be done in making the move."

When Harald returned to Suceava he looked and looked, hoping to find a good job. He tried for the management position in the bodega of a nearby collective, but not being a Communist Party member, he was turned down. There were no openings at the local feed stores either.

Finally he found a sales job for a small independent feed plant that milled and mixed grains for small farmers in the hill country.

He looked at several houses and finally, on the third day, found one that satisfied him—one that he could buy after he sold his property. It was near the mill and a high school that taught the special curriculum Viki needed. It would be available in a month. The owner agreed to settle the costs once Harald sold his property in Vioresca, allowing him to rent in the interim.

Harald returned home the next day and told Sophia and Viki to get ready to move in three weeks. He then arranged to quit his job at the stores and to dispose of his house, land, and personal belongings.

By the first of August 1969, Viki and her mother were living in their new house in Suceava, but it took Harald another year before he could dispose of his property and completely leave Vioresca behind.

PART 3

The Learning Years

CHAPTER 26

Three days after Sophia and Viki were settled in their new house, Sophia called Harald in Vioresca. When he answered the phone, she immediately got to the point. "What are you going to do about getting Viki enrolled in school?" she asked. "Time is drawing near to make a decision, but you're not here to do it."

"No, I'm not," Harald said. "There is so much going on here that I don't think I'll be able to get away. I've got problems with the store inventories, and I'm the only one who can solve them. Plus, the sale of our house and land is not attracting many buyers. There are lots of lookers, but no buyers. So, it looks as though you'll have to enroll her yourself."

"I don't mind doing it, but I know nothing about how it's done. You've always taken care of that chore."

"You won't have any problems doing it. If I were you, I'd get as much knowledge of how the system works there as I could, and then I'd go to the school that is the closest to where we live."

"What school is that?" Sophia asked. "Remember, I'm not familiar with schools like you are. Which one do you like?"

"Well, if it was me, I would select one that specializes in accounting and economics. Then I would go to that school and enroll her. And don't forget to let me know what you were able to do. I'm very sorry, but I must go now. Good luck. I love you."

The next day Sophia entered the County Building, approached the information desk, and waited a moment while the clerk finished a telephone call. As the clerk replaced the receiver, she looked up and said, "What can I do for you?"

"I'd like to see Carmen Cinca, the county scholar administrator. I understand she can answer my questions about the high school system here in Suceava. I have a daughter to enroll in high school, and I'm looking for help."

"She's very busy now, so you'll have to wait," the clerk said, at the same time motioning Sophia to the line of empty chairs.

"I can't wait." Sophia eased an envelope from her handbag. "I've got many other things I have to do."

Eying the envelope, the secretary said, "Since it's urgent, I'll see if she can see you now."

The envelope produced results. Within five minutes, Carmen Cinca came out of her office and waved for Sophia to enter.

"What can I do for you, Mrs. Antonescu?"

"My husband usually enrolls our daughter in school, but he is busy in Vioresca selling our property. My daughter is starting high school. We want to get her enrolled as soon as possible."

"What kind of school do you want her to participate in?" Cinca asked. "We have many different kinds of schools, such as vocational, regular, and university level."

"Oh, university," Sophia said. "She is a good student. We want to get her as much education as she can handle, and hopefully she can qualify for scholarships. Oh, by the way, are uniforms necessary? In the schools my daughter previously attended, uniforms were not."

"Yes, they are necessary. All high school students must dress according to code, maintain neat hairstyles, and keep up a good general appearance. Also, shoulder patches are required showing student numbers, the name of the school, and telephone numbers. That information is necessary in cases where contacts with school officials are necessary.

"Also," Cinca continued, "in the case of the top students who are university material, there are some schools associated with International Baccalaureate that follow strict lines of course study to prepare students with the qualifications that will lead them to a university degree. These schools concentrate on specific fields of study such as economics, agriculture, industrial management, languages, and fine arts.

"I see from looking at Viki's school records that she could easily qualify for a university degree. Have you given any thought to that?"

"No, we haven't," Sophia said. "My husband and I would be happy if she just received a high school education; however, should she qualify for a university degree we would be thrilled to death."

"Wonderful," Cinca responded. "What Viki needs to do now is take the entry exams we require to enter high school. This will give us the knowledge of what course of study to follow for her to get a job in the field she appears to be best qualified to work in. We will let you know when the tests will be given. Good luck."

As Sophia left the building, she wondered if she should have asked more questions about Viki going to college. Apparently, her grades and course work had qualified her to do that. She had always been a good student, and there was no doubt that she was very capable and competitive in everything she set out to do, but Sophia and Harald wanted to see her married so she could give them grandchildren. They didn't want to wait forever for that. Right now, their job was to get her into high school and registered for the courses she was qualified to take.

A month later, Viki started high school. Her entry tests indicated, as her father had counseled, that she was suited to study in the business curriculum, so she was enrolled in courses that taught her economics and accounting. The tests also indicated she had an interest in biology, thanks to her experience with farming and handling farm animals. Because of her affection for and trust in her father, she followed his suggestion, forgoing the biology curriculum in favor of the business curriculum.

Because Viki had passed the tests with such high scores, she was given a state scholarship that paid all her costs, including room and board, books, supplies, and equipment needed to learn the subject matter, plus a monthly stipend for miscellaneous items.

Viki's economics and accounting high school enrolled about a hundred students and housed them in a large manor the government had nationalized in 1950, after forcing the owner to relinquish his property and relocate to one of the new apartment buildings erected near the city. Most students were housed in rooms with about twenty others with only one bathroom to serve them. Because Viki was a scholarship student, she was assigned one of the smaller rooms along with upper graders. Small lockers served as the students' only storage space. Lower-grade students were responsible for cleaning the bathrooms. Students were not allowed to leave the dormitory until beds were made and the rooms were spotlessly clean.

The school had an extensive athletic program. Each student had to participate in at least one sport. Viki was a runner and participated on the track team. She was more academic than athletic. The best she could ever accomplish was to come in second, but she always ran the best race she could.

In her assigned subjects, she was consistently at the top in her class. There were, however, some subjects she disliked. The study of the Russian language topped that list.

"I hate it," she told her parents. "Everyone hates it, including the teachers. It's awful. But I have no choice. In fact, I have no choice in any of the subjects I take."

Next to the school, separated by a two strands of barbed wire, stood a gray two-story residence topped with a rustic red ceramic tile roof. In the backyard grew a stately pear tree fully loaded with green fruit just begging to be picked. As it ripened, the forbidden fruit became more and more tempting to Viki and Elena Eminescu, her roommate. Every day when they scanned the tree, their mouths watered and their temptation intensified.

"Don't they look delicious?" Viki said. "Just imagine how juicy and tasty they would be. If only we could get a couple of them."

"But we can't," Elena quickly responded. "You know that yard is off limits. We've all been told about picking fruit from the tree on Mr. Neascu's private property. If we do it, we will be severely punished for disobeying school rules."

"I know, but I'd still like to have just one of them. I believe there is a way we can do it. Tomorrow night, after dark when the others are asleep, let's you and I quietly leave the building, slip through the fence, and bring back a couple. I'm sure Mr. Neascu won't miss them, as the tree is loaded."

"No, no, no! You know that if we should get caught, we will be punished. No! That is a bad idea."

"If we are careful," Viki argued, "we won't get caught. And I believe this will be worth the effort. Even if we did get caught, probably all we would have to do is pay Mr. Neascu a few pennies for the fruit and be confined to the room for a week or so."

A determined Viki was always successful in arguing her position and usually could convince others to follow her lead. After all, she had had the best teacher in the world—her father, who used his persuasive powers to always get his way.

It didn't take much argument for Viki to convince Elena.

"I still think it's not a good idea," Elena said, "but I'll go along with you because I want to taste those pears, too."

"Good, then we'll do it tomorrow night. Don't mention it to anyone."

The next night, still in their sleeping attire, they silently tiptoed outside the building, softly closing the door behind them. It was a nice cool night with a half-moon casting just enough light to guide their way to an opening in the fence that Viki thought they could pass through quickly without getting snagged on the barbs.

Viki spread the gap, pushing up on the top wire with her hands, and pushed down on the lower wire with her right foot. Elena made it through easily, but Viki didn't. Even with Elena spreading the wires, Viki got snagged. As hard as she tried, she couldn't rip loose the barb.

"Elena, help me," Viki whispered. "I'm caught. I can't reach the spot where I'm caught."

"I'm afraid to let go of this top strand. I'll try with my free hand. So please hold still while I try to find where you're caught."

It seemed to take a long time, but finally Viki realized Elena was not going to free her. Determined to get out of the awkward position, she pushed her way through the gap, leaving a piece of her pajama top attached to the barb. But she was free to pick pears.

Suddenly a dog neither had seen rushed forward, snarling and baring its teeth.

Fortunately, the dog's chain was too short to reach the girls, but that didn't quiet the dog. It made the dog bark loud enough to rouse Mr. Neascu from his night's sleep. Wearing his pajamas, he burst from the back door, his walking stick in his right hand.

"If we hurry," Viki hissed, "we can run to the tree, grab a couple, and get back onto the school side before Mr. Neascu comes around the corner."

They ran as fast as they could, grabbed the closest limb, pulled it down, took two pears each, and scrambled back through the fence. But the limb did not return to its original position. It was too heavily loaded and the strength of the pull was too much, causing it to break and fall to the ground. This happened just as Mr. Neascu entered the front yard.

"Stop where you are!" he shouted. "I want your names. I'm going to report you to Professor Popescu the first thing in the morning."

The girls stopped in their tracks and, shaking with fright, tried to apologize for their mistake. At the same time, between breaths, they gave their names and patch numbers. Mr. Neascu took note. Then, feeling sorry for the young ladies, he said, "Since you went to all that trouble to get a few pears, you may keep them. I hope you enjoy them. However, I'm still going to report you to Professor Popescu first thing in the morning."

"That won't be necessary, Neascu," Professor Popescu said, as he closed his back door behind him. Apparently he had been roused by the barking dog and immediately suspected that some of his students were involved in stealing from the loaded pear tree. He quickly apologized to Neascu. "I know who the culprits are, and I will take care of the matter. I apologize for their behavior. I will see that they are properly punished for their actions, and I will do my best to see that it never happens again."

With that said, he led the girls into the small room he called his office and sternly lectured them on the penalties of violating other people's boundaries and stealing their property. It made Viki think she was listening to one of her father's reprimands.

"I'll arrange for your hearing to start next Monday in the assembly hall," Professor Popescu said. "I'll ask your parents to attend the session, and then to take you home should you be suspended for any length of time. Now, get to bed and get some sleep. From now until after the hearing, you are confined to your rooms except for meals and bathroom needs. And I'll take those pears off your hands."

On Monday morning, the meeting hall was filled with students and teachers. In the first row sat the two sets of mortified parents. Trying hard to be as inconspicuous as possible, they were having little success. First, the girls had to face them and the others in the hall and give a full account of what had gotten them in trouble. And then they had to face the three judges selected from members of the faculty.

After the judges related the charges against the girls, Professor Popescu asked the girls for their replies and comments. All the girls could do was to offer their apologies and beg for forgiveness. They sorrowfully discovered that "I like to eat newly ripened pears" was not a defense that would keep them from being penalized.

The girls were then told to face the attendees and await the decision of the judges. It didn't take long for the judges to make their decision. When they did, they asked the girls to face them as it was read aloud.

"We find you two guilty as charged. Your punishment is as follows: You are suspended from school for two weeks. You will leave the school and go home with your parents. We considered expelling you, but we decided you are good students who just made a foolish error in doing what you did. Since you damaged Mr. Neascu's property, he should be compensated. Therefore, each of you shall pay Mr. Neascu your entire stipend for two months. And lastly, you shall keep up with your studies while at home and be prepared to take special tests when you return. Now, you are free to go to your parents."

The bus ride home was silent. Neither of Viki's parents had anything to say. But she knew what was going to be said once they entered the house.

No sooner had they settled down than Viki blurted out, "I'm so sorry about what I did."

"What in the world were you two thinking when you crossed that fence?" her mama sternly asked. "You knew you were not allowed to do that. Then you took some of his fruit, but worst of all, you broke the limb that held the fruit. Now, you have to pay for your mistake."

"You never thought how your actions would affect your parents, did you?" Papa asked. "You never thought how it would affect your school record, did you? You didn't realize you could have been expelled from the school, did you? Where was your head? What were you thinking about, other than how good the pears would taste? Well, how do they taste now?"

"But Papa …"

"I've told you over and over, don't call me Papa after you've done something wrong! You are not my child. I disown you. When you come to your senses and serve your time, then maybe, just maybe, you can call me Papa again! And Mama feels as badly about this as I do. No child of ours would do such a thing. We are so disappointed in you.

"You have disgraced us, so now we disown you—and it will remain this way for the next two weeks or until we feel you have learned your lesson and until you know how to conduct yourself in an honorable manner. In addition, while you're at home, you will be confined to the house. No telephoning, no television, and no visitors. You can go to church, but only if one of us takes you."

He kept going on and on. Viki just stood there and listened. She couldn't even sneak a word into his tirade. Again she wished he would use the switch across her bare legs rather than making her listen to all those dos and don'ts. His lecture lasted about an hour, after which time he turned her loose to her studies.

Even at dinnertime, everything was deathly quiet except for the slurping of the soup. The food Viki was given was meager, but she brightened when she saw a big and shiny greenish yellow pear resting behind her dinner plate.

CHAPTER 27

Viki and her cousin Doina, daughter of Uncle "Good-for-Nothing" Ilie, attended the same high school. At age seventeen, Viki was a junior; at fifteen, Doina was a freshman. Uncle Ilie's family were the only close relatives Viki and her parents saw regularly. The two girls were good friends. On a Saturday summer morning, Doina showed up at Viki's house. The weather was pleasant enough to permit them to sit outdoors on the glider. They rocked back and forth as they bought each other up to date about the boys in their lives and their plans for returning to school in the fall.

When it was time for Doina to return home, she talked Viki into going with her and staying the night. Her parents had agreed to let her spend the night with Doina, but they urged the girls to take the city bus to Ilie's house because it was so late in the day.

The bus station was crowded with travelers. Buses were coming and going from the terminal in rapid succession. Some of the buses looked old and dilapidated, their tailpipes belching dark smoke, but many were newer models.

The waiting room was packed with people and their luggage. Viki found two empty spots for her and Doina on the straight-backed benches in the front row of the seating area that faced the doorways leading to and from the bus queues. As soon as they got comfortable on the hard seat, Viki and her cousin resumed talking nonstop, oblivious to the chaos around them.

"Viki!" someone yelled from the doorway leading to the buses.

She looked up to see a strange man pointing at her over the heads of the bustling travelers.

"Viki, what are you doing here?" he demanded. He seemed very put out.

The man was of medium build with a heavy black beard and mustache. Under a battered tan felt fedora, his hair was longish and black. Wearing dark sunglasses, he was dressed like a villager in dark work trousers, a blue denim shirt, and white sneakers, none of which were very clean. As he continued to glare at the two girls, Doina moved closer to Viki.

"Viki, I told you to stay home and take care of your sister," he shouted over the noise in the terminal, his anger clearly building momentum. "Didn't you understand me? What must I do to get you to obey me? Just wait until Mama gets here and sees you sitting there when you said you would stay home and look after Eugenia."

The man began to move toward her, weaving through the crowded waiting room and waving his arms.

Who is this crazy person? Viki thought. Why is he berating me in front of all these people? And how does he know my name? This is frightening and embarrassing.

"Who are you?" Viki asked as she stood up, her hands balled into fists. "What do you want from me? I don't know you, I don't know what you're talking about, and I don't appreciate you yelling at me. If you don't leave me alone and go away, I'll call a policeman." As he drew nearer, she started looking around for an escape route.

Still seated, Doina clung to Viki's hand and started to cry softly.

A middle-aged woman in a headscarf and a saggy cloth coat walked up behind the man carrying a paper shopping bag by the cord handle. When the woman looked at her and smiled, Viki recognized her. It was Aunt Ana, who immediately turned to the shouter. "Gheorghe, be quiet," she snapped at her son. "Take off those sunglasses! She is not our Viki; She is the other Viki." Nor knowing what to do, Ana looked Viki in the eyes and said, "Viki, I'm terribly sorry about this encounter. I don't know really what I should do. I'm surprised you didn't recognize Gheorghe … your brother!"

At his mother's insistence, Gheorghe removed his dark glasses. After looking at Viki closely for a second, he blushed deeply under his beard and apologized to her for his mistake. Ana did the same on his behalf. Then without a word of explanation, Ana hooked her son by the arm and led him out of the station.

As Viki sat there, she began to think about her cousin Maria, whom, she knew, was also called Viki. She remembered seeing her for the first time when she was very young at her grandfather's funeral. She remembered that they looked a lot alike then, and she vividly recalled an intense feeling of connection to Maria that, at the time, she didn't understand and couldn't even put into words. Viki had put aside the strange experience. After all, first cousins could resemble each other and feel bonded by their shared blood. But because of what had just happened, she began to question herself. *What if we are really sisters?* she wondered. *Is it possible that Papa and Mama are not my real parents? Or Could Ana and Ion be my parents?* That idea made her shudder. She didn't like Uncle Ion because Papa said he drank too much and was irresponsible. Viki sank back into her seat, confused and distressed.

"I didn't recognize Cousin Gheorghe," Doina said. "He has changed since I last saw him. And with that beard and the dark glasses …" She tried to laugh, but then she stopped, looking at Viki with concern. "Are you all right? You look very pale."

"Doina, I can't spend the night with you," Viki said. "I am too upset. I have to go back now. I need to talk to Mama and Papa about this. I'm sorry to disappoint you."

Viki hugged her cousin and promised to be in touch soon. Then she left the station and hurried home.

When Viki burst into the house, she immediately confronted her parents about the bus terminal incident. "Whose daughter am I?!" she demanded. "Am I yours, or am I really the daughter of Uncle Ion and Aunt Ana? Why did you raise me as your own child without letting me know who my real parents were? Why did you lie to me? Now I don't know what or who to believe."

Her papa turned, seeming to look to her mama for support, but Sophia turned away, folding her arms across her chest. Harald cleared his throat as if something was stuck in it. His face turned red as he began to speak.

"Your mother could not have children of her own," he said, "so it was always lonesome for us around the house. Sophia and all my brothers and sisters were having lots of children, and it was a joy to watch them grow up and have fun together. It was something we both wanted but could not have. When Aunt Ana gave birth to you and your sister Maria, she had to stay months in the hospital to recover from double pneumonia. There was no way your uncle Ion could care for the four boys and two new babies. He could barely take care of himself. So, your Grandma Olga agreed to keep Maria and your mama and I agreed to take you.

"When we took you, I made it very clear to Ana and Ion that we'd raise you as our own child without any arguments or interference from anyone, particularly Ion, given his drinking problem. I assured Ana we would give you good care, get you educated, and see that you had a good life with us. I knew that once we took you, we would grow to love you so much that we would never want to let you go. And your mama felt as I did.

"I tried to tell you about you being our child when we adopted you after we had enrolled you in kindergarten. But apparently you did not fully understand the meaning of what I was saying.

"I knew there would come a day when I would have to tell you all this, but I wanted to wait until you were ready to leave us to establish your own life. Every year on your birthday, your mama and I would discuss when I should tell you, but I kept putting it off, waiting for the day when I knew I had to tell you. I hesitated telling you for fear that we would lose you. I'm sorry you had to find out this way. It wasn't what I wanted. But we are glad you know the truth now. You must remember, we love you very much and want nothing but happiness for you."

"Yes, I remember the times you tried to tell me something about being adopted, but I was so young then that I didn't fully understand what you were saying. I guess I just didn't want to hear what you were saying. I guess my mind was on something more than being told I had been adopted. Actually, I was thinking that when I married, I would marry you, Papa."

Later, after settling down, Viki thought began to think about her situation. Now that I know who my real mother and father are, what difference does that make? I don't feel any less love for those who raised me or any more for the family who didn't. I still feel as though Ana is my aunt and her children are my cousins. Maybe someday that will change. If it doesn't, that's all right, too. I love Mama and Papa. I can't change that. And now that I know who my biological parents are, perhaps I will learn to love them, too. But as far as I'm concerned, Mama and Papa are my real parents. Nothing will ever change that.

Later that month, Viki, with her parents' consent, went by herself to visit her newly discovered birth family. It was both a sad visit and a joyous one. She, Ana, and her five siblings hugged each other and shed a few tears. Ion was not present for her arrival. When he did appear, he was stumbling drunk and loud and made an ass of himself. His behavior terribly upset Viki, and Ana was clearly shamed by it. *At least now,* Viki thought, *I have a better understanding of why Papa feels the way he does about Ion.*

Viki graduated from high school with no plans to do anything other than to get a job and start earning income as quickly as possible. She gave no thought to getting a university education, and her father never mentioned it. He seemed content that she had gotten through high school, graduating at the top of her class. Few within the family had ever accomplished that feat.

Uncle Ilie had been the only one to graduate from the university.

Her father arranged a job for her in the accounts receivable section of Harambie Farms, where she prepared journal entries from shipping orders. For many years he had worked at the state-owned enterprise that produced and sold premixed animal food made from grains raised on Niculescu Collective Farms. Even though he had good connections in the organization, getting her the job had cost him a lot of money in under-the-table transactions. But he believed the expense to be well worth it.

One evening after Viki and her parents had finished watching the government's imposed limit of two hours of television, the discussion between them for some reason turned to marriage.

"Yesterday," her papa said, out of the blue, "I met Boian Hurgoi, my boss's son. He is head of the maintenance department. I like him. When I found out he wasn't married, I thought he would make you a good husband and me and Mama a good soninlaw. He's about the same age as you, maybe a little older. He has a good job and makes a good salary. Plus, he's good-looking, or so the girls tell me."

Her papa's first attempt at matchmaking startled Viki. For a moment she was speechless. "I think of marriage, Papa," she said, "but I haven't met anyone I would be interested in dating. I'm satisfied staying at home, and I'm content with what I'm doing. I appreciate what you are trying to do, but I'm just not interested in meeting this Boian. I will let you know if I change my mind. When the right person comes along, I'll know it. And I'll see that you and Mama know it, too."

Now what should I do? Viki thought. Apparently they have my marriage on their minds. No doubt, they've been discussing it for some time. Maybe I should be thinking about it too. But I haven't met any men I would want to marry. Maybe I need to talk with someone else about it? I wonder if Uncle Ilie would advise me; he always said that if I wanted to make more money and get ahead in this world, I should finish my education. I think I will give him a call and see if he has the time to discuss this.

"Papa is trying to marry me off to some man who works at his company," Viki told her uncle. "I don't know this person, and I'm not interested in meeting him. Since you have a daughter coming of age, I was thinking you might understand my position and help me make a good decision."

"Well," Ilie said, "about all I can do is talk to your father about the advantages of your getting more education now and letting thoughts about marriage rest until a more appropriate time. Who knows, you might find a university student whom you would want to marry and have children with. That would settle the question with your parents and get you qualified for a better job within the government system. I don't see any real problems here. I'll talk to my brother. I believe he will agree with me."

And sure enough, Ilie was right. Viki's mama and papa, now with more confidence in Ilie's judgment and with proof of his ability to achieve, were quickly convinced that she should get more education and let marriage come later.

CHAPTER 28

Education in Romania was controlled and administered by the regulations, policies, and practices of the Ministry of Education. Gaining entrance into the university was based mainly on the results of competitive examinations given to determine the level of knowledge, skills, and understanding of the available fields of study. Those failing to meet the standards were sent home to try another day.

Now that Viki felt free to complete her application, she began to make preparations.

When she discovered that her company's engineers with degrees were earning three times what she was making, she quickly decided she would take the tests as soon as possible. If a university degree would help her make that kind of money, she was more than ready to go for it.

Having taken accounting and economics courses in high school, and since she had a few years of work experience, she believed she could excel in those fields. But she had other interests as well. She considered pharmacy, but saw that it required too much chemistry, one of her weaknesses. When looking down the list of universities that were trying to fill student openings, she discovered there were only seven applicants for three scholarship spots at the university specializing in agriculture and animal husbandry. With her work experience on her family's farm and her father's guidance, she believed she could qualify for one of the scholarships.

She passed the agriculture and animal husbandry tests with high scores and was given a full four-year scholarship. The state paid all her costs, including room and board, tuition, books, and supplies, and gave her a set amount of money each month to spend as she desired.

The university degree required at least four years of studying agriculture, horticulture, and animal husbandry. Viki, delighted, was eager to get started. Finally, she was on her way to completing her education.

"Everything is free," Viki assured her parents when she returned home. "I'll get a good university education, and it won't cost us anything. I'm so happy. I'm going to thank Uncle Ilie for leading me in this direction. I realize you two aren't quite as pleased as I am, but don't worry, marriage will come along some day, as will grandchildren."

To be selected by the university for a full scholarship was a great honor. Her mama and papa could now stick out their chests and boast among their family and friends that their daughter had been accepted to earn an advanced degree.

Students at the university had no freedom in choosing how their degrees would be earned. They were told what courses to take, what books to read, and what activities to participate in. One month a year, both men and women had to wear uniforms and perform military field exercises. All students striving for an agricultural degree had to live, work, and study on the university farm one month each year.

Viki studied hard and was efficient in performing her experiments in the laboratory.

Along the way, she met many nice people and became close friends with them. University life, she quickly learned, could also be fun with lots of dancing, movies, camping, hiking, sports, and competitive performances in organized dancing. She was elated when her dance group came in second in a contest among other universities. She had never felt so free and alive.

She earned good grades and had enough confidence in her abilities to confront any test or examination. She began to appreciate even more the lessons her father had taught her, even though earlier she hadn't always realized their value. He always insisted she study hard and do her homework before anything else, particularly watching television. According to him, school should come first.

Krissy Popovici had become Viki's very close friend. The mud puddle incident had long been put behind them. Krissy was the competition Viki needed to keep pushing her in her studies and moving her toward her goals in life. Krissy and her family had moved from Vioresca soon after Viki and her parents had. The two friends had competed all the way up to and through high school and now at university.

While Viki was accepted into the university on her first try, Krissy missed it by a small margin. She lacked the level of knowledge in biology and science that Viki had acquired. She successfully passed the tests on her second try and was then immediately accepted by the university.

Krissy became the one person Viki could converse with and know that anything said between them would be held secret. She was a good adviser and quick to offer helpful suggestions when Viki needed to discuss something important.

With only a few students in Viki's lab, it didn't take her long to learn their names. One she met by accident was tall and handsome, and engrossed in compounding medicines to cure colic in cows. A full-to-the-brim test beaker had slipped out of his hand and shattered on the tiled floor, spreading a ring of sticky liquid. It made quite a mess.

Viki dropped to one knee and began helping him to wipe it up. He looked at her and said, "You don't have to do this. I let it fall. It is up to me to wipe it clean."

"I know I don't have to," Viki said, "but it has to be done before someone slips and falls. Besides, you looked like you needed help. What is your name?"

"I'm Kornel Negura. I'm happy to meet you. And you are correct: I didn't really know how to clean this mess. I appreciate your help. I've noticed you in lab and was hoping I could meet you, but not like this. What's your name?"

"I'm Viorica Antonescu. I would like to talk more, but we had better get back to our experiments before the professor returns. Perhaps we will meet again sometime, someplace else, and have a chance to talk more."

"I hope so, too. Again, thank you for helping me."

On a day bright sunny day a few days after the laboratory incident, Viki was walking toward her dormitory with her eyes looking up at big white clouds slowly drifting along in the blue sky. It was one of those days when her thoughts were on her good fortune of getting into the university. As she rounded the corner of the administration building, still looking up, she accidently bumped into a person coming the other way.

"Oh, it's you! I'm sorry!" Viki exclaimed.

"No, no, I'm not sorry it's you," Kornel said. "I'm glad it's you. I'm just sorry that I bumped you. If I had to bump into someone, I'm glad it was you, not that I wanted to bump into you. It's just that if I had to bump into someone, I'm glad it's you. I mean, I'm glad to see you, even if it means that, ah, ah … I'm glad to bump into you, but I didn't want to meet you by bumping into you. Oh, ah, I don't know how to say what I'm trying to say."

"No, you're right," Viki said. "Let's each say, 'I'm glad I bumped into to you because I am glad it was you I bumped into.' My mind, too, was far, far away, and I wasn't really watching where I was going."

"Where are you going?" Kornel asked.

"Nowhere in particular. Perhaps to the library to do some research, but I can postpone the research for a little while. Shall we walk together?"

"Yes, I would like that. I don't have anything else to do, and I would enjoy walking with you."

They took a seat in the farthest corner of the reference room on the first floor of the library, where they could quietly talk between themselves without disturbing the others doing research.

"I've wanted to talk with you since we accidently met in the lab. Tell me all there is to know about you," Kornel said.

"Yes, and I have wanted to meet you. As you already know, my name is Viorica Niculescu, but most everyone calls me Viki. What is your name, again?"

"My name is Kornel Negura. I live in the village of Milosoca near Birlad. And you?"

"From Suceava, but I was brought up in the village of Vioresca near Saveni. What brought you to this university?"

"It was the low number of students interested in agriculture. It made the competition easier. I felt I had a better chance of getting a scholarship with less competition to contend with."

"Well, it seems our minds run down the same path," Viki said, a big smile on her face. "That's exactly why I took this curriculum. I too was looking for an easy way into university, although I did grow up on a farm in Vioresca, which helped me with the entrance exams. My father once owned several acres of farmland in the village, but now the farms have been converted into a government-owned collective specializing in grain farming.

"We moved to Suceava when I was ready for high school. Now my father is working for an animal feed company there. He's their top salesman. My mother is a housewife. She hardly got through elementary school. She was a good student, but she had to stay home and care for her brothers and sisters while her parents worked the fields. She is a wonderful mother and an excellent housekeeper. What do your parents do?"

"Well, my mother, like your mother, got just the elementary education and became a housewife and a good mother to me and my sister, Marina."

Kornel stopped, as if he was having difficulty gathering his thoughts. His pause was long enough for Viki to ask, "And your father?"

After a moment, he replied, "My father is a, ahem, ah, ah, highly educated man and, ah, ah, he is a, ah, teacher, ah, yes, a teacher, and a good one." Kornel stuttered and appeared uneasy trying to find just the right words to explain what his father did. He shifted his eyes from Viki's upturned face and looked around to see if there was anyone within listening distance. It appeared he did not want to be overheard trying to answer her question in any detail.

Viki wanted to pursue the matter, but at the same time she didn't want to give him the impression of being too nosy. It was obvious he didn't want to talk much about his father, so she let the matter drop for the time being. *Maybe the next time we get together,* she thought—should there be a next time—*I will bring up the question again.*

To change the subject, Viki asked, "What do you want to do after you graduate from the university?"

"I don't know. I suppose it will be what and where the government sends me. Some collective farm, I suppose, which will be fine with me so long as I will be working with animals."

"That's the same with me," Viki said. "I don't know what I really want to do at this point, so I'll just see what jobs are available, make my application, and complete it the best I can with whatever tests I must pass." After a pause, she said, "Well, it was nice meeting you, but I must get to my research now."

"It was nice meeting you, too, and I also must get going. Would you like to take in a movie, maybe this weekend?"

"Yes, I would like that," she answered.

CHAPTER 29

It was Saturday evening. The air was humid following a sprinkling of rain that had fallen while Viki and Kornel were inside enjoying the movie. The sandy walkways through the park were still walkable without muddying the shoes, and the surrounding greenways were lush with early grass sprouting through the winter thatch. The flowering shrubs and plum trees seemed to swallow the walkers using the path. It was a beautiful evening.

As they walked, Viki observed a few weary souls scattered around the benches as well as some other couples holding hands, some already intimate, and others moving closer and closer to each other.

The park was a place where one could find quiet and a feeling of seclusion, a place where one could talk without fear of being overheard. It was a good place to walk and talk and get to know each other better.

After several minutes of silence, Viki said, "The other day when we introduced ourselves, you were hesitant to tell me what your father did for a living. Why?"

"I couldn't find the words to explain my situation, and I didn't feel I could talk freely in the library. I didn't want to be overheard by informers or listening devices that the Securitate may have placed where people gather. Perhaps I shouldn't be talking to you this way, because I don't know if you are an informant. I would hate it if you were, and I would hate you too. And I don't want to hate you. I like you too much."

"Please continue," Viki said. "I am not an informer."

"My father, Dimitru, is a respected Orthodox priest in my village and is closely scrutinized by spies from the secret police. Everything he talks about, even in the church, is recorded and used against him. He has to report every month to the Securitate in Birlad, where he is made to listen to his recorded messages and forced to explain the meaning of each word and phrase. If the interrogator doesn't like any part of what he hears, they force my father to get down on his knees and recite the laws of the land that relate to the good the country does for the people and the wonderful things its leaders do to protect the people. The way the government treats the clergy is criminal, and unfortunately, the treatment passes on to the clergy's children. That's why I don't talk about my family when I'm in a crowd of people. I can't tell who is and who isn't an informer. And I don't like being interrogated."

Viki realized it was a terrible predicament to be in, all because of the communists' attitude toward religion in general and the people who practiced it, particularly priests. Apparently, Kornel had only a few friends he could confide in and was constantly fearful of his lot in life because of the threat of injury or a jail sentence.

"I've seen some of my friends get arrested for saying something negative about the government," she said. "What they said was only to get people laughing. They didn't mean it, but they were still punished severely. I wouldn't want anything like that to happen to you. I like you too much. So be careful."

Viki had already begun to see the truth in what some of the other students had been saying about the lack of freedoms enjoyed by other countries: freedom of speech, freedom of news media, including radio and television, and freedom to come and go without being constantly checked and harassed.

As they neared the women's dormitory, Kornel said, "Do you like camping?"

"Yes, but I haven't done much of it," Viki said. "My father loves to camp, but my mother doesn't like it. She does not like sleeping on the ground, and she detests cooking over an open fire somewhere out in some wilderness. Do you like it?"

"Yes, I do, but I don't get to do it very often, especially now that I'm at the university. A few of us are planning to take three days of our break at the Black Sea to camp, boat, and fish. And maybe we'll rent a Jet Ski and just have some fun. Could I interest you in going?"

"Gee, I don't know. You mean just the two of us in the same tent?"

"No, no," Kornel said. "Other girls will be going with us. Girls will sleep in one tent, and the boys will sleep in another."

"I don't know. I'll have to think about it."

"Well, think it over and let me know. We still have a couple of weeks. But I do want very much for you to go. I want to get to know you better. I think about you all the time."

"I've never done anything like that before. What will people say? What will our parents say?"

"They don't really need to know. We can do it, and if they ask us, we can just say we didn't."

"No, I can't lie about it. I want to be certain I'm doing the right thing. I'm growing fonder of you also and I would like to know you better too, but like this? I don't know. I'll let you know."

They continued their walk, but now they strode in silence. They stopped at the dormitory and said good night.

Suddenly Viki found herself being kissed by Kornel. After the initial surprise, she decided she liked it and kissed him back. The evening was complete. They went their separate ways.

The next day, Viki called her father and discussed her invitation to go camping with Kornel.

"What do you think I should do?" she asked, after describing the situation.

"You are old enough to know the difference between right and wrong," her papa said, "and you know how to make decisions. You've made a lot of them in the past. Some have benefited you, and some have gotten you in trouble. What is it that you want to do?"

"I don't know. I've never been put in this kind of a position before. I want to go, but I'm apprehensive. I've never been out with a boy like this before. That's why I called you. I want the benefit of your experiences."

Her father laughed. "My father had cut the cord years before I was your age, so I had no choice but to do what I thought was best. Some of my decisions were not good, but most were. I feel I gained more than if I had depended on others to make decisions for me."

"Well, in that case," Viki said, "I want to go, so I will. But I'm still apprehensive about it."

"I'm sure you are. So go and have fun, but be sure you do only what you feel comfortable doing. Right or wrong, it's now yours to decide."

The next day Viki told Kornel she would go with him on the camping venture, but only on the condition that they do as he said they would do: the girls in one tent and the guys in another.

About three weeks later, during the spring break, Viki and Kornel took the proposed camping trip with three other couples to the Black Sea. Once they set up their tents and cooking facilities, they enjoyed full days of boating, surfing the waves, and walking the beaches picking up shells. In the evenings they happily sat around a roaring fire enjoying each other's jokes and discussing student life at the university.

As Kornel had promised, on the first night the girls slept in one tent and the boys in another, leaving two tents empty. But after that, the arrangements changed. On the second night, three boys slept in one tent and three girls in another, putting one couple in one tent and leaving one empty.

"I was led by you to believe that all girls and all boys would share separate tents every night," Viki said to Kornel the next morning. "What happened last night is not how you said things would be. How do you explain that?"

"I can't explain that," Kornel replied, "but apparently Vasile and Andrea became so attracted to each other that they wanted to be together. They are engaged to be married, so I guess they believed it would be all right to do what they did."

"Well, I don't agree," Viki said angrily. "Engaged or not, I don't believe they should have done it."

"Mother Nature is strong and humankind is weak when it comes to sexual attraction," Kornel remarked. "I say more power to Vasile and Andrea. As someone once said, 'The world spins on the sexual instruments of humankind.'"

On the third night, two boys occupied one tent, two girls occupied another, and a couple each slept in the third and fourth tents, making Viki wonder if this was as Kornel had suggested, the way of life. *I'm attracted to him,* she thought, *but I don't know if I can go that far. Perhaps I should change my thinking and get the same enjoyment the other girls say they are getting? I don't know what to do.*

"Kornel, should I spend the night with you?" she asked, as they sat on the beach together watching the sunset.

"You do whatever your conscience tells you to do. As far as I'm concerned, I've fallen in love with you and I want you to love me too. But I don't want to hurt you. It is something you will have to decide. Either way will be fine with me. I love you and I want to marry you."

"Are you asking me to marry you? Are we engaged?"

"Again, that is up to you to decide. But first you have to accept my proposal for us to be engaged."

"Then I have even more to think about. I'll let you know."

On the fourth night, since the other couples chose to sleep in separate tents, only one tent was available for Viki and Kornel.

After a dinner cooked over the hot ashes of the fire and a couple of glasses of wine, they retired to their sleeping bags talking, laughing, and yearning for each other. Kornel, in the dim light of the lantern, reached out to Viki, took her by the hand, softly squeezed it, and whispered, "Why don't we put our sleeping bags together and enjoy each other's closeness and warmth? I want you more and more."

"And I, you," Viki softly replied. "I have to admit I've been wanting to get closer to you ever since you dropped that beaker in the lab. But should we?"

"Let's just do it and enjoy it," Kornel whispered. "I believe it will make our love for each other stronger and more endearing."

With that said, he quickly rearranged the sleeping bags, dimmed the lantern light until only a faint glow filled the tent, and slipped in beside her.

As they passionately kissed, Kornel's hand wandered ever so slowly and lightly over her body. From that moment on it was just pure delight and very gratifying.

"I love you," Kornel said.

"And I, I love you too," Viki whispered as she silently began to doze.

One evening while sitting on their favorite bench in the park, Viki and Kornel decided to set the date for their wedding day. Having been informally engaged since their camping venture at the beach, and now in their third year at the university, they decided they wanted to graduate together as husband and wife and work together on whatever jobs the government assigned to them.

This time Kornel dropped down on both knees, presented Viki with a beautiful engagement ring, and asked, "Will you marry me?"

Without hesitation, Viki took his hands, looked him in the eyes, and said, "Yes, oh yes. I'll marry you, and I promise to be your loving wife."

A few days later, after Kornel's parents had met Viki, they hosted an engagement party, gathering family members and close friends to a hall in the city where they enjoyed a dinner of roast pork, had drinks, and danced to the music of a renowned gypsy band.

On the next morning, the parents gathered with the couple and agreed to the dates for both the civil and religious ceremonies. At the same time, they agreed on who the godparents would be to manage the many details of getting the couple married. It was decided the marriage ceremonies would take place in Suceava because it would be less costly for Kornel's family to travel there from Birlad than it would be for Viki's larger family to travel to Birlad.

CHAPTER 30

The civil marriage ceremony was performed on Saturday, July 28, 1979, in the City Building with only family members and a small wedding party present. The next day, the couple was married in a religious ceremony in Saint Anne's Church, with a larger wedding party of bridesmaids and best men. The bride wore a gleaming white dress trimmed with delicate lace around the neck and sleeves. On her head was placed a shining crystal-studded tiara with an overhanging veil covering her face. She carried a small corsage of pink and white roses, which she handed to her handmaid. Kornel wore a light gray suit with a contrasting black vest and a white carnation pinned to his lapel. The church overflowed with relatives and friends.

Kornel's father, Dimitru, arranged to have Priest Danila Dodrescu, his best friend and college mate, conduct the most solemn wedding service.

The priest followed the Orthodox rites of marriage featuring the two sacraments, the betrothal and the crowning services, which included the exchange of rings, the procession, the declaration of intent, and the lighting of the candles. Remaining standing throughout the service, the congregation participated in singing the marriage hymns and making verbal responses as often as the priest called for them to reiterate their approval of the church's joining of the couple in holy matrimony.

The ceremony was long but beautiful and well received. The couple and their families formed a reception line in the narthex and expressed appreciation to the departing congregation for witnessing the ceremonies and wishing them well in their wedded life.

Following the service, everyone hurried to the reception that had been arranged for the families and close friends in a nearby restaurant. The families and guests celebrated the event with dancing, singing, lots of good food, and a plentiful supply of tuica.

By midnight, the party was over and everyone gone. Since Monday was a workday, most had to get some rest. The wedding couple, however, quickly went to their room, changed into traveling clothing, and left to catch a train to the Black Sea, where they stayed in one of the resorts and enjoyed two weeks of wedded bliss and happiness.

Their first wedded home was with Kornel's aunt, Maricara Negura, who let them use one room of her house until they graduated. Her husband had died, and her children were married and raising families of their own. Kornel and Viki's presence gave her company and a feeling of security and usefulness. She soon became attached to Viki, and for Viki the feeling was mutual. The couple traveled eight miles by train every day to the university.

Viki and Kornel graduated and left the university on May 30, 1980, after successfully submitting papers on assigned projects. Conducted on the university farm, their projects studied the effects of different foods and formulas on the health and growth of chickens and rabbits.

Viki's student group of five kept and maintained records of white rabbits, and Kornel's group concentrated on chickens. At the end of the projects, the classes enjoyed a feast of freshly killed test subjects.

The finale to their course of study was the oral examination by a panel of five professors who themselves were experts. Viki and her group had prepared a fortyfivepage paper on the results of their experiments with rabbits; Kornel and his group topped that with fifty-three pages on feed formulas' effect on chickens. They both graduated with honors.

After they were assured they would receive their diplomas, Viki asked Kornel, "How can we stay together after we leave the university? I don't want to be assigned to work someplace far away from you. I want us to be together always."

"Not to worry," he said. "The government's practice is to keep married couples together, and I want that as badly as you do. I've thought about it a lot, and I suggest that we do this way: I will make a selection of the type of work and then choose the location where the work is to be done, and then you'll make the same selection. Even if your credentials are less strong in the selected type of work than those in line behind me, you will get the post. That way we can make sure that we work and live together."

"Will it be that simple?"

"Yes," Kornel said. "At least that is what I understand. We will know more tomorrow when the work lists are posted."

At 2:00 p.m. the next day, the lists of job openings were posted in the administration building's lobby. Crowds of graduates gathered around, pushing and shoving to see the lists so they could be first to make their selection. In reality it made no difference if two or more people selected the same job, or the order in which they made the choice, because the work would be assigned by a committee of professors according to each student's school achievement score, starting with those who had earned 100 percent. The consensus of the committee was final in the assignment of the jobs.

Viki was selected to be manager of four sheep farms in the Bogoescu sector of the Iordacha Farms Collective, near Vaslui. The other five farms in the sector were devoted to cultivating various kinds of grains to feed the animals. Kornel was assigned to manage those farms.

Once they got their diplomas and knew what their work assignments were going to be, Viki and Kornel said good-bye to the university and boarded the train to travel to Kornel's home near Birlad, where they planned to live until they reported to their workplace in September.

"You know," Viki said, "I have never had to supervise anyone. I'm not sure I know how to give orders, especially to men."

"You'll not have any problems," Kornel said. "I know you will be a good supervisor—a harsh one perhaps, but a fair one. You have the initiative to follow through with your orders and to keep everyone in line with the work that has to be done. And soon you will learn your work objectives and what you have to do to carry them out. Besides, you know how your father had to work with the people he hired to labor on his farm. There is no reason why you can't learn from his experience."

Viki thought about what Kornel was saying and of the experiences she had had on the farm. There were so many lessons she had learned from her father. She recalled the episode with the geese and the lectures her father gave her about following orders and doing quality work every time. And then there was the incident with Krissy and her velvet dress, through which Viki learned the lesson of controlling her temper. She had taken to heart what her father had said about not offending other people, having to face the complaints and wrath of upset parents, and the compensation that had to be paid for the wrongs she had done.

"You cannot look down on anyone," Papa had told her. "You must always respect their thoughts and desires and, if at all possible, go along with them."

"You're right," Viki said. "Thanks to Papa, I do know how to handle myself."

Viki replaced the handset in its cradle atop the telephone and said, "Your sister, Marina, and I just signed up to take a week's tour of Ukraine."

"I'm sure that'll be interesting," Kornel said. "When are you leaving?"

"In three weeks," Viki said. The two of them had just relaxed to watch television in the living area of his parents' home. "We'll be gone five days."

Following their graduation from the university and the assurance of a good job, Viki and Kornel had decided that now was the time to travel and see what other countries had to offer. They were free to visit communist countries, but to travel to capitalist countries required passports—and those documents were virtually impossible to get unless the person held a high office in the Communist Party and had justifiable reasons to go the capitalist country in question.

"That's fine," Kornel said. "I wish I could go with you, but I promised Papa that I would help him remove two dying plum trees and then plant some new ones. So you and Marina go with the group and enjoy the visit."

"Do we need passports? Marina doesn't seem to think so, but I wonder."

"No, passports are needed only if you are trying to go to a noncommunist country. All you need to visit Ukraine is a good guide who will get you through the checkpoints and settle you into a good hotel, one who knows the country and can explain it to you in terms you'll understand and enjoy. What do you plan to do and see?"

"We will tour Kiev and Odessa. In particular, Marina wants to visit the university in Cernauti where your father studied to become a priest."

The guide, Madacina Vartocomti, did a superb job getting the group organized and checked off. She carried the typical green umbrella and used it effectively in leading the group around and through Ukraine as they visited many landmarks and museums, enough to fill five interesting days and four nights. In addition, Viki and Marina took a side trip and toured the university from which Marina's father had graduated in 1935 in preparation for the priesthood in the Romanian Orthodox Church.

PART 4
The Farm

CHAPTER 31

On the morning Viki and Kornel were getting ready to leave to catch the train to the collective where they were going to start work, the telephone rang. It was Viki's papa. Again he was unhappy about the economic and political conditions in the country. And once he got started on the subject, it was impossible to get a word in edgewise, so Viki didn't even try. Eventually she knew he would calm down and listen to what she had to say.

But this time she sensed there was something else wrong. He seemed more rattled than usual, like he had something important to tell her but didn't know how to bring it up.

"What is this country coming to?" he exclaimed. "Now our president is increasing exports of our farm production to repay the foreign debt he has so thoughtlessly built up. Isn't it enough that he keeps increasing our farm production quotas? I don't see how we can go on like this. It's raise after raise. It's bad enough having ration stamps to buy food, but now we must stand in long lines to get what little food there is on the shops' shelves or in their freezers. All we can do is queue up and hope there is enough for us by the time we reach the front of the line—even if it's only bones and scraps."

"So, what can we do about it, Papa?" Viki asked, struggling to get a word in.

"I believe it will get worse," he continued, "before it gets better. Soon, there will be shortages in other necessities, like heating oil and certain services. Already gasoline for our tractors and motors is hard to find. But that doesn't seem to bother our leaders. Now we see in the papers that the president's wife has been appointed first deputy prime minister, the number two position in the hierarchy, right behind the president. Just a year ago she was given a seat in the cabinet. She continues to move up in the world. Do you suppose she will replace her husband when he passes on?"

"I hope not!"

"And now to make things worse," her papa said. Then he paused for a long moment. Viki knew that whatever he was keeping back was about to be revealed.

"Now, ah, now, ah, Mama is not well. She has, ah, ah, Parkinson's disease, and her condition will only get worse. Viki, I don't know what to do."

"Oh, Papa, Papa, I'm so sorry to hear this," Viki said, a knot of emotion rising in her throat. She had to sit down to steady herself. She didn't want to say anything that would make him more agitated. "We just have to take it a day at a time, Papa. I know you've got your hands full, but rest assured, we will help you as much as we can, whenever we can.

"I was just getting ready to call you and Mama," Viki went on. "We are leaving later this morning for Botosani to take over our new jobs. We will keep in touch with you to let you know how we are doing and to keep up with how you and Mama are getting along. I'm so sad about her sickness. If we can help in any way, don't hesitate to call me. I'll give you our new numbers as soon as I get them. Kiss Mama for me and tell her we love her. We will pray every day for the two of you."

As she replaced the handset on its cradle, she turned to Kornel, big tears sliding down her cheeks. She fell into his arms.

"Papa just told me Mama has Parkinson's disease," she said with difficulty.

"There is no cure for that," Kornel said. "I'm so sorry. All we can do is pray and help them as much as we can. The burden on your father will increase as her condition worsens. This is horrible news, but we have to control our emotions and be available when he calls for help. Knowing your father, he'll try to do it all himself before he'll call us."

Kornel gently stroked her hair and said, "I know this is crushing for you, but we must say our good-byes to my parents. And then we have to get to the depot, or else we'll miss our train."

Upon their arrival in Vaslui, Viki and Kornel took the local bus to the headquarters of the Iordacha Collective's regional operations. As they rode, they spoke very little, both staring out the window at the surrounding farm fields, lost in their own thoughts about their future in this place.

"Everything here looks so poor," Viki said. "The landscape, the villages, the roads, and the people—they are dressed in rags. God must have overlooked this part of the world. Why do you suppose he selected us to work here?"

"He must have had good reasons," Kornel said. "I can see where a lot of work is necessary just to renovate the buildings and to improve the appearance and serviceability of the roads and fields."

"There are a lot of barns on the property," Viki said. "I have counted sixteen already.

They must process thousands of sheep every year."

"At least that many," Kornel said, "from the odors I'm picking up."

"We might as well get used to it, because we'll be right in the midst of them."

"It can't be much worse than what we've experienced when we lived and worked on the university farm," Kornel said.

CHAPTER 32

Summer was almost over. All the Iordacha Collective grain fields had been harvested and the hay baled and stacked for later use. Sheep still dotted the hilltops, foraging on the summer foliage and rich grasses. Soon they would be herded back to the valley and into the shelter of the barns. Thunderstorms at the end of August had left ugly ruts and potholes in the lane, and the drainage ditches were filled with all sorts of trash. The road surface itself was dry and dusty. Regional Director Dimitri Dobra was wearing his best walking shoes instead of his usual rubber boots. Though he was not blessed with long legs, his purposeful strides allowed him to cover ground quickly.

Later today he was meeting with his new hires. He wanted to ensure them a place to live while the new house he had planned for them was being built. Because his friend, former director Cojocaru, had a spare room in his house, Dobra had decided to pay him a visit and see if he would rent it to the young couple for a year.

Near Cojocaru's house was the gated entrance to the barns that sheltered the farm's flock of three thousand sheep. Just inside the wire gate was the site where the new hires' house was under construction.

As Dobra passed the men and women toiling on their personal plots of land, he paused and waved. He knew many of them personally. Most were dependable workers. However, there were a few who were lazy drunkards and who spent more time in the taverns than they did working. That was a shame, because they had large families to feed, clothe, and educate.

As he turned the corner, Dobra saw his old friend in front of his house raking a freshly mown patch of grass and placing the cuttings in his compost container. His hair was whiter than Dobra remembered it, and there was a lot less of it.

"How are you, Director Cojocaru?" Dobra shouted. "I haven't seen you for several months. I thought I would drop by and say hello."

Cojocaru looked up from his task, delighted surprise on his face. "I am very well, Director Dobra. It is good to see you again. What brings you out on such a nice day?"

"I last saw you at your wife's funeral," Dobra said. "A terribly sad occasion. I hope you are coping with the loss."

"I take it day by day," Cojocaru said, heaving a sigh. "Day by day."

"I wondered if you were still thinking about renting out your spare room," Dobra said. "I have a young newlywed couple reporting to work Monday. They will be looking for a place to live, as the house I'm building for them will not be ready for at least a year. Are you interested in renting them that spare room?"

Cojocaru leaned on his rake. "Yes, I am," he said. "I'm getting too old for this kind of work, and the house needs a lot of attention that I can't give. It was much easier when my wife was here. I am a teacher, not a farmhand or a housekeeper. I'd like to find someone I could trust to come live with me and help me. I refuse to marry again, and I'm so desperate that I'd be happy to pay them to live here. Now that I've told you my sad story, tell me, how have you been?"

"I've been fine," Dobra replied, "I keep busy with my job and my family. I've more work in the district since our engineers redesigned how our farms will be arranged and what we should do to separate the farms from the villages. The young couple I mentioned will be supervising the operations. They've just graduated from the university and come highly recommended by university officials."

"Possibly I could advise them about the village and the people who live and work here. I know all of them since most of them were students in my school. I believe I could be most helpful to the young couple. I would appreciate it very much if you would tell them about me and my house. Thank you, Director Dobra, for thinking of me."

"You are welcome, Director Cojocaru. I will urge them to come by and discuss renting from you."

"Thank you, but please don't call me Director. I am not a director. I'm just a retired old schoolteacher, and I prefer to be called Professor Cojocaru."

At 10:00 a.m. sharp, Viki and Kornel entered the collective administration building to meet with Director Dobra. His secretary, who introduced herself as Magda Mihnea, immediately ushered them into a well-furnished and immaculately clean office.

The director rose from behind his walnut desk to greet them. Dobra was not a big man, standing about five feet eight inches with a medium build. His stomach lapped a little over his belt, and he used elasticized suspenders to hold his trousers in place. He wore a nice suit and smelled of imported shave lotion. His heavy but neatly trimmed mustache displayed a sprinkling of gray, as did his black hair. It was obvious that the director's desk had been custom-built, as such luxury items were not normally manufactured in Romania. He proudly offered them seats in a pair of richly upholstered chairs, not the usual folddown stackable type.

Beautiful paintings of local scenes hung on the side walls. A map of Dobra's operating region, with colored pins locating each of the fourteen villages comprising his area, was centered on the wall behind his desk. His desktop was clean except for the pencil cup containing all his newly sharpened pencils.

Is it possible, Viki thought, that he starts with new pencils every day? If so, I wonder what he does with the used ones? Perhaps I should find out. I could use some.

"I'm pleased to meet you both," Dobra said, warmly extending his hand to them. "I've heard many good things about you and have really been looking forward to telling you about my operations here and answering any questions I am sure you must have.

"Before we do that, though, permit me to give you a description of the area I direct and of which you will be a part. All my operations here are concentrated on raising healthy sheep for the foreign markets we supply, with emphasis on improving both the quantity and quality of the meat and wool we export.

"Most of our breeding stock is imported from New Zealand because of the excellent quality of their animals. Today, I raise about eighty thousand sheep annually, with plans to increase that once we build more holding pens. In addition, it is my future objective to raise hogs, but we can't do that until a barn is built to contain them. That, Supervisor Kornel, will be one of your first responsibilities. I am under pressure to do everything I can to help the government pay off its huge debt to other countries.

"Here," he said, pointing to the map of the Bogoescu village as he sat down behind his desk, "are the nine farms you two will manage. Supervisor Viki, you will manage the four sheep farms, and Supervisor Kornel, you will manage the five grain farms. Your main tasks are to raise three thousand sheep annually and experiment with the various food mixtures the central laboratory in Bucharest prepares for us. The objective is to improve both the quality of the lamb and mutton meat, and the sheep's wool.

"I operate five farms that grow and process all the grain needed to feed the animals. This, Supervisor Kornel, will be your area of responsibility. Again, as with the sheep, we expect to cultivate and produce better-quality grains each year and increase the peracre production.

"Throughout the entire collective, more than 150 workers are employed to do all the work needed to feed and raise the sheep we produce. That's why we have so many barns on this lot—to hold the sheep until they can be shipped to the processing plant.

"All the collective's farms are mechanized. We have tractors, planters, and harvesters. We have horses, but they are only used in special situations when a motor vehicle isn't practical. While the two of you will not be assigned a stateowned vehicle, transportation is just a phone call away. We have an excellent pool of cars and drivers."

Viki shot Kornel a look. He appeared to be as impressed as she was with the quality of the operation they were joining.

"Supervisor Kornel," Dobra said, "because of the distances between your assigned farms, you will have a motorized four-wheeler available. It is not registered to travel the state roads, but it will get you to where you have to go.

"Supervisor Viki, the barns in your village are near the main road running through our district. They are designed to shelter the sheep during the winter months. They are emptied during the summer months, when the sheep are led to pasture on the hilltops.

"Supervisor Viki, a mechanical system mixes and stores the prepared food into silos. From the silos, the food is spread into the feeding troughs by mechanized delivery carts. And where there is mechanical equipment, we must have skilled and dependable workers to operate and maintain it. When the barns are empty of sheep during the warm months, we utilize the space to raise other meat products like hogs, chickens, and turkeys, mostly to meet local needs."

"Are the sheep of Romanian stock?" Viki asked.

"No, they were bred from stock imported from Australia and New Zealand. When the sheep reach about two years of age, we feed them special diets containing high amounts of vitamins. This helps them produce larger and stronger offspring. After about seven years, the sheep that have outlived their breeding usefulness are culled from the flock and sent to the meatpacking plants for processing and exporting. An inventory record is kept and maintained on each animal from birth until it is sent to the packing house."

"How are the sheep moved from the barns to the hilltops?" Viki asked.

"That is a major operation, as is moving them back in the fall. As you know, sheep don't like to move fast, so the task requires several days of herding the flocks through the village and up to the grazing fields. Our shepherds drive horse-drawn carts loaded with the materials and supplies to keep the sheep safe from predators, control drifting snow, and erect their own shelters for the season. Not to be forgotten are the sheepdogs that herd the animals to and from the feeding areas.

"Ewes are impregnated in the spring by artificial insemination, and because our objective is to produce the best possible meat quality, I spend a lot of time and money gathering the finest sperm I can find. Today, most of our sperm comes from New Zealand."

Viki was grateful for the wellpadded chair. Director Dobra's welcoming speech was longer than some of her university lectures.

"Supervisor Kornel," Dobra said, "you and your assistants will search through the records to choose the ewes to be inseminated. Soon after birth, the new lambs are taken from their mothers, placed in special holding pens, and fed the mothers' milk fortified with the latest growth food supplements recommended by the formulas concocted by the state laboratory as their offering to raise the perfect sheep.

"In the cold winter months, the sheep are sheltered in the specially designed and constructed barns and are fed formulas of hay, grains, and supplements also prescribed by the state laboratory. Extra workers are hired to do menial tasks around the farm and to care for the housed sheep. Often, workers are hard to come by, so it is not unusual to employ chain gangs from the nearby prisons, or students from the local schools, who, as part of their patriotic duties, help plant and harvest the products.

"In the summer months when the sheep are in the upper grazing lands, we hire temporary workers to do the cleanup of the buildings. Barns must be completely scrubbed down, mucked out, sanitized, and repainted. Then the buildings and the automated facilities are used to raise chickens, not so much to raise more money, but more to keep the equipment in good working order. Again, as we do with sheep, we strive to raise quality products.

"At the end of the summer, when the sheep are scheduled to return to the barns, the chickens are sent to the slaughterhouse and the buildings are made clean again in preparation for the sheep.

"During the winter months, the sheep are sheltered in the barns and fed by the equipment on a regular schedule. We don't muck the sheds in the wintertime. We just put down a layer of fresh straw periodically and let it pile up. By springtime, it is a solid mass requiring special equipment to remove, move, and spread to fertilize the croplands."

Viki was relieved when he stopped speaking, as his voice was putting her to sleep. But it turned out to be only a momentary lull.

"Now, about your housing," the director said. "In your village there are about fifty scattered homes and outbuildings. All are old and in need of a lot of major repairs and rehabilitation. So, I would like to see what the two of you can do to make them more presentable. We have numerous visitors each year, and I would like to make this village more presentable to them. It would be a big plus in our ratings if we could arrange some improvements."

Viki couldn't help but wonder why Dobra was using "I" so much, as if he were the only one working in the collective and that it was in fact "his." A big ego he seemed to have, and it was obvious from his long-windedness that he enjoyed reveling in his own glory.

Viki asked, "What about the milk from the ewes? Is it also sold for money?"

"No," replied the director. "I don't sell the milk. It's against the law. I am only in the meat business. The milk is used only to feed the lambs."

Dobra paused for breath, and then he said, "One more thing: you will both find written operating procedures in your office files, and I urge you to closely follow them. Periodically, we are audited by area accountants to make certain our transactions are in line with the state's rules and regulations. I do everything I can to keep improving the quality of the products I raise. That means searching out what other countries are doing to improve the quality and quantity of meat and grains."

"Is it possible," Kornel said, "to visit those countries to observe and bring back the knowledge and skills we can use?"

"Oh, yes. In fact, I encourage it."

"Now comes the bad news," Dobra said. "We have no housing for you on the collective. However, I'm pleased to say that a nice big house is being built for you, but it will take about a year complete it. The rent is reasonable, and there will be no outofpocket costs to concern you. Electricity, water, and sewage are included.

"Also, Supervisor Kornel, there are two other matters that I want to clear up with you so that we understand each other. I read in your records that your father is a priest in the church and has been imprisoned for a period of time. Also, you are not a member of the Communist Party.

"As you may know, in some circles this could be held against you when promotions come up. This is a practice I don't agree with. So, if it does become an issue at the time you are recommended for a higher-level job, I want you to know that I will do my best to get you promoted."

"I appreciate that," Kornel replied. "And I promise I will do my best to get your recommendation. I want desperately to advance in the organization."

"Now I suggest," Dobra continued, "for you to find a room in the village you can rent until your house is finished. I suggest you visit Director Cojocaru and discuss renting his spare bedroom. It became available when his wife died. He is a very nice man and can be very helpful in acquainting you with the village and its people. During his working years, he was in charge of the village's education system. He knows everyone by name and their family history.

"While the villagers call him Director Cojocaru, he has informed me that he prefers to be called Professor Cojocaru, because, as he said, 'I'm just a teacher of the arts and have had little control over the school systems in the villages.'

"He does not drink alcohol, but he always has some on hand for those he knows to be drinkers. He continues to mourn his wife's death, but now he is looking for help in keeping his house clean and orderly and, if possible, in caring for some of his personal needs. Once you get to know him, you'll like him. I suggest you see what you can work out."

Once again Dobra rose from behind his desk and extended his hand, a signal that his guests should also stand.

"I thank you for coming in," the director said. "I've enjoyed meeting you and discussing my operations here on the farm. If you have questions of any kind or need help, my door is always open, as is my telephone line. So, feel free to call me anytime. By the way, I've arranged one of our shuttles to take you to your village. The driver will pick you up out in front of the building. We have a good shuttle service among my fourteen villages, so feel free to use it. We generally meet once a month here in my office, so the next time you come you will get the chance to meet the managers of the other communes.

"Now, for your first meeting with your workers at eight o'clock in the morning, I have arranged to introduce you to your staff. We will meet in the conference room in barn #1. I believe you will learn that all are welleducated and very good workers. I know you will appreciate working with them."

"Wow, can he talk," Viki said softly while she and Kornel waited in the pickup shelter for the shuttle to pick them up.

"I believe he can be of big help to us," Kornel said, "but I think he likes to take credit for everything that gets done on the farm."

"I also get that feeling," Viki replied. "But I hope he doesn't overlook us, especially you with your record, when it comes time for evaluation and promotion. I don't think we should work these farms the rest of our lives. Surely there are better jobs elsewhere."

"Undoubtedly, there are," Kornel said. "But now I suppose we should go and meet this Professor Cojocaru and look at what he has available for us to rent until our house is built."

"Yes, but let's do it early tomorrow afternoon, after we meet with the staff. That will still give us enough time to look for something else if what Cojocaru has to offer doesn't suit us."

"Yes," Kornel said, "let's do it that way. But now, let's find the boardinghouse. I'm tired and hungry."

"Let's get some rest, and perhaps our heads will be clear enough in the morning to make some good decisions," Viki said. "From what I saw, the village houses don't have much to offer. Obviously these people are poor and their properties need a lot of repair. As a matter of fact, the entire village could use a major makeover."

CHAPTER 33

Viki awoke in the pitch-dark and jostled a sleeping Kornel. "It's time to get ready to meet our staff. We certainly don't want to be late."

"What time is it?"

"Five o'clock."

"Give me another ten minutes of sleep."

But Viki was insistent. "It's imperative we are there before he arrives."

"Really?"

"It will show our dedication."

Kornel groaned and rolled out of bed. They showered, dressed, ate breakfast, and walked to the barn. When Viki saw a new car parked near the entrance, she realized that Dobra had already arrived. "I hope he doesn't berate us," she said, "for not being here to greet him."

"He won't. We're on time. I just hope the staff is all here."

They were, all appropriately dressed and anxious to meet their newly appointed comrades.

"Viki and Kornel," Dobra said, "this is our accountant, Andre Anghelscu. He analyzes the financial and statistical reports for my collective and explains the variances to those who need to know. His bookkeeper, Beatrix Bratianu, posts the journals of the financial transactions and prepares the financial reports for the accountant's use. Standing beside Beatrix is his timekeeper, Thialda Tudor. She keeps payroll records for each employee and sees that all receive their paychecks on time each month. In addition, she keeps detailed inventory records of the animals, the farm's buildings, and all equipment and materials.

"Both technicians have completed the required high school education and have at least three years' experience. Comrade Anghelscu graduated from the university and has worked on my collective for more than eight years.

"Meet Vilhelm Vadim, our veterinarian, and his medical technician, Marius Miklos. They are responsible for the health of the animals. And last but not least, this is Eugeniu Ene, my engineer, and Mirca Murgu, his technician. They obtain and service all the mechanical vehicles and keep them in good repair. We all work together as a team and help one another when necessary."

After Kornel and Viki had made the rounds shaking hands, Dobra said, "We are so pleased to meet you, and we look forward to a long and friendly relationship. We will do our best to do our jobs and help you with yours for the good of the collective. Feel free to come see us anytime. We will do our best to accommodate you."

After the staff meeting, Viki and Kornel walked directly to Professor Cojocaru's house following the directions Dobra gave them. They were both impressed by the artistically designed wooden gate welcoming visitors to his property. It was enhanced by an immaculate white picket perimeter fence. The gate was painted in a pleasant variety of colors that blended with the landscaping.

It was clear, however, that the yard had been neglected for some time. Neither the shrubs nor the grass had been trimmed for quite a while. And the side yards and backyard were even worse. In the center of the backyard stood the precariously leaning outhouse. Despite its lean, it appeared to be well built and large enough to accommodate two at the same time.

Kornel knocked on the gate and waited. It seemed a long time before Cojocaru responded. He came out of the house dressed in work clothes that appeared not to have been washed for some time. He was wearing a pair of slip-on shoes that had seen better days.

"Hello," he said, opening the gate and looking at them suspiciously. On his face was what appeared to be a full week's growth of whiskers. "What can I do for you?"

"Hello," Kornel said. "I am Kornel Negura, and this is my wife, Viki. We have been assigned to work on this farm and are looking for a place to live until our house is built. We've been talking to our director, Comrade Dobra, and he suggested you might have a room we can rent."

Cojocaru gave them a big smile. "Yes, I do have an empty room you can use if you think it is suitable. My wife died recently. It is lonely around here. I could use the company. Would you like to see the room and the rest of the house?"

"Yes, if it is convenient for you," Kornel said, as Viki nodded in the affirmative.

"Yes, now is good for me. Come in, come in!"

Viki was shaken by what she saw as she walked through the front door. The house had not been cleaned in a long time. There was clutter in all the rooms—old newspapers, magazines, books, and odd pieces of mail. Dust was thick, and cobwebs hung heavily in the corners of each room.

The kitchen was much worse. It was filled with dirty dishes, unwashed cooking pots and pans, and assorted soiled dishcloths and towels that were strewn about the room or left hanging from the backs of chairs. A thin layer of slippery grease lay on the floor around the tiled kitchen stove built into the corner of the inside wall.

Viki thought to herself, No, no, no! I can't live like this, and I'm certainly not going to clean it up or even offer to keep it clean for him. It's no wonder he's lonely. If he would spend some time keeping his house up, he would not have time to be lonely. He needs to find himself a good housekeeper, and that is not in my job description.

The extra room was actually nice. It was in the same condition his wife had left it. But that had been a long time ago. There was such a heavy accumulation of dust that names could be written in it.

After they had completed the tour, Kornel asked, "How much rent do you want for your spare room?"

"Nothing. You can live here for free."

The answer was baffling, as they had expected to pay something. It didn't make sense. What was he expecting in return?

"I don't understand," Viki said. "If you don't want money to rent your room, what do you want?"

"I just want someone to live in the house and keep me company. Since my Dorina died, I have not been happy and I don't feel like doing anything around the house."

While the rented room was nicer than the rest of the house, Dorina's clothing was spread around and the bedding had not been changed—apparently since she had died. The bedroom chamber pot had been overlooked for the same time period as well. Since it had not been scrubbed for a while, it still exuded an unpleasant odor. At least its cover was intact and seemingly airtight.

"It would make me feel better," Cojocaru continued, "just to have you and Kornel coming and going every day and discussing events to keep me up to date with what is going on in the country and in the surrounding villages. Who knows, perhaps I can be of help to the two of you. Money, I don't need. I have enough to keep me alive and have a decent life. So, I ask you to please feel free to live here, use the house, and let me help you get settled into our humble village."

"We will think about it," Kornel said, "and let you know our decision tomorrow. We thank you for your friendliness and for showing us your house. You have been very nice."

"Well, I thank you for coming. I'm glad to have met you. I hope you will take my room."

As Kornel and Viki walked back to their boardinghouse, they discussed their dilemma: should they accept Cojocaru's offer to live there rent-free or look for another place to rent that was more pleasing to their tastes?

"It isn't the most desirable house," Kornel said, "but it would serve our purpose once it has been cleaned and all the clutter organized. I like the man; he is certainly friendly and seems to want to accommodate us. Personally, I wouldn't have any problems with him or his house, after it's been cleaned."

"I agree with you," Viki said, "but I'll tell you this: I'm not going to be his housekeeper. Did you see that kitchen? My stomach turns just thinking about it. I wouldn't even think about eating my meals in it, let alone cooking for him too. And why is he willing to let us live there and not pay rent? He must be expecting something else. There is no doubt in my mind that he is very lonely without his wife, but I wouldn't want him to expect me to replace her. And, under no condition would I move in unless I paid rent. I would much rather that he be obligated to us than us to him. I'll talk to my father and get his thoughts about what we should consider."

After they settled in their room at the boardinghouse, Viki called her father and discussed the man, his house, and his no-rent offer.

"While it would be helpful financially to pay no rent," her papa said, "you do not in any way want to live there with the constant feeling that you owe your landlord something. You should not burden yourselves with that feeling. If something unexpected happened, he could hold you responsible and cause you grief. But if you paid him rent, then he would not be able to hold anything against you. No, Viki, my advice is, don't live in the house without paying rent. After all, it will be only for a year or so until your new house is completed."

The next afternoon, Viki went back to Cojocaru's place and told him, "We will take your extra room, but only on two conditions: that you accept three hundred leu rent each month, and that the house and outhouse be kept clean and orderly as long as we live here. I will arrange to have it cleaned and see that everything is properly stored.

Since it's your house, you can pay for the labor. I expect you to keep it that way as long as we live here, even if you have to hire a housekeeper to come in and do the work."

"I don't need the money," Cojocaru said, "but if that is the only way I can get you and your husband to move into this house, I will accept it." He looked around and frowned. "Yes, I supposed it is overdue for a good cleaning. I apologize for the mess it's in. I will pay for having it thoroughly cleaned, and I promise I'll keep it that way."

"Fine," Viki said. "Kornel and I will plan to move in when the cleaning has been completed. I will work with whomever you can find to do the work. Is there someone you can recommend who you know will do a good job and do it quickly, someone who is dependable?"

"Yes, that's easy," Cojocaru replied. "You just happen to have the best person in the village already working for you: Veronica Vladu, your building custodian."

"Wonderful," Viki said. "I'll bring her around tomorrow. If she says she will do it, we will work Friday evening and all day Saturday cleaning up. Then Kornel and I will plan to move in on Sunday."

Veronica was a loyal and hardworking woman of about fifty years of age. She was short and rotund and wore a perpetual smile. Viki didn't know what made her smile. If she had problems, she kept them to herself.

After the two of them had looked over the property, Veronica politely said, "This won't be too difficult; I've seen a lot worse."

On Friday evening after Viki and Veronica sorted the rubbish and put away the clutter throughout the house, they cleared the cobwebs and wiped the walls clean. On Saturday they cleaned and scrubbed all the floors and rearranged the furniture. While the women worked inside the house, Cojocaru straightened the yard and cleaned the outhouse.

Everyone was delighted with the results. Cojocaru gladly paid Veronica the money he had promised. He marveled at how the house seemed as clean and sparkly as it had when his wife was alive.

On Sunday, Viki and Kornel settled into the house and began their working life in the new environment as employees of the state.

CHAPTER 34

Viki began her first supervising job by looking over the day's work orders, and then she handed them to her technician, Mirca Murgu. After scanning the orders, Murgu passed them out to the employees who performed the specified duties.

Most of Viki's regular employees were young and had completed at least a technical high school curriculum. A few of the older ones had just a smattering of elementary education and generally were alcoholics prone to missing workdays or being late in reporting to work. Viki knew who they were, having discussed her employee list with Professor Cojocaru. He knew each one and eagerly relayed his thoughts on how to manage them.

"Only fifteen have shown up," Viki said, looking at her technician. "Where are the others?"

"This being Monday," Murgu said, "the absences don't surprise me. They happen frequently, but mostly on Mondays following some special village event that carries through the weekend. As you know, there was a big wedding here Saturday with lots of dancing and drinking. When that happens, it's generally these same people who show up late, and usually with big hangovers. But I do give them some credit; they almost always get here within an hour of the start of work. I suggest we wait for about a half hour or so and hope they show up to get their orders."

"I have to rely on your good judgment," Viki said. "And since you know these people, I believe you know what you are doing. But this tardiness is still wrong. Not only is their work being delayed, but also look at the effect it's having on the rest of us. As you and I stand here waiting for them, our own work is not getting done. And the other workers who depend on them to do their jobs are being held up too. This isn't right. It must stop."

Sure enough, three of the missing workers finally showed up, obviously still inebriated judging by their staggering gait. The only one who did not make an appearance was Circu Costache, the maintenance specialist who worked on the electrical and mechanical food storage and feeding systems.

"His system will have to be shut down," Murgu said, "until he shows up."

"Well," Viki said, "there is nothing we can do about it until he shows up, so we might as well get to our own jobs. Let me know if he does show up."

"I will," Murgu replied. Then they went their separate ways.

Inside, Viki was seething, but she knew better than to show her temper, particularly on her first day as supervisor. *Don't these people realize that in their absence, others have to do their work for them?* she asked herself. *Or maybe they just don't care? Is it like this all over the country? These people get paid good money. Something must be done about this problem.*

At 10:30 a.m., Murgu stuck his head in Viki's office and said, "He's here, and he says he is ready to go to work."

Costache appeared behind Murgu, still wobbling drunk.

"We were wondering when you were going to show up," Viki said. "We have work orders to repair equipment, and since no one else knows how to do your job, I have to hold up the work until you get here. That is unacceptable. Either you show up on time or I'll have to take action to remove you from the job. We have a lot of skilled workers here. Murgu tells me you are one of our best, but we can't operate efficiently if people don't show up for work on time. Do you understand what I am saying?"

"Yes, I understand, and I'll try to do better."

"From now on then, you'll have to be on time to get your assignments. And even if you are here on time and it is obvious you've been drinking, be prepared to be sent home. I don't want anyone coming to work who might endanger himself or others working around him. And another thing: if you are sent home, you will miss that day's pay and the following day's as well. Do you understand me?"

"Yes, I understand what you are saying. I promise I will do better."

For the rest of the day, Viki walked around her farms to get more familiar with her surroundings and to observe how each of her workers was performing. She was pleased with some, but she quickly learned that not all were doing their best. She had little experience directing people, but something had to be done to get them all to produce more effectively.

She discussed the matter with Kornel, Director Dobra, Professor Cojocaru, and her father. All told her the same thing: treat your people fairly and get them to understand their responsibility to do the best-quality work they can. And punish those who break the rules.

"What should I do about the drunkard?" she asked her father.

"Appropriate and prompt action must be taken to punish him," he said. "And send a message to the others in the group to let them know who is boss now and what can happen if they don't follow the rules. You don't want to fire him, because that not only punishes him but also adversely affects his family. Besides, it is virtually impossible to fire anyone in the collective system. You would have to transfer the offending party to another area, and that just moves the problem instead of solving it. It also puts a burden on you, because now you have to train another to take his place.

"You should send him home and not pay him for the days he misses. True, that action will hurt his family, but not as much as firing would do. He probably spends most of his salary on his tuica rather than on food for the family. Withholding his salary will hit him in his wallet and hopefully teach him a lesson. So you might consider suspending him for a given number of days without pay."

Costache did well reporting to work on time for about two weeks. However, it was obvious he still drank, because of the body and breath odors he gave off as he passed by. Based on her experience with meaningless promises made by alcoholics—most notably, Ion Pavenic, her birth father—Viki knew it was only a matter of time before Costache was back to his old habits.

Sure enough, after three weeks Costache was two hours late on a Monday morning, and when he arrived at work, he was seriously impaired.

"Where have you been?" she demanded. "Certainly you know we can't operate this way. I've warned you more than once about tardiness and coming to work drunk, and you know what the penalties are because I made them very clear to you and you acknowledged them. So you leave me with no choice but to send you home without pay for this day and tomorrow. I expect to see you back Wednesday on time and ready to do your job. Do you understand what I'm saying?"

"Yes, I understand, and I promise I'll not do it again. But please don't send me home today. I can't afford to lose two days of pay."

"I'm sorry to have to do it, but I've heard those promises before. Again, you've let me down and you leave me no other choice but to send you home." She quickly turned and walked away, but then suddenly she stopped and turned back. "I can assign other work for those who depend on you to do their jobs. So the equipment can be repaired whenever you decide to work free of alcohol. Or else I can train another person to fill your position. I am prepared to do that if you are unable to comply with the workplace rules."

Viki immediately picked up the phone and called Director Dobra to tell him what she had done.

"You did what had to done," Dobra said. "He knows the rules. He has had this problem a long time. Perhaps time off without pay will make him accept the seriousness of his condition and force him do something about it. Just keep doing what you're doing and continue to keep me informed."

Costache returned Wednesday. He was on time, sober, and clean of body and mind. Apparently, the time off did what Viki had hoped, and she was grateful, but her gratitude didn't last long. As each weekend passed, Costache grew more reckless and began to arrive later and later—only a few minutes at first, but then it worsened. By the end of the month he was back to his old habits.

On the first day of the new month, after a weekend of heavy drinking, Costache did not show up until noon. Viki was fuming and let him have it.

"As I have told you over and over, we cannot work this way. You are hereby suspended without pay for the rest of the month. And, as I told you before, I'm going to train another person to do your job."

"But I can't afford to lose my pay for a month. My family needs it to live." He removed his old woolen cap and clutched it firmly to his breast as he begged her. "I promise I won't be late again. Please, oh please, don't do this to me and my family."

"You've made the same promises before and never kept them. It's obvious you are not willing to try to be here when you are needed. You leave me with no other choice than to suspend you. I have nothing further to say."

With those last words, Viki spun on her heels and walked away, leaving him stunned, not knowing what to do or say. Trotting after her, Costache kept pleading for her to change her mind, but she had closed her ears. She was not going to do it. She walked faster and faster until finally, she was out of sight.

Costache could do nothing but replace his cap on his head and slowly start walking down the lane to his home. He was devastated and didn't know what to tell his wife. So, rather than go home and face her, he decided to take the next shuttle to the district office and appeal his suspension with Director Dobra.

"Yes, I heard about it from Supervisor Negura," Dobra said. "And I uphold her actions. It's her job to produce, and to do so she must rely on you and the other workers to do your jobs. The only suggestion I have for you is to do your job as you know how it is to be done and make it a point to show up on time for work each day. Limit your drinking to Friday and Saturday nights. Do you understand what I am saying?"

"Yes, but I think it's too harsh a punishment. I have a family to think of. I need my pay each month."

"You should have thought about that when you spent your pay buying the alcohol you drink. Now you must pay the price for your actions."

Almost once a week, Costache approached Viki and appealed to her to take him back, literally falling on his knees begging with his old wool cap clutched in his hands. But Viki held firm and sent him home each time to consider his actions and accept what he had to do to follow the rules. She regretted having to function this way and truly was sorry for him and his family because he could be a capable worker when he was not drinking.

Viki kept asking herself if she was doing the right thing. She discussed it with Professor Cojocaru and her father. Both offered the same advice: "Don't give in. Continue to do what you are doing. If you let him return before he has served his time, you will lose face with your other employees, and the drunk will never learn. Your other employees look to you to be firm in your convictions and trust you to do what is right for everyone."

Viki wondered from time to time whether she might be the proverbial black sheep of all of Dobra's supervisors. She sometimes felt her people didn't like her because she was being too strict.

In the first two months on the job, she was forced to temporarily suspend others for various and assorted reasons: drinking on the job, not doing their work as scheduled, missing work, and being tardy in reporting to work.

Her people soon realized she was a fair supervisor. They knew that they would get the same treatment if they didn't shape up. And sure enough, Viki soon began to see a decrease in the drunkenness of the other workers and an increase in the productivity of all the employees' work.

After the month passed, Costache made up his mind: he had enough of suspension and absolutely no desire to go through it again. He was sober and ready to return to work. But best of all, he had given up alcohol. Physically, he hadn't felt so good in a long time. He promised himself and his wife that he would never let himself get that way again. In a sense, he felt grateful to and had more respect for Viki for putting him through the ordeal. So, one of the first things he did upon his return was apologize to Viki and then to his fellow workers. From that time on, he was one of Viki's best workers. He also set a good example for the rest of the workers.

CHAPTER 35

As time passed, Viki became much more comfortable working with her people. She began to realize she was using the same mannerisms and vocal expressions her father had used on her when she failed to follow family rules and adhere to their working standards. She had been a good student even though she hadn't realized it at the time.

Her people began to tell her how much they liked her supervision and how much more efficiently and pleasantly their working objectives were being achieved. Projects were getting done faster with better quality, and even the appearance of their village was improved. Everything was cleaner to work around.

Not only was Kornel responsible for managing the production and quality of his five grain farms, but also he was charged with improving the outward appearance of the old and dilapidated village. Over the years, roads, houses and outdoor structures had been neglected to the extent that most were now in immediate need of rehabilitation, which required new funds and governmental assistance.

Observing that the people were indeed interested in upgrading their properties, Kornel kept after Dobra to use his contacts to get the public works department to improve the road surfaces and to clean and deepen the drainage ditches. The shrubs, trees, and other foliage bordering the roadways needed to be trimmed, pruned, or removed and replaced, as the case may be.

This attention inspired the people to plant more flower gardens and to improve the appearance of their property by refurbishing the structures, ridding the ground of all trash, and replacing unsightly foliage with blooming shrubs.

Within weeks, the village began to display a new look. It was obvious that everyone was taking a lot more pride in their dwellings. There were smiles as people greeted each other and praised each other's efforts in improving the appearance of their properties. This was evidence of a bond of togetherness that had long been missing in the village.

One evening after dinner, and with only two hours of television on one broadcasting channel, Viki and Kornel took time to discuss how well the people were doing their jobs and how proud they seemed to be of their achievements.

"There should be something we can do to show our appreciation for their good work," Viki said. "We can't give them more money or any of the products we produce on the farms, but there should be something we can do."

"I agree," Kornel replied, "and it doesn't have to be anything spectacular, just something to make them feel we appreciate them."

"The only thing I see we have to offer," Viki said, "is that piece of land near the entrance to the farm that is not being used for anything. Why don't we let them share it? They can make gardens to supplement their food supply, and sell their surplus products to make a little extra money for themselves. Do you think that would work?'

"That's a great idea," Kornel said. "Yes, I believe that could work—and work well. I'll run it by Dobra and see what he thinks. If he agrees, I'll tell the people and let them decide how to share the land. I believe they will appreciate this."

"Comrade Viki, I need some freshly made feta cheese," Comrade Dobra said during one of his afternoon visits. "Could you see to that for me?"

Viki was a bit startled at the director's request. "Ah, yes, of course, but I believe you had said that we aren't allowed to use the sheep's milk for ourselves."

"Yes, I remember saying that. However, there are times when we can perhaps bend the rules a bit."

"But how do I account for the milk I would need to make the cheese? As you know, records have to be kept of how the milk is used, and making cheese is not authorized."

"That's easy," Dobra said. "I'll show you how we can do it when you deliver the cheese to me."

"Well, I don't wish to brag," Viki said with a big grin on her face, "but I believe you'll find my cheese very tasty."

"Good!" he said. "And if there is a time when you want something, just let me know and I'll show you how to account for it."

On one of her special visits to observe the way another district village functioned, Viki was invited into the home office of one of the supervisors and was immediately dazzled by a colorful oriental rug spread across the living room floor.

"Where did you get that beautiful carpet, Camelia?" she inquired.

"I bought it from a carpet dealer in Suceava."

"How much did it cost you?"

"Not much, just one truckload of newly shorn wool."

"I surely would like to have one for my living room."

"Discuss it with Director Dobra. Maybe he can help you as he helped me."

"Why do you want an oriental rug for our living room?" Kornel earnestly expressed himself, saying, "I don't see any need for it. What we have is sufficient, even though it isn't as attractive as the one you saw in Camelia's house. And you know I don't approve of what you have to do to get it."

"I just want one like it," Viki answered. "It will greatly improve the appearance of the room. And besides, I want to keep up with the other women in the collective."

"Well," Kornel said, grunting. "If you want it that bad and are willing to take the risk, then go ahead and do it. But leave me out of it."

The next year after shearing time, Viki filled five truckloads of wool. She decided four loads would go to the wool-processing plant and one would be exchanged for a newly made oriental rug for her living room. Knowing she needed Dobra's assistance in completing the transaction, she hand-delivered a large container of freshly made cheese in exchange for his showing her how to complete the papers to divert the truck to the carpet dealer.

Viki had always had help from her boss and felt comfortable even though she knew she was skirting the law. And as time went by, her cooperation with contacts in the other departments paid off when she wanted quick service and scarce products. She had learned how to haggle with her peers and how to exchange products for services received: a lamb here and a piglet there always put her in good favor with the other managers handling gasoline for the vehicles or furniture for the house, or getting someone to stand in the long lines for her to buy scant rationed produce not readily available on the farm.

It was a hot and dusty day in August when a strange-looking lonely man wandered down the lane toward the barn. He was dressed like a peasant farmer and acted as though he might be lost. He hesitated until Viki sent her workers off to their assigned duties. Then he made his way over to her.

"Hello there," Viki said. "What can I do for you? Are you lost?"

"Oh no, no, no. I'm Nicu Nechita. I'm looking for work and I saw you from the road, so I thought I would ask you for a job. I'm a good worker, but I lost my job when they shut down one of the farms in another district. Can you use me?"

"No. I have all the people I need. But even if I did need help, I couldn't hire you; hiring is done by Director Dobra."

"That's what I guessed, but I thought I'd stop and talk to you anyway. Have you hired anyone since you've been here?"

"No, I haven't! As I told you, I don't have the authority to hire people. Go talk to the director!" Viki was immediately suspicious and wondered if she was talking to a Securitate spy. Nechita's appearance and line of questioning reminded Viki of Kornel's stories of his experiences with the secret police and the tactics they used for gathering incriminating information. Rather than antagonize the stranger, Viki decided to play his game long enough to get him off her back and on his way.

"Yes, I will go see the director," Nechita said. "But do you mind if I ask you about what you do on this farm? I see you have many barns. Do you raise animals? I don't see many around."

"Yes, we raise sheep."

"Where are they? I don't see any."

"I believe you know where they are! It's summertime! They are in the hills feeding on the summer grasses. And I'm sure you know that they are sheltered in the barns during the cold weather."

"How many sheep do you raise here?"

"You're asking a lot of questions that I am not in the position to answer. You'll have to get that information from Director Dobra."

"I will. But really what I stopped here for was some food. I'm very hungry. Do you have some good cheese or other food I can beg from you?"

From that request, Viki knew that he was an agent from the Securitate.

"No, I don't have any sheep cheese. The only cheese I have is what I bought in Vlasca. We are not allowed to milk the ewes except to feed the lambs. We produce sheep for meat and wool production only, not for milk products."

"Oh, I didn't know that. I had heard that good sheep cheese can be obtained on the sheep farms."

"I don't know about that. I can only speak for my farm."

"Well, with the holidays coming up in a few months, I would like to get a lamb from you. I have a good color television set I could trade you."

"Again, I don't have lambs to sell or to exchange. Every lamb we produce is carefully inventoried and accounted for. We have strict instructions on how to raise those animals and keep them safe until they reach the size for being sent to the processing plants. Only then are they removed from our inventory records."

"I know it's being done," Nechita countered. "Sheep get lost, are ravaged by other animals, or die of natural causes. And I know that it is done on other farms."

"I don't know about that, but I can assure you, it's not being done here."

"I've heard that it was being done by your predecessors."

"Again, I don't know anything about that."

"You're not being very helpful to me. All I want is to get a job, not a lecture on how you follow the practices. Can't you help me?"

"I think I've helped you enough. I can't give you a job, and I can't give you products from the farm. That's all the help I can give you. Now, I must go about getting my job done. You've already taken too much of my time. Good-bye."

"I'm not ready to leave yet," the man said, taking a pencil and notebook from his coat pocket. "You see, I'm from the Securitate. The only reason I'm here is to investigate a rumor that you have a fascist working for you. Is that true?"

"Of course it isn't true. Why do you say that?"

"I understand that some of your storage boxes have the Nazi swastika painted on them."

"If they do, I'm not aware of it. I've never seen any here."

"Show me your boxes. Then we'll see if what I understand is true."

Viki led him to the barn where empty boxes were stored. She pointed them out. Much to her surprise, some boxes indeed had the swastika symbol showing on them.

"I don't understand," Viki said. "The red *X*'s I understand, because I had my technician paint in red to indicate that they housed newly born lambs that had to be separated from their mother's milk while being fed with the milk formula prescribed by the veterinarian. Someone has added with black marker, the wings to make the *X*'s look like swastikas."

"So you do have them on the boxes. What's your tech's name? I'll have to arrest him."

"Why do you want his name? I know he didn't do it. Someone else added those wings. See the change in color and notice the difference between the paint and the marker? I don't know who did it, except there are always young kids running around the farms painting graffiti on everything. They must have done it, certainly not my technician."

"Will you sign that on my report?" He had been writing everything down as they talked.

"Of course I will." She took the paper from him and began to read it over. She noticed he had left out her statement about the neighborhood kids, thereby still implicating her technician. "I'm not signing this unless you correct the error you made."

She made him take the report back and rewrite it, freeing her technician of any suspicion. Once Viki signed it, the agent angrily turned on his heel and left, much to her relief.

Later, when she discussed the session with Kornel, he said, "You handled that very well, just like an expert would: answer their questions and don't lie, but be careful."

"Is the Securitate holding me back because my father is a priest? Or is it because I refused to join the Communist Party?" Kornel was furious. He had been called to see the director about a promotion he had been recommended for but for which he had been turned down by the regional office. "I feel that I shouldn't be treated this way. Will this be held against me the rest of my life? If indeed that is my destiny, then what do I have to look forward to?"

"I understand your position," Dobra said, "but I can't help you. I've tried arguing with them the best I could, but they told me they were not approving your promotion. They said that if I continued to argue with them, they would see that I was given a lesser job in some godforsaken village. So, the only advice I can give you is, stay with the job you have and continue to do the good work you are doing, and wait until conditions change."

"When will that be?"

"I don't know, but changes have been made in other areas. It's possible that someday they may be made here."

CHAPTER 36

Now that Viki and Kornel both had good jobs that paid good salaries, they decided they wanted to tour other countries to observe and learn how people there lived. Aware that passports were virtually impossible to obtain to travel to capitalistic countries, they decided to concentrate only on visiting the surrounding communist countries, which required only personal identification to cross the border. They agreed to take one guided tour each year to learn the differences in cultures and to appreciate the many historical sites only tour guides could fully explain. Most of all, they wanted to study living conditions so as to compare them with those they were living under in Romania.

From June 15 to June 20, 1981, Viki and Kornel visited East Germany, a tour Kornel had arranged in the travel office in Vaslui. From the lists of available tours, the one to East Berlin attracted his attention the most. He thought it would be good to see the country that had been the subject of so much world publicity during the Cold War between Russia and the United States. He added his and his wife's name to the long list of the others wanting to take the same tour and then paid the posted fees.

On departure day, Kornel and Viki took the local bus to Vaslui, assembled with the others going on the trip, assured themselves their names were on the guide's list, and listened to his descriptions of what all they would see and do in East Germany.

"To get to East Germany," the guide said, "we will fly out of Bucharest and land in Budapest, Hungary. There we will board the train to East Berlin. We will pass through Hungary, Slovakia, and the Czech Republic. As we are checked at each border crossing, I will clear each of you through with the border guards to save you the trouble and delays. To do that I must hold your identification information to show when needed. I'll return the documents after we complete the trip."

The passenger car Viki and Kornel were traveling in was full when they took their seats. They placed their baggage under their seats, stretched their legs, and leaned back to relax for the long ride ahead of them. Seated beside them was a young couple who appeared to be newly married and going on their honeymoon. The couple snuggled close and held hands all the way. Seeing the young couple's eagerness to get on with their honeymoon gave Viki a feeling of being much older, but she didn't let it bother her. Kornel seemed oblivious. She knew his mind was on arriving in East Berlin safely and settling into the hotel room, where they could relax, eat some good German food, and be near the sights the guide had chosen for them to visit.

After a long period of silence, Viki said, "Tell me again what you want to see the most in East Germany."

"I want to see the infamous wall separating East Berlin from West Berlin and get the story of how it was built, how many escaped to the West, and the number killed trying to climb the wall. Also, I'd like to go to the opera, visit the museums, and tour the city."

"Do you know how to get around the city without a guide?" Viki asked. "I think it would be very difficult without one."

"We already have a qualified local guide. He speaks our language and has a good grasp of the city sights and events that have occurred since Berlin was split among the four powers: France, England, United States, and the Soviet Union."

"That's all well and good, but will I have a chance to shop in the stores while we are there? I'd like to compare the goods they offer to those that the stores in Romania offer. And if I can find something different, I just might buy it."

"Yes, we can do that. I also want to see if they have long queues for food products like we have."

"Whatever. I guess that any way we look at it, it should be an interesting and educational vacation."

Their hotel was located near the center of the city, reasonably close to everything they wanted to see and learn about. While not luxuriously furnished, it was clean and had its own bathroom.

Their German guide, Hans Gruber, met the group in the lobby the next morning and explained the day's itinerary. It covered everything they wanted to see. While he spoke with a heavy accent, his Romanian pronunciation was easily understood. He carried a green umbrella in the event of inclement weather. He also used it as a signaling device to keep the group together.

"The division of Germany began after World War II ended," he said. "At the time, Germany was occupied by Russia in the east and by the Americans, British, and French military forces each in their own zone in the west. Later, the three western zones chose to merge into a single economic unit that became the Federal Republic of Germany. A new constitution was written by the United States, and the Federal Republic of Germany was later integrated into a new antiSoviet military alliance, the North Atlantic Treaty Organization, or NATO. East Germany then became the German Democratic Republic under the rule of the German Communist Party and patterned after the Russian model.

"Despite the advantages of free medical service and free education," Gruber continued, "East Germany was less affluent than West Germany, where the attraction of higher salaries and better working conditions remained strong, so strong, in fact, that East Germany lost a goodly portion of its professional population. Most of its engineers, doctors, educators, lawyers, and highly skilled workers fled to West Germany, attracted by higher wages, interest-free loans, low-cost apartments, immediate citizenship, and compensation for property left behind.

"East Germany decided to take defensive measures; it couldn't afford to continually lose its skilled people to the West. Therefore, in an effort to put a halt to this severe loss of its people, the East placed walls, fences, minefields, and other barriers along the length of the border to keep its people in. However, in 1961, when these stringent tactics proved to be ineffective, East Germany decreed the infamous Berlin Wall be erected.

"Since then, hundreds of East German escapees were caught, shot, drowned, or blown apart by mines. Or they committed suicide after being captured. Many served prison sentences. Yes, even I was caught in 1978 trying to scale the wall. I endured one year in prison."

The group then walked to the most infamous sight on the tour: Checkpoint Charlie, one of several checkpoints along the perimeter of the wall.

"Charlie," Gruber said, "was the site of the start of the Cold War between the United States and Russia. It began soon after the crossing opened to people and motor vehicle traffic going in both directions. Westbound traffic into West Berlin was virtually eliminated. While traffic entering from the west did not need entry permits, it was denied entry by the East Berlin border guards.

"This unwanted action created a furor between the two jurisdictions, to the extent that hundreds of tanks from both military sides were lined up along the route to support each side's position. However, after several days of squabbling, Russia and

East Berlin gave in and permitted westerners to gain entry without official documents."

Of greater interest to Kornel and Viki was taking the opportunity to talk with local people. Fortunately, Kornel had a basic understanding of German, just enough to communicate.

One gentleman stood looking at the gate. He was sobbing because he had not seen his aged mother since the wall had been built. Yes, he had been able to correspond with her, but he had not seen her. Another older couple had not seen their children or grandchildren since the wall was completed. Others mourned the deaths of children trying to escape over or through the wall. It was pitiful standing there, watching the personal injustices, and wondering if and when it would end.

Hans led the group to the site of the Stasi Prison, where the buildings had once been used to house orphaned boys. Later it was converted to a prison used by East Germany's secret police. This was the prison Hans had spent a year in.

Rounding out their visit in East Berlin, Viki and Kornel visited several of the museums and took in one performance of the Komische Opera. The theater had been built around 1892 and underwent many openings and closings until the auditorium was destroyed by Allied bombings in 1945. After extensive repairs, the theater had reopened in 1966.

They enjoyed their visit and tour of East Germany, but it had nothing to offer that would entice them to move there. While Viki had opportunities to visit department stores, she found little difference between what East Germany had to offer and what she could find in Romania, except perhaps that Romania had fewer products and longer lines.

On a Sunday afternoon, while awaiting Viki to finish dressing for a visit with her inlaws, Kornel watched a television documentary of a sheep farmer in New Zealand operating a large farm. As the informative film skipped from scene to scene, Kornel thought, *I can do that. With my education and all my experience working on the university farms and the farms for the state, I believe I could manage a farm just as easily as it appears he does. In fact, the more I think about it, the stronger I feel about leaving Romania for New Zealand. That might be my best opportunity.*

"Viki," he said when his wife came out of the bathroom, "I see where the government is sending specialists to different countries to observe their methods and systems for operating sheep farms. They want us to adapt new ideas to our production that will enable us to perform our tasks easier and faster and produce a better quality of meat and wool."

"How does that affect us?" she asked.

"I'm thinking I could go somewhere, stay a while, and save enough money to bring you over to wherever we locate, and then we can decide where we want to reside. I think we would like either Australia or New Zealand. There we could buy a sheep farm, make a good living in a free country, and be free from the hassle of the Securitate and this socialistic system we are living under with its rationing and long lines."

"What will you have to do to do that?"

"I must have a passport and then get permission from the Ministry of Agriculture to leave the country, which means getting a visa to travel to the country of our choice. And as you know, obtaining those papers will require a lot of time and Spaga—incentive gifts."

"Well, it sounds like it could work. But I don't like the thought of living here without you. So, wherever you go, I will go, too."

"Good. Then I'll get started by applying for permission from the ministry's office."

He prepared a request and submitted it to the office of the ministry for a signature. After what seemed like a long wait, he was given the approval for the trip. Now he had to get that much-needed passport. So with Spaga in hand, he went to the passport office and made out the application.

Spaga entails gifts of anything that is in need at the time, not necessarily money, but gifts of scarce items like gasoline, meat, butter, wine, cheese, TV sets, and electronics. Most of these items were almost like gold and could open doors if given at the right time in the agreed amount.

"How are you?" Kornel asked.

"I'm good," replied the agent. "And how is your family?"

"We are doing well," Kornel answered, "but with the economy being what it is, like everyone else we cannot get enough food to satisfy our needs. And what little we can find is inferior. Plus we have to stand in line for such a long time to get it."

"Yes, I agree," the agent replied. "My wife and I have experienced the same thing. So often we stand in a long line for just a small piece of lamb, only to get small scraps of meat and lots of bones. What can you do with bones?"

"Perhaps I can help you," Kornel said in a confidential tone. "If you can help me get a passport, maybe I could come up with some lamb chops and maybe a leg."

"That sounds interesting. Are you party member?"

"No. I never had any good reason for belonging to the party."

"Well, I regret to say it, but without party identification, I cannot give you a passport."

"But this trip was approved by the Ministry of Agriculture," Kornel said. "Wouldn't that be enough to get the passport? Doesn't the minister have some authority in the matter of getting passports?"

"Your minister has no say over the passport office, so I couldn't care less if he approved your trip to New Zealand. I cannot give you a passport."

"Why not?" Kornel pleaded.

"Let me reiterate." By now the agent's vision of roasted lamb was fast fading away, as was his patience. "You are not a member of the party!"

"How do I become a member of the party?"

"I don't know. You'll have to find that out for yourself. But if you want me to get you a passport, you'll have to belong to the party. Good-bye, comrade."

Kornel met with the party leader of his district and explained the reason why he wanted to become a member of the party.

"We find in your files," the party chairman said, "that you are the son of a priest who has spent time in prison for not cooperating with the Securitate. Also, we find that you had refused to join the Communist Youth Movement when you were in elementary school. With that information, the committee met and discussed your request to join the party, and then unanimously decided you would not be good for the organization. We like you as a person and for all the benefits you have brought to the community, but we believe you will not be good for the party."

"Why are you holding those incidents against me? They happened many years ago. Times have changed."

"It's true times have changed, but the committee stills holds to its decision. Come back later. Perhaps our minds will have changed."

In the latter weeks of September 1981, Viki realized she missed her menstrual period. "I think I may be pregnant," she said as she hustled about pretending to be busy making the morning coffee.

Kornel quickly lowered the morning paper, thrust his head over the top, and said, "What did you just say? Did I understand you to say you're pregnant?"

"No. I didn't say I was pregnant. I said I think I'm pregnant. I'm not sure yet. I just missed my period, and being pregnant was the first thing that came into my mind. We'll have to wait until I miss another one or two before I'm certain. Then I'll visit the doctor to be absolutely certain. We'll just have to wait."

"Well, you know I've always said we would have children whenever we believed we could give them good care and a good education. Do you think we are at that point now? I haven't given it a lot of thought lately. But, thinking about it now, I suppose we are as ready as we'll ever be."

"Yes," Viki said, "we've got good jobs making good money and a good place to work. Even though our house isn't finished yet, I believe we are ready. And I'm happy I may be pregnant. I want so much to have one or two children so that our parents will be able to enjoy them before it's too late, particularly with Mama struggling with Parkinson's disease."

"Well, I'm also happy, and looking forward to the day he or she arrives."

"I've decided I want to have the baby in Birlad close to your parents. I'll wait a couple of months and then visit a doctor in the Birlad hospital to make all the arrangements."

"Yes, I was thinking the same thing. The doctors and medical facilities are better there than here. And that's where we'll spend our time off caring for the baby."

Two months later, a very excited Viki returned home. "Kornel, the doctor said I'm pregnant and that I should deliver our first child in the latter weeks of June next year."

"Wonderful! Do you know if it will be a boy or girl?"

"No, I don't know. And I don't want to know until it is born."

"If it's a boy, what will we name him? Or what will we name her if it's a girl?"

"I don't know. I haven't got that far along in my thinking and planning. But don't let me hold you back from thinking up names. I want your thoughts also. The two of us can come up with the names we really want. So we'll make that decision when the time comes."

Viki then advised Dobra of her condition and began to make plans to leave about the time the baby was due and have the birth in Birlad hospital. Periodically, she traveled to Birlad for her examinations.

Professor Cojocaru was excited about her pregnancy and said how nice it would be to have a baby in the house again. He even wanted to attend the baby shower the village women planned for Viki but they wouldn't let him. He did give Viki some infant clothing and a bunch of diapers, and arranged to place his old family crib in their bedroom.

On Sunday, June 27, 1982, Viki traveled to Kornel's parents' place in the village of Noica to await the birth of her first child. Two days later she went into labor and was taken to the hospital. She gave birth that afternoon to their first daughter, whom they named Christina.

Viki and Kornel thought Christina was the most beautiful baby in the whole world. Not a quiet infant, she was demanding and full of energy. She let it be known when she was hungry and when a new diaper was needed. Otherwise she chose to sleep through all the commotion made by the other babies who surrounded her in the hospital's nursery room.

"She's so beautiful," Kornel exclaimed as he held her. "Let's have another one to go with her."

Viki looked at him and quietly said, "Later, buster. Much later."

CHAPTER 37

After Christina's birth, Viki and Kornel stayed with Kornel's parents. During that time, Kornel had taken his six months of paid absence and helped Viki care for the infant. The young family then returned to Professor Cojocaru's house in late February.

Cojocaru was happy after being alone for so many months. He was especially proud of having the baby in the house. He had scrubbed his long-stored crib with hot water and soap and furnished it with colorful bedding. Then he hung a circling carousel decorated with tiny sculpted animals that circled above the baby to attract her attention.

"It is times like this," Viki told Cojocaru, "that we appreciate the government's medical benefit. Just think: my pregnancy didn't cost us anything, plus I was paid 80 percent of my salary to stay home to care for the baby. And Kornel too was paid 80 percent of his salary to assist me. We both believe it's a gratifying benefit, particularly for those who can't afford to lose their income."

"Yes, and I certainly agree with you," Cojocaru said. "It is a beneficial program. On the other hand, those services don't come free. It comes down to us, the people, to pay for these kinds of services with our annual taxes."

From December 19 to December 23, 1982, Viki and Kornel traveled to Budapest, Hungary, a four-day tour. Kornel's parents took care of the baby while they were gone. It was the Christmas season, and the streets and stores in the city were adorned with a multiplicity of brightly colored lights and holiday decorations. Everything looked clean and inviting.

"Why can't Romania look like this?" Kornel asked. "And the people are so friendly. I've never seen anything like it, except in movies, television, and magazines."

Queues for food and other products were noticeably much shorter than they experienced back home, and food seemed to be more plentiful.

"What a pleasant change," Viki said, especially seeing people in line actually chatting with each other and smiling.

They visited Notre Dame du Budapest and many other attractions and were enthralled with the beauty and the cleanliness of the city and the surrounding countryside. It was depressing to think about returning to Romania with its dirt and the dismal attitudes of its citizens.

On the last day in Budapest, their guide gave them free time at the hotel to rest and pack for their return trip. It was a very pleasant day to sit in the shade under an umbrella covering a café table. As they relaxed and sipped tea, they were approached by a woman, one of their fellow travelers, who asked, "May I join you? I've noticed you in our group and I wanted to meet you."

"Yes, please do. We've also enjoyed the tour and, like you, have met several of the others. We're pleased to meet you. We are having a sandwich and tea. May we order the same for you?"

"Yes, thank you," she said, taking a seat across the table from Viki. "My name is Corine Cosmescu. I live in Bucharest."

"What kind of work do you do?" Viki asked.

"I'm a doctor of psychology and have been working in Bucharest for the military for thirty years in the office of the Minister of Defense. I have a good position and have enjoyed the thirty years I've worked there." Corine was a bit chubby and stood about five feet four inches tall. Her coarse black hair had sprinkles of gray peeking through. She and her husband had been married twenty-eight years, with no children. An engaging and friendly person, Corine wanted to be helpful to everyone, like lending a hand with luggage, assisting with seating arrangements, pointing out unusual and artistic artifacts in the museums, and describing the picturesque places of interest included in the tour package.

As their introductions continued, they discovered they all had attended the same university, but in different years. As they continued their discussion, they each felt closer to one another, enough that Viki and Kornel began to talk about their likes and dislikes about living in Romania, particularly their mutual fears of the secret police and of Kornel's desire to leave the country.

After learning about the difficulty Kornel was having obtaining a visa to New Zealand, Corine, after looking around to see if there was anyone near enough to overhear their conversation, surprised them by softly whispering, "I don't know anything about getting visas to New Zealand, but I have a friend who can get you a visa to Greece. And once there, you can obtain your visa to New Zealand."

She took a piece of paper from her notepad and wrote down some names and telephone numbers and handed it to Kornel. "These might help you," she said. "And if you need more information, I wrote my telephone number for you. Don't hesitate to call me if you need help."

"How can we ever thank you?" Kornel asked. "I'm going to continue my search for a New Zealand visa via Yugoslavia, and if that fails I will be in touch with you."

On April 15, 1984, a second child, Anka, was born to Viki and Kornel in the Birlad hospital. A tiny black-haired bundle of delight, Anka let it be known that she was around and always ready for mother's nourishment.

"Isn't she beautiful?" Kornel beamed. "Now Christina will have a sister and a playmate; they'll have good times together."

"I agree." Viki waited for Kornel to suggest their having a third child, but he said nothing. That pleased Viki. *I'm not having another child,* she thought. *I'm not going through that again. Two is enough.*

Viki again stayed in Noica with Kornel's parents until she was ready to return to Bogoescu to work. She had arranged for a new basinet for Anka in their bedroom and moved Christina, still comfortable in Cojocaru's crib, to another bedroom.

From October 1 to October 6, 1984, Viki and Kornel traveled to Bratislava, the capital of Czechoslovakia, and found it likable. People there spoke French. They visited Bratislava's castle, a plant that made crystal glass, including a replica of a set made especially for the queen of England, and other interesting sites.

Again, they were impressed with the friendless of the people and their seemingly easier life compared with the life in Romania.

From July 1 to July 8, 1985, Viki and Kornel traveled to Prague in the Czech Republic just to get away from the daily grind of running the farms. They found the city and country clean, and the Czechs more at ease and friendlier than the Romanians.

I wonder why they are so relaxed? Viki thought.

They stayed at the first-class Don Giovanni Hotel, and on one afternoon they visited St. George's Church and the Royal Gardens with their marble monuments. They visited the Bohemian town of Kutna Hora the next day, as well as the ossuary chapel with its artistically displayed decorations and furnishings formed with human bones.

"How did you like this tour?" Kornel asked.

"I liked it very much," Viki replied, "especially the shopping. I found some nice goods for me and the girls, and I liked the attitude of the salespeople. They seemed friendlier and more helpful than those we have back home. How about you? What impressed you the most?"

"I thought the people were friendly also, and I found the sites interesting and plentiful. I especially liked Kunta Hora and the interesting display of the sculptures of human bones in the Sedlec Ossuary."

"I didn't like that," Viki said. "I wasn't comfortable being surrounded by all those bones. They made me feel creepy, particularly in the sanctuary."

"That didn't bother me. I was fascinated by the skills of the artist.

"But more than everything else I experienced," Kornel continued, "in the Czech Republic and in several of the other countries we've toured, I've noticed the friendliness and intelligence of the people. I don't experience that so much with Romanians.

"Do you suppose the people in those other countries have more freedom to speak out about the government, or is it just my imagination? Whatever it is, I like it, enough that I'm becoming more anxious to get away and take up residence in another country where we can come and go wherever and whenever we please, and where we can say and do whatever we want without fear of being hit upon by the Securitate."

"Well, if you are thinking about relocating to a country other than the communist countries we've toured, you know the task of acquiring the necessary papers will be difficult and expensive."

"Yes, I know it will be not easy."

CHAPTER 38

The minister stood nervously before his nation's great leader, a clean-shaven man with thick wavy hair who wore a fine suit from Saville Row.

"The people are unhappy, Comrade President," the minister said, trying to still the quaver in his voice. "The lines for food are too long, and the products are scarce and inferior. Now they are wondering why more goods are not available since the national debt has been paid. Perhaps we should start letting the stores have more of the products the country produces and cut back on some of the quantities we export."

"No," the president said. "We need all that money to help beautify the grounds around the new administrative compound I'm building in Bucharest. We need to finish that project."

"But how will we get more food to the merchants? The people are clamoring for it and becoming more restless and agitated."

"Then they will have to work harder and produce more. Surely there are places in the country where there's plenty of food. And there are some stores in the bigger cities where they seem to keep good stocks. Maybe we should show on television me and my wife visiting those stores to show the people that the country is in good condition and that there are plenty of foods available. We will not reduce the government's demands for quality products to export."

"Very well, we will set it up as soon as possible."

On February 3, 1986, Director Dobra received a copy of the state's annual production report of the state's collectives. Much to his surprise and delight, he saw that Kornel's farms had come in first place. Dobra knew his farms were among the best in the nation, but *first* place? *This calls for a big celebration,* he thought, and quickly summoned Kornel into his office.

"Comrade Negura, we've got a big job to do," he said. "Your farms came in first place in the nation's quality and quantity of sheep meat and wool produced, and I believe that achievement is deserving of something special, something that can be televised throughout the country or, perhaps, around the world. So, I went ahead and set the date for the first day of May."

"The date for what, Comrade?" Kornel asked warily.

"The celebration of the award. I want you to take charge and make all the arrangements for a good showing. There are so many things that have to be done. We've got to improve the appearance of the village and find an attractive place to gather, eat, drink, and dance. We'll have to work hard to clean and beautify the village and everything we wish to display. It was your good result that put us in first place, so whatever you are doing, keep it up. In the meantime, let's celebrate."

"May first is awfully close, isn't it?" Kornel said. "Do you think we can be ready by that time?"

"Yes. If we get busy now and plan what we want to do and get it on the schedule, we can be ready."

"Do you have any thoughts about what needs to be done that you can discuss with me now?"

"Yes, I have many thoughts. For one thing, the working equipment has to be replaced with new, and the fields must be made to look as neat and as well managed as you can possibly get them. We need to improve the appearance of the village. All homes and outside structures need to be repaired and made to look new again. And we have to gather and fatten up the best-looking animals we can find, and paint and repair the barns in which we house them.

"No doubt, more ideas will come as time passes, so do what you know you have to do, even if it means bringing in the best of animals, buildings, and equipment from other farms. We want to make a good impression on our visitors and officials.

"Oh, I almost forgot, we must prepare a place to park the cars, as some officials may drive rather than use the train and bus. We'll plan to get together each Wednesday morning at 9:00 a.m. and discuss how things are progressing. You are dismissed. Good day, comrade."

"Great news," Kornel shouted as he came through the door. "Our farms came in first in the country last year, both in efficiency and production. I feel great about it, and so does Director Dobra. He wants to have a big celebration and invite all the government officials from Bucharest and the many directors from other collectives to come and celebrate with us."

"That's wonderful," Viki said, throwing her arms around Kornel and giving him a kiss. "You deserve it. You've worked hard to achieve that honor. When will it be?"

"Dobra suggested May first, and he put me in charge of making all the arrangements. It will take a lot of work, as there's only a short time period to do it, but it's feasible."

The next day Kornel assembled the section leaders and asked each to take charge of their group and instruct them how to clean and display all assets they were responsible for, including all buildings and equipment. "Impress upon your workers," he said, "that they need to help each other if necessary to reach our goal.

We want to show our guests what a quality functioning collective should look like, an operation to be envied."

Kornel asked Anghelscu the accountant to create separate records for the costs of the celebration and to prepare to display his office, his people, and the equipment they use to do their work to the guests. He asked Vadim the veterinarian to display his office and his people, and to prepare charts showing the results of his activities in ensuring the production of healthy and highly marketable animals.

Vladu the village custodian was asked to see that all the village properties were cleaned, painted, and made orderly for better appearance, including the houses, garden areas, and outbuildings.

Kornel asked Ene, the engineer, to clean, paint, and replace, if necessary, all equipment used on the farms, including the most up-to-date equipment borrowed from other farms just for the event. They chose to meet once a week and report on progress made.

Kornel then arranged to visit the managers in the collective's other farms to discuss the need for their cooperation and support.

By the first of April, the village began to reflect its new look: buildings appeared cleaner and brighter with new paint and the absence of old trash and junk that had previously littered the grounds. All abandoned buildings were either cleaned and painted or dismantled and hauled away. The roads were scraped and fresh gravel put down, and the drainage ditches cleaned.

Near the end of April, Kornel was called to report to Dobra's office for a discussion. He was optimistic that Dobra was going to commend him for what he'd been doing to brighten the appearance of the village.

"I thought you should know," Dobra said. "You've been asked for by a director in another collective to replace one of his managers who was promoted to another collective. While it isn't a director position, it would be an upgrade in your responsibilities with a higher compensation. But I turned down the transfer. I need you here more than he needs you. And you are too valuable to leave me now with our big celebration coming up."

"But there are others behind me who can do what I have been doing!" Kornel protested. "I feel like it is time for me to move on and get more experience. I, too, want to be director someday."

"No!" Dobra said, slamming his hand down on his desk. "You are needed here. After the celebration, I will try to get you and your wife promoted. In the meantime, I want you to keep up the good work you are doing here so that we may have the biggest and best celebration we can achieve."

Everyone pitched in and worked hard in anticipation of the coming event. Even the peasant workers were given new clothing and good food to eat. The best of food and drinks were brought in from other collectives and were displayed to appear as if all had been produced on Dobra's collective and represented the quantity and quality that was available throughout the country.

The evening after the festivities ended, Kornel and Dobra took the delegation to the best restaurant in Vaslui to entertain them while they waited for their transportation home. After dinner, when they were in a relaxed mood and had enjoyed a couple of bottles of wine, Paul Albu, the supervisor of a large collective in the north, rose to his feet and began to relate a joke he had heard about the secretary general of the country.

"Stop me if you've heard this one," he said. "It seems our fearless leader was approached by a voluptuous lady of the night as he was walking one evening on a main street in Paris. He was receptive to the invitation and got more excited as she described what would take place in her hotel room. He agreed to go with her. And sure enough, once they were in the room and she undressed, our leader could hardly wait to remove his clothes. He was nervous and excited. His hands shook as he removed his trousers. The woman too, was anxious and held out her arms to receive him. He quickly responded."

Perhaps thinking of the punch line, Albu paused and started laughing to himself. Out of the corner of his eye, Kornel noticed that a man at a nearby table had removed a small recorder from his briefcase. It appeared he was taping the story as it was being told. Realizing he had to do something and do it quickly, Kornel got up from his chair and whispered to the man sitting beside him that he had to go to the restroom. As he passed by Albu, Kornel "accidently" bumped him and sent his napkin falling to the floor. As the two of them bent down simultaneously to retrieve it, Kornel said, "Don't look around, Paul. You are being recorded."

Kornel continued on to the restroom. When he returned, Albu and the secret policeman were nowhere in sight. No one seemed to know where the supervisor had gone.

As Kornel and Viki strolled through the village the next morning, he said, "I'm glad the gala is over. It seems like it has been a long adventure, but now we can sit back and be proud of what we've accomplished. The village has never looked better. It's cleaner and more orderly, and the people are happy with their achievement. They deserve something in return for their time and effort; there should be some way we can show our appreciation."

"I agree," Viki said. "You all did a fine job. I believe we should do something for them."

"I agree, but what?"

"Ever since we moved here, I've noticed that large vacant lot on the far side of the village and wondered why it has not been used for something. It just sits there and does nothing but collect trash. Why not turn it over to the people for their use? It's ideal for growing fruits and vegetables they can use for themselves or sell in the marketplace."

"An excellent suggestion," Kornel said, "I'm sure they'll be grateful. I'll advise the boss and get his blessings."

"Good. Then I'll have Veronica get the word to everyone. They can begin dividing the lots and cleaning them up."

A week later, Kornel received an anguished telephone call from Paul Albu and was told the full story of his disappearance. "After receiving your warning," Albu said, "I immediately excused myself and headed for the restaurant's entrance. When I was struck by the cold of the night, I realized I had forgotten my coat hanging on the back of my chair and my briefcase. But I was not about to turn back to retrieve them. Instead, I hurried to the train station to catch my train. I just wanted to return to the comfort and safety of my home.

"But that was not to be. When I arrived at my home, I was seized by a waiting member of the Securitate and taken immediately to the agency's local headquarters. At first I denied that I was the one telling the story. However, after they played the recording, I had to admit it was me. 'I was only trying to put a little fun in the dinner party,' I said. 'I wasn't trying to belittle our leader. I was just telling a joke I had heard someone else say.'

"They disagreed with me and decided they would punish me to teach me a *nevertobeforgotten life-size* lesson.

"They placed me in the corner of the room and gave me a book that detailed the leader's responsibilities to the people of the country. One of them said, 'We want you to start at the very beginning. Read it loudly and convincingly enough that you make us feel you really mean everything you say. Do you understand?'

"'Yes, I understand.'

"After I read the first two chapters, one of them stopped me and said, 'You are not convincing me enough of what our good leader is doing for this glorious country. So start back at the beginning again, and this time read it louder and put more emphasis on what the leader is doing for us. Otherwise you will go back to the beginning. And if you don't show excitement and gratefulness enough to satisfy us, you will start over—and over and over again—until you get it right.'

"They repeated this punishment for six hours before they let me go. When I arrived at my home, and before I could enter the door, another agent met me and took me back to headquarters, where they had me start all over again. This time they turned their radio volume up and tuned it to play Radio Free Europe. They ordered me to read again and to be certain everyone in the room heard me clearly.

"After an hour, one of them stopped me and said, 'Are you reading the book convincingly, or are you listening to the radio? You don't sound convincing to me, so start over, and this time be louder and more believable.'

"This stopandgo torture persisted for another six hours, and then I was once more released to go home. But again, as fate would have it, I was met at the door of my home and taken back to headquarters, where the punishment was started all over again. 'Why don't you just beat me and let me go home?' I begged them.

'I can't take this treatment much longer. I just want to go home, get some sleep, and go back to work.'

"'We will let you go home whenever we feel you have been punished enough. So start reading!' They were relentless and kept it going for two full days before allowing me to go home.

"However, they still were not through with me," Albu said in a shaking voice. "I almost passed out when they told me I had been fired from my manager's job. Now I'm working as a farmer on a sheep farm near Suceava. I lost my house. I'm supporting my family on a farmer's meager wage and living in an old broken-down peasant's shelter."

CHAPTER 39

After sipping his hot coffee, Kornel said, "Viki, have you heard that Mirhas Marga and Mugur Mizilu plan to tour Yugoslavia? They are two managers from other villages in the collective. They worked on different farms and have different specialties. Marga is an accountant, and Mizilu is a veterinarian."

"I think you should go with them," Viki said at once. "It will be an opportunity to see another country."

"And leave you behind?"

"You know I'd love to go with you," Viki said, "but we just finished moving the sheep to the hills and I have too much work to do cleaning the barns and then getting everything ready for the chickens. And don't forget, I have two young daughters who need my attention. Go with your friends and enjoy what Yugoslavia has to offer, but don't forget to bring your girls something nice, and that includes me."

"It's too bad you can't go with me, but I understand. My friends are not taking their wives either, as they too have work and families to care for. They are anxious to go now because Yugoslavia is hosting the International Music Festival. There will be some popular singers from the United States. And I'll try not to forget you and the girls."

"You'd better not! Do you have everything you need?"

"I think so. If not, I'll buy it in Belgrade."

It was a dreary, drizzly morning. Kornel had been waiting on the train at the station for almost half an hour when he saw Marga and Mizilu arrive in the queue with their wives. They hurriedly kissed their spouses and leaped on board just as the train began to move out. Taking their seats in the compartment with Kornel, they quickly removed their rainwear, pulled out their handkerchiefs, and wiped their faces and the tears flowing down their cheeks.

There is nothing unusual about wives weeping when seeing their spouses off on a trip, Kornel thought, *but husbands?* Marga and Mizilu stood at the window wiping their eyes and their dripping noses, waving good-bye at the same time. *I wonder why they are crying so hard?* he thought. *After all, it's only a sevenday journey.*

As the train pulled away and the women were out of sight, his friends turned to him and smiled weakly. Then they began to talk about what they would do after their arrival and if they had free time during the guided tour.

It proved to be an interesting trip. The weather was fine, and their visits to the museums and city sights were educational and thought-provoking. At the International Music Festival, Kornel took pleasure in the events and displays, the excitement of the carnival rides, and the exhibits from other countries. He particularly enjoyed the musical program and seeing and hearing the two famous singers from the United States. He gathered their brochures and bought tapes of their music. *The girls will love these,* Kornel thought as he stuffed them in his pocket, *as well as the stuffed animals and a collection of colorful balloons.*

Kornel was glad he made the trip. He found the country and city clean and orderly. And the people seemed more at ease, open, and friendly. If there were secret police agents in the country, they were well hidden. Even though he had had a good time, he looked forward to going home.

The entire tour group returned to the train on time except his friends, Marga and Mizilu. They were nowhere to be seen. The guide had the conductor hold the train for thirty minutes. Still they failed to show.

"Where are your comrades?" the tour guide asked Kornel. "They should be here now."

"I have no idea. I'm expecting them also. I don't know where they are."

"Do you suppose they are trying to leave Romania?"

"I have no idea. I've only known them for a couple of years, but they never once said anything about leaving the country. Your guess is as good as mine."

"Well, I hope you are telling me the truth, because my director is holding me responsible for guiding them and bringing them back home. So be prepared to answer to the Securitate when you get home."

With that the guide turned to the conductor and, in an angry voice, said, "Let's get the hell out of here; I can't wait any longer."

Viki also was perplexed and baffled when she heard about Kornel's friends leaving the group in Belgrade. She was a bit more confused when Kornel said, "I don't blame my friends for leaving. At least they are free from this godforsaken life."

"What about their wives and children?" Viki asked. "What will they do? The secret police will be harassing them because of what their husbands did. It's too bad the families couldn't have gone with them."

"No doubt they discussed all this before they decided to leave," Kornel said. "I feel they will work out something to get their families to wherever they've settled. If it wasn't for you and the girls, I too would be leaving this country. The more I stay here, the angrier I get. The Securitate keeps harassing me and preventing me from getting promoted. I look around and observe what people have to do just to eke out a living under such a corrupt government and then standing in long, slow-moving lines just to get a small ration of inferior goods and products."

"Yes, but we don't live that way," Viki countered. "We have a good job with good pay, and we live in a nice house on a busy farm. We have easy access to everything we need and want. Do we want to give all this up and start all over again in some faraway country where we don't know the language or the customs and have to adjust to a new lifestyle? Is that what you want?"

"Yes, I'm seriously thinking of leaving Romania, if for no other reason than to get away from the Securitate's harassment. I don't know when or how it will be, but it'll happen, someday."

"What about me and the girls? Does that include us?"

"Of course it includes you and the girls; I couldn't live without you and the girls. I'll have to work out the arrangements. We'll take it one step at a time."

"Well, leaving Romania and our families isn't something I want to do," Viki sadly said. "I dread the thought of having to leave what we have. But I understand your position, and I don't blame you. I realize that if we are to keep the family together, we will have to go wherever you decide."

Sure enough, it wasn't long before the Securitate called Kornel in to interrogate him about his friends leaving the country. Not only that, but also they had called in Director Dobra, because the two in question worked for him—and if he didn't know what was going on, it reflected badly on his stewardship. In spite of all the questions the two men were asked, they both told the secret police they knew nothing about the two managers leaving the country.

"I don't know how much more of this I can take," Kornel told Viki when he got home. "They won't let me forget I'm a priest's son. Why does that make me an enemy of the state? It's obvious they won't ever stop holding that against me. Every time I go through an interrogation, I become more determined to leave Romania."

Around this time, he began to think that the safest way to exit Romania would be a governmentsanctioned business trip to another country. Fascinated with the quality of animal husbandry in New Zealand, he started to quietly investigate how such a trip could be arranged.

Dobra called Kornel into his office and gestured for him to sit down in one of the plush chairs. "In March," the director said, "after I would not let you take a promotion because of your value to me in organizing our big celebration, I promised you I would do my best to rectify matters. Well, I've got some good news for you. I recommended you for a collective director's position near Suceava, and our district director has accepted my recommendation.

"I have already arranged an appointment for you at his office this afternoon. You are to listen to his explanation of what the new job entails and the added responsibilities that go along with it. Then if you take the offer—and I don't know why you wouldn't— he will give you the certificate and the necessary documents that go with the new title."

"Thank you. Thank you very much," Kornel said, as the director rose from his chair.

Dobra rounded his desk and forcefully shook Kornel's hand. "You are welcome, comrade. I wish you nothing but the best. Keep up your good work and you'll go far in the organization."

"Thank you again," Kornel said. "I deeply appreciate all you've done for me. I'll call the car pool and arrange for one of the drivers to take me to the district office this afternoon."

The ride to the district office was not long, but it gave Kornel time to savor his promotion and wonder what his new responsibilities might be. He was glad he'd had time to tell Viki the good news before he left. As the car pulled up in front of the brick office building, he was very excited and could hardly sit still.

After the introductions were completed, Kornel started to take a chair in front of the area director's desk. The fat, balding man stopped him with a raised hand. He had very short and pudgy pink fingers.

"There is no need to sit down, because this interview will not take long," the director said. "I have decided not to offer you the job. While I was waiting for you to arrive, I read your file and discovered that your father is a priest and has had repeated problems with the Securitate. That information put me in an awkward position, as you can imagine. How could I promote the son of a counterrevolutionary? After considering the matter carefully, I realized my only option was to select one of the others who had been recommended for the job. That is the end of it."

Kornel was stunned. "I, ah, eh, I don't know … ah … what to say. I, ah … can't understand …"

"There is nothing to understand, comrade. You do not get the job. There is no need to discuss it any further."

"But I, ah, eh …"

He pointed a fat finger at the open door behind Kornel and bellowed, "Good-bye!" Kornel angrily returned to his car and told the driver to drive him home.

Is this the way my children and I are going to be judged and treated? he asked himself. Will our children be subjected to the same discrimination? If so, then I want nothing more of this country. I want my children and grandchildren to have the freedom to go wherever they want, whenever they want, and to be treated with dignity. If I have to immigrate to another country to ensure them of these freedoms, so be it.

Viki knew the news wasn't good the moment Kornel stepped through the front door. She had never seen him so furious.

"It looks like I'm never going to get promoted in this country," Kornel told her. "The Securitate has gotten word out that I'm the son of a priest. Nobody is going to accept me at a higher level. I don't want to see this treatment passed on to our innocent daughters. Surely there are other nations in this world where we can live with the freedom to go and come as we please and not be continually followed and interrogated."

"I agree," Viki said, giving him a hug. "It's very important that the girls receive the best education possible. We need to go where there are good schools. The school on this farm has only two rooms: grades one and two, and then grades three and four, with only one teacher. I don't want them to have to walk or ride long distances to get to school as we had to do."

"How would you like to move to Bucharest?" Kornel asked her. "Yesterday I saw a notice of job openings in the husbandry laboratory in the capital city. They won't be promotions, but it will get us to another place where we may have a better chance of getting a promotion. I can make applications for both of us tomorrow and see what happens."

"Yes, let's do it."

"Tests will be necessary to pass. Are you still agreeable?"

"Yes, indeed. We have taken lots of tests and have passed them. So another one won't bother me. And I know it won't bother you."

"Not at all. I'm confident we will do well."

"There is another good reason why Bucharest will be a good move," Kornel said. "It may make it easier for me to leave Romania. The passport office is headquartered there, as are the many embassies from other countries."

"You have decided to leave?"

"Yes, as soon as I can make the arrangements. It's imperative no one else knows of my intent, because I don't want the Securitate prowling around and calling me in for more interrogations. I've already got too many black marks in my file. I'll go see the boss tomorrow and let him know of our intention to apply for the lab jobs in Bucharest."

The next morning, Dobra was not happy about the possibility of the Neguras leaving the farm and moving to Bucharest. "You can go ahead and take the test, but I won't let you go," he warned Kornel. "I believe you are more valuable to us here than to the lab in Bucharest."

"But if I'm not going to get promoted from here, why should I stay here?" Kornel asked. "At least being in Bucharest we might have more opportunities for advancement."

"Well, you might as well get used to the situation, because I will never let you go just to take a lateral job. And that is final."

"But Comrade Director, what if I …"

"I said it is final, comrade. Now good-bye!"

Kornel stormed out of the building and kicked a fence post so hard it hurt his toes. He decided to walk the three miles to the village to cool off and think of a plan to get him and his family out from under these unbearable conditions. Long before he arrived, he had concluded that no matter which country he chose to immigrate to, he had to have a passport and a visa.

The ministry agent was emphatic. "No, I cannot give you a passport."

"Why not?" Kornel asked.

"For two reasons: First, you are not a member of the party. Only party members can get passports. Second, you plan to leave Romania and not return."

"What makes you think I won't return? Who told you that?"

"I am not empowered to give out names."

"It doesn't matter. Whoever said it is wrong. Of course, I intend to return to Romania. I plan to go to Yugoslavia and get a visa to New Zealand to study how they carry out their animal husbandry program. See, I have permission from the Minister of Agriculture to go, and New Zealand takes specialists from a communist country, only if it is Yugoslavia," Kornel said as he carefully laid out the papers on the agent's desk.

"And I have a wife and two daughters here whom I do not plan to leave. I love my family and I love Romania. I have no plans to leave either of them. The government has been good to my wife and me by giving us a good education and meaningful jobs after we finished the university."

"Even if what you say is true," the agent countered, "and I must say I don't believe you, you must be a member of the party to get a passport from me."

"How do I do that?"

"I don't know. I can't help you with that. You'll have to find out for yourself."

When he returned home, Kornel threw himself down on the couch beside Viki. "They refused to issue me a passport again, but they added a new reason. Not only are they turning me down because I'm not a party member, but also now they say I'm planning to flee Romania. I tried to make them believe that that is not true, that someone was feeding them false information. Of course, they refused to tell me who it was."

"Oh my, it could have been me," Viki said, her cheeks turning red. "One day I was having lunch with Patricia Pauker, one of my coworkers, and I mentioned you needed a passport to leave the country. I had no intention of telling her that. It just slipped out. I wasn't thinking. I had no idea she was an informer. Please forgive me; I feel so bad about this."

"Of course I forgive you. It isn't the end of the world. But there is one thing we must do starting this very moment. We must vow never to mention to anyone, including our families, any thoughts about leaving, or actions I plan to take to leave, the country. I believe this is a good time to put the collective behind us and move to another area where we are not so well-known, and where I can renew my efforts to obtain the documents I need to leave Romania. So, I've decided that we take those laboratory jobs in Bucharest and move as quickly as we can. What do you think?"

"Dobra said he would not let us go," Viki said.

"We'll have to find out if he really has the power to stop us."

"Well, you know how I feel about you leaving us." Viki said. "I realize I have to go along with you for the sake of keeping the family together. I'm ready to make the move. If I can be of any help to you in any way, don't hesitate to ask me."

CHAPTER 40

Answering the questions on the laboratory entrance test was easy. Both Viki and Kornel passed with high grades, and both were accepted and ordered to report to work.

"I'm certainly glad that is over and we have the jobs," Viki said to Kornel. "Now we've got to get busy and be ready to move by the end of the month."

"I'll break the news to Dobra in the morning that we've been accepted by the labs and that we'll be leaving the last day of the month."

When Kornel told his director of their plans, Dobra was surprised and upset. He had not yet received word from the labs about them leaving.

"No, I can't release you," he shouted. "You two are valuable to me. I can't afford to lose you to Bucharest. Yes, you are experienced and you do outstanding work, but I could care less about how well you two passed the tests. I will not let you go. And that is final."

Kornel didn't let it stop there. "May I use your telephone?" he asked calmly.

When Dobra nodded, perhaps thinking Kornel was going to tell Viki the bad news immediately, Kornel quickly dialed his new boss in Bucharest and explained the situation. The lab's executive director told him to put Dobra on the line. When he spoke, he shouted so loudly that Dobra had to hold the handset away from his ear. Kornel could hear every word.

"Either you release them to transfer to Bucharest or I will exercise my authority and report your insubordination to the minister of agriculture. That couple has the best qualifications to do the lab work here in Bucharest. It and the nation need them far more than you do in your little collective. So, release them at once."

Dobra did as he was ordered.

Kornel and Viki were thankful to be leaving the village but were sad about having to sever their relationships with the village people, whom they had learned to love and appreciate. They spent their last day saying good-bye. The chairman of the village committee expressed appreciation for what they had done to help the villagers. He mentioned their work and also their having their best interests at heart in improving the villagers' lifestyles and the overall appearance of the village. Especially, the villagers thanked the Neguras for the use of the empty lot and gave them small gifts of appreciation. But the saddest good-bye of all was with Professor Cojocaru, whom they had learned to love and appreciate. He had become their *other* father, and to Christina and Anka, their *other* grandfather.

CHAPTER 41

The laboratory to which Viki and Kornel were assigned was part of the animal husbandry division, tasked with finding ways to improve the quantity and quality of farm animal products such as meat and wool. Technicians collected various sorts of data from the collectives' farms and, in return, supplied them with new recipes for feed mixtures based on the lab's analyses. The objective was increased size and weight of the animals. It was detailed work, demanding of their time and knowledge. And they were both grateful for the experience they had gained on the university's and collective's farms.

At first, Viki had problems caring for the girls after school while she was working. Christina was five years old and Anka three. Viki tried hiring sitters, but that didn't work out; those she tried were not dependable and refused to do what she wanted. Then she tried day care for Anka and kindergarten for Christina, and although that worked for a little while, it didn't last long. It took too much of Viki's time and patience getting the girls to school in the morning and picking them up in the afternoon.

"What are we going to do?" the worried Viki cried. "We can't leave them by themselves. And neither of us can afford to quit work to care for them!"

"Perhaps the church can help us," Kornel said. "Surely we are not the only family in this area with this same problem. I'll call my father. He may know someone who could help us in this time of need."

Kornel immediately got on the telephone and called his father. "Yes," his father said in reply to Kornel's question. "I personally know the minister in one of the churches near you. Call him and see what he would recommend."

Kornel immediately called the church. Much to his appreciation, he found the solution to the problem: the church would gather the girls after school and keep them busy until Viki could come by after she quit work.

After six weeks, the uniqueness of the move to Bucharest had worn off and the Neguras awoke to the realization that living conditions were worse than at the collective. They were living off the local economy, and there were shortages of most everything. To get wanted foods and staples, it was necessary to stand for hours in lines that often encircled the block. They could no longer have fresh meat for the dinner table. No longer did they have willing employees to stand in long lines to purchase the staples and nonperishable foods they needed for their house.

"What have we gotten ourselves into?" Kornel asked after standing two hours in line for meat, only to bring home the last two bones the butcher had left of his day's ration of beef.

"What am I going to do with these bones?" Viki said in dismay. "Make another pot of soup? What about mad cow disease?"

"I don't know, but they passed the government's inspection. See the blue-lettered stamp on each bone? The government is assuring us the bones are safe to eat."

"That makes me feel so much better," Viki sarcastically said. "Now it's time to find out what my father thinks."

Once Viki's papa understood their predicament he said, "Don't worry. I'm still working and making good money. I will send you a package of meat and other foods each Friday by the train."

So each Friday, Kornel went to the train station and picked up the packages of food, which helped them to live decently for the rest of their days in Bucharest.

Scarcity was typical of living conditions at that time. Even at the lab, most of Viki's colleagues, who had been working there several years or so, brought only small bits of cheese or meager meat sandwiches neatly wrapped in napkins in their purses or pockets. It was usually a sandwich they nibbled on during the lunch period. Then if they did not eat all of it, they wrapped the remains in a napkin and took it home to eat for dinner.

After Harald began helping the couple with food, Viki often shared it with a few of her close friends. Soon, she stopped giving it away, because she felt it implied that she and Kornel were somehow rich. She began eating lunch in nearby restaurants and paying cash for each meal. She didn't think about it much until her fellow workers began to insinuate she must be wealthy to afford such luxury. In Romania, being put into upper-class status like that was not a compliment.

"Some of the people at the lab are beginning to think we are rich," she told Kornel.

"Why so?"

"Apparently it's because I'm an only child and your father is a priest. What can I do?"

"I don't really know. Perhaps if you were to bring yourself down to their level of living, it might help. Otherwise, let them think what they will and then learn to live with their opinions."

"Well, that doesn't help me much, but thanks anyway."

Kornel quickly changed the subject. "I've got to start over again and change my tactics if I want to get my passport and visa to Greece."

"So you're still planning to leave Romania?"

"Yes. I can't take this country any longer. I must do it."

"And you're planning to go to Greece?"

"Yes. After what Corine Cosmescu told us in Budapest, I've decided to go through Greece to get to our ultimate destination, wherever that may be. This effort to leave Romania is turning out to be the biggest challenge I've ever had to contend with. But on the positive side, with everything I've learned in all my failed attempts, I believe I'm better equipped to acquire those documents I need. I'm still interested in immigrating to New Zealand or Australia. If I'm not successful in getting visas to those countries, then I'll take any other country that will offer to take us in, like England or Canada."

"Not the United States?" Viki asked.

"No! Absolutely not. With everything the Russians have told us about how unsafe it is to live in America, I don't think we want any part of that country."

"Well, as far as the girls and I are concerned, we will go wherever you decide. I'm determined the family must stay together. I'll do whatever I can to help you, and I can assure you that Papa will help us too."

"Well, I appreciate that. I need all the help I can get. As you know by now, passports and visas are almost impossible to acquire. Only the top officials of the party can obtain them. I've never been a party member, but I know what I must do to convince the chairman of my need for a passport. We must be prepared to entice him with money and gifts. And I'll have to rely on your father's help to do that.

"Now that I have Corine's contact in Greece, I feel more confident I'm on the right track to get out of Romania. I'll telephone the contact as soon as I arrive in Greece and find out how he can help me find a new home in a capitalist country. He is connected with the United Nations and is responsible for aiding refugees from communist countries like ours."

It took time, patience, and a lot of Spaga to attract the attention of the local chairman of the Communist Party, but it got Kornel invited to a meeting of the local membership council, where he pleaded his case to become a party member. After his third meeting, the committee voted to admit Kornel as a member of the Communist Party. Now that he had been given his membership card, he was prepared to go to the passport office and get the document he needed to leave the country.

A week later, Kornel submitted his party membership card and a hefty amount of Spaga to the embassy clerk and was given a passport that enabled him to travel outside the communist bloc countries. More Spaga was passed to the clerk to keep the Securitate from getting involved in the transaction.

The secret police paid close attention to anyone who attempted to get a passport to leave the country. There was the very real fear that such people were leaving Romania for good, which would create losses in the business and professional ranks. Much like the East Germans did with the Berlin Wall, the Romanians were not trying to keep foreigners out. Instead, they were trying to stop the skilled professionals from leaving to find the better-paying jobs and better living conditions that were readily available elsewhere.

Now all Kornel needed was the visa to enter Greece, but that proved to be the most costly to obtain more than all his other efforts put together. He called his father-in-law.

"Do you think you can help me come up with about fifteen thousand leu?" he asked Harald. "That is what I've been told I will need."

"Yes, I believe I can help you," Harald said, "but it won't be in cash. As you know, money these days is not all that beneficial, and not all benefactors want to handle it. It's the scarce products they want. So I believe I can get you some ration books to purchase rationed products with and, from the underground, almost any other products you can use, like cheese, gasoline, cooking oil, meat, and fish, and anything else that is available."

"Well, I really appreciate what you are doing for us. I don't know how you do it, but we're most grateful and indebted to you for your generosity."

"Fortunately," Harald said, "I'm still in a decent financial position to help. And we know just how costly things are. Sophia and I don't want to see you leave us, but we understand your position. We want to be as helpful as we can in seeing that you find the place where you and Viki want to live and where you can be happy and make a good living for your family."

"I don't know how he does it," Viki said after Kornel hung up, "but he always comes through for us."

"I hope someday we can repay him for all he is doing."

"I'm not going to worry over it," Viki said. "I believe that we will be able to repay him, with interest. In the meantime, you've got to get your visa and your traveling clothes together and be on your way."

"I've already been doing that," Kornel said. "As soon as I have visa in hand, I'll purchase the train ticket to Greece and leave. My biggest fear now is getting through Bulgaria. I've heard the border guards carefully check each person traveling through there. I certainly don't want to be interrogated and returned to Romania."

Once Kornel was settled on the train, he became concerned that the train security people would find the name and phone number on the slip of paper Corine had given him. One part of him realized that the fear he felt was irrational. The name and number would mean nothing to anyone but him. But he kept turning it over and over in his mind. His experience with the Securitate had taught him that they suspected everyone and everything, and that they could smell fear and guilt. He convinced himself that he had to hide the paper or risk discovery, return to Romania, and an even worse life than the one he had left.

He was certain that at some point he would be interrogated by communist border guards and forced to display his documents before they would let him leave Bulgaria and enter Greece. He realized he had to slip that tiny piece of paper from his wallet and hide it without being seen by the other passengers in his compartment.

Under the pretext of looking for a picture of his family, he removed the paper and, hiding it from view, used his fingers to roll it into a tiny wad, which he then casually dropped onto the floor. There was a lot of other debris on the floor—paper, food wrappers, and the like. He put his right foot on the wad, pinning it to the floor.

At the border, the guards checked his documents and found them all to be legitimate and passable. He did not have to rise from his seat to present his papers—there wasn't enough room in the compartment for them all to stand at once.

At the first stop in Greece, he reached down, recovered the tiny wad, and slipped it back into his wallet.

As soon as he disembarked at the train station, he found a telephone and called the number. As Corine had said, the contact was a United Nations adviser. After explaining his reasons for leaving Romania, Kornel said, "Can you give me information on how I can leave Greece and immigrate as a communist refugee to another country, perhaps Australia or New Zealand?"

"I don't have knowledge of what countries are looking for in refugees and the state of their quotas, but I can give you a telephone number of a person who can be very helpful to you, someone who has that kind of information and knows how to get visas."

After writing down the name and number he was given, Kornel asked, "Do you know where I can find an inexpensive place to stay for the night?"

"I'll give you the telephone number of the university. It offers hostel programs. Even though the school is still in session, the housing section may have rooms for visiting dignitaries that could be available for you."

"Thank you very much," Kornel said as he wrote down the information. "You have been very helpful. I appreciate it."

"You're welcome, and good luck in your search."

"Thank you, and good night."

Sure enough, Kornel was able to get an inexpensive room at the university. That night when he lay down to sleep, he realized he was free from the Romanian constraints and the harrowing and frightened feelings he had experienced since leaving Romania. He was exhausted and ready for a restful night.

He awoke the next morning feeling good and ready to do what he had to do to find a welcoming friendly country he could enter and settle down in with his family. After he had breakfast at the hostel, Kornel found a phone to call the number the United Nation's adviser had given him. After the third ring, a very pleasant female voice answered and made it known she would try to be as helpful as she could. Natalie—he didn't catch her last name— being experienced in processing immigrants from communist nations, was able to give him all the information he needed to obtain the documents to immigrate to New Zealand or Australia.

But she said immigration to those countries would take a two-year wait and required that a New Zealand or Australian citizen sponsor him. Kornel was unprepared for this news. He didn't know what to do or say, but he realized he had to say something. He finally asked, "Are there other countries taking immigrants seeking asylum from Romania without such long waiting periods?"

"Yes, there are two other possibilities: Canada and America. Their waiting periods are only six weeks, but that can change quickly. Both have sponsors who will take refugees, particularly those who are formally educated or well skilled in their line of endeavor. The sponsors will help you find work and provide food, money, and shelter until you are established in your own place and successfully employed."

"Well, I dislike being picky, but I feel Canada is too cold for me. And I've heard the communists say so many bad things about the American capitalistic system that I'm not sure I want to go there. On the other hand, I don't want to have to make my way here in Greece for the next two years. And most of all, I'm not about to return to Romania now that I'm experiencing my freedom here in Greece. What do you think I should do?"

"Well, what I'd do if I were you would be to visit each embassy and learn for yourself how quickly you can move, and then decide which country is best for you. Also, if I were you, I wouldn't believe everything the communists say about any country or economic system, particularly America. It isn't as bad as you've been led to believe."

"Thank you. I appreciate how well you have treated me. I can't tell you how much I am indebted to you."

"You're welcome. And good luck."

CHAPTER 42

Kornel arrived in Athens on the fifth of May 1987 and checked into a cheap but clean hotel. After an hour's nap to revitalize his mind and body, he set off in search of the embassies he planned to visit. The first two on his list were Australia's and New Zealand's.

Despite the information Natalie had given him about the two-year waiting periods, he wanted to assure himself there weren't any recent changes that would allow him to immigrate sooner.

Although neither embassy could process him faster than that, the agents were helpful in recommending he visit the Canadian and US embassies next, and consider what each had to offer. They said if it was necessary for him to wait the full two years, he could stay in Greece, find employment, and save as much money as he could to pay his way to the other country after he got his entry papers.

Kornel's visit to the Canadian Embassy a few days later was unproductive. Refugee quotas were filled, and as with Australia and New Zealand, it would be at least two years before the country would open its gates again. While he was disappointed, he was also relieved. He didn't really want to go to Canada because of the cold climate.

Now it was beginning to look like he might have to stay in Greece for at least two years before reaching the promised land. That meant he would have to find some employment to pay the cost of living in Greece. He was depressed by this outcome, but one thing was certain: he was not going to return to Romania.

The only option he had left in Athens was the United States Embassy, but he and Viki had sworn they would never relocate to the United States. But he was feeling desperate. Maybe the Russians were wrong in their view of the United States and the Americans. Maybe the criticisms of the US system were created to make people be thankful for communism. *America must have something going for it,* he thought. *Maybe there is no equivalent of the Securitate in America.* At that instant Kornel decided he had to visit the US Embassy.

The next day, Kornel stepped into the lobby of the United States Consulate. "What can I do for you?" the receptionist asked. "Do you speak English?"

"Only a little bit," Kornel said. "I speak Romanian and a little French. I want to leave Romania, and I understand America has a program to help refugees like me get away from the communist countries."

Fortunately, the embassy agent who came out to greet him knew enough Romanian that she could converse with him.

"Yes, we do have a program," she said. "What is your situation that you want to leave your home country?"

Kornel proceeded to give her the details of the reasons why he had left Romania, thereafter mentioning why he wanted to find a friendly country where he and his family could settle down and make something of themselves.

After getting a feel for Kornel's situation, she said, "I'll refer you to Kristina Preda. She's from America, but her family migrated from Romania in 1950 after the communists took control of the government. She understands and speaks Romanian fluently. She'll take all your information and then determine if, how, and when we can get you into America."

After Kornel was introduced to Preda, a tall blonde woman who was very well-dressed, he repeated his need to get away from Romania. "I understand you might be able to get me into America. I want to start a new life for me and my family. I've had a bad time living and working for the communists, and I feel I must get away from there. I am a university graduate and believe I can be an asset to America. My wife, too, is a university graduate and a good worker. She and our two daughters are still in Romania and are anxious to join me as soon as they can. I have here my resume, which will give you more information about me."

"We do have programs to help persecuted people to immigrate to America, particularly educated people like you," she said after scanning his resume. "I'll look over your resume more closely and check to see what's available. Can you come back tomorrow? We may have something for you in about six weeks."

"Yes," Kornel said as he rose from the chair. "I'll see you tomorrow."

As he left the building, he couldn't help but ask himself, Am I doing the right thing? We had ruled out America because of the ups and downs in their economic life and all the terrible social and political problems we were led to believe by the communists that exist there: all the drugs, killings, and racial tensions. How much of that is true? Surely America can't be all that bad. If it were, why do so many foreign people want to go there? I'm still apprehensive about getting American documents and wondering what Viki will say when she hears what I'm doing. I can hear her now admonishing me for even thinking about going to America, the country we always said we wouldn't even think about going to, but it will be great if I can get there in six weeks. That isn't too long a wait.

He liked having hope that he might have finally found his way out of Romania, but he was still bothered about the United

States. *I've got a decision to make*, he thought. *Do I or don't I? I can't make up my mind. But six weeks is just what I'm looking for. Would it be worth going for? Would I like it when I got there? What would I do if I didn't like it? I'll have to really think long and hard about what I should do, but I am certain of two things: I will not return to Romania, and I won't remain in Greece unless I absolutely have to. I'll talk to Viki and get her feelings, but in any event, I'll have to get some kind of employment to cover my expenses here for at least another six weeks.*

That evening, when Kornel knew Viki would be at home, he telephoned her. He wasn't sure how to tell her about his experience at the US Embassy. Was he elated? Yes, but he also was uneasy and questioning making the decision.

After the fourth ring, Viki answered. "Guess where I was today?" Kornel said.

"I don't want to guess. Just tell me."

"I went to another embassy and got a positive answer to my request for a visa," Kornel said. "The American Embassy."

"What?" Viki shouted into the phone. "I thought we had agreed we did not want to go to there! I find it difficult to believe you would even go there and do that after the way we have talked against living in America."

There was a long pause at the other end of the line, as if she was thinking about this sudden change in plans and what it would mean to their future. Then she said, "What did they tell you? How will it affect us?"

"A very nice person said the embassy could arrange to get us into America and said that I should come back tomorrow. Then she will take my application and make arrangements to give us visas to get into America. That is just the first step. Tomorrow she will go over the other steps we will have to take if we decide we want to live in America. I'm to meet her at ten in the morning."

"What do you mean when you keep saying 'we'? Does that include me and the girls?"

"Of course it does!" Kornel spoke up more brightly, relieved that Viki seemed to be considering the opportunity. "You know I include you and the girls in all my plans. That is, if you agree with me and will go."

"Well, you know how I have always said I would never live in America. And I don't like the thought of raising the girls in America, where there are so many drugs and gangs running around attacking foreigners and stealing from them and raping the women and girls. Is that what we want for us?"

"Don't believe everything the communists say about America. We have as many drugs and assaults of that kind there in Romania. That'll be the same wherever you go in this world. It's up to us to see that the girls are raised safely and properly." He took a deep breath and then said, "Viki, I can't force you to go. You'll have to make that decision. If you decide you can't go, then I will go by myself and you and the girls can stay in Romania and do what you want. But I'm not coming back to Romania."

"Now don't get upset about what I just said," Viki told him. "This news has taken me by surprise. I need to think about it. Let me have a few days, and then I will let you know my decision. I don't want to be separated from you, but I do have the girls and their lives to think about growing up in America. I just need more time."

"I wasn't getting upset with you. But now that I have an opportunity to go to another country, I don't want to lose it. And besides, America can't be as bad as the communists say it is. Why is it so many people you talk to want to go to America? What is it about America that is so attractive? They say it's because in America there is more freedom and good work. What is freedom? If we have freedom in Romania today, then why do I want to leave it? They say it's a different kind of freedom, like you can go anyplace and say anything you want to say and there is no Securitate around to interrogate you or take you to prison or, even worse, get rid of you. If that is true, then America's for me. Now the more I think about it, the more I'm willing to take that chance. And I hope you can learn to see it that way too. I'll call you again tomorrow evening after my morning visit with the embassy. I love you."

The next morning, Kornel was at the embassy promptly at the appointed hour. He took his seat in front of Kristina Preda's desk and waited until she got off the telephone with another person wanting to go to the United States. After what seemed like a long time, she said to the person calling, "Well, thank you for letting me know. Good-bye."

With that, she cradled the handset and turned to Kornel.

"Good morning. It's good to see you again, but I'm afraid I have bad news for you. We recently got new orders from Washington. Tens of thousands of Jews are leaving the Soviet Union and want to immigrate to the United States. We must concentrate our workload to accommodate them. I'm sorry, but that fills our quotas for at least two years, which means there is nothing I can do for you until that time except put your name on the waiting list."

"Quite frankly, this is extremely disappointing. I was thankful I could leave Greece in six weeks, but now I have to find work here that will keep me occupied for two years. That part I don't like, but what else can I do? Returning to Romania is certainly not an option. I've made up my mind that I want to go to America. While I know nothing about it, I'm anxious to find out."

"There is no doubt in my mind," Preda said, "that you will like it and you will realize it is the best decision you ever made. You soon will appreciate that life is easier there and freedom is enjoyed more than what the communists have led you to believe. You will also understand that if you want to achieve financial security and happiness, you will have to work hard at it. As we say in America, the rows are long and difficult to hoe, but success is achieved in the harvest. I wish you luck and ask that you keep in touch with us. I hope that the wait time will be shorter than the two years."

"Thank you for your help. I appreciate what you have done for me so far. Good-bye!"

That evening, Kornel called Viki with the terribly disappointing news.

After he'd gone to bed, he tossed and turned thinking about what he had learned and how long he would have to wait. Sleep finally came, but only after he resigned himself to the fact that eventually he was going to the United States come hell or high water. *Nothing ventured, nothing gained, so they say.*

The Securitate's contacts verified that Kornel had overstayed his visa return date. To get an explanation, they summoned Viki to their headquarters.

When she entered the grim building, she was greeted by a receptionist who directed her to a chair to await her turn. She waited there for more than two hours before she was called into a security agent's office. The policeman who had his hair cut so short he might as well have had a shaved his head was on the phone. There was no chair for her to sit on, so she stood for another forty-five minutes until he hung up.

"Do you have your papers with you, Mrs. Negura?" he asked.

"Yes."

"Show them to me!"

She removed them from her purse and put them on his desk. He gave them a cursory glance and then shoved them back to her. In a nasty voice he said, "Hereafter, when you come see me, have your papers ready without my having to ask for them. Do you understand me? Otherwise, you are wasting my time, and I don't have time to waste with you."

"Yes," she replied. "I understand."

"I see that your husband did not return from Greece before the end date posted on his visa. Are you sure he is coming back?"

"Yes, he plans to return. It's just that he is running late on his scheduled contacts with the Grecian sheep farmers. He is very much interested in their insemination programs to breed larger and better-quality sheep. It is taking longer than he estimated to see everyone he had on his lists. He's just being delayed. He will return."

"Well, I certainly hope so, for your sake," the agent said, "because I don't believe what you are telling me. I think you are lying. I'm more inclined to believe that he is trying to leave Greece for another country."

"You can believe what you want, but he tells me he is coming back, and I believe him. Kornel loves Romania and all it has done for us and our daughters. He has no thought about leaving for another country. Financially, we are well-off and have good jobs. We appreciate all that the country has done for us. Why would he want to leave all that and his family just to have to start over in another country?"

"We'll see. I want you to come back and see me next month if he hasn't returned. Good-bye."

"Good-bye."

CHAPTER 43

It took until the end of May before Kornel got his first job in Athens. It consisted of moving and cleaning slabs of marble. It was definitely not to his liking, but it was the only thing available.

In Greece, marble floors are commonly found in houses and apartments. While it is a strong material and easily cleaned, marble is intolerably cold to walk on during the winter months. To counter this drawback, the marble is covered with heavy carpets. To add more warmth to the walking areas, heated rocks are placed in spots.

But rocks and carpets get dirty and must be cleaned, which in the summertime is done by companies that specialize in this sort of business. The rocks and carpets are then stored until needed in the fall, at which time temporary workers are employed to carry the carpets and rocks back into the houses and replace them on the floors.

While carpets are not that heavy to carry, marble rocks are a different story. Kornel soon discovered he had a weak back. Being the most recent employee, he struggled to carry the rocks while his older partner carried the lightweight carpets.

In multistory buildings where there were no elevators, the materials had to be carried up flights of stairs. Kornel's partner kept shouting for him to hurry up, which did nothing but add to the frustration of his task. Eventually, the weight of the rocks took its toll on his back. It got so sore from the repeated abuse that he had to lie on the floor to change his clothing. Then his back got so painful that he had to quit the job for two weeks. Without income, he couldn't pay his hotel bill. The manager took possession of all his luggage.

"No payment, no luggage," the manager said.

"But I need my luggage. I need to change my clothes if I'm to continue working," Kornel angrily complained.

"Again, I repeat," the manager said, "no money, no luggage."

"Unless I get my luggage," Kornel threatened, "I will go to the police station and get them to help me get my luggage back."

"Go right ahead, but you won't get your luggage until you pay me what you owe. What is it you don't understand? As I keep saying: no money, no luggage."

And sure enough, the manager was right. The police repeated the manager's words: "No money, no luggage."

On July 6, a month after her first visit, the Securitate called Viki in for a second interrogation. She dreaded this visit, as it was becoming more and more obvious that Kornel had no intention of ever returning. *But how do I cover for him in this situation?* she asked herself. *I don't want to side with the government, but I may have to in order to protect myself and the girls from its wrath. I don't want to lose my job, but if I can't convince the Securitate agent that Kornel will return, then I have no other choice but to agree that he isn't coming back and convince him that what my husband has done isn't my fault, that I am a victim of the traitor too.*

"The last time we talked about your husband overstaying his visit to Greece, you assured me he would return," the agent said. "Why hasn't he?"

"I don't know. He keeps assuring me he will return, but then he doesn't."

"I don't believe he will come back. Why don't you divorce him?"

"Yes, probably I should. I'm beginning to feel he doesn't care about us anymore, that he cares only about himself. However, at this point I still want to believe he is going to return as soon as he finishes his research in Greece. If he doesn't, I will divorce him and start a new life without him."

"Well, you had better do that if you want to keep working at your laboratory job. Again, I think you are lying to me about all this, but I have to go along with you until I can prove different. I will see you here again next month, when I hope you have something better to tell me."

"I've got my two girls to care for. If I have to do it alone, I will."

Once he recovered sufficiently to return to work, Kornel quit the cleaning company and started working at a plant that made plastic drawstring storage bags. His job was to insert the plastic drawstring into the loop at the top of the bags. It was a terrible job. The plastic ties were sharp enough to cut flesh, but he held on until he had earned enough money to pay his delinquent hotel bill and get his luggage back.

He then quit that job and went to work for an apartment complex, where he cleaned stairwells and hallways for three months. Because it was night work, from 1:00 a.m. to 11:00 a.m., he couldn't get any decent rest. The noonday heat made his room an oven. With the windows open for ventilation, the outside noise from the street traffic of Athens was so loud that all he did was toss and turn. Eventually, he grew so tired that he felt as though a tiny push would topple him to the ground.

I have to find easier work, he thought. I can't go on like this.

He looked and looked for an ideal day job but had no luck finding one. The only day job he could find involved pushing wheelbarrow loads of large heavy rocks for a lady building a retaining wall. It was backbreaking work, but it allowed him to get some much needed nightly rest.

When the wall was finished after three months, Kornel was able to get a better-paying job with a construction crew keeping the skilled workers supplied with the materials they needed to do their jobs. Again, it was day work and he could get his night's rest. Contented with this job, he was able to accumulate enough savings to carry him until he got his entry into the United States.

When the waiting time had elapsed, Kornel again applied to the US Embassy to get his visa.

"I'm sorry to have to disappoint you again," Kristine Preda told him, "but that United Nations program of taking in thousands of the Soviet Union's Jews is still ongoing and the United States has agreed to take an additional ten thousand of the Soviet Union Jews. We must give this additional order our full attention until it is completed. I realize this is not the news you want to hear, but all I can tell you to do is keep in touch and we will get you there as soon as we can. You are at the top of our list."

Now what do I do? Kornel thought as he left the building. I certainly do not want to remain in Greece that long, but what else can I do?

He immediately called Viki and gave her the bad news.

"What are you going to do now?" she asked. "Do you plan to leave Greece?"

"No, no," he replied. "I plan to stay here and continue working for the construction company. For sure, I'm not going to return to Romania. I've been happier here in Greece, enjoying my freedom from the Securitate and being able to go and do as I please. I do regret, however, that I'm not there to help you and the girls, but there's nothing I can do about that now."

"Don't worry about us," Viki quickly replied. "I am doing well, and the girls are happy living with their grandparents. But I miss you terribly and pray that you soon will get something permanent so that we can be together again."

The first week of August 1987, the Securitate ordered Viki to come to the office for yet another interrogation. The meeting was set at 9:00 a.m., but the agent didn't appear until after lunchtime. Showing no consideration for Viki, he snarled at her, "Do you have your papers?"

"Yes."

"Well, where are they?"

"They're in my purse."

"Why didn't you have them ready to show me without me having to ask for them? Can't you see I'm in a hurry? Why do you waste my time? Where is your husband, that good-for-nothing, that selfish traitor? He is a disgrace to Romania and to the party."

"He's still in Greece."

"And you haven't divorced him yet?"

"No, but I'm going to. He should have returned by this time. I realize now I need to get on with my life without him."

"Well, regardless, he's been gone long enough to make me believe he is just trying to immigrate to another country but hasn't been able to find one that will take him. That is the way with those capitalist countries: all talk and do nothing.

"I still believe you've been lying to me all along. Now it is time to stop it. You are now fired from your job in the laboratory. The Securitate intends to see to it you will never work in your chosen field again."

"But what will I do? Why do you punish me and my children? We had nothing to do with him leaving Romania."

"Perhaps you didn't, but you've been lying to me all along, so my action is to punish you."

"But what am I to do? How can I care for my children?"

"I don't know, and I don't care. Good-bye, Mrs. Negura. You're taking too much of my time. Can't you see I'm busy? I said good-bye!"

Viki left the building with tears running down her cheeks. *Now, what do I do?* she asked herself. *I could kill that Kornel for putting us in this position.*

In midAugust, Viki moved to Suceava with Ana, her biological mother, who had finally divorced Viki's alcoholic biological father, Ion. The move forced her to separate the girls. She kept Christina with her mother and took Anka to Kornel's parents' place in Birlad. Then, after settling the girls into their respective schools, Viki began to look for a job, one free of Securitate meddling.

She still wasn't sure what would happen to Kornel and where he would finally settle, but she knew he would stick it out in Greece until he could immigrate to another country. *I'll just have to take it one day at a time,* she thought, *until we can determine our destiny. In the meantime, I'm going to work.*

When Kornel called, Viki told him that she had found another job, one not related to agriculture. "It's working for the government in the local accounting office as a line supervisor in the receipts division. I have twelve clerks under my supervision. We account for the payments the customers make for their electric and gas usage."

"Well, that's good, and it's right down your alley. With your experience supervising people on the collective, you shouldn't have any difficulty at all."

"I decided I had to go to work," Viki continued, "not knowing how long you were going to be delayed getting out of Greece. I need to be busy. And besides, I need the money. Do you remember Claudiu Comeaga? He was one of our classmates at the university. He is my boss."

"Yes, I remember him, but only vaguely. Does he know you were fired from your job in Bucharest?"

"Yes, he has my records and he knows the full story. He also knows you are in Greece looking for a way to leave Romania permanently. He says he understands and won't hold it against me as long as I do a good job for him. But he doesn't know for a fact that I plan to work only until I can join you wherever you are located. However, I believe he suspects that I will join you."

"There is no change here in Athens. I've got several more months to work before I can get to the American Embassy and get my visa. So you might as well work and get as much money as you can to join me in America."

Viki's new job went well. She was happy with her people, and they felt the same way about her. But the smooth sailing didn't last long. One of her best workers was overheard telling a joke about the president's wife by an employee informer who immediately notified the secret police. The Securitate confronted Manager Comeaga, demanding that the culprit be fired and released into their custody. Comeaga complied at once, calling the woman into his office and then firing her. She was handcuffed, paraded through the office, placed in a police car, and driven away.

"But it was only a joke," Viki pleaded with her boss. "She meant no harm to anyone, particularly the president's wife. It was just a harmless funny story. And besides, why did you fire her and turn her over to the Securitate without coming to me first? After all, she was my worker. If she was to be fired, then I, not you, should have been the one to do it! Is this the way you are going to operate? If so, then you don't need me. What are you going to do to free her and keep her from going to jail?"

"Comrade Negura, you are out of order. You work for me and you will do what I want you to do. If I had wanted you to take action against her for what she did, I would've ordered you to do so. I took the action because I wanted the Securitate to know I was with them. She knew what she was doing when she made those remarks. She got caught, and now she must suffer the consequences."

It was obvious that he was not going to change his mind. Even though at the university Viki had known him as a nice, quiet, and friendly person, he had let his position with the government, and the Communist Party, go to his head. He had become mean and overbearing, and it was clear he did not get along well with his people. He didn't trust them, and he gave them no reason to trust him. The longer Viki worked for him, the more she could see he was not the person she remembered.

Viki counseled with her father. His response was, "Why do you let that bother you? Just quit and concentrate on going to America."

She didn't quit right away. Instead, she held onto the job until the end of March 1989, when she handed in her resignation and started working with her father to prepare herself and her girls for the move to the United States.

CHAPTER 44

At the end of the two-year period, Kornel returned to the embassy and was given the wonderful news that he was going to Dallas, Texas, USA. Finally he had a dependable sponsor. And everything that he needed to settle in Texas would be provided.

Kornel immediately called Viki. As soon as she said hello, he shouted, "Hallelujah! Someone up there has finally come to the rescue. I'm going to Dallas, Texas, in America!"

"You are?" Viki said. "When?"

"I have all the necessary documentation and will leave Greece as soon as I can board the plane. This morning I collected my last paycheck and reserved a flight to Chicago, where I'll change planes for my flight to Dallas. There is nothing I can do now to make any changes to the plan. We may be happy we made the move, or we may be miserable. Only time will tell."

"Well, I keep praying you are making the best move for us," Viki said, "But as you say, time will tell."

"I still don't know how we're going to get you and the girls to Texas, but I'm sure we'll surmount each obstacle that comes up."

"Don't forget," Viki said, "that my father will help us. So we'll take it one step at a time and do the best we can to get all of us settled there."

"At this moment, everything is moving so fast that my feeble mind is not able to keep pace. All I can think of now is that my flight leaves tomorrow morning at eight o'clock. It will take many hours to arrive in Chicago."

"Well, just take it easy," Viki said. "Relax and enjoy the trip. I love you and long to be in your arms again. Have a good flight. Call me again after you arrive."

The plane left Athens on time and made good time across Europe and then the Atlantic. It felt strange yet comfortable for Kornel to be flying in such a large US plane with almost two hundred other passengers from Greece, the United States, and other countries.

Much of the flight was at an altitude of around thirty-five thousand feet. Little could be seen except the bright blue sky and the cloud cover beneath the aircraft, until the plane made its descent into Chicago O'Hare International Airport. Once the aircraft broke through the clouds, a new world opened to Kornel. He marveled at the spread of residential areas and the size and number of industrial and commercial buildings. He was amazed by how quickly the captain made the final descent into the airport and came to a stop at the international terminal.

Kornel was weary and anxious when he arrived. Surprisingly, he cleared customs without even a simple question from the customs agent, whose voice, Kornel was pleasantly surprised to discover, was friendly as he stamped his documents and smiled. Once finished with the task, the agent said in a cheerful voice, "Welcome to America. We hope you have a pleasant stay in our country."

I never experienced that kind of welcome in all my travels to communist countries, Kornel thought. The communists always acted like they were doing me a big favor letting me visit them, and to top that, they always expected an envelope containing some Spaga for having to take the time to check my documents. Now that I'm finally standing on American soil, I'm beginning to wonder if all the horrible incidents I've heard and read about are just a lot of malicious mistruths. If the Americans are as organized and as pleasant as that customs agent seemed to be, I know I'm going to be changing my attitude.

Kornel claimed his luggage at the international terminal and made his way to the Dallas gate to board the plane for the last leg of his flight to Dallas. There he checked his luggage and then sat down to await boarding.

As he looked around, he was amazed at the size of the airport and the number of carousels delivering luggage to the huge crowds waiting to grab their bags before hurriedly scrambling outside to meet awaiting transportation.

While standing and waiting for his luggage, he couldn't help but think of what he had gone through the past two and a half years after escaping Romania. *One thing I'm certain of,* he thought, *is that I've done it. My wishes and prayers have been answered. I no longer fear the Securitate. But now that I'm in America, why do I not feel completely relieved? Why am I not jumping up and down with joy? Why do I worry that I might have made an unforgivable error by coming to America?*

PART 5

Kornel Discovers the United States

CHAPTER 45

Immediately upon entering the baggage claim area, Kornel noticed a white-haired man holding a piece of white cardboard with his name—NEGURA—scrawled across it in bold black letters. It had to be Glen Becker, his savior from the church, standing at the edge of the crowd with a big smile on his face, waiting to rescue him from all the pushing, the shoving, and the echoing noises filling the claim area. *What a wonderful greeting*, Kornel thought as he weaved his way through the bustling crowd to shake Becker's hand.

Glen Becker had arrived early that day and made his way to the carousel to unload the baggage from Chicago. He was a lay leader of St. Ignatius, the sponsoring church. Today, his task was to meet Kornel Negura, get him to his apartment, and introduce him to the church's program for assisting refugees from other countries.

Becker, of average height and weight, had a ruddy complexion and white hair that once had been red. A jolly person, he was quick to speak out. He had emigrated from Ireland after the Second World War and worked in housing construction, eventually coming to own his own company. He had been waiting about forty-five minutes before the crush of passengers from Chicago crowded around the carousel.

Surprisingly for a Sunday, it was a busy day of travel. Something must be going on in Dallas, Becker thought. Perhaps a baseball game? Oh yes, he remembered, the Texas Rangers are playing the Chicago White Sox in a fourgame series. I hope they win. Becker was not a big fan of the Rangers, but he did like to keep up with how they were doing in the league, hoping, of course, they won their way into the World Series. This must be one of the big reasons for the noisy crowd, he thought.

Becker had been doing these greetings since the church inaugurated the program years ago. He was in no hurry to acquaint Kornel with the church's program or to introduce him to what life was like in the United States. He remembered how bewildered and awed he had been when he first arrived in Dallas from his Irish home in 1975. Even though he had little difficulty with the language, except perhaps the strange American accent, he was amazed at how different the atmosphere of the United States was compared with that he had left in Northern Ireland. Here, the people mingled, talked, and laughed at the littlest instance.

"Welcome to America and Dallas," Glen said as the man he recognized from photographs walked up to him. He could sense Kornel's unease at being so far from his home in Romania. The reaction was typical of many he had helped over the years.

"Do you speak English?" Becker asked. "I speak only a little Romanian, but maybe we can communicate enough for you to understand who I am, how my church functions, and where we go from here. Please ask questions. I'll try to answer them enough so that you'll feel at ease and understand how we do things."

"No, I only understand a few words of English," Kornel said in Romanian. "But I understand what you are saying in my language; you speak good Romanian."

"Well, that's a matter of opinion. But over the years that I have been doing this for the church, I've met many people speaking many different languages. And, much to my surprise, I've been able to retain enough to communicate a little with each. I'll be with you several days getting you settled in Dallas, so we'll have many opportunities to communicate with each other."

"As soon as we gather your luggage from the carousel we'll go to my car and I will drive you to the apartment we have reserved for you—and for your family when they arrive. It will take only a few minutes."

Kornel asked Glen, "Are other American airports this big? I have never seen anything like it. I'm amazed."

"Oh yes," Glen replied. "There are many big airports like this across America, particularly in the larger cities. American people do a lot of traveling. It takes many planes to handle the enormous traffic. Here at Dallas, thousands of planes land and take off every day carrying hundreds of thousands of people. It takes a lot of equipment, buildings, and working staff to handle it all."

"Are the people as happy at their jobs as they appear? They all smile and say, 'Have a good day.' Do they really mean it?"

"Yes, most of them do. A few, however, do it only because they are told to do so by their employers. Not every person is happy with his or her work here, but most are pleased with what they do. Most like working with people. If they can make the people happy, then they are happy."

"People in Romania, under the communist system, have very little to smile about," Kornel said. "There are too many shortages, too much interrogation and suspicion, and too few incentives to work hard. Unless you belong to the Communist Party, and most people don't, there are no reasons to smile and be friendly. That's one of the big reasons why I'm here and why I want to bring my family here."

As they talked, the carousel began moving the luggage from Chicago. Kornel pushed his way to the front and then grabbed his bag as soon as it came around to him. He and Decker then rushed out of the terminal, heading straight to where Decker's automobile was parked.

Kornel placed his suitcase in the trunk of Becker's car. It was early evening. The sun had just settled behind the tall buildings, and the streetlights were beginning to cast their soft glow upon the streets, lighting the way for the slight Sunday traffic. The men made good time and soon arrived at the apartment building, a four-story redbrick structure.

Becker parked his car near the entrance, removed the luggage from the trunk, crossed the lobby, and took the elevator to the fourth floor, apartment 417. After opening the door to the four-room apartment, he handed the key to Kornel.

"The key is yours now," he said with a big smile on his face. "Please don't lose it. While we find this neighborhood to be relatively safe, one never knows how someone might use a lost key."

By Becker's living standards, the apartment might have been small, even cramped; to Kornel, however, it was huge. He was astonished at the open space inside what was now his apartment. Viki, he thought, was going to have a big task filling the rooms with furniture and decorations.

"This building," Becker said, "is the church's main housing unit and where many of our needy parishioners and sponsored refugees live. It was built in the 1950s during the building boom that followed World War II and has been kept in prime condition. The first three floors are used by our parishioners, and the fourth floor is reserved exclusively for immigrants, such as you, from troubled countries."

Becker carried the suitcase down the short hallway, turned into the smallest bedroom, and placed the baggage on the floor beside a large mattress with bedclothes in the center of the room. A small fourdrawer dresser sat against the wall.

"You don't have a lot to start with, but at least you'll have a nice, soft, and safe place to lay your head at night." Becker said with a grin on his face. "The church can help you get started, but the rest will be up to you and your wife. The church will support you for three months. After that, it will be up to you to pay the rent and utilities, and to subsist on your income. It may not be easy, but no one said it was supposed to be. From what I have seen so far and from what little I know about you and your family, I believe you'll do well. We in the church have faith in you and your obvious capabilities."

Becker continued into the kitchen and proceeded to explain how the appliances worked. Kornel sat in one of the collapsible chairs around the folding card table as Becker moved around the kitchen and its contents. The table and chairs would have to serve his basic needs until Kornel could afford more comfortable furnishings. Glen showed Kornel the coffeemaker, the utensils used to prepare food, and the supply of foodstuffs, enough to get him started.

"Tomorrow morning," Becker said, "I'll pick you up and take you to the Westeastin Hotel and introduce you to the people with whom you'll be working. No doubt, you'll be given menial tasks to start with, but don't fret. Just do your best. You'll have plenty of opportunities to progress to better-paying positions.

"Tonight, it's important you get a good night's rest. You'll need it tomorrow, as it'll be a busy day. And, in case you don't know, it'll take you at least a couple of weeks to get over the jet lag. I'll pick you up at 7:15 a.m."

With all the information Glen had given him racing through his brain, Kornel closed the front door, leaned his back against it, and stared at the emptiness surrounding him. Suddenly, he felt all alone and weary from the long journey.

Now, what do I do? What have I accomplished for myself and my family? Are we that much better off now than how we were? Well, it's kind of late now, to be thinking about that. Maybe if I can get a good night's rest, I'll better appreciate the American freedoms I've heard so much about. We'll see. But there's one favorable thing that pleases me: this apartment is so much nicer and more comfortable than Cojocaru's grubby cluttered house we lived in on the farm.

He picked up the telephone, put it to his ear, and was surprised to hear an instant dial tone. *Great,* he thought, *the phone is working.* He dialed the number and almost immediately heard the ring on the other end.

Knowing her husband's itinerary, Viki had sat by the telephone all day awaiting his call. She had lain awake for hours every night since Kornel had told her about the possible move, wondering, worrying, and trying to visualize what living would be like in Dallas. All she knew about Dallas was the television series portraying how one very rich Dallas family lived, loved, and hated each other. *Surely there is more to Dallas and the United States,* she thought, *than what is being shown on television. Now that Kornel is in Dallas, all I can do is to wait and hope.*

Suddenly the telephone rang. It had to be Kornel calling as he said he would. "Hello," she answered.

"It's me, calling from Dallas. How are you today?"

"I am good but tired. How are you?"

"Well, I feel a little better, but I too am tired. It's this jet lag everyone keeps talking about. They say it will take about two weeks for the body to catch up with the time zone. And I believe it.

"When I arrived, a man named Glen Becker from the church met me at the airport and drove me to the apartment I'm calling from."

"I'm glad you arrived safely," she said. "What's it like being in America?"

"It's overwhelming," Kornel said. "Everything is much bigger than I ever imagined; that includes the Atlantic Ocean, America, and the state of Texas. I was beginning to believe I would never get here. Texas is spread over a vast area with millions of acres of open space and a variety of tall buildings in the cities. Even our apartment is bigger than I expected it would be, much bigger than the one we had in Bucharest. Also, it's much cleaner than I had imagined. It seems the Americans do a better job of keeping everything neat and clean. The airport is spotless, and the streets are clean and in good repair. From what little I have seen and heard, America is much different in all respects than what we were taught to believe by the communists."

"Please now tell me about the apartment and your job and how we will live once the girls and I get there. That's what I'm mostly interested in hearing. And the schools? What are they like? Are they close to the apartment?"

"Whoa! Let's take one thing at a time. Remember, I just arrived and I haven't had any chance to find out about those things. You are correct, they are important, but we have lots of time to find out about them. I can tell you about the apartment now, but that is all. It's a very nice fourroom apartment, with two bedrooms, a living room, and a kitchen, awaiting your creativity to decorate it and fill it with furniture. In the kitchen we have a nice big refrigerator and a gas stove with a large oven. Even though they've been used, they are clean and look almost new. I'm sure you'll appreciate them. They are certainly much better than the oilburning stove and icebox we found in Cojocaru's house on the farm. In the kitchen we have a folding card table and four folding chairs."

Viki waited patiently while he caught his breath from speaking so quickly.

"In the living room," he continued, "we will have my dreamy big color television I will buy as soon as I get some money. In the meantime, we now have a tiny TV that will have to suffice until we can afford the larger one. The TV sits on the floor and is the only furniture in the room. For us to watch it now, we will need to sit on the kitchen's folding chairs. The only bed that came with the apartment is in the master bedroom. It's a floor mattress with pillows, sheets, and a blanket. There is nothing else except a small fourdrawer dresser. The bathroom contains a bathtub with a builtin shower, a nice commode, and a big sink complete with hot and cold running water. There is also a nice big medicine cabinet built into the wall with lots of room for everything we need."

"We will have to sleep on the floor?" Viki asked him.

"Only until we can afford to buy a proper bed."

"Good Lord, we will have to rough it?"

"Yes, if that's how you choose to think about it."

"So we will have nothing. I don't like the thought of having to start all over again!"

"Well, you had better get used to it if you want to get out of Romania. But as I've told you many times, I can't make you leave. You'll have to decide what you want to do with yourself and the girls. As for me, I'm staying, least until I begin to feel I made a huge mistake. If I fail, I can always come back to Romania and take my chances there. Pray over your decision. The Lord will direct you. I pray you will come here. I believe strongly we can make it in America."

"You'll have to forgive me," Viki said. "I'm a little flustered. You know I want to be with you, but I'm also thinking about the welfare of the girls. I want them to get the best education possible."

"Very well. I'll start inquiring around here tomorrow to try to get some ideas about the quality of education in Dallas."

CHAPTER 46

Becker was on time the next morning, but Kornel was tired and sleepy. Because of his jet lag, he had gotten very little sleep after finishing his telephone discussion with Viki. *I'll get to bed earlier tonight and see if that will help,* he thought as he was trying to memorize the route Becker was driving. *After today, I'll have to find my own way to the hotel.*

Becker must have been reading his mind, because he said, "Starting tomorrow, you'll have to take the downtown bus to your workplace. The bus stop is only two blocks from your apartment. I'll show you when we get back."

"The cleanliness of the streets and the new and massive buildings I'm seeing here in Dallas are amazing," Kornel remarked. "Construction is newer and the buildings more uniform in color and workmanship than what I'm familiar with in the older communist countries."

"And that's as it should be," Becker said. "The older countries are just that: old. You must remember that America is a much younger country than those you came from. Who knows what the Americas will look like when they too are old."

Finally, they reached their destination. After parking the car in the employee parking lot at the rear of the building, Becker led Kornel through the employee entrance, to the elevator, and up to the seventh floor. There he was introduced to the manager of housekeeping, Lowell Follendorf, a Swedish immigrant from Stockholm. He had been in the United States more than fifteen years and had worked his way up the ladder to his present position.

He knew his job and worked at it diligently. He had earned his degree at a university in Sweden.

Shaking Kornel's hand, Lowell said, "I am happy to meet you, Kornel. Welcome to Dallas. We have been looking forward to this day since the church told us about you and your wife and your struggles to leave Romania. Isn't your wife with you?"

"I am happy to meet you, too," Kornel said in broken English, trying to be as cheerful as he could be even though he was exhausted after his long journey and had had very little sleep. "No, my wife is not with me yet. With the political situation in my country, she is having difficulties getting a passport and visa. But I expect her and our two daughters to come over soon."

Becker acted as interpreter and did the best he could.

"Well, please tell her we have a job for her as soon as she arrives," Lowell said. "Now I will take you to the personnel office and get your paperwork completed. You will begin work tomorrow. I'll introduce you to your supervisor, and she'll get you started when you arrive in the morning."

"I'll meet you in the lobby," Becker said, "after Lowell finishes with you and you are ready to return to the apartment."

Follendorf led Kornel to the elevator and up to the twelfth floor, where the new immigrant met his immediate supervisor, Madeline Brosy. She was cordial and anxious to get him started on the job. Having emigrated from Poland, she'd been with the hotel eleven years, the last six years as supervisor of eleven housekeepers, now twelve.

Madeline was quite attractive. A little on the plump side, with short black hair and brown eyes, she stood about five feet four inches tall, in her stocking feet. Kornel knew he would have no problems working for a female boss. He had grown accustomed to working with females in Romania. Under the communist system, men and women were treated as equals.

Follendorf led Kornel to the elevator and to the personnel office on the mezzanine floor, where he was introduced to the employment manager, who turned him over to one of his clerks to prepare the necessary papers for Kornel to be placed on the hotel's payroll. After the paperwork was completed, Kornel was welcomed as an employee to begin working the following morning. He made his way to the lobby and found Becker sitting on one of the sofas reading the morning newspaper.

The return journey seemed shorter and took less time, as traffic had thinned. On the way, Becker drove by the bus stop where Kornel would catch his bus. His workday started at 8:00 a.m., which meant he had to catch the 6:30 bus to allow him sufficient time to get to the hotel.

At the apartment, they took seats around the kitchen table, on which Becker spread out a city map. Before starting to read the map, Kornel suggested they have a cup of coffee.

After taking a sip of the coffee, Becker said, "I noticed yesterday that you weren't taking notes, so I want to repeat some things that I mentioned. I will also repeat some of the things that I will mention today that might be beneficial when talking with your wife." As he sipped his coffee, Becker handed Kornel a small notepad and a ballpoint pen. "You might want to take notes," he said, "so you have something to refer to when talking with your wife."

"As I said last evening, the church will pay your basic expenses for three months, which will include your monthly rent and all utilities plus trash removal. And the church will reimburse you for your first month's bus charges. You'll have to pay for your telephone usage." As he handed Kornel an official-looking paper, he said, "You will have to sign a one-year lease for the apartment." As Kornel signed the lease, Becker continued: "Periodically, someone from the church will meet with you and your family, once they get here, to see how you are getting along and offer any help that you might need to keep going."

"It sounds like a wonderful program," Kornel said. "I'm deeply grateful to be able to be included in it. And I'm certain my Viki will feel the same way once she arrives. I want to thank you and the church for all you are doing for us."

"This church program was started by Boris Popov," Becker said, "a native Russian who immigrated with his wife and six children in 1956 with nothing but the clothes on their backs and just enough money to pay their way to Dallas. He had to depend on members of the parish for financial assistance until he could earn enough income to pay his own costs. He was a good carpenter and immediately got work in the construction business building houses. Eventually he started his own company, reaping a fortune. When he retired, he firmly believed it was God's plan for him to create a program to help others like him who were being persecuted and forced to leave their homelands. So, Kornel, it is he who made it possible for you to be here. He has since died, but his family continues the program today."

Viki was unable to sleep. Her mind was constantly on the United States and worrying how Kornel was progressing with his job, the apartment, and the schools for the girls.

It's only been a few days, she thought, since I last talked to him, but it seems like forever. What should I do? I can't arrive at any reasonable decision I think is right. I need to talk to someone. Ana hasn't been much help in giving advice, but she means well. She has been exceptionally kind since the girls and I returned from Bucharest. I hate the thought of having to leave her here by herself, but what else can I do? I've been hesitating to call Papa, wanting to make the decision myself, but I'm getting to the point where I doubt that I can do it without his help.

She tossed and turned for what seemed like hours before dropping into a deep slumber with ghastly nightmares. In a blurred picture, she saw Kornel involved in a terrible automobile accident. She and the girls were not there to see him before he passed away. She shuddered, screamed in her sleep, and awoke realizing she it was just a horrific dream. It jolted her so much that she knew she had to make her decision. *I can't go on living this way. I must talk to my father.*

The next morning, as soon as she thought he would be up and about, Viki called her papa. She was nervous and not sure how she wanted to start the conversation, but she didn't have to, as her father spoke up for her. He knew.

"You can't make up your mind, can you?" he said in a gentle voice. "You don't know which way to turn. You know you've got the girls to think about rather than just yourself. What's holding you back?"

"I don't know, and then again everything. I don't know the language, and I can't see myself going to school to learn it. And I can visualize the girls having to struggle so hard with learning English that I'll let them take their minds off the subject matter they will be taught. For the same reason, I will not be able to help them. I doubt that Kornel will be much help, having to work such long hours. I can think of many more reasons to stay here than to leave. Here we have something; there we have nothing. We will have to start all over again. We have no house, no furniture, and no car to get around in. No anything. And I'm getting too old to want to have to go through those hardships again."

"What does Kornel want?" her papa asked. "Does he plan to stay? Do you want to be with him badly enough to forget the disadvantages and work hard to make a better life in America than you can make here? Have you forgotten what I taught you about working hard to fulfill your wants? Do you really believe you are too old to make a new start? Does America really frighten you, or is it just the unknown? If America is the land of milk and honey, why don't you tackle it and see how much of its riches you can gather? I have a lot of faith and confidence in you and Kornel and your abilities to take advantage of all freedoms you will enjoy. I believe you can instill in your two daughters the same work skills and habits you learned and applied in getting your education, giving them the strength and the aptitude to use the education to achieve their goals in life. I say, do it. I know you can make it, but it's your decision to make, only yours. What do you say?"

"I suppose you are right, but I'm still confused. I need to think about it some more. I will let you know my final decision. Goodbye, Papa," she said, replacing the receiver in its cradle.

What to do? What to do?

As Viki leaned back in the chair, and before she could close her eyes, Ana walked in, looked intently at her, and said, "What did my brother tell you that you don't already know? Do you feel any better? I could only hear one side of the conversation. I can only guess his responses, but I know him all too well. I never did forgive him for taking you away from me. But I do have to admit, he and Sophia did a good job in rearing you and giving you the opportunity to make something of yourself. Your real father never would have done that. While I still don't like my brother, I realize now that he did the right thing for all of us."

Viki realized that Ana was about offer her some advice.

"Now, I'm not one to interfere in anyone else's business," Ana continued, "but I can't help but tell you what I believe you should consider. I know you love your husband and your children and you care about their life and how they should live it, at least according to your beliefs and standards. I know also that you want to see your girls grow up well educated and capable of carrying on a happy lifestyle without a bunch of worries. That's what we all want, and I'm sure that is what Kornel wants. Kornel has made a great sacrifice leaving Romania, his family, and all that the two of you had accomplished. He is willing to start over in a new and strange land he could never have envisioned. And it is my belief that you should join him. You belong together. Remember your wedding vows?"

"Of course I do," Viki said.

"And your children need both of you, together in America. If it were me, tomorrow I would get all the necessary papers, pack as much stuff as I could manage, and board the first plane leaving for America. I would leave all my worries and cares behind me and think only good thoughts about how I was going to make a good living in America. And that is all I have to say."

With that, Ana paused, took a breath, and then added, "No, that is not all I will say. There is one other thing I observe about you that I feel should be mentioned. You are too negative about all this. You have not thought enough about the advantages of living and working in America, or about the educational benefits the girls might have from being taught in the American schools. You cannot rely on what the communists say about how terrible life is in America, about the crime and the poor and how inferior their education system is compared to ours. That is only propaganda trying to downgrade the capitalist system to the level of the communist system. Certainly, I do not know which system is the right one. I only know what I have heard and seen that makes me believe America does offer a better way of life. It must have something good going for it. Think about that as you sit there moping and worrying."

With that, Ana left the living room and retired to her bedroom.

Viki was amazed and grateful. She had no idea Ana was so observant and knowledgeable, and so positive about the benefits of the United States. And on top of that, what she said made sense.

Perhaps, she thought, I have been too negative about all this and have worried more about knowing what to do rather than just going ahead and doing it. I realize now, I must take a more positive attitude toward all of this and think more about what I have to do to make our life in America much richer and better than what we have here in Romania. I'll be more positive with Kornel when he calls the next time. Now, maybe I can sleep better tonight.

CHAPTER 47

A couple of weeks passed before Kornel called again. It was the Fourth of July: the United States was celebrating its birthday. With the jet lag behind him, Kornel sounded more relaxed and desirous of bringing Viki up to date.

"How have you been?" he asked tenderly.

"Good," Viki replied. "I'm very good now that I've decided to join you. Until I had discussions with Papa and Ana, I'd been letting my doubts and fears overwhelm my better judgment. I realize now that for the girls' sake our life together must go on. Now I'm asking my father to help me get my traveling papers as quickly as he can accomplish it."

"Thank you," Kornel said. "That is the best news I've had in years."

"What are you doing now?" Viki said. "How is the job going? And for the apartment, have you bought any more furniture?"

"The job is going well. I'm working with Junal Barnarsky, an immigrant from Poland. Language is a barrier, but we are able to talk with each other by drawing pictures and using hand motions. Can you imagine a Greek speaking Romanian and working with a Polish immigrant who speaks only Polish, with a Spanish Mexican boss looking on wondering what in the hell is going on? We're removing furniture and fixtures from rooms to enable renovators to repaint and paper the walls and replace the carpeting and drapes. The hotel has begun a big renovation program of their guest rooms. We began by starting and finishing just one room at a time, but moving the furniture around and waiting for the renovators to complete each room was inefficient and wasted a lot of our time. After finishing several rooms that way, I suggested to the director that since an empty room could store as much as five rooms worth of furniture and fixtures, we should clear out the rooms to be renovated before starting work and eliminate all that wasted time. It worked! The boss thought I was a genius."

"That is wonderful," Viki said.

"I haven't gotten any more furniture for the apartment, yet," he continued, "but I'm looking and considering what is the cheapest and most attractive. There are so many brands and styles that I can't make up my mind. I'm waiting for you to get here. The entire apartment is screaming for your attention. I miss you so much; I can't wait until I again can have you in my arms. You truly are coming, aren't you?"

"Yes, I'm coming," Viki said. "I'll make a start as soon as Papa and I can gather the necessary papers. That will probably take a while. No doubt, we'll have to offer spaga envelopes and do a lot of haggling to get the ministry to move."

"Well, as you can imagine, there are lots of nice things here that will make good gifts to convince the ministry to give you the papers you need. After I get paid next week, I'll start sending you money and gifts."

"That is perfect!"

"After we get you settled in and we know our way around," Kornel continued, "we'll bring the girls over. I believe that it's best they remain in Romania until we know what we are doing, both in terms of our work situation and their school situation. It's imperative they be enrolled in their new school the first day of the new semester."

"I agree with that wholeheartedly," Viki said.

"Oh, I almost forgot," Kornel said, "more good news. I've lined up a job for you working as a maid in the Triple Branch Hotel, which is near where I work. I talked to the supervisor there, and she is anxious to get you on board. She always needs good help. She knows you're efficient because I told her you were."

"I don't know about that," Viki said. "I have no idea what a maid is supposed to do. I don't even know how to use a vacuum sweeper, let alone clean toilets and sinks. We'll just have to wait until I get there and try it. And by the way, now that you have been there for more than a month, what are your impressions of America? What are your likes and dislikes?"

"Well, the first thing I had to do was get rid of that fear of the Securitate persecuting me. Here, there is no secret police. And what they say about the CIA isn't true—it does not operate within the borders of the United States. Here, there is the personal freedom to do and say what you want as long as you do it lawfully. It took me several days before I stopped looking through the cracks in the window drapes to see if anyone was following me. I don't know how to describe the feelings; you just have to experience them yourself. And another thing, adult men and women do not wear backpacks every place they go. If they have anything to carry, men use nice leather briefcases and women hang large purses from their shoulders or carry handbags. Here, only schoolchildren use backpacks. In fact, the other day I went to the Goodwill place, a charitable organization that receives and sells donated goods and merchandise, and bought each girl a backpack. They are well-built and look like new."

"They are used?"

"Yes, but they look new."

"I won't like them if they are used. I believe the girls should have new clothing and new supplies. That's what I want and that's what they'll get, not someone else's junk."

"They're not junk; they look like they just came from the factory."

"I don't care where they came from," Viki reiterated. "If they are used, I won't have them. The girls deserve the best. That's the only thing I'll accept."

"Well, you're the boss. Now it looks like I'll make another trip to the Goodwill place and make a donation of two like-new backpacks. When you get here, I'll let you do the shopping to buy whatever you wish.

"One other thing I found out the hard way: you have to be careful asking for directions, especially if you're walking. Americans think in terms of automotive distances and times. For example, just last week I was looking for a place to buy a cold beer, so I asked a man who was standing on the corner waiting for the traffic light to change. He pointed up the street and said, 'There's a nice bar just up the street. You can't miss it.' He said, 'It will take only a few minutes to get there.' So, I walked and walked for what seemed like a half hour before I found the place. The man didn't realize I was walking; he must have thought I was using the bus."

"That is very difficult for me to visualize," Viki said. "So much space."

"Everything here is clean and well lighted," Kornel said, "and the people who work in the stores are very friendly and always smiling. When parting, they say, 'Have a good one.' I don't know which one they're referring to as good, but I'm guessing they mean, 'Have a good day.' And people are more than willing to help you with the language problems. They always smile and, knowing you have a problem, will give you all the time you need to make yourself understood. It's not like in Romania when a stranger wants to understand Romanian. People there think the stranger is an idiot, a Securitate agent, or an informer, and silently pass him by."

The next day, Viki called her father to talk about making arrangements for her journey. "Papa," she said, "what are the procedures for obtaining a passport and visa just for me? The girls won't be going with me. We plan to wait about a year before bringing them over. We want to wait until their school year is completed."

"I'll take care of getting those documents for you," he said. "All you need to do is decide what you should take with you for traveling and what you will need after you get there. Then you can shop around and buy what you want. Just keep the weight of what you leave here with as light as possible and you'll be all right. I'll arrange to get your passport, but you'll have to get your own visa."

"Can you please explain the difference?"

"I believe it would be virtually impossible for you to get your own passport," her papa said, "because of what the Securitate has already recorded about Kornel leaving Romania. I doubt that they would give you the time of day. It wouldn't surprise me if they tried to persecute you even more for aiding and abetting in his escape. No, I'll take care of the papers. All you have to do is get there. Just tell Kornel to send nice gifts that I can use to entice the agents to give me the documents I want. And keep in mind, your girls will get good care while you are gone."

At first, Harald made progress obtaining Viki's passport, but then activity slowed down.

Kornel was regularly sending impressive gifts—money, wristwatches, and hardtoget nonperishable food products. The key was that they were small and expensive enough that they could be concealed and easily passed between Harald and the official parties.

On the day Harald was supposed to finally pick up Viki's passport, he found that the paperwork had not been completed as promised. He didn't want to make a scene and lose the deal he'd arranged, but he was upset.

Maria, the office clerk, apologized and said, "I couldn't get the approvals for you because everyone has been out of the office for the past two weeks. Some kind of meeting they had to attend. But they promised to be back next week. Can you come back then?"

"Yes, I can come back," Harald said, smiling agreeably but still upset. "I know you have been working hard and doing the best you can, but we are in a hurry and time is running out. And speaking of time …" He reached into his jacket pocket and took out an envelope. Maria's eyes grew wide. Then he opened the envelope flap and gave her a quick peek at the gleaming gold ladies' wristwatch inside. Her eyes grew even wider. "I would appreciate it greatly if you could speed things up," he said as he closed the flap.

With an excited but pleasant smile on her face, Maria said, "Yes, I believe I can move her request up a bit more."

"I thank you for whatever you can do," Harald said, placing the envelope on her desk after assuring himself that no one was watching.

After he left the office, he couldn't help but wonder what else could possibly happen to hold up getting the passport for Viki.

What actually did happen in the next few days was something he had not anticipated. Before he could return to the office to collect the completed documents, all hell broke loose literally, creating a huge vacuum in the governmental structure.

CHAPTER 48

After the room renovations were finished, Kornel was assigned a housekeeper's job cleaning rooms: providing clean bedding and supplying items for bathing and lounging. Kornel had a daily quota of seventeen rooms to make presentable to the hotel guests. The rooms had to look as though they had never been occupied.

He was proud of the quality of his work. He considered himself to be the best bed changer on the floor and the best bathtub cleaner in the whole building, but after a few months he was ready for a change. Because his supervisor recommended him, he was given the position of public restroom attendant and was put in charge of all the public restrooms in the building. To make him look more distinguished and official, he was given a dark blue monogrammed jacket, a white shirt with a black tie, and gleaming black shoes. He was proud and elated—this was his first position of responsibility. "It was," as he later said, "as if I had died and gone to heaven."

In her next telephone conversation with Kornel, the first thing Viki said was, "Is there a lot of television coverage there about this terrible situation here in Romania?"

"Yes," Kornel said, "and they say it is spreading like wildfire across the country. The local police and Securitate are having problems keeping the crowds under control. What's it all about?"

"Well, all I know is what I've heard on the radio from other countries. If our local radio and television stations do mention the disturbances, the announcements are brief and there are no details. All they broadcast is the usual propaganda about how great our government is and what it's doing to develop Romania into a world power. It all started, I understand, when local officials tried to send a Protestant pastor to the countryside, claiming he stirred up religious loathing among those who would listen. His members gathered to prevent his removal, and soon many others joined them, believing the government was attempting to suppress religious freedoms. When the crowd tried to enter the government buildings, the mayor called in the city police and the Securitate. Many in the crowd were beaten and arrested. And when the mob was turned back with force, it regrouped and started another protest march. But that too was turned back.

"The next morning, the crowds were able to break into the district committee building, where they destroyed documents and then attempted to set fire to the building. This time military units were called in to assist. As riots and vandalism continued, the soldiers opened fire with rifles and cannons, killing and injuring many of the protestors. It was awful. Despite the bloodshed, the protests continued to grow in number and volume, demanding the president and his wife's resignation. Now, as I understand it, even more violent protests are springing up across the country, resulting in lots of injuries, deaths, and arrests."

"What is the president doing about it?"

"Nothing," Viki said. "He is in Moscow with his wife. He's left a bunch of stooges behind to put an end to the devastation caused by the rioters. Both of the opposing forces believe the fighting will soon be over because they think the people love them and will do whatever is asked of them."

"Well," Kornel said, "our president is totally mistaken. The people don't like him. They detest what he has done to the country. They are expressing their frustrations and demanding that immediate changes be made. I'm anxious to see what is going to happen next, but I am concerned about your safety and the safety of our daughters. Please call me again soon, so I know you're all okay. And I'll bring you up to date from this side of the world."

"I see on the television and in the newspapers that the revolt has spread across the country and the rioters are getting vicious," Kornel said as he talked with Viki.

"Yes," she replied, "it has spread and the crowds are getting angrier. The president has returned from Moscow with the belief that the revolts are just interferences caused by foreigners. I understand he and his wife are really shaken over what is happening to the country.

"The next day, from what I hear, his cabinet ordered him to appear before a fixed crowd of supporters and promise to give them whatever they want just to get them to go home. He reluctantly agreed, but still believing the people loved him, he made his appearance on his balcony and tried shouting over the boisterous crowd, mentioning his many achievements in recent years. Only his organized crowd cheered him on to make it seem like he really was the loved one. But they were only a small minority of the rioting mass of noisy people. The majority made it be known that he was not the loved one, calling him a thief and murderer.

"His attempts to gain silence only made the crowd grow louder, so loud and rowdy that his security men pulled him from the balcony and placed him in a safe room. But being a persistent person, and still believing he was loved, he insisted on talking to them again.

"But the next day, the makeup of the crowd was not the same as the day before. Absent were his selected few who had been urged to agree with all he said. Still convinced he was loved, he shouted even louder with this speech.

"Again he had difficulty attracting attention. The threatening crowd jeered him and drowned out his hellos and the prompts from his wife, who was standing in the background shouting, 'Talk to them, talk to them. Promise them salary increases and the extra help they must have during the planting and harvesting seasons.'

"His pleas, however, fell on deaf ears. The people were sick of hearing promises that never materialized. Their shouts and screams completely overrode his raspy irritating voice.

"Even the leaflets dropped from the helicopters pleading with the people not to listen to the enemy but to go home and enjoy Christmas dinner were tromped on, balled up, or torn into thousands of pieces. Surely, the people thought, the president and his wife were fully aware of the shortages and long lines the people had to endure just to eke out a meager living. How could the people celebrate a hearty Christmas dinner when the only available foods were bones, legs, and claws, with hardly enough cooking oil to prepare it? Hadn't he seen the long lines of frustrated and angry people hoping and praying there would be enough edible foods to buy when they reached the front of the line?

"Then, suddenly, sounds like fireworks, bombs, or guns were heard, scattering people in all directions. Loudspeakers, having been taken over by the protestors, were saying the Securitate was firing into the crowd. The event was turning into a revolution. Then the president's security team, fearing for his life, pulled him off the balcony and put him into the safety of the building.

"Soon the entire downtown area was overflowing with people being hounded by police, the Securitate, and the military soldiers attempting to break up the screaming, rioting, and damage-doing perpetrators. Rioters were being shot at from building tops, alleyways, and tanks. Many were killed and many more injured.

"And here in Suceava," Viki concluded, "I heard that Claudiu Comeaga, the director I worked for, was kidnapped, taken into an alley, and nearly beaten to death. He suffered a broken arm, a flattened nose, and numerous bruises over his face and body. His house was completely ransacked and burned to the ground. Then, adding to his pain and misery, he was chased out of town."

When Kornel called on Monday, December 26, Viki brought him up to date on what had happened. "As you have undoubtedly already heard," she said, "the president and his wife are no longer with us. They were executed by military firing squad."

"Yes, I know. It has been big news here in America. But what I don't understand is how it could happen so quickly. The last news I'd heard was Friday, and he was in still in Bucharest trying to settle the turmoil but having no success."

"Well, on Saturday," Viki said, "he and his wife were put aboard a helicopter. The pilot was ordered to fly them to the district office in Tutu. But before they could leave for their destination, they were captured by a mob of people and imprisoned in a locked room to await the verdict of a hastily organized court. Yesterday, on Christmas Day, the president and his wife faced a military tribunal and were charged with many crimes against the people. Their responses and appeals fell on deaf ears. Both were sentenced to death and were immediately dragged to the courtyard, placed against the wall, and shot to death. It happened so quickly that the photographer had no time set up his equipment. It is said that about 120 bullets entered their bodies. It is also said that the president's wife tried to run away when she realized what was about to happen."

"Are the people happy now?"

"They say they are happy," Viki said, "but who really knows? Everyone now is asking, 'Where do we go from here?' At any rate, the revolt is over and many people have died needlessly, because no one knew which side was the winning side. It happened so quickly and was so disorganized that there was no advance planning for a government takeover. Only the communists seemed ready to assume the new roles. Now people are beginning to realize that very little was gained from changing the political system. All we can hope for is to be able to enjoy more freedoms of life and less of the government's snooping and recording people's lives we shall see."

On Sunday, March 1, 1989, Harald called Viki and said, "Your mama has gotten much worse and is not able to get out of bed, so I've made arrangements for a nice young lady to come three times every day to clean and feed her, and keep her comfortable. Also, she washes and irons our clothes. I'm with your mother the rest of the day and through the night. Because of the continuing turmoil in the government, I haven't been able to get your travel documents yet. And this horrible turn of events with Mama makes it impossible for me to devote the time necessary to get it done. I'm sorry, but what else can I do?"

"There isn't anything else you can do," Viki said. "You must care for Mama; she needs your full attention. Is there anything I can do for either of you?"

"No, but if I think of something, I'll let you know.

After hanging up the phone, Viki added another worry to her already heavy load. When her mother would die was anybody's guess, but it was certainly closer now that she was beginning to fail. Viki knew Parkinson's was a terrible disease that slowly stole the life of the afflicted person and sapped the mental and physical strength of the caregiver.

I wish there was some way I could help Papa through this, Viki thought sadly, but I can't. And the truth is, I'll probably be in America when Mama dies.

CHAPTER 49

It took Viki another full year to get through all the red tape before she was clutching her passport and visa in her trembling hands. In their ongoing discussion about bringing the girls to the United States, she and Kornel decided to leave them with his parents until he and she were adequately settled in their jobs, had comfortably furnished their apartment, and had gotten acquainted with the local schools and determined what transportation the girls needed.

And when the time finally came to bring them over, they had to find someone who would secure the girls' documents and escort them to Dallas. Harald still was not available because of Sophia's failing health.

Anka was five years old and Christina seven when Viki told her daughters she was going to the United States alone and they would come later. In the meantime, they would stay with their grandparents in Birlad.

"I don't want to go, Mama," Christina cried. "Why do I have to? I don't know anyone in the United States, and I don't want to learn English. It's too hard to understand. And my teachers have nothing good to say about America. They say there are organized gangs running around fighting and killing one another, and lots of drugs. They also say the schools are so bad that we can't get a good education. Besides, I don't want to leave my friends. And I don't know how to make new friends when I can't speak their language."

"I know you don't, honey," Viki understandingly said, "and I also have reservations about going, but we have little choice. Your father is getting settled in America and is working very hard to move us there. He misses us as much as we miss him. And he is anxious to get us settled in our apartment and arrange to enroll you and Anka in school. Moving to any foreign country isn't easy, but we have no other choice. We know practically nothing about the school system, but we are very desirous of getting you into the best schools we can find. And if it's any consolation, I too have problems. I don't know what kind of work I will be doing or whom I will be working with, and I have the same problems with the language as you girls will have."

"Well," Christina said, pausing in her crying, "then you can send us some chocolates and other gifts, but I don't want to go. I still think I will hate it."

Viki asked Anka, "And how do you feel about leaving Romania and flying to America? It will be a long, long trip, and it won't be easy."

Anka dropped the book she was flipping through and shrugged her shoulders. "I don't care, Mama," she said. "If you tell us we have to go, then we will just go. I think I will like flying in an airplane and seeing the big ocean. I don't know anything about America, but I think I would like to try to like it."

"That's fine, Anka. I'm sure you will get along well with whomever you meet with in Dallas."

Now, Viki thought, if I can just get Christina to look at the brighter side of the adventure, I will feel better. Plus, it will make it easier for me to accept America. Still, the complexity of changing lifestyles is daunting.

Normally, Ana preferred not to interfere in her daughter's parenting of her children, but she now spoke up. Looking directly at the children, she said, "Listen to what your mother says and do it. If you don't, you'll regret it the rest of your lives. When I was about your age, perhaps a little older, my parents, your grandparents, ordered me to leave our home with four of my brothers and sisters and travel to a distant place far in the country to begin a new life. This occurred during a severe worldwide depression. They had twelve of us children to feed and clothe. The only solution my parents could reach was to reduce the size of the family or face the possibility that we would all starve to death. People in our village already were dying of starvation. Our parents did not want that to happen to us. But I didn't want to go. I couldn't tolerate the thought of leaving my parents and my friends. I begged and pleaded with my parents, but to no avail. But after a switching by my brother, your father, who was in charge of the move, I reluctantly agreed to go. Still, I remained adamant in my position, disliking the journey itself and the life I had to live away from home.

"Our father had arranged with the landowner to take over some godforsaken barren land in a very small village named Vioresca, near Saveni. We had to start from scratch to make it livable: clear the land, cultivate it, and harvest it well enough to eke out a living. It was difficult. Then we had to build shelters for ourselves and for a large variety of animals and birds.

"We had nothing, nothing at all, and the worst part about it was I couldn't finish my education. I had made it through the fifth grade in Niculesca, our home place, but in Vioresca I couldn't go to school because I had to work on the farm. It took all five of us to clear the land, build the buildings, and plant and harvest the food.

"It was terrible, but we did it, and we benefited from what we had accomplished. But I was always homesick and wanted to go home. Finally, after several years of making trouble for all of us, I convinced my brother Harald, your father, to let me leave.

"After I got back home, however, I began to realize that life was not the same as I had left it and that my homesickness for home had overshadowed my need to accept and appreciate the joy and happiness of my new surroundings. I sorely regretted that I had made such a big issue of nothing. And I have regretted my actions ever since.

"My life back home was miserable, and my marriage was a big mistake. I should have stayed in Vioresca on the good farms we had developed for ourselves. I realize now I would have been much better off. When I got back home, I couldn't stay with my parents, so I had to work as a livein maid until I got married and started having children.

"So, I urge you, go to America and make a good life for yourselves. You'll soon learn to forget Romania and take on a new appreciation for your new land. My only advice is, don't fight it, just do it! You'll be glad you did."

With that, Ana walked out of the room.

Viki was glad Ana had added her two cents, even though it had surprised her when she rose from her chair and faced the girls. She was especially pleased to see Christina's look of astonishment as she received the lecture, and the contrition and acceptance in her eyes when it was over. The girls were going to the United States, but not until later.

Every evening after Kornel had dinner and before he started watching television, he scanned the help wanted ads in the Dallas newspaper. He liked to practice reading. Now that his English was better, he was beginning to think about getting a better job. Even though working at the hotel paid a reasonable wage, cleaning toilets wasn't what he wanted to spend the rest of his life doing. He wanted something more in line with his education, like the supervisor's job he'd had in the collective in Romania. *Better still,* he thought, *why not start a farm of my own?*

He glanced through the property ads looking for land where sheep or cattle might be raised. His experience with sheep in Romania gave him confidence that he could make a go of farming in the United States. *Why not become a landowner and raise sheep?* He clipped an ad that looked promising and decided to visit the property on his next day off.

"Why do you want to be raise sheep out here in Texas?" the farmer who had put the land up for sale asked. "Are you familiar with what we sheep ranchers have to contend with? Many are going bankrupt because of the terrible market conditions. Do you know Willie Nelson?"

"I don't know him personally, but I know who he is," Kornel said, wondering what a country singer had to do with sheep farming. It was brutally hot in the sun in the man's front yard. There was no grass, but there were a few weeds. The reddish soil looked baked and brittle.

The farmer went on, saying, "Why do you want to start raising sheep when Willie Nelson is doing telethons to raise money to help us Texas sheep farmers avoid bankruptcy?"

"I understand what you are saying," Kornel said. "And I thank you for the information. At least I'm getting a better understanding of this capitalist system of ownership. It is much different from the socialist system, where the government owns everything and you are just an employee working for the government. I need to rethink all this and see where I want to go from here. Thank you for spending time with me. And I assure you, when Willie Nelson puts on another of his telethons, I will watch it with a better understanding of what the farmers have to contend with here in America."

Kornel then looked the farmer in the eye and said, "There are times I do stupid things, but it doesn't take a baseball bat between the eyes to make me realize that possibly, just possibly, farming isn't what I should get into in America."

Viki left Suceava on May 15, 1990. She took the train to Bucharest, where she boarded her plane to fly to Munich, Germany. There she changed planes and flew across the Atlantic Ocean to land at the John F. Kennedy Airport in New York City, where she was to change planes once more to end her journey at the airport in Dallas.

Plane boarding in Bucharest was no problem, but the hustle and bustle of the crowd entering the plane was nerve-wracking and aggravating. It was as if Viki had started out on the left foot, as they say in Romania: nothing seemed to go right. As soon as she took her seat, she began weeping and wiping tears, all the while trying to hide her crying from the other passengers. The flight attendants kept watch on her and tried different ways to pacify her, but their kindly efforts were futile. Finally, in deference to the passengers around her, Viki was moved to an empty seat in the first-class section.

Thanks to the move, she was able to get close attention. And with a fresh packet of facial tissues, she was able to relax a little. But being a natural-born doubter, Viki couldn't completely shut out all her troubling thoughts. *Have I done the right thing?* she asked herself. *Why am I putting myself and my family through all these heartbreaking moves when I'm not sure I know what I'm doing? Why am I following my heart instead of my head?*

Was I unhappy with Romania? No, Romania has been good to me and I love the country. Yes, there are things about it I don't like, but that would be true of any other country in the world. Why does Kornel believe I would be happier in America? Is there more freedom to do and say, as he believes? I'll believe it when I experience it.

Already I miss my girls so much, and I just left them.

With Becker's help, Kornel made all the arrangements for Viki to fly from New York to Dallas. But while Viki was en route to New York, a change in plans had to be made: she would have to layover in New York and catch another flight the next day.

Knowing Viki's itinerary, Shirley Padgursky, secretary of the church's refugee assistance group, had arranged with her counterpart in New York City to meet Viki at the airport and assist her in making her connection with the plane to Dallas. But since Viki was already in the air, there was no way to notify her; she would have to find out when she arrived in New York.

The flight from Munich arrived at the airport on time. As Viki disembarked, she was met, to her surprise, by a woman pushing a wheelchair the flight attendant had arranged before the plane landed. The woman led her to US Immigration, where she had to show her documents to a uniformed officer. After the documents were stamped, the woman shepherded Viki to the baggage area. She seemed happy to be helping Viki, but they could only communicate with gestures and smiles. When they had collected her luggage, the woman led Viki first to the customs counter, and then to the waiting area at the gate for the plane she planned to take to Dallas.

But the plane was not there. For some reason she could not understand, the flight had been cancelled. Viki was confused and about to burst out crying again. But she knew she was scheduled to go on to Dallas, and that someone from the church would meet her at the gate and see that she safely boarded the plane to Dallas. Where was that person?

She called Kornel to let him know that she had safely arrived and had gotten through the entry checks.

"Well, I finally made it to New York," she said. "The flights were fine, but I've been a poor traveler. Leaving the girls and home has made me very sad. I'm waiting for the person from the church to help me get on the plane to Dallas, but no one has shown up. And the sign says the flight has been cancelled."

"There's been a change in your itinerary," Kornel said. "You were booked to fly to Dallas at 5:00 p.m., but now you are scheduled to fly out tomorrow at 11:00 a.m. Someone from the church will meet with you and see that you get aboard that flight. So be patient until he or she gets there."

Viki waited and waited for that someone to show, but no one did. She tried to communicate with the attendant at the gate desk, but she found it almost impossible to do so, as she couldn't speak or understand English and the desk attendant didn't understand Romanian.

Viki called Kornel, and again he told her to be patient, saying that someone would soon appear and take care of her. No one came, and again she called Kornel. It was now 11:00 p.m. He told her to remain calm, saying that a representative of the church would soon arrive and help her to catch her flight.

"I've been in touch with the man," Kornel said, "and he promised he will see that you get to a nice hotel and get you aboard the flight to Dallas tomorrow. So calm down and be patient. I know this is not what you wanted, but here you are, and all you can do now is wait. I promise that you'll be well cared for."

As it neared midnight, the desk attendant told her Viki couldn't wait overnight in the airport. She explained how airport security was always looking for homeless people who tried to use the airport for sleeping and said that she did want them to treat her as a homeless person. She'd have to go a hotel.

Viki called Kornel again and turned the phone over to the attendant, who explained that her shift was over and that Viki could not spend the night in the airport. She would have to go to a hotel. Kornel explained that someone was coming who knew what to do. He was held up in a huge traffic jam, but he would soon be there to collect her."

The attendant consented to stay with Viki until the escort arrived, but she had to leave by midnight. Kornel thanked her for her consideration and her willingness to help Viki through this difficulty. After hanging up the handset, the attendant pointed to the dial on her wristwatch and said to Viki, "Midnight. I have to leave by 12:00 midnight. I will stay with you until then."

Viki felt better, even though she didn't understand what the attendant had said to her. The woman's pleasing smile and warm pats on her hand calmed her down and put a slight smile on her face.

Finally, at about 11:45 p.m., Jim Iones, the New York church's representative, approached Viki introduced himself and showed his credentials to both Viki and the attendant. He and the attendant then tried to explain to Viki that he had been asked to take her to a hotel for the night and then bring her back to the airport in the morning to catch a flight to Dallas.

Now Viki was faced with a dilemma: should she or shouldn't she go with him? Iones was a big black man. She had heard about many bad incidents in the United States about the black people. The prospect scared her.

Again, she called Kornel who urged her to go with Iones. While Viki was on the phone, Iones had conversed at length with the attendant. After Viki hung up, the attendant urged her to go with him.

So Viki did. However, she was extremely apprehensive all the way to the hotel. And because of the language barrier, there was no conversation between them. She cried all the way to the hotel.

After about a thirtyminute ride, they stopped at what appeared to be an apartment building in the courtyard of a church. Iones checked her in at the desk and then escorted her to her room. He handed her a piece of paper on which he had written, "I will return at 6:00 a.m. and take you to the airport to catch your plane." She could read the number and figured out what he meant. Still she was afraid, shaking, and completely overwhelmed by a day she would never forget.

Still wary of her benefactor Iones, Viki wouldn't let him place her baggage in the room; she did it herself. After he left, she doublelocked her door and pushed the dresser against it.

Finally, she was alone. She was tired and frustrated but thankful that she had arrived safely in the United States. She slept fitfully until she was awakened by a knock on the door. It was 6:00 a.m. Iones was back to help her.

He drove her to the airport, checked her in at the airline's desk, and waited with her until the flight to Dallas began boarding. By this time, Viki realized she had not treated Mr. Iones very nicely. In some way, she wanted to express her appreciation for all he had done for her. So she took him by the hand and, with a smile on her face, apologized in Romanian for her unpleasantness. Then she thanked him for all he had done for her. He didn't understand what she said, of course, but the change in her attitude and the big smile crossed the language barrier.

The plane, which took off on time, climbed skyward to reach its assigned flight altitude. Viki was seated in coach, in a middle seat between two businessmen. While they appeared to be working, they also tried to engage her in conversation, but gave up once she let it be known that English was not her first language. In addition, she was so shaken and frustrated that she wouldn't know what to do or say if she had been able to speak the language.

Soon she was crying again. It was obvious to her that the men were disturbed by her actions. They kept looking at her. She didn't understand their offers of help, and they couldn't understand what she was trying to communicate to them.

Finally, one of the men touched the attendant's call button and discussed their concerns with the flight attendant. Viki knew they were talking about her, but she couldn't stop crying. After being summoned a third time by the businessmen, the attendant beckoned with a finger for Viki to follow her. The attendant led her to the first-class section of the plane, and once again she was directed to an empty seat.

When she continued to cry, the other crew members took turns trying to calm her. Still she couldn't stop. The personal attention, a little food, and three glasses of red wine, however, worked miracles. As the alcohol took effect, Viki began to relax and calm down. She stopped crying and felt a little better. She looked around and saw that all the other passengers were either occupied in their work, reading, or sleeping. She began to relax even more before nodding off into a light slumber.

Eventually the wheels touched down on the runway in Dallas. The plane came to a halt at the concourse. Viki had reached her destination. She was happy that she had arrived safely, but she was still apprehensive about whether she was doing the right thing and if there would be more such unhappy days to contend with.

PART 6

The Family in the United States

CHAPTER 50

When Viki's plane arrived in Dallas, an anxious and eager Kornel met her at the gate. After squeezing and ravenously kissing her, he took her hand and led her to the correct baggage carousel. As they stood waiting for the luggage, Kornel again kissed her and whispered, "I've missed you so much. It's been such a long, long time."

"And I've missed you, too," Viki said. "Three years is a long time. But right now I'm tired and frustrated. I long for a good night's sleep. This trip has been a nightmare. I'm so glad that it is over."

After Kornel grabbed her baggage, they passed through the revolving door to the outside.

Viki immediately began fanning herself with the magazine she had carried from the plane. Even though she couldn't read it, she could enjoy the photos. "Wow, it's hot! Is it always this hot in Dallas? What's the temperature?"

"No, in the summer it gets a lot warmer and we have much more humidity. Right now it's ninety- three degrees Fahrenheit."

"What is that in Celsius?"

"That's about thirty-four degrees."

"It never gets this hot in Romania this time of the year."

"You'll get used to it, and also to the high humidity the summer months bring to Texas. You'll also experience many comfortable days as you acclimate to the area. But you will have to recover from the jet lag before you begin feeling like your old self. What I think you will appreciate more once you get acclimated to life in

America are the freedoms here. It may take a while, but eventually you'll be taking them for granted as I did when I realized I could come and go as I please, and say and do what I felt like, without the fear of informers and secret police breathing down my neck."

"Yes, I've heard a lot about that, but I'll believe it when I actually experience it."

Soon, the shuttle picked them up. After a comforting air-conditioned ride, they were dropped off at their apartment. Viki left the magazine on the shuttle seat.

"This is a nice apartment," Viki said as she scanned her surroundings. "How much does it cost us?"

"You get right to the point, don't you?" Kornel said.

"Please excuse me. I'm just so tired that I can hardly think," Viki said.

"You are excused. It will take a while to get over the jet lag. If you're like me, it'll take two or three weeks before you begin to feel comfortable. Now to answer your question: for the first three months, the church paid the rent. After that I signed a yearly lease at a cost of $450 a month. That probably sounds like a lot of money to you, but believe me, it isn't by American standards.

"Glen Becker, the owner of the building, is a meticulous and faithful member of the church and is totally dedicated to leading its program of finding persecuted immigrants from Eastern European countries and relocating them to Dallas. While helping immigrants get settled in America, he keeps his apartments rented and assists the church in building its membership."

"That's very interesting," Viki said, "but let's talk more about the apartment. Where's the furniture? All I see in the living room is a big television set, and in the bedroom, a mattress on the floor. Except for the folding table and chairs in the kitchen, there is nothing else in the house. I thought that by this time you would have found some comfortable furniture to relax on and from which to enjoy the television?"

"No, no," he said, "now that you're here, we'll go shopping together and buy what we need. We've got $1,500 in the bank, and with you also working we can add to that balance. I would have had more in the bank, but I had to pay $1,200 for that junky old Oldsmobile we have parked on the lot.

"Also, there are lots of yard sales every weekend where we can buy good, hardly used pieces of furniture and fixtures at low prices. And with your decorating skills, we should be able to get by with a lot less than that. I've been anxiously awaiting your arrival so you can furnish and decorate the apartment the way you want it."

"Do we have to go shopping tomorrow?" Viki asked.

"No, not tomorrow. We can shop on the weekend after you are rested and feel like driving around the city. We have lots of time. First, we must get you settled in and familiar with the ins and outs of Dallas."

"Will I be doing the same type of work as you, like changing beds, cleaning toilets, and sweeping floors? Don't forget, I'm completely ignorant of the English language."

"You'll soon learn the language as I did. Now, let's go eat something and get you back here to sleep. Rest won't come easy tonight, and tomorrow promises to be a long day."

They walked to the nearest restaurant and ordered a full meal of soup, salad, steak, french-fried potatoes, and dessert. Viki was starved, not having eaten much since leaving Suceava. She consumed all she had ordered.

As they ate, Kornel said, "Tomorrow you will meet the staff at Triple Branch Hotel. It is located near the Westeastin, where I work. The human relations people will take all your information and introduce you to the people with whom you'll be working. When I talked to them, they said they will hire you as soon as you are ready to work. I could have gotten you the same kind of job where I work, but in deference to your wishes, I contacted the Triple Branch."

"It isn't that I don't want to work with you," Viki said. "It's because I don't want to lean on you to help me with English. I can't learn as fast if I have to depend on you for everything. I've got to do it my way.

"I know nothing about cleaning rooms. I don't have a clue about what I'm supposed to do, and I don't want you interceding on my behalf. I repeat, and let me emphasize, I must do this my own way. While I appreciate all you are doing for me, I believe it is better we work in separate hotels, at least for the time being. I'll be happier that way."

"Well, if that is what you want, then I'm happy too."

"Good. Now let's go home," Viki said. "All I can think about is how much my weary body is yearning for that flat mattress spread across the floor and, ah … ah … how much more I've yearned for you. It's been such a long, long time, and I've missed you so very much." She reached across the table and touched his hand.

Kornel took her hands in his, looked directly into her eyes, and said, "I love you so very much. I've been looking forward to this moment for what seems like forever. I want you, now. I promise you, it won't take long."

They hurried back to their new home, set out their night clothing, stretched out on the mattress, and immediately were in each other's arms.

Kornel was right: it didn't take long at all.

After dressing for sleep, they again spread out on the mattress. Within a few minutes, both were sound asleep.

Morning came too soon. Still tired and suffering from a lack of restful sleep, Viki did not want to leave the warm mattress. But she did, soon readying herself to leave with Kornel and go to the Triple Branch Hotel.

Following a quick breakfast of cereal and fruit, they made their way downtown to the employee entrance, where Kornel dropped her off at the application desk. She was taken to the hotel's personnel office, where she completed all the paperwork and was introduced to Louise Kopinski, her supervisor.

Kopinski was a small, rather slim champagne blond with a few dark roots begging for treatment. Kopinski had emigrated from Poland and settled in Dallas in 1982, immediately taking employment with the Triple Branch Hotel. During her eight years, she had worked with and supervised many women and a few men who had immigrated from a variety of countries with different governments, cultures, and languages. Without exception, all came with the hope of finding opportunities to make more money than they ever could in their home countries.

Working closely with them, Kopinski had learned their cultures and a little of each of their languages, enough that she could teach them how to do the quality work demanded by hotel guests and company management. Her love for the United States was so great that she mastered enough of the English language and the United States' spirit of life to persuade her to attend night school and get her papers. Her husband had obtained his citizenship papers a year before. She was so impressed with the certificate and the moving ceremonies that went with it that she had vowed to get her own papers that year.

"You can start today if you like," Kopinski told Viki in fractured Romanian. "One of my girls called in sick and I'm short of help.

With thirty-nine rooms on this floor to get ready, it will take us all day to finish. I can surely use your help."

"I would like to work today," Viki said. "We need the money to live on and to cover the costs of bringing our two daughters from Romania."

After Kopinski introduced Viki to the others, she took her aside and gave her personal instructions on how the work was to be completed and how the equipment functioned. She described the supplies she needed, and showed her where they were stored and how they were to be arranged on her new maid's cart, which contained all her working tools. It was sometimes difficult for Viki to understand what her boss was saying, but Kopinski good-naturedly repeated herself until the instructions were clear.

At the end of the day, Kornel came by and drove Viki home. Near the apartment, they noticed, piled on the curb, a small variety of used furniture. Hand-painted FREE signs were taped to the offerings, inviting passersby to help themselves. In the middle of the pile was a dark blue velvet sofa that looked almost new. They quickly decided it would fit nicely in the living room.

As soon as they reached the apartment, Kornel called one of his friends. Once he arrived, the two of them carried the sofa from the curb and placed it in the living room directly in front of Kornel's pride and delight: his giant television set.

"Someday," Viki said, "I'll find a nice shiny wooden table on which to place the television set, and a couple of overstuffed chairs on which to relax and nap while watching the programs."

CHAPTER 51

After one month in the United States, the newness had worn off for Viki. While the aggravating effects of the jet lag had disappeared, she missed her daughters, family, and friends. The depression she had experienced on the flight was now intensified. *Will I ever get over this homesickness?* she kept asking herself. More and more she was beginning to sympathize with the homesickness her biological mother had suffered as a young girl when she was compelled to leave her family and journey to Vioresca to begin a new life in a strange place.

Times, of course, have changed, she thought. It took almost a week for the five siblings to complete that fiftyfive-mile trip by horse and cart, whereas my fiftysix-hundredmile journey from Romania to the United States took only a couple of days and was much more comfortable.

Thank goodness, she thought, that my girls are only a long distance telephone call away. I can talk to them and the rest of the family as often as I want. If it weren't for that, I don't know what I could do except pray and pray until they got here.

Being a dedicated and intelligent person, Viki didn't take too long before she understood all the nuances of her new job. She soon became one of the better housekeepers in her crew. From her previous work experience in Romania, she had learned that tasks had to be completed quickly and the work had to be of the best possible quality. She applied those same ethics to her job as a hotel maid.

After four months of working at the Triple Branch Hotel, Viki was approached by Kornel to quit the job and take similar employment at the Westeastin Hotel.

"I've been talking to Dorothy Strelco, Westeastin's human resources manager, about you," Kornel said, "and she wants you to come and work at the Westeastin. She says she likes what I tell her about you. She wants to meet you."

Both Strelco and her husband, Ed, nicknamed Sock, had served in World War II and had completed tours of duty at air force bases in Texas. They had immediately fallen in love with the state. After their discharges, they moved to Dallas and found work with the Westeastin Hotel. Dorothy started working in the housekeeping department, and Sock in the maintenance department. Eventually, both were promoted to supervisors, and then they became managers.

"Why should I leave my job to take the same job at the Westeastin for the same wages?" Viki asked. "I'm content at the Triple Branch, and I am good at what I'm doing. Why should I leave?"

"She says you are the kind of person they are looking for, someone who has the qualifications to move up in the company."

"I don't know about that," Viki said. "I can't see any advantage for me to change, unless they want to hire me now as a supervisor. Otherwise, I'm staying with Triple Branch."

"I'll tell her how you feel and let her decide what she wants to do."

That evening after dinner, Kornel said, "I talked to Strelco this morning and told her what you said. She said she would like to visit with you and explain how much they would like for you to come and work for them."

"Well, that's okay with me, but I'm not changing my position. I just can't see any advantage for me to make that kind of change. And that is final. She can come anytime she wants."

"I'll tell her tomorrow."

The next evening, Kornel said, "Strelco came by this morning and said she would like to come and talk to you Saturday morning at ten. Will that be convenient for you?"

"Yes, I'll be ready. I'll make some coffee and serve some of my poppy seed cookies. However, with my lack of English, I don't know how I will talk to her."

"She realizes you don't know English. She has worked many years with foreigners and knows how to communicate. If it will help, I'll be there also to act as interpreter."

On Saturday morning, promptly at ten, Strelco arrived carrying a large bouquet of radiant aromatic red roses in a colorful sculpted ceramic vase.

"Hello, my name is Dorothy Strelco. I'm the one who has been talking to your husband about you and your qualifications. We at Westeastin are pleased with Kornel and his dedication to his work. He tells me that you work harder than he does, which I find hard to believe. We would like to have you on our payroll so that when an opening for a supervisor comes up, as happens frequently, you would be in a position to be considered for the job. Now, however, the best we can offer you is to come on with us as a housekeeping maid."

"Well, it's like I told Kornel," Viki said. "I can't see any advantage in moving to what is essentially the same job I have now. I don't know, but I might be able to get the same kind of promotion here at Triple Branch. I'm sure they have openings from time to time. I don't want to make the move and have to go through the paperwork and getting used to working in a new environment with new people just to do the same work for the same pay. I'm glad to have met you. I thank you for thinking about me, but I'm just not interested in making that kind of move."

"I'm sorry to hear that. I wish you the best of luck with Triple Branch. I thank you for the coffee and especially those delicious cookies."

Two weeks later, Strelco returned to visit Viki, this time bearing gifts of colorful dishware and a tablecloth with place mats to match.

Viki refused to budge. "I really appreciate those lovely gifts, and I feel honored that you think so well of me," she said, "but as I said before, I won't give up my job at the Triple Branch to go to the Westeastin and serve in the same position. I'm pleased with what I have been able to achieve there. And I …"

Strelco interrupted her. "Would you join us if all you had to do was detail the bathrooms, only eight a day? You get a raise of fifteen cents an hour."

Viki had to make a quick decision since the offering had changed. Whereas as a maid at the Triple Branch, she had seventeen rooms to prepare each day, at the Westeastin she would have but eight bathrooms to detail—and she'd make more money. *What's to lose?* she asked herself.

"Yes, I could do that. I've never had to do detail work of that kind, but I'm sure I can learn it quickly. When would I start?"

"Tomorrow, if you can get away from Triple Branch that quickly. But I believe it would only be fair to give them at least a week's notice of your resignation."

Viki submitted her resignation on Monday and left the Triple Branch following the completion of Friday's shift. On the following Monday, she reported to work at the Westeastin, where she met with Susie Harah, personnel manager, who placed her on the payroll.

Harah then reviewed, with the aid of her computer, the nature of Viki's job and the quality standards she was expected to adhere to. While Viki didn't fully understand Harah's English, the images on the monitor were clear enough to enable her to inject an "okay" here and a nod there to indicate she understood what she was being told. After the interview, Harah introduced Viki to Mariana Rivera, her immediate supervisor.

"Why are you still moping around?" Kornel asked, unable to keep the strain out of his voice. He had observed Viki's actions and attitude more closely the last couple of weeks and was puzzled about what she was doing and saying. "Aren't you glad to be here in America? It's obvious to me you are upset and suffering from homesickness, as I was when I first went to Greece. It's a natural feeling one gets after the initial wonderment wears off and before one begins to appreciate where they are and what they are doing."

"You've been here longer, and you seem to prefer America to what you had in Romania," she countered. "Look at the kinds of jobs we have here. We didn't leave Romania to be maids in a hotel! We had good managerial positions on the sheep farm and honorable jobs working in the country's leading laboratory. The money here is much better than what we earned in Romania, but then the costs are much higher, too."

"I don't like doing maid's work either," Kornel said, "having to clean public bathrooms and guest rooms, but the work supports us financially. Yes, I want more, as you do, but we have to take it one job at a time until we get what we're looking for. And if we continue to work hard, it will come to us. You'll have to admit, though, that our lives and our living standards here are much better than what we experienced in Romania."

"Are you happier being away from your children and other members of your family?" Viki asked.

"Of course not, but these are the sorrows I thought we understood we would experience and accept when we made the decision to make the move."

"You're right, they are," Viki said as she began to loosen up. "I guess my biggest problem is the language. For me, English is difficult. I don't seem to be making any progress learning it."

"Well, my advice is, just study it. I haven't observed you making any strong effort to learn. You need to go to school and get some books to read and start practicing it more with those around you. Talking with your neighbor across the fence about the weather won't do it. You need to read more and watch more television. That's what has helped me. I found that as my English improved, my attitude brightened and I gained more confidence in myself.

"I'm convinced that everything will work to our benefit. I believe we are much more educated than most of the others around us, and that too will be helpful. You'll see once we get settled and know what we want to do with the rest of our lives."

"That's easy for you to say," Viki told him. "I still don't like English, and I hate the thought of having to take the time and expend the energy to learn it. I just want to be left alone to do my job. And I have to admit that there are many times I wish I was back in Romania with my daughters."

"Well, you're free to go back whenever you want. As for me, I'm here to stay. I like it, and I look forward to making us a better life in America. I realize that will take time, but we are still young and we have lots of good years ahead of us to achieve our goals, whatever they might be."

Viki and Kornel had just finished dinner and were sitting in the living room watching the evening news when the phone rang. Viki answered. When she realized it was Kornel's sister, Marina, she shouted for Kornel to pick up the extension in their bedroom.

After exchanging pleasantries, Marina got right to the reason for her call.

"Your daughters," she said, "are doing well staying with Kornel's parents. However, as you know, our parents are getting along in years. I would like to see them relieved of the duty of looking after your daughters. I know it will take you a long while to get settled in Dallas, so I thought perhaps you would let them remain here with us until you are ready to bring them over. What do you think?"

"Well, that is very generous of you," Viki said, "but we don't want to pass that burden on to you and your husband. You've got your own family to care for. Plus, now that we are in the United States, we are depending on you to care for your parents in Kornel's absence. He wishes he could help you, but being so far away, it's virtually impossible for him to do anything."

"Well, that's what we're thinking also," Marina said. "You and Kornel are struggling to get settled in the new country having to work two jobs and doing menial work making beds and cleaning toilets. We thought we could care for the girls until you are finally at the point where you feel you can bring them over there. Also, I'm thinking about Kornel's health problems, especially his back trouble. That's why we are willing to care for the girls, even if it's only for another school year."

"That is very generous of you, Marina. I appreciate your thoughts about our well-being and your offer to help us," Viki said. "But I'm thinking of the girls and how they'll have to adapt to this new country once they are here. I believe it is to their advantage if we get them here as soon as possible without interrupting their school attendance. I believe they can get a better education here than there. That's the big reason I'm working at these menial tasks, plus taking on any other work I can manage. But you might want to talk to Kornel and get his thoughts. He's on the bedroom extension."

"Kornel, I'm only trying to help you get settled there," Marina said. "I keep thinking about your health and back problems and the fact that you're working two jobs every day. I feel there should be some way for us to help you and Viki get settled. And helping with your daughters is one way my family could do it."

"It is very thoughtful and generous of you to make that offer," Kornel replied. "However, I must agree with Viki. I too believe it is imperative that we get the girls here as soon as possible to get them settled in school so they can adjust to the customs of living in America. The customs here are rather different from those we were familiar with back there, like study time, freedom of movement and transportation … Many of the students here have their own motor vehicles.

"And so many foreign languages are spoken here that getting used to those languages is a task in itself, especially the Spanish language. More than half of the population here speaks Spanis, or so it seems. It's to the girls' advantage to get here as quickly as possible. Mama and Papa will have only a few months to care for them. Then we can get them here and enrolled for the coming school year."

At this point in the conversation, Viki broke in and said, "Thank you, Marina, for calling and offering to help us with the girls. You've done me a big favor. Now I've got to get busy and make the arrangements to get them here. I would ask my father to help with that task, but with my mother's illness, he won't be able to help as had offered to do in the past."

"Well, there's no way we can help you move the girls there," Miranda said, "but if you have something else we can, do just give us a call."

"We'll do that," Viki said. Hanging up the phone, Viki thought that now she was in a predicament: she had to get help to get the girls to America as quickly as arrangements could be made.

That night, Viki found sleep hard to come by as she thought about the situation. Whom else could she trust to arrange for the two girls to come to the United States in time for school to start?

Then she remembered Corine Cosmescu, the friend she and Kornel had met on their tour of Prague, the person who had helped Kornel get his papers to get into Greece. *Why not call her and see what she can do?* Viki thought. *What with the changes in the Romanian government following the revolution, travel restrictions are completely different. I'll give her a call tomorrow and see what she can do for us.* With that possibility to explore, Viki dozed off and slept soundly through the remaining dark hours.

The next day, Viki placed a call to Cosmescu and was pleasantly surprised when she said she would take care of the arrangements to get the girls to Dallas in time for school.

With that, Viki took a big breath and exhaled a big sigh knowing that a big load had been removed from her shoulders. During the conversation, Viki told Corine about Kornel's sister wanting to care for the girls.

"That is certainly generous of your sisterinlaw, but I'm like you. I would take care of my own also. So don't fret it. My husband, Cosmin, and I will be pleased to help you get the girls to America. And coincidentally, it just so happens I have a nephew, Petru

Pavlenco, who is going to Dallas to study for his doctorate degree. I'm certain he will be more than happy to escort the girls." Viki was elated and couldn't wait to give Kornel the good news.

And sure enough, Corine and Cosmin made all the arrangements. Kornel sent them the funds needed to fly the girls from Bucharest to Dallas, plus any miscellaneous expenses they would incur. In addition, Viki offered Pavlenco a little gratuity for his trouble, but he refused the offer. "I'm going to Dallas anyway. It is my pleasure to help you with this pressing need. Perhaps someday I will need your help with my own pressing needs."

CHAPTER 52

As the plane rose from the runway and turned its nose toward the west, Christina and Anka, along with Petru, their escort, settled back and tried to get comfortable. They were flying to the United States. All that could be seen through the small windows was the bright blue sky above and the billowing white clouds below, creating a relaxing scene conducive to a long nap.

But Anka was uncomfortable. With white knuckles, she clutched the armrests and asked Petru, "We won't crash and fall into the ocean, will we? I heard there have been lots of crashes lately."

"Where did you hear that?" Petru said. "I don't remember seeing or hearing anything like that in the newspapers or on television."

"That's what my girlfriends were saying when I told them about going to America."

"Well, you shouldn't have believed them. They were only telling you that because they were envious of you going to America. Get those thoughts out of your mind. We will be all right, and hopefully we will arrive in Dallas on schedule. You have nothing to fear." Petru smiled as he patted Anka gently on the shoulder. "Just relax and think good thoughts about how wonderful it will to be with your parents again."

That pleasant approach and the big smile worked wonders. Anka relaxed her grip on the armrests and slowly slipped into a peaceful sleep.

Though Christina was acting like she had flown many times before, she was actually scared and apprehensive about the journey. She couldn't help but wonder what she would feel like when she was on the ground in the new country.

"I've heard so many nasty comments from my friends about how bad America is to its citizens," Christina said, "and how difficult it is to get acquainted with American teenagers because they are mean and intimidating. They don't like foreigners because they can't speak the language, and no one is willing to learn Romanian. They also say they will call you bad names and push you around because they are nothing but a bunch of, ah ..."

Petru quickly interrupted her. "Don't believe everything you hear. Most Americans are just like us. They want to get educated and get a job and get married and raise a family just like we do. You will find that most are friendly and willing to help you get settled and become familiar with their ways. Yes, their customs are different from ours, but they enjoy more freedom of movement and speech. And yes, some do use drugs, but no more than in Romania, maybe even not as many.

"You won't like America at first, but as you learn the language and become accustomed to the new ways, you will recover from your homesickness. You'll soon learn to like it more than you thought you would.

"It took me a long time, but now I like America better than Romania. I plan to get a work permit after I finish my education; I plan to become an American citizen. Someday, you'll get your citizenship papers, and then you'll enjoy all the benefits that citizenship has to offer. First, however, you must get your education. It will be up to you to determine how badly you want to progress in America. You'll be free to go as far as you want. Who knows, maybe you'll even become president, provided that the Constitution is changed to allow naturalized citizens to vie for the office."

"But we didn't want to leave Romania," Christina continued. "We have lots of friends and were happy there. I don't think I will like America."

"But you haven't tried it yet." Petru countered. "It will take you some time to get settled in, but you'll learn to like it, I promise, just as your mother is learning to like it now. I emphasize, don't believe all the appalling things you've heard about the country. Before you realize it, you'll like America more than you ever thought you would—perhaps even more than you like Romania."

It was late in the afternoon when Christina and Anka arrived in Dallas, met their parents at the baggage claim, gathered their luggage, and rode out of the airport in the ancient lumbering Oldsmobile.

Before returning to the apartment, Kornel and Viki drove the girls around Dallas and past the school where they would be enrolled. On the way, they stopped into a nice restaurant for some food. Not a fast-food place, it was a nice sitdown restaurant with white tablecloths and napkins, and a menu that featured many good entrees and desserts that Viki and Kornel had learned to enjoy since leaving Romania.

The girls were amazed at what they saw in Dallas: the theaters, large modern buildings, and heavy traffic with nothing but big cars and modern-looking buses and trucks. How Americans dressed, and the laughing and singing they often heard, was unlike anything they had ever experienced in Romania. But still they had reservations about living in the United States. Most of all, they missed their grandparents and old friends.

The girls occupied the second bedroom. Viki had furnished and decorated it for them, including comfortable furniture and fixtures for both studying and sleeping. To top it off, Viki had purchased and arranged, in the girls' clothes closet and dresser, enough new clothing and school supplies to last them a lifetime.

When Viki enrolled Christina in the fifth grade and Anka in the third, she discussed school policies and practices with the counselor. Communication was difficult, but she thought she understood what was being said—with one exception. She thought the counselor said the girls would have little to no homework to detract from their quality time at home. What's this *quality time*?

This information created a problem for Viki. With no homework, she asked herself, how was she going to keep the girls occupied until she or Kornel returned from work? They would be alone, and in the absence of homework, it was hard to tell what kind of problems they could get into. What was needed, she thought, were some kind of learning exercises to fill this time instead of watching television or reading magazines. *Is it possible I can make the girls do some kind of homework? I'll discuss it with Kornel.*

"I've got a problem," Viki said after dinner when she and Kornel had retired to the living room and the girls to their bedroom. "Students at this school have little or no homework. The counselor told me it was the school's practice not to assign homework, that the time normally allotted for homework was considered quality time and should be spent with the family."

"Why does that trouble you?"

"To begin with, I don't want the girls sitting around watching television until we get home. You know that television here is full of sex and drugs and everything else not conducive to studying and learning classroom subjects. I know there are ways to block television channels, but it's literally impossible to block all of them."

"I agree, but what else can we do?"

"I've been thinking about having them concentrate on learning English at home, in addition to what they are doing now. There should be some way we can do it. There must be learning tools available I don't know about."

"Why not go to one of the outlets the teachers use to get teachers' materials? Surely there are store personnel who can help you."

"That's a good idea. I'll do that tomorrow after work, so I might be a little late getting home."

The next day, Viki came home with plastic bags filled with English primers, flash cards, dictionaries, and other learning materials, along with complete instructions on how they should be used by the home teacher. So, not to waste any time, immediately after dinner Viki began the task of teaching the girls how to use the materials, mentioning the amount of time each afternoon they were to study until she and Kornel returned home from work.

While Viki was doing this, Kornel cleaned up the kitchen and washed the dishes.

Getting a college education was mandatory to Viki's way of thinking. Touching the back of the television to see if it was warm was her way of ensuring that the girls had been studying their lessons rather than watching the tube.

She was exceedingly focused on getting her daughters the best education possible, so much so that they began calling her their "communist mother" because of the threat that hung over their heads: "If you don't study hard and make all A's I will see that you receive your education under the communist system while living with your grandparents."

For several months, Christina was frustrated with being in the United States. She, like her mother, couldn't understand or speak English. She missed her friends, her grandparents, and the freedoms she had enjoyed the year she and Anka lived without their parents hovering over them. Now the girls found it a little strange living with their father. It had been about four years since they last had seen him. Christina barely remembered him; Anka, not at all.

Although Christina was an intelligent student and a good leader, she felt isolated, believing she wasn't being accepted by her peers. Being one of the brighter students in Romania, she believed her classmates looked up to her. In the United States, however, she thought the opposite. *I'm just another foreigner,* she thought. *I'm struggling with the language. I'm not trying hard enough to learn it.*

"I hate it here!" she told her parents one day. "I dislike the students in my class, and I detest America. It isn't anything like Romania. And now I'm beginning to hate you for bringing me here."

"Young lady," Kornel said, "you'd better learn to change your attitude about us and America, because I can very easily send you back to Romania to live with your grandparents. Aunt Marina would love to have you stay with her."

"You must give yourself more time," Viki said, "to get adjusted to this new life. Make up your mind that this is what you're going to have to live with for a few more months. Who knows, perhaps you'll like it better than you do now. Just give yourself more time. That's what I have had to do, and now I like America better than I ever thought I would. I miss my family too, but not the country."

After her daughters had been in school for a few months, Viki noticed that Anka was speaking a lot of Spanish when she came home. *That won't do,* she thought. *It's more important she learn to speak English.*

Viki was keenly aware that the Dallas schools were heavily populated with Spanish students, so it was only natural the girls were exposed to that language, particularly in the lower elementary grades.

Also, like Romanian, Spanish is a romance language, so it was easier for the girls to pick up Spanish than it was for them to learn English, which is a Germanic language. But Viki didn't like it. She insisted the girls concentrate on and become more proficient in English.

On October 14, 1991, Viki received a sad but not unexpected telephone call from her father. Sophia, her beloved mother, had succumbed to pneumonia, one of the ravages of Parkinson's disease.

"What can we do?" Viki asked Kornel after she had hung up. "I want very much to return for her services, but this is not a good time for us."

"I agree. We can't afford the costs to make the trip, and we don't want to lose the earnings from the lost time it would take us to make the journey."

"And," Viki added, "I just enrolled the girls in school and I don't want to interrupt their education for the length of time the trip would take."

"Also," Kornel said, "we don't have American passports. We would have to use our Romanian passports. I fear that I might be arrested and punished for illegally fleeing the country, particularly since there remains much confusion following the breakup of communism. No, there is just no way we can go."

Viki tried soothing her emotions with the thought that she had said her good-byes to her mother when she left Romania. Also, she knew her father would ensure that all the funeral arrangements would be carried out. It did, however, sadden her to think she would never see her mother again.

But life goes on, as it must, she thought. Now I've got my own family to care for. I must help them achieve whatever life dreams they set for themselves. That is, if they want my help.

CHAPTER 53

On Sunday, December 1, 1991, Viki's father finally arrived in Dallas to begin his long anticipated visit. He was almost eighty years old but looked physically and mentally healthy. He thought the United States was the most wonderful place in the world, but he didn't understand why Viki and Kornel hadn't decorated their entrance door as people did in Romania. He had several ideas about how it should be done, but they all fell on deaf ears.

"Americans do not decorate their front doors," Kornel said. "However, you will soon see how businesses and residences decorate their buildings, houses, yards, and even their golf carts with strings of bright sparkling lights to celebrate the holiday season. I promise, you'll be amazed."

And he was. He could not get over how much imagination and care the decorators put into the placement of their holiday lights and decorations. What really got his attention was the hustle and bustle of people shopping the malls and department stores making preparations for the holidays. And best of all, he enjoyed taking pictures of Christina and Anka sitting on the lap of Santa Claus telling him what gifts they wanted and how he should place them beneath the Christmas tree.

Harald was fascinated and comforted by how Viki and Kornel decorated their small apartment with a Christmas tree covered with many strings of multicolored lights, ornaments of many shapes and sizes, and strips of tinsel. But more than that, he was thoroughly amused at how they were able to package and stack around the tree the large number of gifts they pretended that Santa Claus had delivered. Especially, he wondered which ones were his.

"I deeply regret that Sophia couldn't be here to help us celebrate the birth of the Christ child," Harald said as he wiped his eyes. He was reminiscing of those days gone by and letting his voice flow with his heartfelt memories of the sad and anxious times he and his beloved Sophia had lived through.

He spoke softly. As tears filled his eyes once more, he said, "Sophia would have loved to see all of these Christmas festivities, and how much better you all have made your lives here in America. She so much enjoyed going to church this time of year. She missed you all so much when you left Romania to live here."

While Harald could not help but dream of the past, he realized he was living a new life now. While he missed the love of his heart, his family was growing and, from all appearances, doing quite well in this new land. Still, the future offered a lot more. The opportunities were there. The family gave the strong impression that they would take advantage of all they could and benefit from it.

But it took their first Christmas season to solidify the girls' love for the United States. It awed them, as it did their grandfather, to see firsthand how the Christmas season was celebrated in the United States with all the colorful, sparkling lights and the beautiful and extravagant decorations.

While shopping in one of the department stores, Christina saw a giant white and black panda that was almost as tall as she stood. She immediately fell in love with it and pleaded with her mother to let her take it home. Viki, however, in her smooth and persuasive style, talked her out of it, but it did not leave the clever mother's mind. She immediately added it to Christina's ever-growing Santa Claus list. She kept a list for Anka too.

Viki got her one wish from Santa and that was for a high-quality camera that would take exceptionally good pictures. Sure enough it was under the tree. She made good use of it, taking a myriad of photos of the colorful decorations and the smiling faces of those receiving the gifts they had asked Santa to deliver. But the best picture of all was one of Christina hugging the giant panda bear she wanted so much for Santa to bring.

Finally it was necessary to gather the wrapping paper to be used for wrapping next year's presents.

On New Year's Eve, the Neguras and Harald all stayed up late watching New Year celebrations around the world. Then, following a drink of sparkling grape juice, they silently made their New Year's resolutions for the New Year, 1992. Harald, however, had his favorite drink, tuica, the plum brandy condensed and bottled in Romania.

After two brandies, he raised his glass high in the air and shouted, "Here's to America, the most wonderful place in the world, and to my wonderful family, who are making the most of their new opportunities."

He had stayed two months, enough to give him a comfortable feeling for US culture, US attitudes, and the hard work Viki and her family had put forth to achieve their dreams. He admired Viki's and Kornel's loyalty to each other and to their girls, and all the efforts they had made in creating a comfortable life with modern fixtures and conveniences. More importantly, he was pleased with the way they had accepted their new life and the newly discovered freedoms that the United States offered.

Now he felt he could die happy, as he was proud of the part he had played in helping Viki reach out to snatch a few luscious pears in a life she never dreamed could happen.

As time passed, Christina became proficient in English, enough so that she was asked to participate in the annual spelling bee held among the schools in the state. In her first year, in fifth grade, she did not do well, but in her second year she was much improved. She would have taken first place had she not stumbled on the word *motorcycle*.

One early spring day, Anka came home from school with a small clear plastic envelope containing a white crumbly substance of some sort. She showed it to her mother and said, "Mama, look what I got at school today. I bought it for only fifty cents."

"Who did you get that from?" Viki asked, immediately suspecting it was one of the illicit drug dealers she had been hearing about who were selling drugs to unsuspecting students.

"I bought it from some older student. He said it would be good for me."

"Well, you may think it will be good for you, but I don't agree. Let me have it. Tomorrow I am going to take it to your teacher and talk to her about it. I think it is some kind of bad drug that will harm you. I don't want you spending your lunch money on stuff like this. Do you understand me?"

"Yes, Mama, I understand."

The next morning, after advising her boss she would be late reporting to work, Viki took Anka to school and visited with the teacher before the early class bell rang.

"Yesterday," Viki said, showing the plastic packet, "Anka brought this packet home and showed it to me. She said she bought it from some young man for fifty cents after he claimed it would be good for her. I believe it is some kind of drug. I want to bring it to your attention."

"I agree, it looks like drugs," Anka's teacher replied. "They are illegal on our campus. In spite of all our efforts, drugs remain our biggest problem on campus. There is little we can do about it except to keep trying to keep them out of the school. We have security people who are supposed to be on the lookout for this sort of thing, but their hands are tied. We find that it isn't our students who are the sellers, but outsiders who find their way onto the campus and search out the unwary student like Anka with the hope she will keep coming back to buy more of their drug. There is very little we can do except warn the parents and ask that they help us make their children understand the ill effects of bad drugs and tell them not to buy anything from strangers.

"I thank you very much for bringing it to my attention. I will see that the principal is made aware of the situation. I will also alert the proper authorities so they can search out the culprits and take care of the problem. We want to keep drugs off our campus."

That insistence didn't ease Viki's mind about drugs, but it did make her more attentive to what went on among young people in US schools. She became even more stringent about the activities of her daughters with their friends. She forbade them to accept sleepover invitations. She had heard from her fellow workers about what can occur at these events, as boys and girls attempted to get together during the night. And sleep wasn't uppermost in their minds.

When time permitted, Viki babysat young orphaned Romanian boys for her friend Ginny King. Ginny, a plumpish middle-aged member of the Orthodox Church sponsored orphaned boys and prepared them for adoption by American families. King could speak conversational Romanian, and Viki, by this time, could do the same in English, enough to carry on a relaxed conversation.

On one such occasion, Viki decided to bring up Anka's buying drugs on the school's campus and coming home in the afternoons speaking Spanish instead of English.

"Yes," King said, "I have experienced the same problems with most of my charges. The solution I've found is to change schools. In fact, just last week, I enrolled three of my older charges in a school in Carrolton that has an excellent graduation record and is reputed to be drug-free. The school offers an advanced curriculum that guides students all the way to college."

"I've been coming to the same conclusion also," Viki said. "While I don't like the agonies of having to change schools, I will do it if it benefits us and our children. I'll discuss it with Kornel. If he agrees, we will make the change."

That evening, she discussed it with Kornel. He agreed. "By all means," he said, "let's do it."

The next morning, Viki was excused to take the morning off work to arrange changing the girls' enrollment to the new school. The school district's counselor was in complete agreement and advised her to make the change. However, she cautioned, "You should understand that the entrance tests are not easy. If your daughters qualify for entry, you may come to consider it one of the best decisions you ever made to educate them."

While the entrance exams were indeed difficult, the girls easily passed the tests. They were immediately enrolled and placed in the special college preparation curriculum.

However, in making the change, a new problem arose: transportation. While Viki could drive them to school in the morning, there was no way that either Kornel or she could drive them home in the afternoon because of their work schedule. Also, she doubted the old Oldsmobile would hold up under the strain of having to be used that much. So, as a way of solving two problems at the same time, it was decided that the old Oldsmobile would be replaced and Viki would hire a taxi company to pick up the girls in the afternoon and drive them safely home.

On the following Saturday, the family drove to a Toyota agency and traded up to a more recent, little-driven, more attractive Toyota sedan.

After the girls had been in the new school for two months, it was obvious to Viki that they were not putting a lot of effort into their homework. They appeared to be just going through the motions of studying their assigned lessons.

"Why aren't you girls studying your lessons instead of reading magazines and watching television?"

"It's because we already know this stuff," Christina said. "Most of these lessons, we learned in Romania. This school is behind the schools we left in Romania."

"We'll see about that," Viki sternly replied. "I can't have you girls sitting around here after school doing no schoolwork. I'm going to talk to your teachers about it. Now, get busy and clean up this room."

"We will have to do something about this study situation," Viki said to Kornel that evening after the girls went to bed.

"The girls say they do not have much homework to study after they get home from school. They claim they know the subject matter already and that the Romanian schools are far ahead of the American schools. If indeed that is the case, then we should have the girls moved up in their grade levels. What do you think?"

"I agree. I, too, believe the schools here are behind those in Romania, but there is little we can do about that situation except, as you suggest, push the school to allow them to skip a grade."

"Well, since you can speak English better than I do," Viki said, "I believe you should go to the school and discuss it with the counselor. Then come to some conclusion about what the school can do to assign them more homework."

"Since you think it will produce good results, then tomorrow afternoon I will talk with the counselor, the principal, or whomever I can visit who can advance the girls to a higher class."

The next evening when Viki returned home after work, Kornel sat down with her and gave her a full report on how the meeting went with the school's counselor.

"This morning," he said, "I met with the school's counselor. After the counselor reviewed Christina's and Anka's records, after a lot of discussion, it was decided it would be appropriate to upgrade each of them by one year. They'll make the changes effective immediately."

CHAPTER 54

It took Viki a while to feel at ease living in the United States among people of many colors and races. Yet when she thought back to all the adverse and frustrating events she had to endure in Romania, she was glad she had made the move. She still found it difficult to keep her mind from slipping back to the times when she was forced to visit the Securitate and lie to them about Kornel leaving the country, the times when Kornel had been pressured by the secret police to inform on his father, and the and the times Kornel was passed over for promotions just because his father was a priest. And how much anxiety and fear Kornel must have had to endure because of the punishment his father received being sentenced to prison for a year, and his long train rides to Bucharest each month to be tortured by the Securitate for refusing to reveal the details of his personal conversations with members of his congregation.

Viki was beginning to understand the meaning of freedom in the United States. She had quickly learned that the US population was not infiltrated with government informers and that she did not have to be careful of what she did or said that might adversely reflect on the country's leaders or on what the government was or was not doing. She was beginning to relax and enjoy the freedom of saying and doing whatever she felt like without fear of being hounded by government agents.

Recognizing that Kornel was a hard worker who took great pride in doing a quality job, his manager offered him the position of maintenance supervisor.

At first, he thought the task was impossible because of his deficiency in English, but the personnel manager, Susie Harah, insisted he take it. "We know you are a hard worker, Kornel," she said, "and you take great pride in doing a quality job on whatever task you undertake. We realize you have difficulty with the English language, but that's the situation we have with whomever we put in that position. Our languages are so mixed that any person we put in a position of responsibility has that same difficulty. But it's easily overcome.

"Many times, even we are surprised at how easy our managers communicate despite language differences. So, don't let that hold you back. We want you to take the job. We will help you as much as we can. And, to help yourself, you might want to take some English courses. Many schools offer periodic weekly and evening classes."

"Okay," he said. "I'll take the job for a while until I can get a good grasp on my performance. Then we can go from there."

Shortly after Kornel's promotion, Viki was advised of her promotion by her supervisor, Marian Rivera. "Congratulations Viki," she said. "I've been moved to a new position in the front office, and you've been promoted to supervisor to replace me. You are highly qualified for the task. We believe you can become a good supervisor."

Not understanding everything Marian said, Viki hesitatingly responded by saying, "Okay," as Kornel had once suggested she try. He told her there would be times when she wouldn't understand everything being said, but oftentimes, she could get by just nodding her head or saying "yes" or "okay."

"Management," Rivera continued, "is convinced you are an excellent worker and very detailed in the attention you give to every task you undertake. Your bathrooms are always sparkling clean and neatly arranged showing originality and thoughtfulness. You have passed every bathroom inspection with the highest number of points. Do you understand?"

Again, not fully understanding what she had heard, Viki answered with a weak, "Yes."

"Tomorrow, I'll take you to the personnel office and complete all the paperwork, see that you receive your new uniform and name badge, and review the supervisor's handbook with you. I apologize for not having a handbook written in Romanian, but we are limited in the number of languages in which our handbooks are written. However, I am in a position to strongly suggest that you take an English course in the community college. The company will reimburse you for all your costs. Will that be all right with you?"

Viki paused for a second and then softly said, "Yes, ah, okay."

"What are you so sad about?" Kornel asked as they were riding home from work. "I thought you would be shouting for joy now that you are a supervisor."

"What do you mean, I'm a supervisor?"

"Didn't you have a discussion with Rivera this afternoon?"

"Yes."

"Didn't she tell you about your promotion to supervisor?"

"She told me a lot of things, but I didn't understand most of what she was saying. I thought she was telling me I didn't do good work and that I may be let go. Are you sure she was promoting me?"

"Absolutely. You are replacing her starting Monday. She got promoted. She insisted that you replace her, and management agreed with her. You are now Supervisor Viki, making more money than you ever have before. We must celebrate. We'll take the girls and go to a nice sitdown restaurant with white tablecloths, good champagne, and a waiter with a white cloth napkin spread over his arm anxiously waiting to serve us. What do you think of that?"

"Are you sure about me being a supervisor?" Viki asked.

"Yes, you are a supervisor," Kornel replied.

"I can't believe it. But if I am, then I agree. Let's go someplace nice and have a good time. But I don't want to be too extravagant. Let's just go to our favorite pizza place and have some pizza and maybe a small glass of wine. Or, if you want, we could have a small glass of cold beer. What do you think of that?"

"Whatever you say, madam. You're the boss."

Viki had eight girls under her supervision. While she continued to have difficulty with her English, she was able to communicate by drawing pictures and demonstrating how the work was to be done.

She was not without her problem employees, however. What should I do with Juanita Spardo? she asked herself. She continues to reuse sheets and pillowcases when they should be changed. I'm inclined to fire her.

She discussed the problem with her supervisor, who was sympathetic, saying, "You have the authority to fire her. I urge you to do so. But have you discussed your concerns with her and assured yourself that she understands the consequences of her actions? If you haven't, then I urge you to do so. And if you do, I emphasize that you keep detailed records of your conversations.

You never know when you might need them. For example, she could decide to appeal the decision."

Viki randomly inspected the work of each employee to ensure that the quality rules were being followed exactly as prescribed by the company and as they had been taught in the training courses. Had the sheets been changed? Were clean towels placed neatly on the proper rods? Did the drinking glasses pass visual bright-light inspections? Was the bathtub scrubbed down from top to bottom to remove water and soap spots so as to produce that smooth, clean feel to the touch? Were the floor coverings completely swept, or had only the walkways been done?

Viki's checklist itemized each task to withstand the close scrutiny of inspections by the hotel's management and by organizations that inspected hotels and motels and awarded star ratings.

In late September, Viki had no choice but to discharge Juanita Spardo. For the third time, she had failed to change the sheets in one of her assigned rooms.

A very likable person, Spardo was one of Viki's better-performing employees and could be depended upon to do a good job except when she was rushed to finish her daily quota on time. She'd take shortcuts by reusing the bedding instead of replacing it with clean bedclothes. Twice she had been warned about the failures, and twice she said she would not let it happen it again. After the second event, Viki had told her, "If it happens again, I will have to fire you. Do you understand?"

"Yes, I understand, but I think that is being a little harsh, don't you? After all, I work hard and my work quality is generally very good. Why should I be fired because I reused bedding that I know I should have replaced?"

"Juanita, there are eight of you in our unit, and management considers us one of the best in the building. Supposing, however, I let every one of you do as you please and reuse dirty linen. What would management say, especially after getting a load of complaints and rental losses because of dirty beds? If that was the case, then we'd all lose our jobs. You may think I'm being unfair, but I'm held responsible for the quality of work coming out of our unit. Again I say, if you do something irresponsible like reuse the bedding again, you will be fired. Now, come with me and I will show you what you did. And then I'll review with you again what you should have done."

With Juanita looking on, Viki exposed the bedding. It obviously had been slept on given the wrinkles of the sheet and pillow coverings. There was little doubt: the top sheet and pillowcases had not been changed.

"What do you have to say?" Viki asked.

"Yes, you are right. I didn't change the bedding. I was running late because of the late vacancies. I didn't want to work overtime, so I made the decision to reuse the items. They looked clean enough to me to reuse, so that's what I did. I'm sorry. I won't let it happen again."

"That's what you told me the last two times it happened. I'm at the point where I can't trust you anymore. As I told you before, if it happened again, I would have to let you go. I'm sorry I have to do it, but you no longer have a job here at the hotel. You can pick up your check tomorrow afternoon."

With that, Viki turned on her heel and left the room. She made her way to the personnel office with tears flowing down her cheeks.

One week after Viki fired Spardo, she was asked to bring her back. It was rather gloomy outside, and Viki was having one of her "What am I doing here?" days. It seemed everything she touched turned sour. *What more can happen this day?* she thought. *I'll be happy to get home and relax a little.* But it was not to be. Adding to her growing pile of disappointments, she was approached by Rivera with a request.

"I've been thinking about Spardo lately and wondering if you would be amenable to bringing her back to the job. She was one of our best workers. Her fellow workers liked her and enjoyed working with her, and they all feel that she has learned her lesson. Also, she is a single mom with three young children to feed and clothe and is having problems finding another job."

Viki's response was quick and loud. "Absolutely not. I have my other employees to care for, and I don't want to confuse them with a mind change. They are doing good-quality work. I want them to continue that way."

"But you have to admit," Rivera said, "Spardo is a good steady worker and we need her. It's difficult to find good maids. Plus Spardo is ready to come back. She says she has learned her lesson and feels she has been punished enough. Will you bring her back?"

"My answer is still the same. No, I will not do it! And, if you take it upon yourself to bring her back, then you will have to find someone to replace me. I can't work under those conditions."

"I understand your position, Viki, and I support you, but in this case, I believe we need to be more tolerant and give her another chance. Why don't you discuss it with your husband and let me know your answer in the morning."

"Yes, I can do that. I'll let you know in the morning."

The next morning, Viki met with Rivera and told her that after listening to what Kornel had to say, she decided change her mind and rehire Spardo, but with the understanding that she'd be penalized two weeks' wages and warned that if ever again she failed to do her work as prescribed and lied about it, she would immediately be fired and become ineligible to collect unemployment compensation.

Early in the morning of May 15, 1993, the telephone rang. Kornel answered.

"Kornel, this is Kristopher Cristescu. I have sad news for Viki and, of course, you. I'm the next-door neighbor to Harald Antonescu, Viki's father. I have the sad task of reporting that he died during the night."

"Hold on, Cristescu, until I can get Viki on the other phone," Kornel said.

Kornel called for Viki to pick up the extension phone. After she said hello, Cristescu said, "Viki, I have bad news for you. Your father died last night."

"Oh my God!" she cried. "How did it happen?"

"I don't know, but it must have happened while he was sleeping. When he didn't answer his telephone this morning, I knew he was having a problem, so I broke through the gate, rushed into the house, and found him in his bed looking as though he had slept through a pleasant dream. The medics who picked up the body said it looked like it was his heart. Is there anything I can do?"

"Nothing I can think of, but I appreciate you calling me. How did you know to call me?"

"Soon after your mother died, year before last, your father gave me your telephone number to call should anything happen to him. I'm so very sorry that I had to bring you this dreadful news."

"Well, I appreciate very much that you called. Kornel and I will have to get our thoughts together and do what we must do. I'll try to keep you informed of our plans. Let me have your number, please."

The trip to Suceava was long but uneventful. The memorial services were long but memorable. Viki and Kornel had a day to visit with family members and discuss their experiences in the United States, expressing their likes and dislikes. Needless to say, their difficulties in learning English topped a long list.

They returned to Dallas on Friday, May 21, which gave them a weekend to rest up and get ready to return to their work and school routines on the following Monday.

CHAPTER 55

"You know, Viki," Kornel said, breaking the silence in the living room one Sunday evening, "I haven't really decided what I want to do with the rest of my working life. I know I don't want to work in the hotel business forever. I keep rereading the employment ads and seeing the benefits of the nursing profession. The field is wide open. Apparently nurses are scarce in all medical areas and the salaries are good. What do you think? Should I become a nurse?"

"Well, if you feel strongly enough about it to spend another four or five years in school," Viki said, "then I say go for it."

"I believe I will," Kornel said with an enthusiasm that Viki hadn't witnessed in a long time. "My education in chemistry, biology, and animal husbandry, plus what I learned working on the university farms and the sheep farms we managed, makes me realize there aren't so many differences in caring for people. And it will only take two years at community college to become a nursing assistant. I could work in a hospital or nursing home and earn about the same salary I'm now earning in the hotel. I could go to school every day and then work in nursing on the weekend."

"If you want to go that way," Viki said, "then I will continue with my job. Also, I'll take care of the girls to relieve you of any of that burden. So, if that is what you want to do, then do it. But remember, we still have to live. You'll have to keep your current job, too. We can't afford for you to quit your job while you attend classes and do home study. Do you think you can manage that?"

"Yes, I do," Kornel said. "I'll juggle my schedule and make it work somehow. If I have to, I'll work as a nurse at night and take my nursing classes during the day."

That September, Kornel enrolled in the local community college, with the goal of earning his certified nursing assistant (CNA) certificate.

After living in the United States for five years, Kornel finally became a citizen. He took evening classes to learn English and studied government manuals on how to become a citizen. He answered all the questions put before him and then proudly stood with his large class at the graduation ceremony to pledge his allegiance to the United States.

Viki looked on, smiled, and applauded during the ceremony and the presentation of the certificates while, at the same time, dreading the thought of what she would have to do to earn her own certificate.

"Now it's your turn to do it," Kornel told her after they returned home. "You've seen me get my papers; now it's up to you to get yours."

"But you made it look so easy. You know I have difficulties trying to learn English. I can't even read the instructions on the application papers. How do you expect me to pass all the exams?"

"You're not giving yourself much credit for what English you already know. Even your daughters think you know the language. They've heard you talking with your neighbors."

"That's only over-the-fence English, the same I use when working with my employees. It isn't enough to answer all those test questions. I'd have to study very carefully and attend many night classes to do it. And I have the girls to care for. When will I have the time to go to school?"

Viki was scared. This was the first time in her life she let anxiety overtake her initiative to take action. She never before had let any obstacle block her way to achieving her objectives. She thought of the occasions when she was forced to physically put up her fists and fight her opponents to protect herself and her animals. *There were no hesitancies then to make up my mind,* she thought, *so why am I being so stubborn now about doing what I realize I must do? I must get those papers!*

"You'll find the time," Kornel continued. "I'll help you all I can. I'll make it a point to keep the children while you attend the classes. It's surprising how much you can learn in a short while."

Finally, after much thought, Viki followed Kornel's advice and enrolled in the first night classes available to her.

With his lawyer's help, Kornel applied for citizenship papers for the girls. It was not a difficult process, as Kornel was now a naturalized citizen of the United States and the girls were under eighteen years of age. All he had to do was deliver their applications to the proper government office.

When he did, he was told to return in a week when the papers would be ready. A week later, he went back to pick up the papers, but the office had only the papers for Anka.

"Where are the papers for my other daughter, Christina?"

"Apparently," the clerk said, "we didn't get an application for her. If we had, we would have prepared papers for her."

"But I know I gave you applications for both of my children at the same time," Kornel said. "I don't understand what you are telling me."

"What is it you don't understand? Without an application, we can't process the papers for the person you name. I suggest you have another application prepared and bring it in. Yes, we have records of her entry into the country, but we don't have an application for her citizenship papers."

The family was infuriated. What had happened? They knew all the filings had been completed, so what could possibly have gone wrong? They kept blaming the agency, and the agency continued to report that papers were never filed. Finally, Kornel went to their lawyer and told him what had happened.

"Don't fret it," he told Kornel. I'll make another copy, personally take it to the agency, and have them make further searches of your daughters' files to see if the original has been misfiled. Go home and relax. I'll let you know what I find."

A few days later, the lawyer called Kornel and advised him that the passport office had indeed made an error; they had misfiled the forms. That same day, after the office apologized for their negligence, Christina received her certificate of naturalization.

Big sighs of relief echoed throughout the house, and telephone calls were made to family members in Romania extolling the achievement. All in the family except one were US citizens, and Viki vowed to become a citizen by next year.

The mere fact that the girls were now American called for a big dinner in a nice restaurant, where gifts were given to the girls and a good time was had by all.

In early June of 1994, Viki got a telephone call from Krissy Popovici, her good friend from Vioresca and her days at the university. Krissy and her husband, Vasy, had emigrated from Romania a few months after graduation and had settled in the West Valley near Phoenix. After reestablishing contact, the two women chatted frequently about current events and the progress each family was making in the United States. Krissy seemed very familiar with the area and with the frustration of having to select suitable schools for their children.

"How are you doing now, Viki?" Krissy asked. "Are you satisfied you made the right decision about coming to America?"

"Yes and no," Viki said. "There are things that still frustrate me. I'm not so happy about the schools here. Perhaps I liked the Romanian education system better. I don't like the school the girls now attend, and I'm at a loss how to find others that may be more satisfactory."

"What's the big problem?"

"The school they are attending here is too lenient and liberal. Both girls are still ahead of their peers. I might be dreaming, but I believe the curriculum in the Romanian schools far exceeds that which I'm finding here in the American schools. But what do I know?"

"I'll look around," Krissy said, "and determine what might be available in this area. Maybe you just need to get away from Dallas."

"There is something else," Viki continued. "We both have to find new jobs and easy access to community colleges. Kornel wants to get his nursing degree. We are still working at the Westeastin Hotel, but as Kornel says, 'We don't want to spend the rest of our years working for someone else.' He wants to develop our own business, one we can successfully manage and make profitable— something that was never possible in Romania. What are the opportunities in your area?"

"I understand what you are doing, and I agree that the girls should get the best possible education, even if that means a sacrifice. I'll check out the schools here and let you know what I find. Then you can decide what you want to do. Also, there are lots of work openings here in the Valley. With the knowledge and skills you two have, you won't have any problems getting decent jobs."

"The girls come first," Viki said. "That is the main reason I came to America. I will appreciate whatever you can do to help us."

A few days later, Krissy called back and reported, "I've got a couple of leads that sound interesting. First, the school: Howling Storms, a remarkable elementary school in Scottsdale, has a good reputation. It offers what appears to be a good challenging curriculum and is highly rated. Second, the job climate here is good with many positions available. One that I would recommend is the Workingman Clothing Company. It's an old, old company that has been in business since the 1920s marketing Western workmen's clothing. Today, it manufactures mostly sporting goods for men and women. It operates in Phoenix employing tailors, seamstresses, and machine operators. With your abilities, you shouldn't have any problem getting a job with them. It is a strong business, and as I understand, they compensate their employees well.

"If this one is not to your liking, there are plenty of others you can choose from. You and Kornel shouldn't overlook group homes. There are lots of them in the Valley. Most are owned and operated by Romanians. They pay well and yield a good return on their investment. But it's demanding work. You must expect to operate 24/7 as the job requires. Because of the hours and the nature of the work, it's almost impossible to keep good people for any length of time. I guess that's one reason why so many Romanians get into the business. They aren't afraid of hard work and long hours. And remember, if all else fails, you can always get work at the local hotels."

"What about the community college?" Viki asked. "Is it easy to get to, and does it have a good reputation and graduation rate?"

"Yes, it is considered one of the best in the state."

"It all sounds good to me," Viki said. "I'll discuss it with Kornel tonight. Thank you. You've always been so helpful."

"Oh, something else before I hang up," Krissy said. "Tell Kornel to look into working at the Triple Palm Nursing Home. They are always looking for nursing help, and I understand they pay well."

"Thank you," Viki said. "I'll let him know. He can check it out."

"Well, I wish you nothing but good luck. Let's keep in touch."

CHAPTER 56

Early in July, Kornel flew to Scottsdale and immediately rented an apartment near Howling Storm, the school Krissy had recommended. The next day, he visited the Triple Palm Nursing Home hoping that it had an opening. It did, and it offered the wages and working environment Krissy had described.

After he had taken the tour of the home, he submitted his application to work as a nurse's assistant. To his astonishment, it was immediately accepted, with the provision he start work on the following Friday. *Apparently, nursing homes are as desperate for nursing assistants as I am for the work,* he thought.

The next day, Kornel took public transportation to the local community college to get information about enrolling in the school's next session. He gathered a fistful of brochures describing the school and the curriculum it offered. He was deeply impressed with what the school had to offer and decided he would enroll in the winter session to complete the second-year courses that would enable him to get his CNA certificate. *Then,* he thought, *I can continue my education and training to eventually become an RN, a licensed registered nurse.*

Getting his RN degree had become his number one goal despite the strain it would place on him and the rest of the family to earn the degree. *Hopefully,* he thought, *I can accomplish that goal in only two or three years. With that,* he thought, *the family and I can live a lot easier with the increased compensation I will earn as a full-fledged nurse.*

That evening, he and Viki had an hour-long telephone discussion about the move. As he told her about his discoveries and his ideas for the future, he could tell that his excitement about work and school was passing on to her. By the end of the call, she was completely on board.

Since the Scottsdale apartment Kornel had rented was unfurnished, he decided to lease just basic furniture until Viki and the girls arrived. To minimize costs, he rented a floor mattress with bedding, a card table with one folding chair, and a large television set. Because he loved watching television, he wanted the largest television set with the clearest picture he could afford.

As agreed upon, Kornel reported to work on Friday. He had signed on to work thirty-six hours total each week: a twelve-hour shift on Friday, Saturday, and Sunday each week, beginning at seven o'clock in the evening and ending at seven o'clock the next morning.

He was responsible for the care of thirty-three ailing and demanding patients. The work mostly consisted of menial tasks such as helping patients to and from the bathroom, or calming irritated patients awaiting responses to their call buttons, demanding fresh water or a bedpan, or to be moved into a more comfortable position. Then there was the frequent necessity of changing patients' clothing and bedding because they'd had nocturnal accidents.

But that's what nursing assistants were hired to do: free up the productive time of the nurses so they could maintain patients' charts and records, administer medications as scheduled, and most of all, accommodate the demands of the doctors.

Kornel had his hands full with his load of patients. His workload was much more than any conscientious nursing student could effectively manage.

On the first of August, Viki and the girls flew to Phoenix and shuttled to the Scottsdale apartment. Kornel had already flown back to Dallas and rented a moving van. With the help of friends, he loaded the truck and then drove it to Scottsdale. Viki, the girls, and a couple of new Scottsdale neighbors unloaded the truck and put its contents in place. Kornel then returned the truck to the nearest rental center.

A week later, Viki visited the Howling Storm School and enrolled the girls. The campus was spread across several acres of nice level land. From all reports, the school produced outstanding students, most of whom moved on to college.

On August 15, Viki submitted her application for employment at the Workingman Clothing Company. Much to her surprise, it was immediately accepted by the personnel office. She was told to report to work the following week.

She was assigned a sewing machine in the workshop and given the task of sewing zippers into men's trousers. It was a good job that paid well. Viki was pleased, and it showed when she told Kornel and the girls all about it that first evening. When the girls pronounced that their communist mother to be the world's fastest zipper sewer of men's trousers, they all laughed.

It wasn't long before Viki was the best producer in the shop.

When school started for the girls, they quickly settled into their new environment and made new friends. It wasn't long before they began to get invitations to attend special events and, to Viki's dismay, were invited to sleepovers at others' houses. It was obvious the girls were outclassed by the richness of the locals in their dress and in the automobiles many owned.

Shortly after the girls started their school, Kornel enrolled in the local community college. While it required two years to become a CNA, it was necessary to devote another two or three years of study to become a registered nurse. Schooling was costly, as was living, making it necessary that he continue to work while attending classes.

On school days, it took a lot of effort for him to leave work at 7:00 a.m. in Scottsdale, drive several miles to the community college, shave and wash up at a nearby automotive service station, change clothes, and be in class by 9:00 a.m. Many of his fellow students thought he was homeless. After he explained his goals, they were amazed at his stamina and drive.

His schedules were so tight that he had little time for anything but work and school. After he finished classes and got home, he only had time to get a few hours' sleep, get up, and go at it again. But it was worth it.

After working only three months at the Triple Palms Nursing Home, Kornel injured his back.

"What are you doing home at this hour of the day?" Viki asked when she opened the door and found Kornel stretched out flat on the living room floor. "Did you hurt yourself?"

"I hurt my back this morning trying to get a large heavy man to the bathroom. It's the same disc I ruptured in Greece lifting and carrying those heavy stones. The patient was too much for me to handle; I should have known better."

"Couldn't you get help?"

"I tried, but there was none available. I thought I could do it myself, but as you can see, I couldn't."

"Well, you're not in Greece anymore, so let's get you to the emergency room and see what they can advise us to do. A back injury is too important to ignore."

Viki drove him to the emergency room, where his back was x-rayed. The attending doctor studied the x-rays and surmised there was nothing further Kornel needed to do. "Just go home and take it easy," he said. "Don't do anything that will make it worse. Allow about six weeks for it to recover, and then you may go back to work. But don't do any more heavy lifting."

"How about attending classes?"

"Wait a week. Then if you feel like it, attend your classes. Just take it easy."

At the end of the girls' first school year, Viki decided she was not satisfied with the way the place was run and decided to call Krissy.

"Here I am calling again, and again it's about changing schools," she said. "We're not happy with the school the girls are attending. I want to find one that is stricter and more like the schools in Romania, where we never had to worry about drugs, or sleepovers, or lack of homework. Schools in Romania offered a curriculum similar to what the International Baccalaureate program emphasizes."

"I somehow get the impression you are not happy with the schools in your area," Krissy said with a laugh. "What's not to like?"

"It seems to me the schools are more interested in the students having fun rather than studying. There are too many sleepovers, which I don't allow. I've heard too many ugly stories about what goes on at those events, with boys breaking into the houses or the girls sneaking out to meet the boys. It seems to me there's very little adult supervision. Also, the kids here have way too much money and too many fancy automobiles. Golly, some of those cars are much newer then the one we own. My girls envy their classmates and keep begging us to trade up to a more up-to-date model, but we can't afford it. And the work and school schedules we have to follow don't give us much time to stay at home to keep them busy. I miss the strictness of the Romanian schools where we had to wear uniforms with identity patches. Students there didn't have the luxury of leaving the campus whenever they wanted. They had to stay in their rooms and study."

"It sounds to me like you wish you were back in Romania?"

"I used to think I preferred being back in Romania, but not now. Romania is behind me. Now all Kornel and I want to do is educate our daughters, take home a good living for ourselves, and retire to enjoy peace and harmony with no financial worries. We believe we now have the freedom to choose what we want and the flexibility to do it how we desire. Now we are Americans. It has taken me a long time to make this adjustment and then to admit it, but now I feel more contented and free to do what I want, and what I want now is to find the best schools for the girls. I hate to keep bothering you like this, but again I come begging for recommendations."

"It just so happens," Krissy said, "I do know of a high school here in Phoenix that uses the IB program, but there are many who do not believe in it because it's too controversial. Others don't like it because it's too rigorous and difficult for the average student. Some believe it leans too much toward worldly affairs and less toward the business world's needs for highly educated and trained employees. It's the West Phoenix High School. It has a good reputation, but entry tests are not easy to pass. Oh, incidentally, there is also a West Phoenix Middle School that Anka can attend."

"That's exactly what I'm looking for. Thank you, Krissy. I can always depend on you. I'll get in touch with the schools and go from there. It'll be wonderful when we can finally settle down and live in a place we can call our own and not be concerned about having to move so often. Thanks again. It will be good to see you again, which will happen as soon as we decide to leave Scottsdale."

On June 1, 1995, Kornel and Viki purchased their first home. It was in Phoenix, near the schools Krissy had recommended. Built in 1955 as a model, the home cost them almost $100,000, including the furniture and fixtures that decorated the house and surrounding grounds. It offered two bedrooms, two bathrooms, and a huge open great room consisting of a living area, dining area, and open kitchen. Finally, after living six years in scant rental housing, they owned their dream home.

That fall, the girls were enrolled in their new schools, Christina as a sophomore and Anka as an eighth grader.

CHAPTER 57

The United States offered lots of opportunities for entrepreneurs to invest in, own, and operate their own businesses. Viki was determined to do all three. With her accounting knowledge and financial skills, she believed that she and Kornel could develop their own business, something virtually impossible to do in Romania.

First, however, the reluctant Viki would have to finally get her citizenship papers and Kornel his RN license, while at the same time continuing their jobs to maintain their income and lifestyle.

"But I don't know enough English to take the tests," Viki protested one evening when the family was insisting she get her papers. "There are many other things I want to complete before I can think about getting my citizenship papers."

This was the girls' chance to get back at their mother.

"You'll do it now and let those other things fall into place," Christina said. "We insist you enroll in the next class and stay with it until you become a citizen. There's no way we can threaten to send you back to Romania to get it done, as you did to us about studying, but we promise you that we will continue to hassle you until you do it. We know that once you have completed the course and passed the final test, you'll be much more relieved and satisfied. Then, after you get it done, we'll call ourselves Americans and have a big celebration."

Viki was moved by and grateful for their encouragement, so much so that she enrolled in an evening class at the community college. She found the courses challenging, but she did well, getting good grades. The English class was the most difficult, but by studying hard, she made an A on her final test. She received her citizenship papers on July 4, 1996. She felt as good about her citizenship papers as she had about the university diploma she received in Romania. And she was very comfortable with the others in her graduating class, laughing with them and shaking their hands.

"Let's celebrate," Kornel said. "Let's all go out to the finest family restaurant we can find and enjoy this wonderful occasion."

The girls waved their arms in the air and broke into one of their favorite Romanian dances.

With huge tears welling up in her eyes, Viki could not speak. She could only stretch out her arms, hug the girls and Kornel, and thank them for pushing her to get the deed done.

Viki stayed with her job and remained one of the best at sewing zippers onto men's trousers, causing her to attract the attention of management. Viki loved being appreciated, but she was not satisfied with her education, so she enrolled in an Accounting 101 course at the community college, where she used the computer and learned its sophisticated business software.

When the company became aware of what Viki had done to improve her understanding of accounting, she was immediately moved from the sewing department into the business office, with an appropriate increase in salary. She was happier and worked just as hard doing that job as she had on the sewing machine.

It wasn't long before the less experienced entry clerks were coming to her with their questions about account classifications and coming away with answers that completely awed them. Once Viki had established her niche in the bookkeeping department, she was promoted to supervisor of eight entry posters, which meant a higher salary. As time passed and her unit's production was good, she was offered more responsibility, preparing and explaining financial results to company management.

Christina had a young bearded handsome mathematics teacher named Mr. Black. He was a good teacher, but he came from the laissez-faire school of learning: If you don't want to read that book this week, then next week will be okay. If you can't get that assignment done today, then tomorrow will be okay.

Christina adored him. She repeatedly would say, much to her mother's chagrin, "Oh, Mr. Black, he is the most wonderful teacher in the whole world." Then she'd go on, saying things like, "I believe everything he tells the class, and I find myself learning more from him than I do from you. Plus, his English is better than yours and he can explain things better than you."

Initially these comments only served to embarrass Viki and make her want to do something to better answer her daughter's questions. However, when Christina continued repeating her teacher's name in such adoring fashion, Viki decided something more had to be done.

She discussed it with Kornel. They both agreed someone must have a discussion with Mr. Black and come to some conclusion to blunt Christina's attraction to him. Viki called the school and made an appointment to meet Mr. Black.

When Viki first set eyes on him, she saw why he had such a powerful effect on young females. He projected empathy, warmth, and a deep personal interest.

"Mr. Black," she said, "what are you doing that has such a strong impact on my daughter? When we discuss her schoolwork at home, all she can do is talk about you. She doesn't want to tell me what she is learning in your class. She only wants to talk about how good a teacher you are and discuss your good looks and your bearing. All she says is, 'Mr. Black said this' and 'Mr. Black said that.' She doesn't want to listen to me anymore and is quick to quote from you about subjects I believe do not belong in a mathematics classroom. I don't like it. I don't know what you can do to distract her, but please do something."

He blushed and began to stammer, "Well, ah …"

But before he could get words out, Viki said, "It is your job to teach your students mathematics. Leave these other subjects up to the parents to discuss with their children."

"I have never before had parents challenge either my teaching methods or my subject matter," he said defensively.

"That's because most American parents are soft and more inclined to leave those kinds of matters up to the teachers. I'm not that kind of mother. I have my own philosophy of how I want my kids raised and what I want them to achieve. I don't need or want help from outsiders. I understand you are a very good math teacher. If so, then teach them math and leave the rest of your subjects to the parents to cope with."

Mr. Black seemed dumbfounded. Apparently, he had never been challenged like this before, particularly by a meddlesome communist foreigner telling him what he should or should not teach.

Having made her point, Viki turned and quickly walked away, leaving Mr. Black searching for something to say.

After that meeting, Viki never heard Christina say another word about Mr. Black. He must have understood her position and taken action to change his way. Either that or he convinced Christina to keep quiet about him when talking to her mother. In any event, his name never came up again when Viki discussed the mathematics class with her daughter.

"I know nothing," Viki said, "about handling patients or medications, or the procedures for operating a group home. I'm completely lost." She was conversing with Marianna Popa and her husband, Vali, a young couple who owned and operated Silver Times Assisted Living, a group home in the West Valley.

"Not to worry," Popa said, trying to be as encouraging as possible. "I can teach you. I'm a registered nurse. I've had several years' experience in the business and I believe I'm qualified to teach you the fundamentals of how to operate group homes, at least the way we operate our home."

"I see that your group home is in a residential area." Viki asked, "Is that permitted by the government?"

"Yes, it is. You see, group homes have been doing business in residential areas for a long time. Initially they were called foster homes, which cared for needy children. Now, with the advent of needy adults whom busy families can no longer care for, they are referred to as group homes."

"I'll discuss it with Kornel, my husband. He is studying for his RN certificate. Then I'll let you know. It scares me, but after this discussion with you, I believe I'm becoming more interested in pursuing it further."

"I met Marianna Popa and her husband, Vali, after church this morning," Viki said, making Kornel look up from the nursing course books spread all over the kitchen table. "And we got to talking about group homes in the area and the number of Romanians who operate them.

"They own Silver Times Assisted Living, a group home. They've been in America eleven years and seem to be well established in the business. The conversation got me to wondering if that might be a business we should consider starting. After all, we've decided we want to own our own business and work for ourselves rather than for others. So why not group homes? As you know, we have always said that caring for humans is not a whole lot different from working with animals. The more I think about it, the more I'm inclined to want to try it. What do you think?"

Kornel paused a second or two, and then he said, "I agree that there is very little difference between treating animals and treating humans, but it's not as simple as it sounds. There are many other things that we would have to consider, items like, first, converting our residence to serve as a group home and providing furniture for sleeping, eating, and resting, and then living items, like food, clothing, and medications. Then we have the costs of organizing a business, such as insurance, licenses, and taxes, and operating costs like salaries. Then there are the costs of room and board and clothing for employees who will be on the job twenty-four hours a day. In addition, we will have the costs of transportation, property maintenance, and tools and equipment. And another thing: I can leave my job when the shift is over and leave the problems at the nurse's station for someone else to deal with. In a group home operation, I couldn't do that. I'd be carrying home problems every day, every week, every year. I don't want to work in a group home. But if that truly is what you want, then you have my blessings and support. All I can say is good luck and God bless you."

"Well, in that case," Viki said, "you continue what you are doing and keep your nursing jobs. I will operate the group home. I would appreciate it, however, if during your off-hours you would help me by caring for the buildings and grounds and seeing to the tools you need to do that work. I'll care for the patients."

"Well, if that is how you want to divide the responsibility, we both can look into the business and determine if it is something we should pursue."

By the first of January, what had been the two-car garage became a bedroom complete with bathroom facilities. The Neguras' beloved residence in Phoenix had been converted into an assisted living group home. While construction was progressing, they studied and visited other homes, and learned all that was necessary to obtain building certificates and licenses to operate the business.

"While I'm thinking about it," Kornel said, "don't you think we should have a name for our business?

"Yes indeed," Viki replied. "I've been thinking about it, too. Now that we are well organized and soon will be fully operational, we should go ahead and do it. Then we can have business cards and brochures printed. How does Golden Peaceful Assisted Living sound?"

"That sounds good to me," Kornel said. "If you are satisfied, then we can go ahead and make it official."

With that said, Viki picked up the telephone and called their lawyer. After discussing their needs for a few minutes, she hung up the phone, looked at Kornel, and said, "The lawyer will have all the paperwork done and ready for our signatures about this time next week."

Around the middle of the month, George Hensley, an elderly man suffering from Parkinson's disease, became the first patient at Golden Peaceful Assisted Living. He was virtually bedridden except when Viki roused him early each morning, showered him, and fed him his breakfast before she reported to work at the clothing plant. Viki made it a practice to prepare the next day's meals each evening before retiring.

Obviously, because Viki was still working at the clothing plant, it was necessary she hire another person to care for her patient during her absence. She was fortunate when she found, at a local church, a good list of refugees from Romania who were looking to get established in the United States.

One such person was Rodica Roman, a middle-aged former teacher at a Romanian high school who was looking for daytime work. Viki immediately interviewed her and was delighted when she agreed to take the 8:00 a.m. to 6:00 p.m. shift Monday through Friday.

Viki always dropped the girls off at school each morning on her way to her job. She depended on Rodica to look after her patient until she returned from work in the evening. One day Rodica failed to appear on time, so Viki asked her daughters to remain home with Hensley until Rodica arrived. As fate would have it, Hensley had an unexpected accident with his lower digestive system, shocking the girls and leaving them wondering who was going to handle the task of cleaning him and changing his clothing, and changing the bedclothes.

Christina pleaded with her sister to do it.

"No!" Anka shouted. "You do it! You are the oldest and should be able to do it better than me."

"No!" cried Christina. "I don't want to do it either. I've never done it before, and besides, what would my friends think about me if they found out what I had to do? No, no, no! I think you should do it."

"Well, I have friends too, and I don't want them to know about it either. But one of us is going to have to do it, or else we will be grounded again for another month. Neither of us wants that to happen, so get on with it!"

"I am not going to do it!" Christina said. "And I don't care if we do get grounded. I'm not going to do it, and that's final!"

Finally, Anka acquiesced and proceeded to undress and clean the patient, fuming at her sister and Rodica the whole time. After successfully completing the task, she stood back and admired her handiwork, but she knew she had no desire ever to work in a group home or have anything to do with caring for sick people.

When Viki listened to her daughters' account of the morning's events, she realized neither of them was interested in working for the group home. And as far as she was concerned, that was just fine; she preferred that her daughters complete their education and find work more suited to their personalities and educational achievements.

Early one morning as Viki was leaving the house for work, Marana Johnson, a young lady from two blocks over, approached her and said, "I understand you and your husband are caring for a sick person in your house. Is that a group home?"

"Yes," Viki said, "we are starting a group home and just took in our first resident."

"Do you have room for two more?" Marana asked. "I've been caring for both my mother and father, and it's gotten to the point where I can no longer manage it. Could you possibility take them in?"

"Well," Viki replied, "we don't have the room right now, but we do plan to rearrange the house so we can comfortably add more patients. How desperate are you to get them into a home?"

"It isn't an emergency," she said, "but the sooner space is available, the better it will be for us. It's becoming more and more difficult for me to care for them by myself."

"Well, I'll discuss it with my husband tonight and see what we can work out for you. I'll call you as soon as I can and give you a time. Is that all right?"

"Yes, that'll be fine."

That evening, Viki related her conversation to Kornel and asked, "Can we do something to accommodate her?"

"It'll take about a month to rearrange our bedroom to accommodate two patients," Kornel said. "So if you're willing to give up our bedroom, select a date and then call her tomorrow to let her know when she can bring her parents here."

"Yes," Viki said, "we'll definitely have to give up our bedroom. You and the girls will have to find another suitable place to live. Until it's needed to add two more patients, I'll use the girls' bedroom for an office and my bedroom."

"I'll start searching for a nice comfortable place to live near the school so the girls can walk to and from classes."

"Good idea," Viki said. "But with three patients living here, I'll have to give up my job and hire a couple of certified caregivers to help me."

"Yes, you will," Kornel said, "and while we're at it, let's go ahead and renovate the rest of the house so we can care for as many as seven or eight patients."

"Can we afford the increase in the second mortgage we will need to do all this?" Viki asked.

"Not now," Kornel responded, "but we will be able to do so after we add the Johnsons."

On October 1, 1995, Kornel and the girls moved into a four-room condominium near the school.

As soon as the bedroom and bathroom alterations were completed, Viki informed the Johnsons they could move in.

Within a week, with the help of their children, the couple settled into their new home under the capable care of Viki and her newly hired caregiver, Rhea Davis.

Once the Johnsons were comfortably situated, Kornel and Viki converted the remaining space in the house to handle four more patients and two live-in caregivers.

By the end of the year, Viki and Kornel had seven patients under their care, with the help of two certified Romanian caregivers. They had started out using American caregivers, but that didn't work out, so they decided to stick with the more tolerant and compassionate workers from Romania.

They were well established in the group home business, and it was prospering. Viki was gratified knowing that the patients' families appreciated the quality of life she and her staff were giving their loved ones. While a very few were mobile enough to move about, most were helpless and relied on the assistance hands that only she and her staff could render. One or two, in the later stages of Alzheimer's disease, were occasionally capable of speaking with their caregivers. It was obvious, however, that their mental defects from the late stages of dementia prohibited them from carrying on meaningful conversations. But from the looks of contentment in their eyes, it was clear that they appreciated what the staff was doing for them. There were a few patients who resisted being handled because of the pain and the stress of being moved, but with kind words and gentle urgings, they too conceded to whatever the staff wanted them to do.

Demand for the group home's services remained high. Viki and Kornel had no problems keeping their house full. The work was hard and, at times almost impossible, but they were satisfied with what they were doing, and the patients appeared to be comfortable and accepting of their surroundings.

When they took on the eighth resident, the additional compensation was welcome, but it meant that Viki had to move into the condominium. Finally, the family was back together again.

"Now that we have experience working as owners of a group home, are you ready to consider expanding the business?" Viki asked Kornel, hoping for a positive response.

"Well, I have to admit," Kornel said after a long pause, "it's something I have thought about, but do we have to discuss it now? I've had a bad day, and I'm not sure I want to get into a long conversation about it. To me, that sounds like a lot of work."

"I can see that you're tired, but maybe talking about it this evening might help you to relax and perhaps sleep better tonight. I know it will help me. It's been on my mind for several days. I would like to get your thoughts."

"As I've told you before," Kornel said, clearly a bit aggravated by her insistence, "I don't like group homes. I like working my scheduled hours and then having the rest of the day to do what I want. You have to be working twenty-four hours a day, seven days a week, to ensure that everything is being done to best care for your patients. Your whole life is built around them. You hardly get a moment's rest. If you're not on the job, you're thinking about all that has to be done and wondering how effective your staff is in caring for the patients."

"Yes, that is true," Viki said, "but I love it. I like what I'm doing, and I get a lot of satisfaction when I see the patients' contentment. Yes, it's hard work. We must always be ready to respond to every plea or sign of a problem. If we were to expand, I'd have to increase the staff to help with the additional patients. I realize I can't do it myself. And yes, I want to expand."

"Well, if you are so intent on this," Kornel said with resignation, "I'll go along with you, but I don't like buying a newly built house and then having to renovate it to function as a group home. It's too much work, and it's costly. If we are going to expand, and it looks as though we will, I suggest we have a contractor build the houses to our specifications and save all those renovation costs."

"You're absolutely right. Let's do it that way: you build the houses and I'll staff them. Where do you think we should locate the houses?"

"Well, if you are ready to start, I recommend we build in Surprise," Kornel said. "It's a rapidly growing area with many contractors building lots of homes and business structures. The home selling prices are very competitive, and the houses are readily available. Yes, I believe Surprise would be our best location."

"Surprise. That's an unusual name for a town. Where is it located?"

"It's about twenty miles west of Phoenix. While it is small, it's bordered by several large age-restricted communities. Property owners must be at least fifty-five years of age to live there. The area is attracting thousands of new residents, and the demand for new homes continues to increase each year. And it will continue to expand for many years because of the availability of many thousands of acres of agricultural land becoming available as the population continues to grow. There are many group homes now operating in the area, and most, they tell me, are owned and operated by Romanians. I believe that's where we should build."

CHAPTER 58

In May of 1997, the couple signed the papers to have group home no. 2 built on Spanish Drive in Surprise. It would have adequate space for eight to ten patients and at least two live-in caretakers.

"Did the contractor look over your blueprint showing how we want the interior rooms arranged?" Viki asked Kornel.

"Yes, he did, but he said the company couldn't do it our way because their houses are constructed according to standard specifications to reduce costs. He said he can't change that. But he did say that he would lower his building price by constructing only the weight-bearing walls, and then we could contract someone else for the interior."

"That sounds better to me. I'd rather do it ourselves and have the interior finished and furnished exactly the way we want it."

After his recovery from his back problem, Kornel accepted a job at the nearby hospital in Phoenix rather than returning to the nursing home. While his income was better, his scheduled twelve-hour midnight shifts each weekend were long and tedious. That plus the hours he was spending in school to earn his RN certificate left him little time to help Viki with her group home duties and with looking after the girls.

Kornel soon also realized that his hospital duties were much like those he had been assigned in the nursing home. There was too much work and not enough staff to effectively get it done.

On the plus side, however, he appreciated the increase in compensation he had gained by earning his CNA certificate.

"What bothersome thoughts are you filling your head with now?" Viki asked him. "It's obvious you've got something on your mind. Do you want to talk about it?"

"It's just something I'm beginning to understand about the job I have at the hospital," he answered reluctantly. "I am assigned too much work, and there is no one to help me get it done. I have more responsibilities than I had before and there is a lot more pressure. I'm not comfortable, and I don't know what I should do about it."

"You could always quit," Viki said, "and do something else. There's a heavy demand for nurses. You shouldn't have any difficulty getting another job."

"Yes, I've been thinking about doing that. But if I quit the hospital, where else could I go? It certainly wouldn't be in a nursing home. I tried that and didn't care for it."

"You could always work as a private nurse. There are lots of health care companies that need nurses to do private duty."

"I've thought about that too, but I still prefer working with several patients rather than just one. As you know, I'm physically not capable of moving or turning patients because of my back, so I don't want that to be a hindrance in my getting another job."

"Have you thought about doing palliative care? All you would have to do is keep your patients comfortable and their loved ones calm when there is no curing the patient. You'd be working with fewer patients and families. Of course, the job would require more travel time visiting your individual patients."

"That's a good thought; it never entered my mind. I'll look into it and see what's involved. Thank you."

Christina was absorbed in rearranging the contents of her hallway locker when she was startled by a deep male voice behind her.

"Would you go to the junior–senior prom with me?"

As Christina turned to face the voice, the book she was holding slipped from her hand. When she realized who the speaker was, she dropped another book. "You, ah, you want me to go to the prom with you?"

"Yes, I do."

Well, I, ah, ah, don't know what to say. You scared me."

"I'm sorry. I didn't realize I was scaring you. But I want to take you to the prom. I'm Zach Martin."

"Yes, I know who you are, but, ah, ah, I need to think about it."

Both were juniors, about to become seniors. While Christina had noticed him noticing her from time to time, their classes and schedules never enabled them to meet. Needless to say, she was thrilled to be asked to go to the prom by one of the most popular boys in school.

After about a five-second pause, which to her seemed much longer, she said, "Yes, I would love to go to the prom with you, but first I need to discuss it with my parents. If they agree, then I want them to meet you. Would that be all right with you?"

"Absolutely. I want to meet them as much as I want you to meet my parents."

"Would you go to a movie with me this Friday night?" he asked.

"Yes, I'd like that very much."

"Good. I'll come by and pick you up at 6:00 p.m."

"Do you know where I live?"

"Yes, I looked it up in the student directory."

"I'll be ready. That will be a good time to meet my parents. As you may know, we are originally from Romania and both my parents still struggle a little with the English language. I may have to interpret for you."

"Fine, I'll keep that in mind."

After he walked away, Christina turned to her locker, pumped her right fist in the air, and whispered, "Yes, yes, yes!"

When Christina got home from school, she exclaimed, "Mama, guess what?"

"I have no idea of what's on your mind, but it must be very important judging from the look on your face."

"Well, I'm not going to keep you guessing. I think I'm in love. His name is Zach Martin. He's very handsome, and for some reason he seems to be attracted to me. He comes from a good family and is one of the better football players on the team. Also, he is at the top of the class. He says he wants to stay with sports, particularly football, and wants to go to college and hopefully play professionally with one of the National Football League teams. Zach just invited me to the prom. I want very much to go with him."

"Can you bring him home and let us meet him?"

"Yes, I will do that Friday night. He is going to pick me up at six o'clock and take me to a movie. You and Papa can meet him then."

"Well, I am anxious to meet him. I know your father will want to shake his hand."

On Friday, Zack arrived promptly at 6:00 p.m. Christina introduced him to her parents and sister. They all spent about an hour getting acquainted before the two went on to a movie.

"You know, I like him," said Kornel.

"Me, too," Viki said.

On the evening of May 9, 1996, a long gleaming yellow limousine drove up to the apartment building, reminding everyone who saw it that it was once again prom night.

Zack entered the apartment and presented Christina, beautifully dressed in a white prom dress, with a gorgeous wrist bouquet of miniature white roses. She was glowing with happiness.

As Viki observed the young couple, her eyes slowly welled with tears. Kornel was almost speechless too. All he could manage to say was, "Have a good time."

Viki quickly added, "And be good."

Christina and Zach were good. Both had a most enjoyable time at the dance. As they prepared to part on her doorstep, Zach encircled her waist with his arms, looked into her eyes, and said, "I don't know about you, but I don't want this to stop."

Christina placed her hands on his broad shoulders and softly said, "I want very much to keep it going, too."

"Wonderful," he said. "Let's go to another movie Friday night." Then he leaned down and kissed her for the first time.

It made her toes curl.

By that October, Viki was managing two group homes, the older one in Phoenix and the new one some twenty miles away in Surprise, with a one-way driving time of about thirty-five minutes.

While Kornel did not help Viki with her patients, he was available during his off-hours to do whatever was necessary to maintain the appearance of their properties.

Viki soon had staff members in both homes trained to maintain a smooth and efficient operation. She had them start each morning by getting the patients out of bed, taking them to the bathroom, getting them showered and dressed, and seating them at the dining table awaiting their breakfasts by 8:00 a.m.

After breakfast, the patients were seated comfortably in their lounge chairs in the great room, where those who were alert enough could watch programs on a large television or flip through periodicals and newspapers.

Those living in mentally confused worlds relaxed and napped, paying little attention to their surroundings. Others played with their fingers and muttered incoherent sounds as if carrying on conversations with family members, some absent, some present.

"You had better listen to me, Bobbie, or I will punish you," Mattie Romanesque said from her wheelchair. "If I see you again dragging that cat across the floor by its tail, you're going to get the paddle and sit you in the corner for an hour. Do you understand me?"

"Yes, Mama, I understand. I promise I won't do it again," the man sitting next to her replied.

Mattie didn't realize it was not her son's hand she was clutching. Instead it was that of her husband, John. Knowing that the cancer that riddled her body and the dementia that impaired her mind would soon take her life, John always soothed her and supported her fantasies. It was his way of comforting her. He did so knowing that soon he would be left with nothing but memories.

Steve Pulaski, a three-hundred-pound male patient, was wheeled into the room by his caregiver, Dana Dobo, who then used the mechanized sling lift to ease him onto his bed. Viki was always searching for new equipment that would make difficult tasks easier on her staff. When the occasion called for it, she would rent, at a cost of $1,000 per month, mattresses that virtually guaranteed no pressure sores.

There was never a shortage of patients in the Surprise area. Virtually surrounded by senior adult communities, the group homes were almost always filled to capacity by families needing places to care for relatives who were unable to care for themselves.

Anna Fecek, a beautiful eightyyearold lady, had been in the home since it opened. She was suffering from advanced Alzheimer's disease, which brought terrible memory loss. She was not bedridden but had the freedom to wander through the great room and from the front door to the back door. Finding the doors locked, she would smilingly return to her chair and take a nap.

One day when Anna tried the front door, she found that it easily opened. Apparently someone had failed to set the lock. She decided to step out into the bright Arizona sunlight and look around.

Walking to the end of the block and not seeing anything that interested her, Anna decided to walk to her home and take a nap. But which way was home? Confused, she continued walking, looking for the street that would lead her to her home. After walking a few more blocks but seeing nothing that looked familiar, she turned up an alleyway, hoping she would see something she recognized. But there was nothing to see and no one to help her. She was lost.

Meanwhile, Viki was finishing changing the dressing on a diabetic patient's leg. When she entered the great room, she immediately shouted, "Where's Anna?" No one answered. "Where is Anna?" Viki yelled even louder. Her caregivers came running. They admitted they had no idea where she might be.

When Viki tried the front door, she found it unlocked. *Anna must be outside,* she thought. *We've got to find her before she gets hurt.*

"Alexa, you remain here with the other patients. Dona, come with me. We'll try to find her before she wanders too far. If we can't find her, we'll have to get the police to help us. I don't want to have to do that."

They searched on foot for about an hour with no luck. "There's a small park a couple of blocks over," Viki said. "Let's go take a look. If she isn't there, I'll just have to call the police." *By this time,* Viki thought, *Anna could be anywhere.*

As Dona and Viki entered the park, they could see it was occupied. Children and adults were using the swings, exercise bars, waterslides, and other facilities. Dogs, too, were plentiful, running, barking, and chasing sticks and Frisbees. But there was no Ana.

"Let's split up," Viki said. "Dona, you go one way, and I'll go the other. Check all the benches, chairs, and restrooms, and all over the grounds. Then we'll meet back here in about half an hour. If we don't find her, I'll call the police and fire departments and let them take over the search."

When the half hour expired, Viki sat down on one of the benches and began looking for Dona to appear. Fifteen minutes passed and still no Dona. *I wonder what happened to her?* Viki thought. *She should have been here by now. I hope she didn't get lost, too.*

Another ten minutes passed. Viki was about to give up and call the police, but as she turned to her right, she saw Dona slowly leading Anna toward her.

"Hallelujah!" Viki shouted. She ran to meet them. "Where were you going, Anna? We've looked all over for you."

"Home," Anna said. "I can't find my home."

"Come with us," Viki said. "We know where you live. We'll see that you get home."

In late May of 1997, Kornel completed all his nursing courses with good grades. After passing the necessary state tests, he was awarded his certificate and license to practice as a registered nurse. When he applied for a job with the Surprise hospital as a nurse in the oncology section, he was immediately accepted.

Again to free up his daylight hours, he agreed to work from 8:00 p.m. to 8:00 a.m., Friday through Sunday each week, leaving him Monday through Thursday as free days to help Viki maintain the two group homes she was managing.

CHAPTER 59

In April of the following year, Viki and Kornel doubled the size of their business. They bought two side-by-side houses that became group home 3 and group home 4. Located on Sunset Drive, the homes were only a block behind group home 2, on Spanish Drive. Group home 2 was being operated as a unisex facility, but they decided to take only males in group home 3 and only females in group home 4 to determine if that was a more efficient operation. By the end of the year, all four houses were full of patients, and the staff members trained and functioning well under Viki's guidance.

With four homes to oversee, Viki had her hands full. She still had that thirty-five-minute drive from the group home in Phoenix to their group homes in Surprise. She was gallantly working hard to keep up with the expanded business. The hours were long and the moving about among the homes was tiresome, to say the least.

One day as Viki was discussing the menu with her cook, her cell phone rang. Seeing that the call was from the manager of the home in Phoenix, she immediately answered. "What's the problem?" she asked.

"It's Mrs. Johnson. She collapsed in the shower as we were trying to wash her."

"Is she breathing?"

"Yes, but weakly."

"Is she hurt in any way?

"There's no visible injury—no blood or bruising. She didn't fall as much as she just sort of slid down the wall of the shower."

"Did you call 9-1-1?"

"Yes, and they're on their way."

"Well, there is nothing more you can do but keep her comfortable until the EMS arrives. I'm on my way. I'll be there in about thirty minutes or so. Let the EMS attendants have their way should they decide to take her to the hospital. Go ahead and call Mrs. Johnson's daughter to explain what has happened to her mother. She'll come over and stay with Mr. Johnson, her father. No doubt, she'll want to talk with the EMS people once they get there. I'll try to get there as quickly as I can. You might want to offer everyone a cup of tea and one of those delicious sticky buns you baked yesterday."

As Viki was driving from Spanish Drive with her mind intent on what she was going to say to the Johnsons, she didn't notice the parked car ahead in her lane. When she saw it, she turned her steering wheel hard to the left and slammed her foot onto the brake pedal. Fortunately, that slowed her down so that the inevitable impact was minimized. Her right bumper and wheel smashed into the left bumper and trunk area of the parked car, and then her car came to an abrupt stop, throwing her face-first into the ballooned air bag.

The noise of the crash brought the car's owner out of his house in a run. He opened Viki's driver's-side door, helped her from her car, and steadied her until she could regain her composure and balance.

"Are you hurt?" he asked.

"I don't think so."

"What happened?" he asked. "You sure made a mess of your car. What little damage there is to mine can easily be repaired, so I'm willing to let the insurance companies settle the issue. Then the two of us can go about our business as if nothing happened. I'm thankful you didn't get seriously hurt."

"I don't have any problems with your suggestion," Viki said. "I have an immediate need to get to Phoenix. I own a group home there and I just got word that one of my patients fell while being showered. I need to discuss with her daughter what the prognosis is and if she will be all right."

"Well, the police will soon be here, so I suggest you wait until they leave. Then I will take you to Phoenix."

"No, you won't. I'm calling my husband now. He'll come here and take me. But I thank you for making the offer."

Soon the city police arrived. It was not long before they had gathered all the information they needed. Since no one was hurt and both parties had agreed to let the insurance companies settle the issue, they gave Viki a warning about safe driving on city streets. She was not charged with any wrongdoing. As the police left, Kornel arrived.

Viki did not get to talk with the Johnsons until much later that evening. All news was good news. Mrs. Johnson was not hurt. She apparently experienced a momentary blackout that temporally weakened her legs enough to let her body slide down the shower wall.

"Now that the group homes are doing so well financially," Kornel said one evening as he was reading the financial news in the evening paper, "why don't we buy a couple more and bring in more patients? The housing market continues to generate more construction, and home values continue to increase."

"Do you think it wise to invest in more houses at this time?" Viki asked.

"Oh, absolutely. At least the newspaper is optimistic. It forecasts continued growth for many more months. Yes, I believe now is the time to buy."

"Why should we do that now?" Viki asked. "I believe we are doing well with the four we now own."

"Not only would we benefit from handling more patients," Kornel continued, "but also with this building boom being what it is and with the way houses are selling, I'm confident the structures themselves would make good investments."

"But what about operating them? I'm having difficulty operating the four we now own. I can't handle two more at this time, especially with the traveling I have to do between these we have in Surprise and the one we own in Phoenix."

"When the girls get enrolled in college," Kornel eagerly continued, "we can sell the one in Phoenix and invest the proceeds in the stock market, thus protecting it until we decide to buy more homes, if that is the direction we want to go. No doubt the demand for group homes in this area will continue increasing as older residents find the need to be placed into assisted living facilities."

"Why not buy just one more, work out the operating problems we know we will encounter, and then think about buying more?" Viki asked.

"Yes," Kornel said, "we could do it that way, but I'd like to buy at least two now and take advantage of the growing market. I'm confident we can make some money. After all, we won't be working all our lives. There will come a time when we will want to retire and enjoy our family. Hopefully we will have some grandchildren we can spoil. So I suggest we buy two houses, make one a group home, and use the second one as a rental property until the timing is right to sell it."

"Well, if you're confident that's what we should do, then let's do it."

As Kornel entered the house, Viki excitedly called out, "Guess what?"

"What?" he asked.

"I sold the house in Phoenix."

"Wow, the sale went faster than I thought it would. How much did you have to lower our asking price?"

"I didn't. I sold it at the price we listed it for."

"How did you do that?"

"I just took a firm stand," Viki said, "and argued that the listed amount was reasonable and that the house would be a good investment for them, especially since it produces about $200,000 a year in income. 'Where else can you find jobs that will give you that kind of a profit?' I asked them. The buyers wanted to haggle with me, but I held out and let it be known that we wouldn't let it go for anything less than what we were asking."

"When do we have to give it up?"

"In thirty days. That'll give us time to remove our personal belongings and clean it up."

After the sale closed, Viki reduced her both workload and travel time with only group homes no. 2, 3, and 4 to manage. However, the Neguras had to continue living in the Phoenix condominium until both girls were enrolled in the university.

Christina graduated from high school in May of 1998 and made preparations to enroll at South Desert University. She had been accepted by the school and awarded a four-year scholarship, including tuition, books, and supplies. Viki was proud of her daughter's achievement and the roles that she and Kornel had played in helping Christina to bring it about.

"What do you plan to do after you graduate college?" Viki asked her.

"My primary interest is in Spanish, but I also want to be able to understand and translate other languages. I plan to continue my studies in the school's ROTC program, and enlist in the US Army when I graduate. I think my language skills would be useful in the military."

During the months before Christina's first semester, the family had spent a lot of time getting her ready for college life. They began to accumulate and pack everything they could think of that Christina might need to live on campus, including clothing, bedding, a computer, a cell phone, a television, and supplies. What they couldn't think of, they decided could be purchased in town.

What they completely overlooked was the availability of dormitory rooms. Much to their dismay, none were available. They would have to search off campus for a place for her to live.

"There's a practical alternative," Viki said. "We can buy a large residential property near the campus for Christina and rent the extra rooms to other students. That way we can make enough money to pay off the mortgage. And Anka, coming here in a couple of years, can also use the house during her four years in the school. What do you think?"

"Can we afford it?" Kornel asked.

"Yes, I believe we can. I think it'll be a good investment."

Kornel selected a real estate agent. Within a month, he and Viki took possession of a four-bedroom house and had it completely refurbished. It would be an excellent and convenient place to live and a good source of income.

That August, Christina formally enrolled at South Desert University.

"Did you sign up for all the classes you wanted?" Viki asked.

"Yes, surprisingly I did. I thought some might be closed, but I was able to schedule all the ones I really wanted."

Getting Christina and three of her fellow students completely settled in the rental house took all day. All four families gathered bags, suitcases, radios, television sets, computers, and kitchen needs from their vehicles and crammed it all into their children's respective bedrooms.

After all was said and done, Viki and Kornel invited everyone to a nearby restaurant, where they enjoyed a nice dinner with wine and all the trimmings. After dinner, the parents dropped the girls off at their new home and wished them good luck with their studies.

While everyone appeared happy and delighted with their children becoming students of a nationally acclaimed university, the parting was difficult. There were hugs, kisses, tears, and quiet sobs as parents literally tore themselves from their offspring and silently scurried away.

It wasn't until Kornel and Viki were about halfway to Phoenix that Viki began to feel the loneliness that came with the idea that she and Kornel were beginning to lose their children.

"Now, in a couple of years," Viki said, still wiping tears from her eyes, "Anka will be entering college and we'll be completely by ourselves. I wonder what life has in store for our girls."

"Who knows, but I'm confident they will do well. You've been a caring mother and have worked long and hard getting then educated. You were strict, but in a motherly, loving manner. They may not be grateful now for what all you've done, but as they continue on their life's journey, they will become more appreciative of all your endeavors and express it in their love for you—and hopefully some for me, too."

In July, while lifting a heavy patient, Kornel reinjured his back: the same disc that troubled him in Greece carrying heavy stones to build a restraining wall, and in Scottsdale when he lifted a heavy patient onto a gurney.

After looking at his x-rays and MRI, his doctor said, "The injury is not severe enough to risk an operation at this time, but I do recommend complete bed rest for a couple of weeks. That should improve your back enough to enable you to move about and do small chores. Please take six weeks off before thinking about going back to work, and when you do return, do not even think about attempting to move heavy people or any other heavy load."

Kornel followed the doctor's advice and did very little for three weeks. During the last three weeks, he was able to do light work in and around his and Viki's business properties.

"Do you plan to return to work at the hospital?" Viki asked one evening after he began helping her with the group homes.

"That's been my intention," he said. "But there are times when I wonder if I should return to the hospital. Undoubtedly, there will be times when heavy lifting will be necessary, and that makes me wonder if I'd be better off working someplace else where lifting is not a problem."

"Have you ever thought about working for West Valley Hospice? They use nurses, and heavy lifting is not a prerequisite."

"Good suggestion," Kornel replied. "I hadn't thought about it, but it sounds like a possibility. I'll look into it."

He did, and after his six weeks' recovery, he returned to work as a nurse for West Valley Hospice.

CHAPTER 60

In the spring of 2000, Viki and Kornel bought group home no. 5 in the same neighborhood as their other houses. Having investment in mind, and after refurbishing it to serve as a group home, they placed it on the market at a hefty selling price. They hoped it would sell quickly, but it didn't.

"I don't know why it hasn't sold," Kornel said. "It's all ready to be placed into service as a group home, but we can't seem to attract any serious buyers."

"It's too expensive," Viki responded. "We've had many inquiries, and a few offers, but all were too low. I don't want to lose money."

"What else can we do then?" Kornel asked.

"I believe that if we put the house in production," Viki said, "and show the income potential, we might be able to sell it, but I don't want to have to manage another group home. I've tried managing four homes. That's too many of them and not enough of me."

"What do you suggest?" Kornel asked.

"Why don't we rent it out with an offer to help the tenant start his or her own group home business? Then, once the business is established and the renter gets to the point where he or she realizes it is financially better to own rather than leasing, we'll sell it."

"Do you believe that'll work?" Kornel asked.

"Yes, I do," Viki said.

"How much will you rent it for?"

"I don't know now," Viki said. "I'll determine that when we get some inquiries. I'm still convinced we can get a good return on the investment. It's a beautiful house in a good location, and it will accommodate eight or ten patients."

"If we rent it, I'll have to maintain it," Kornel said.

"That shouldn't bother you. Just consider what I have to look forward to: obtaining the business license, hiring and training a complete staff, and then helping to admit and set up a regimen of caregiving for six or eight patients. Then, once I'm assured the owner can operate without my help, I'll be able to determine what the asking price to purchase the home will be."

"I agree; you've got a lot of work to do."

On May 16, 2000, the telephone rang at 3:30 in the afternoon. After the third ring, Viki, who was attending a patient, hurriedly answered it before it went to voice mail. It was Anka.

"What's wrong?"

"It's Papa. He is on the floor and I can't rouse him. I called 9-1-1. The paramedics are on their way."

Through the phone, Viki heard the doorbell ring and the door opening. "It's four paramedics with their equipment," Anka shouted.

"Don't hang up!" Viki screamed, "I want to talk to them before ... ah ... ah ..."

Before she could get her words out, one of the paramedics took the phone from Anka and said, "Who is this?"

"I am Viki Antonescu. The girl you are talking to is my daughter Anka. The person on the floor is my husband, Kornel Antonescu. Can you tell me what his problem is?"

"Not yet. We're just attaching the equipment. We'll have an answer in a couple of minutes. Just hang on. I'll keep you informed." He returned the phone to Anka.

"What can I do, Mama?" Anka asked between sobs.

"There's nothing you can do but wait," Viki said, trying to calm her. "Just hang on to the phone and wait."

In about five minutes, the paramedic returned to the phone and said, "We believe your husband has had a heart attack. We're going to rush him to the emergency room of Mountain View Hospital. We're ready to leave now, so I'm hanging up. Get in touch with the hospital for reports on his condition."

But before he could hang up, Viki asked tearfully, "Is it serious? Is Kornel going to die?"

"I can't answer that, ma'am. While it doesn't seem too serious, we must assume the worst and take every precaution to prevent further damage to his heart. I can assure you, though, that we will give him the best care we can and get him to the ER as quickly as possible. You might want to get there as soon as you can. I'm turning the phone over to your daughter now. I must say she acted very promptly and calmly. If it wasn't for her finding him on the floor and then calling us, it could have been worse."

"Mama, what can I do now? I don't know what I'm supposed to do!"

"Don't fret about it. There is nothing you can do. Just get a soft drink, sit down, and try to get it out of your mind. I'll be there as soon as I can, and then we'll immediately go to the hospital and stay with your father until we can get answers from the medical people. There is nothing more either of us can do. We'll work things out."

Anka approached her mother as she was preparing dinner for the family. "Mama," she said, "I've been asked to go to the senior prom by a very nice boy named Bob Bartlett who's in several of my college placement classes. I was hoping he'd ask me, but I wasn't expecting it."

"Are you in love with this Bob Bartlett?"

"Oh, no, Mama, he's just a good friend. He says he's not ready to go steady yet, but he occasionally likes to date different girls. I suppose it's my turn now."

"That sounds a little odd, but I suppose it's all right."

"And guess what Mama?"

"I'm not guessing about anything," Viki said. "I don't like these guessing games when it comes to you girls dating. Just tell me."

"This is not about dating Mama, not at all. It's about getting to and from the prom, and to the restaurant we have chosen to celebrate our graduation, and going off to college."

"And what will that be?"

"Well, unlike what Christina, Zach, and their group did, we are not going to rent one of those long limousines."

"Oh? Then how do you plan to get there and back? Neither I nor your father will be able to drive you there, because then we'd have to wait up most of the night to go pick you up."

"No. No, Mama. We don't expect you to do that. We are going to take the school bus."

"What?"

"Yes, the school bus, and it will be full. We plan to have a good time at the prom and then at the restaurant after. We've booked tables at Tres Primos Restaurante, where we can relax, eat, and continue the fun of the evening."

"You mean you all are going to use a school bus to take you around to all the places you want to go? I don't believe it."

"Yes, Mama, that's exactly what we are going to do, and we all believe we will have more fun in the bus than what the limousine crowd will have in their little ol' limos."

"Well, all I can say is, to each his own."

In July of 2000, Kornel returned to light work. It was six weeks after his heart attack, which required four stents. He felt good and strong enough to help Viki around the group home doing cleanup and also repairing some electrical problems. A week later he returned to West Valley Hospice and resumed his palliative care work visiting patients in their homes. He also attended to patients residing in group homes.

In August 2000, Anka enrolled in SDU, following in the footsteps of her sister, who would be graduating in a couple of years. Like Christina, Anka was granted a four-year scholarship for her undergraduate studies.

Getting her girls settled in their off-campus house was a busy and emotional experience for Viki. Christina was returning as an upperclassman, an Anka was starting as a freshman. Viki and Kornel were proud and giddy getting the girls ready for their year of university life.

The entire family gathered and stuffed the girls' clothing, radios, televisions, computers, and kitchen needs into whatever bags, boxes, and suitcases they could find. Then they crammed it all into their SUV.

Kornel drove the SUV, and Viki and the girls followed in the small automobile the girls would have at their disposal during the school year. Upon arrival, everyone pitched in and moved everything from the SUV into the girls' rooms. While everyone appeared happy and delighted about going to college, it was a sad time for Viki and Kornel, as they would be returning home to face an empty house. After getting the girls settled in their rooms, the good-byes were tearful.

As she and her husband drove away, Viki knew it wouldn't be long before the girls were truly gone, having moved on to walk the paths that lay before them. She and Kornel were going to miss them terribly, but they were committed to helping them with whatever assistance they needed. Like all good parents, they wanted to see their children be successful and happily settled in the environment of their own choosing. But most of all, they wanted to see cute little grandchildren toddling around their feet.

Viki maintained close communications with her girls with frequent telephone calls and occasional visits. The university was close enough that she could get in her car and, within an hour or so, be talking face-to-face with her daughters. She made the trip often, and often the girls didn't appreciate it.

A month before Thanksgiving, Viki had one of her bad days. One of her patients had died. She thought the day would get better, but it only got worse, particularly after she had talked to Anka.

"I thought I'd give you a call and see how you are doing," she said. "Hopefully your days are better than the ones I've been experiencing here in the homes."

"I'm doing fine, Mother. Everything is going well. I like my classes and am getting good grades, although I didn't feel real well this morning when I got out of bed. I had a little cough and a little temperature, but after I had my breakfast, I felt fine. I've since decided it must have been something I ate yesterday that didn't agree with me. But now I'm okay."

"Did you go to the infirmary?"

"No."

"Don't you think you should?"

"No, I'm okay now. I don't need to see a nurse or doctor."

"Well, if you don't get completely better, you should go and have it checked out."

"I will, Mama. Don't worry."

Viki hung up, but she was worried. She believed her daughter should have medical attention, if for no reason other than to be certain she was not coming down with something serious. *What to do? What to do?* After thinking about it for about an hour, she decided she had to find out for herself. *I'll just go down there,* she thought, *and make certain she is all right. If she isn't, I'll take her to the emergency room.*

She hurriedly changed her dress, jumped in her car, pushed the accelerator to the floor, and sped down the highway toward the university. She would normally have made the journey in about an hour and a half, but today she didn't.

About halfway to her destination, she heard a police siren, and in her rearview mirror she could see red and blue flashing lights. *Oh no,* she thought, *not now.* But she had no choice. She pulled to the side of the road.

As the patrolman approached, Viki lowered her window. Before the patrolman could say anything, she said, "I guess I was speeding a little bit."

"A little bit, you say? Just how fast do you think you were driving?"

"I'm sure I was driving just a little over the speed limit."

"Well, you weren't. Actually you were traveling at seventy-seven miles per hour, which is twelve miles an hour faster than the legal limit."

"I was? I didn't realize I was going that fast. I'm sorry."

"Ma'am, being sorry doesn't change the fact that you were speeding."

"Well, you see, I was hurrying to see my daughter who is going to the university in Tucson. I talked to her this morning and she didn't sound well. She refuses to get medical attention. I'm very worried about her."

"Well, ma'am, I too have a daughter in school, so I can appreciate what you are going through. So, even though you were speeding and deserve having it on your record, I'm going to let you off with just a warning, which could add points to your record. But if you attend our safe drivers' training course, the points will be dropped. The choice is yours."

"I'll go to the school," Viki weakly responded. "I don't want the points on my record."

"So go ahead and meet with your daughter," the officer encouraged, "but stay within the speed limits."

"Thank you, officer. I really appreciate that. I promise I will watch my speed more closely.

When Viki rushed through the front door, Anka asked, "Mama, what are you doing here?"

"I had to make sure you are all right."

"Of course I'm all right. You didn't have to make this trip to check up on me. I think you're spying on me. You're still being a communist mother, always wanting to be near us to keep an eye on us. Don't you trust us?"

"Of course I trust you, but I miss you. And I always want to be certain that you are both safe and well. You know I'm a hands-on person; that's the way I treat my patients. While I have good staff to help me, I still like to treat the patients personally to make certain they are as well as they can be and as comfortable in their surroundings as their physical and mental health will let them. That's just the way I am. And I'm the same way with you girls. Please come with me and let's have the doctor check you out."

Anka made an exasperated face.

"Please?"

"All right, all right, Mama; let me get my coat. You never give up, do you?"

"No, and I never will. We love you, and we want only the best for you and your sister."

As her daughter opened the closet, Viki smiled, thinking, *My Anka, just like her sister, is a very smart girl.*

Now that the girls had moved into their own worlds, Viki and Kornel decided it was time to think more about themselves. So in October 2000, they bought their sixth home with permanent residence in mind. It was a small house, but they believed it had everything they needed. Located in an attractive community, it offered many amenities, like golfing, tennis, shopping, and a nice array of service facilities. The price was right, and the drive to their group homes was an easy one.

They had waited for what seemed like forever to enjoy a feeling of achievement. Now they wanted to make the most of it and live out their lives in peace and quiet, the American way.

In late October, Kornel and Viki moved their belongings from the condo to their new residence. There was very little furniture and few appliances to move. Most of what they had owned was now serving the patients in the recently sold Phoenix group home, so they had to purchase new items for the house. Kornel searched for the largest television set he could find to satisfy his addiction of watching the excellent US programs that had never been available in Romania.

"Why do you want such a large television set?" Viki asked him. "Not only is it costly, but also it's too large for one person to handle."

"I have never lived any place where there was too much television to watch until I came to America, and now that I'm here I want the biggest TV set I can buy. I love all the channels and programs available to me."

"Well, if you're that fervent about American television programming and are willing to spend the money to buy a large TV set then do it. But I hope you can find enough space in the house to display it."

Much to Kornel's disappointment, the TV was too large to fit into any of the spaces in the house except the dining area. But sitting at the dining room table to watch television was out of the question.

"I don't like it," Viki said. "This is too awkward an arrangement."

"I agree, but what else can we do?"

"I suggest you sell that ugly huge set and purchase a smaller TV, one that will fit nicely in the living room."

"No, never," Kornel countered. "I would rather sell this little house and buy a larger one that could accommodate my large television set."

"But look at the extra cost we would have," Viki said. "That would be ridiculous."

"Yes, I know it will cost more, but that is what I want. And I don't want to be talked out of it. You've been insistent all along that we had to spend what we needed to buy the best of everything that went into the group homes. So I think we should treat ourselves the same way. With all we are spending to establish a good business, we should treat ourselves well. In fact, I insist on it."

Viki finally agreed, as she, too, had become leery of the house. As she contemplated how she wanted to arrange it, she began to realize how small it was. She wanted something larger, something she could decorate to her satisfaction.

She and Kornel looked around and finally decided to buy a suitable home in Bella Zona, a new development bordering on one of the retirement communities. They settled the purchase on December 1 and moved in on December 18, just in time to help the neighborhood celebrate its annual preChristmas party.

With everyone gathered around their neighbor's new giant-sized rotisserie eating hot dogs and hamburgers while drinking wine and beer, Kornel and Viki were overwhelmed. Since Viki thought she might become addicted to alcohol, seeing as her biological father was an alcoholic, she abstained from the beer and wine, drinking only her favorite, green tea.

The new residence was closely located to Viki and Kornel's group homes, and travel consisted of an easy drive. It was such a relief to be free of that long travel distance to and from Phoenix. They outfitted the new house and found a nice large space in the Arizona room that appeared to be built just for the TV Kornel had selected. It and its related equipment fit nicely and proved to be easily accessible for complete enjoyment. The space actually took on the regal appearance of a nice big theater and could seat at least six viewers.

Unfortunately, their small house sat unsold for a long time. The local housing market was experiencing a troubling downturn, and Viki and Kornel were caught right in the middle of it. They decided to rent the small house in order to earn some income to help cover the cost of keeping the small residence, but the income wasn't enough to match the mortgage payments. They were losing money every month. Finally, to rid themselves of a bad investment, they sold it at a loss. But in so doing, they learned a new lesson about how housing markets functioned in the United States. They were fortunate, however, in the long run, because they were making a lot more money selling their other properties.

Since Viki and Kornel had their affairs in order regarding his nursing position and her group homes, they invited Corine Cosmescu and her husband, Cosmin to come to the United States for a visit.

Corine and Cosmin accepted the invitation and spent a month with Viki and Kornel visiting the many places they had heard and read about and wanted to visit. They went to the Grand Canyon, Las Vegas, San Diego, San Francisco, and Mexico, as well as places of interest in Arizona. They enjoyed their stay but had no desire to move to the United States permanently. While they were not truly happy in Romania, they loved their home.

"Romania has changed a lot since the economy improved," Corine told them, "but the communist attitudes of the country's leadership haven't changed at all. And corruption continues to be a big problem. Everyone has his or her hand out expecting something of value to be placed in it in order to seal any transaction."

"The Romanian people are experiencing some basic freedom of speech and movement," Cosmin said. "It is easier to get visas and travel documents to most any country, but the price is a lot higher. The people are looking forward to even better conditions as time passes."

"If we were younger," Corine said, "and just getting started in life, we would consider coming to America. Now, for us it's too late."

They thanked Viki and Kornel for their generosity and hospitality and invited them back to Romania whenever they could get a break from everything they were doing in the United States.

CHAPTER 61

When Viki answered the phone, she was surprised to discover it was Gheorghe Pavenic, her biological brother, calling her from Romania. Her moment of joy disappeared as soon as he began to speak.

"Our father died Saturday," he said, "and we plan to have his memorial service next Saturday, February 16. Can you come? We know you're busy and that it is a very long trip, but it would please us very much if you could come. Mama, especially, would love to see you."

Viki was stunned, unable to speak for a long moment. She was not close with Ion Pavenic, but she knew her brothers and sisters still loved him and spent time with him. Gathering herself, she said, "I'm so sorry to hear this news, Gheorghe. Our sympathies go out to you and the rest of the family. I'll discuss the trip with Kornel this evening and let you know tomorrow what we can do. I can't promise anything."

"I understand. But we would all love to see you."

That evening Viki discussed the situation with Kornel. Both agreed that what with their having to keep all the group homes running and not wanting Christina and Anka to miss classes at the university, the trip was out of the question.

"Call him back tomorrow," Kornel said, "and express again our sadness over Ion's death. Tell him why we are unable to leave at this time. Perhaps we can go later when conditions here are better."

The next morning, Viki called Gheorghe and said, "We are so sorry, Gheorghe, but we can't make the trip. We love you all very much and regret we can't be with you. Especially tell our mother how much we love her and how much we really miss her. We'll send some flowers and be thinking of you when the service is held. Perhaps sometime in the near future we all will be able to make the trip. God bless you all."

In May 2002, Christina graduated from SDU and was commissioned as a second lieutenant in the United States Army. Initially, she was transferred to an army base in Texas to enhance her administrative skills in language intelligence. After three months, she was sent to Germany, where she learned and became fluent in a number of foreign languages. Her first assignment was to oversee a unit of interpreters in the Intelligence Department.

Dinner was over, dishes were put away, and Viki and Kornel had just settled into their lounge chairs to read the newspaper and watch television. It had been a busy day for both. They looked forward to some relaxation before going to bed.

How was your day?" Kornel asked as he reclined the back of his chair. "A good one, I hope."

"They don't make good days anymore." Viki said. "I've had a bad day, much like most of the days I've been having lately."

"I'm sorry to hear that. Is there anything I can do to help you?"

"No, thank you. These are things I have to take care of myself."

"Well, if there is anything, please, ah, ah ..." Kornel was interrupted by the telephone ringing. "I'll get it," he said. Then he hurried to the kitchen telephone.

He picked up the receiver on the fourth ring. "Hello? ... Oh, hi. ... Is that right? ... Well, it's about time. When will it take place? … I don't know. I'll have to discuss it with Viki and let you know … Yes, I'll let you know in a couple of days. Tell everyone I said hello, and hopefully we'll see you all then and help you celebrate."

Now what? Viki thought as the conversation continued. What is he getting us into this time? It sounds like a call from Romania, so it must be Marina. If it is, what does she want now? I hope everything is all right with the family, because I'm certainly not interested in taking another long, tiresome trip to Romania with all the work I have on my plate.

"Ah, yes, in a couple of days. Good-bye."

"What was that all about?" Viki asked.

"It was Marina."

"What does she want now?"

"She just called to let us know that her son Ragu is marrying Marcia Mircea on August 13. She is pleading for us to attend the festivities. What do you think?"

"I've been wondering when Ragu was going to marry Marcia," Viki said. "From what I've heard, she is a beautiful and intelligent young lady and should make him a good wife. I'm anxious to meet her. But this is not a good time for me."

"If you want my opinion," Kornel said, "you should thoroughly think this thing through. There's no doubt in my mind that there are others who can cover for you for a week or two to enable you to make the trip."

That night and the following day, all Viki could think about was the wedding and how she could arrange for someone to cover for her. Considering all the plans she would have to make was agonizing. She was about to throw up her hands and tell Kornel that he could go without her when a loud scream from one of the patients' rooms startled her.

She recognized the voice. It was Viola Buchak. She and her husband, Justin, had been working at the home for six months as caregivers. Viki ran to the room and found her patient Susan Hensley struggling to breathe and nonresponsive, apparently in a coma. As Viola tried to comfort the poor woman, Justin slipped the oximeter on her right index finger. He showed Viki the readout. Susan's blood pressure was dangerously high. Her blood oxygen level was low, and rapidly dropping.

Viki knew that given Susan's physical deterioration, there was little that could be done for her. Susan had been in the home under hospice care for several months. Viki thanked the Buchaks for their assistance, and then she called Susan's husband, Bob, who came over immediately and agreed that there was nothing anyone could do for her but try to make her as comfortable as possible. Bob and Viki sat with her.

As Viki sat quietly with Bob, her thoughts returned to Ragu's wedding. She knew she had to make a decision today. *I want to go, but I need coverage,* she thought. *Who can do it?* Then it occurred to her: why not ask the Buchaks? Viola, in addition to her caregiver role, had proven to be a good cook. Justin, a strong and loving caregiver, also helped manage the operations of the home and the storage shed positioned in the backyard. *They are very thorough and have been doing a very good job for me. They should be able to continue in my absence. I will ask them.*

Just before Viki was ready to leave for home, she approached the couple and asked if they would cover for her for a week while she and Kornel were in Romania.

"Yes, of course," Viola said. "We would be happy to do that for you. Go and have a good time. We will take good care of the home for you."

"Thank you, thank you!" Viki said. "We will only be gone for a week. You have my telephone number in case you need to call me for any reason."

During dinner, Viki looked over at Kornel and said, "I've decided to attend the wedding. It was a hard decision for me to make, but I know how badly you want to go. I asked the Buchaks to cover for me, and they agreed to do so. That couple is turning out to be among the very best caretakers I've ever had. I know they will take good care of the home and the patients."

"How much did you offer to pay them for their services?"

"I increased their salaries by 25 percent for one week. They were happy with that."

"Thank you for working it out. I appreciate it very much. I'll return Marina's call tomorrow and tell her we will be there. Then I'll start making the travel arrangements."

The next morning, Kornel placed a telephone call to Marina and caught her at home. It was Saturday. Viki had taken the morning off to listen in on the conversation and help him with the arrangements.

"It's me returning your call to let you know we plan to be there for the big event," he said.

There was a pause as he listened to his sister speak.

"No, it'll just be Viki and me. The girls are starting their new semester, so they won't be coming with us. But they send their best wishes to all of you and wish the couple many happy years together."

Viki observed another pause as Kornel listened to Marina.

"You want us to do what? … Well, I don't know about that. I'll have to discuss it with Viki. Aren't there others you can ask? Remember, we'll only be there for just a few days."

Kornel sat and listened.

"I know why you want us to do it, but I'm thinking of the time it will take us to decide what must be done and how we'll carry it out."

Viki again watched Kornel as he sat and heard what Marina had to say.

"Yes, I'll call you back in a couple of days with our answer."

After Kornel hung up, he turned to Viki and said, "Guess what Marina wants us to do at the wedding?"

"You know I don't like guessing games. Just tell me what she wants!"

"She wants us to be Ragu's godparents."

"What?"

"Marina wants us to perform the duties of godparents at the wedding."

"Why does she want us? Surely there are others there who could do it better than we."

"She said they wanted us because of what we've been able to achieve since leaving Romania. The pride we display, she said, is contagious, and they want the wedding couple to follow a path similar to the one we took to get where we are today. If you will assume the role of godmother, then I'll become the godfather. You know, we would be replacing their parents and be responsible for arranging and guiding the wedding services and festivities. And that means, of course, that we would have to leave here sooner than we'd hoped. Can we afford to take that much time away from our responsibilities here?"

"Well, I don't want to be the godmother or anything else. I just want to make the trip, visit with the family, and enjoy the wedding. However, if you decide we should do it, then I'll help you. But don't forget, you wanted to spend a lot of time with your parents and catch up on everything. It's been several years since you last saw everyone. This added responsibility could make that more difficult."

A few weeks later, Viki gave Kornel some bad news. "I just had a call from Marina," she said. "Your father has fallen and shattered his right hip bone. The family is trying as hard as they can to have him treated, but they can't clear the bureaucratic hurdles. She says the hospital won't admit him and the private doctors refuse to do the necessary surgery to repair it."

"I don't understand," Kornel said. "Is it because he was a priest? Is he still paying for that? Or is it socialized medicine in action?"

"Perhaps he's too old for the surgery. Marina didn't say. She just said that he's suffering excruciating pain and that over-the-counter medications do little to relieve it. They alternate ice bags and heating pads, but they don't ease the pain enough for him get a good night's sleep."

"What can we do?"

"Nothing. There isn't anything we can do."

"Did she say anything else?"

"Yes, we talked about the upcoming wedding. They plan to go ahead with it as planned despite your father's broken hip. He won't be able attend the big event, but we can still visit with him. I wish there was something we could do from here, but it is not to be."

At 10:30 a.m. on Friday, August 13, 2005, the wedding party of Ragu and Marcia appeared at the City Building in Suceava to acquire the wedding license required for their religious ceremony and for them to be married in a civil service. The bride, groom,

and godparents participated in the ceremony. Viki and Kornel acted as witnesses.

The civil service went smoothly. The couple nervously sighed and their tears flowed when the legal marriage document was handed them. Now they could be married by their priest and his deacon in the church's sacred ceremony.

Immediately after, Kornel led the party to the chosen restaurant to begin the first of three days celebrating the couple's new life as husband and wife. There was eating, drinking, and dancing to the music of the best band in the area until midnight, after which guests began to leave so they could get some rest to be ready for the religious ceremony the next afternoon.

The church service was beautiful and emotional. The priest followed the church's long established religious rites. The guests chorused responses during the ceremony as established in the scriptures and cultural traditions.

After the church service, Kornel and Viki, acting as godparents, led the assembled guests back to the restaurant for more eating, drinking, and dancing. On Sunday morning, the festivities were still continuing and everyone was having a grand time. The bride danced with her male guests, and each dancer pinned money to the bride's wedding dress—money the couple could spend on whatever they wished. What the couple had wished for was enough money to finance their honeymoon, with whatever was left going toward furnishing the house Ragu and his friends had just completed.

Since things seemed well in hand, Kornel and Viki excused themselves from the wedding festivities long enough to visit with Kornel's father to describe how the wedding celebration was progressing and to tell him how much his presence was missed.

As they entered the room, Dimitru appeared to be alert, but as they neared the bed, Viki could see he was motionless and obviously unaware of his surroundings. While his eyes were open, they appeared glassy and unseeing. Something was terribly wrong, but he appeared to be without pain.

"I don't like this," Viki said. "I believe he is dying."

"I agree," Kornel said. "I've seen it so many times in the hospital, and I know you've experienced it in the group homes."

"What can we do?"

"There's little we can do but keep him as comfortable as we can. I'll let Marina know. We can begin making the arrangements." Suddenly overcome, Kornel began to sob. "Why, oh why, does he have to go now? I've prayed so much to see him improved by the time we left for home. But that is not to be."

Seeing Kornel weeping, Viki knelt down and began praying. Then she almost immediately broke down herself and began crying. Kornel joined her in kneeling. Together they prayed.

"At least he is without pain," Kornel said.

"Amen," Viki said as she wiped her eyes. Then she rose and lightly kissed her father-in-law on the forehead.

As Viki and Kornel stepped back from the bed, Dimitru wheezed his final breath and died.

Kornel approached his father, put his arm around him, kissed him on the forehead, and whispered, "I love you, Father." Then he slowly pulled the sheet up and over his lifeless body.

They left the room. Kornel immediately called Marina and gave her the sad news.

Weeping, she said, "We'll be right there."

Kornel immediately called Christina and Anka to let them know what had happened, telling them that they should not to try coming for the services. "We'll keep you posted on the details, and we can talk about it when we get back," Kornel said. "We love you and miss you both." Then he hung up his cell phone.

Viki got in touch with Justin Buchak. "Kornel and I have to extend our time here because Kornel's father has passed away," she said. "He and his sister have funeral and estate matters to take care of. When that is completed, we will be on the first plane out of here. I know you are planning to quit your jobs at the home, but I would greatly appreciate it if you would stay on until we get back."

"Not to worry," Justin told her. "Viola and I will be here to take care of everything. When you return, we'll bring you up to date."

"Thank you so much, Justin. Please continue doing what you're doing. We'll see you soon."

"Have a safe journey. We all miss you."

Funeral services were held the following Wednesday at 11:00 a.m. After the service, Dimitru was buried in the church's cemetery. For the rest of the week, Kornel worked with Marina handling the settlement of the properties. On Saturday, Viki and Kornel returned to Arizona. They took Sunday off to relax and rest up so they would be ready to return to their jobs on Monday morning.

CHAPTER 62

As Viki drove onto the driveway of group home no. 2 the next morning, she breathed a big sigh of relief. It was good to be home after all they had gone through in Romania. Now they had to pick up where they left off. *I hope everything is all right in the home,* she thought. *I haven't heard anything from anyone in a while, so I'm hoping that the absence of news is a sign of good news.*

When she tried the front door, she was startled to find it unlocked. *I wonder who let that happen?* she thought as she stepped in. Everyone knew that for patient safety, this door had to remain locked at all times, except when visitors and others came and went.

Once she made her way through the receiving room and into the kitchen, she was greeted by Stefania, her cook. "Oh, Viki," Stefania said, throwing her arms around her, "it's so good to see you. We've been having an awful time here without you."

"Why isn't breakfast ready?" Viki asked. "It's almost 8:00 a.m. and only about half of the patients are at the table and ready to eat. What's going on?"

"Well, the food is ready. Both caregivers are doing the best they can to get the patients to the table, but it's not been a good morning for them."

"Where are Justin and Viola? They should be here."

"You know they quit, don't you?"

"Well, I knew they were quitting, but I expected them to still be here when I got back."

"They left a week ago. They said they had this new job and they had to take it right away. All they said was they would be back, but they didn't say when."

"Did they say anything about getting someone to cover for them until we returned?"

"No. All they said was good-bye."

Viki hurriedly made her way into the dressing area, where she found her other caregivers, Dona Dobo and Alexandra Gusa, rushing to dress the other patients to get them to the dining table. After greeting them, she asked, "Why are you so late getting the patients to the breakfast table?"

"We had some problems getting two patients out of bed and into the shower," Dona said. "Then one of them, while being showered, lost her grip on the handrail and slid to the floor. Fortunately, she didn't get hurt, but it took all the strength Alexandra and I have to get her back on her feet. We didn't have any other help, so it put us behind schedule. And we still have two more patients to get ready."

"Well, I'm here now, and I'll help you. What do you know about Justin and Viola?"

"All they told us was they had this new job in a new group home and they had to leave us. As they left, they asked us to explain this to you and to tell you they would be back to see you, but they didn't say when. They just walked out the door and never said good-bye—or anything else."

"Did they say anything about someone covering for them until we got back?"

"No, they never said anything."

The rest of the day was spent cleaning and freshening the rooms and furnishings. All bedding was changed and clothes closets restored to their neat and orderly arrangement.

When 5:30 came around that day, Viki was exhausted and ready to go home. She needed rest to recover from the jet lag after the long trip.

Just as she finished filling her briefcase with night work, the doorbell rang. Much to her surprise, it was Justin and Viola. After hugs and greetings, she led them into the visitors' room and seated them around the table she used to conduct business. The atmosphere was cool: Viki was still seething from having to solve all the unpleasant problems that had arisen during her time away.

"What do you have to say for yourselves?" she asked, barely able to conceal her anger. "How dare you leave us without having someone cover for you! I'm disappointed. I expected more of you than that."

"We didn't want to do that to you," Justin said, "but you placed us in a difficult situation when you called and said you had to stay there another week because of the death of Kornel's father. When we discussed that with our new employer, he gave us the ultimatum: you either come with us now, or we'll take another couple we like. We tried to get him to wait a week, but he wouldn't listen. He claimed he had a demanding situation that needed immediate attention and that we were the ones who could resolve it. He couldn't wait a week. Viola and I discussed his demand and decided to go with him even though we realized it wouldn't be fair to you. We are sorry it worked out this way. We hope you will understand our position and won't hold it against us."

"What other choice do I have?" Viki said. "You didn't even try to find someone to cover for you. That put our patients and my business in jeopardy. I suppose you are here now to get your final checks? If you'll wait a few minutes, I'll get them for you."

As she handed them their checks, Viki looked them each in the eyes and simply said, "Good-bye."

That evening, Viki described to Kornel all the adversities she had dealt with that day.

"Well, you handled them properly. I'm proud of you for that. Now, let's get to bed and get some much-needed rest. Then we'll feel better in the morning. But you have to admit, in spite of all our recent problems, it's wonderful being back home again."

At the end of May 2004, Anka graduated from SDU with a bachelor of arts degree. It was a moving experience for Viki to see her second daughter graduate from the same university as her firstborn. Anka ranked among the top 5 percent of her class. On her diploma were the words magna cum laude—"with highest honors."

Following the ceremony, Viki and Kornel took Anka, her three housemates, and their families to a big dinner in the best restaurant in town. There they raised their champagne glasses high and toasted the graduates and their achievements. Tears flowed, and lots of hugs and kisses were passed on to the new graduates.

"Anka, now that you've got schooling behind you, what are your plans?" Kornel asked.

"Annie Williams and I have plans to travel to New York and get teaching jobs in the Manhattan School District," Anka said. "We've been in touch with them, and they assured us they have positions waiting for us to teach Spanish to their elementary grades. We will leave next week and settle into a two-bedroom flat they've arranged for us. It won't be cheap, but it's going to be a great experience."

"If you ever need help, just let us know and we'll do what we can," Viki said.

"I appreciate that, but I hope that won't be necessary. We've made inquiries to three East Coast colleges and found there are fellowship funds available for us to earn our master's degrees. Once Annie and I get settled and have a better feel for the city, we will apply to all of the schools and take the best offer we can get."

"You can rest assured, your father and I are really proud of you. We wish you nothing but the best in whatever you attempt to achieve, and we stand ready to help you if ever you need it."

With that, Viki and Kornel said their good-byes and took the girls back to their house. Then Viki headed the car in the direction of home.

On their way back home, Viki and Kornel spent several miles in complete silence. The only sound was the purring of the engine. Both were deep in thought about the excitement of the day and wondering what it was going to be like now that Anka was off to make her own decisions and to suffer or rejoice in the results.

"Do you think she can really make it on her own?" Kornel asked.

"There is no doubt in my mind that she can," Viki said. "She has a good head on her shoulders, and she knows how to use it. Of course there will be times when we will question her judgment. But I believe her way will be the best way, even though we may not agree."

"We'll see," Kornel said. "Now, in thinking ahead, we've got a house to sell. We no longer have any need of the residential property the girls and their schoolmates have been using as a dormitory."

"I agree," Viki said, "but don't forget, we still have Beth and Sally, Anka's friends, in it. We can't very well toss them out. Both will graduate next year, and then we can sell it. We'll just have to add two other students to occupy the empty rooms with the understanding that we can only rent it to them for the coming year."

"I agree," Kornel said. "In the meantime, I'll start making plans to get it sold as soon as it is vacant."

"I can't take it anymore!" Viki cried one evening as she entered the house.

"Now what's the matter?" Kornel asked, not looking up from the newspaper article he was reading. Titled "Another Bad Day with the Patients," it was about an immigrant Italian owner of an Arizona group home.

"What's the matter?" Viki echoed. "I'm so tired and worn out with all that has been happening these last few months that I feel like I'm losing my mind, what with our girls leaving us to go out on their own, us having to take that trip to Romania to attend your nephew's wedding, and that being followed by your father's unexpected death and funeral services. Then there were the extra days we stayed assisting your sister with the distribution of your parents' properties. Now, back here, I'm trying to operate three group homes that I haven't been able to adequately staff. I'm trying to keep them going with people from Romania, but the good workers are scarce and no one is trained. Look at what happened when we went to Romania. I left Justin Buchak and his wife to manage the homes in my absence. When we got back, however, we found they had left without finding anyone to take their place. Then they had the audacity to show up only to get their paycheck. I can't put up with this anymore."

"What do you want to do?" Kornel asked, his newspaper lowered, the article forgotten.

"We've got to do something about either giving me some relief or cutting my workload," Viki said. "As a matter of fact, the more

I think about it, the more I'm inclined to sell two of the homes, leaving me with just one to operate. I don't care how you feel about selling the homes, as I'm determined you're going to sell them. So get in touch with our realtor and let's get it done."

By the end of September 2005, Kornel had sold group home no. 3 and group home no. 4, leaving Viki with only group home no. 2 to operate. As before, they sold their properties at premium prices.

On New Year's Day 2006, with a mischievous smirk on his face, Kornel said, "Lately I've been seriously thinking we should buy two more houses, convert them into group homes, operate them for a couple of years, and then sell them at for a profit. What do you think?"

"What do I think?" Viki said. "Well, buster, I'll tell you what I think in just four English words: *Over my dead body!*"

Having gotten that off her mind, Viki leaned back in her chair with a contented smile on her face and thought, *I never believed I would ever be comfortable with the English language, but now I am! And I love it!*

ABOUT THE AUTHOR

Bob Bennett was born in the coal mining village of Junior, West Virginia, on March 29, 1924. His father, being a coal miner, moved from coal town to coal town seeking steady work until finally settling in Bobtown, Pennsylvania, in the spring of 1928.

Bob completed his elementary and high school education, graduating in 1942 from Point Marion High School and thereafter working for several months in the Shannopin Coal Company coal mine.

In early 1943, Bob enlisted in the United States Navy and served three years as a navy bugler, both in the United States and during two tours of duty in the European Theater of World War II. In June 1945, Bob married Mabel Hensley of Morgantown, West Virginia. A year later, the couple became proud parents of their son, Thomas.

After his discharge from the navy In December 1945, Bob immediately enrolled in West Virginia University, from which he graduated in 1948 with a degree in business administration. He accepted a position with the Chesapeake and Potomac Telephone Company of West Virginia and worked for the Bell Telephone System for almost thirty-seven years.

In August 1952, Bob and Mabel became parents of their daughter, Joan Renee.

In 1978, the company transferred Bob to Tehran, Iran, to work for American Bell International in its contract to assist the Iranian telephone utility to expand its telephone system. However, because of the unrest in the country and the exile of Shah Pahlavi, Bob and his fellow expatriates returned to the States. He resumed work with the telephone company in Silver Spring, Maryland, and in Denver, Colorado, until his retirement in 1985. A year later, Bob and Mabel moved to Sun City West, Arizona. In 2008, the love of his life passed away.

In 2010, Bob met the loving and caring Marion Rivera. The two began an endearing relationship that grows stronger each day.

Printed in the United States
By Bookmasters